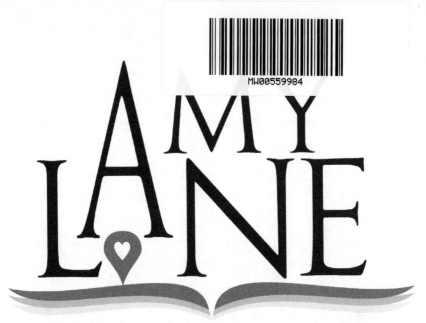

Choose your Lane to love!

Readers love
Beneath the Stain
by AMY LANE

"*Beneath The Stain* by Amy Lane is a journey of pain and love that is lost, found and rediscovered anew. It is the transformation of a group of boys into men whom one would be proud to call friends. It is truly storytelling at its best and I highly recommend this novel to you."
—Joyfully Jay

"*Beneath the Stain* isn't a roller coaster ride so much as it's a life journey."
—Shameless Book Club

"One of the best books I've ever read. I will never forget these guys, their pain, their love. Amy, you did good. You did better than good. Be proud of yourself, I know I am."
—Rainbow Book Reviews

By Amy Lane

An Amy Lane Christmas
Behind the Curtain
Bewitched by Bella's Brother
Bolt-hole
Christmas Kitsch
Christmas with Danny Fit
Clear Water
Do-over
Food for Thought
Freckles
Gambling Men
Going Up
Hammer & Air
Homebird
If I Must
Immortal
It's Not Shakespeare
Left on St. Truth-be-Well
The Locker Room
Mourning Heaven
Phonebook
Puppy, Car, and Snow
Racing for the Sun • Hiding the Moon
Raising the Stakes
Regret Me Not

Shiny!
Shirt
Sidecar
String Boys
A Solid Core of Alpha
Tales of the Curious Cookbook
Anthology
Three Fates
Truth in the Dark
Turkey in the Snow
Under the Rushes
Wishing on a Blue Star

BENEATH THE STAIN
Beneath the Stain • Paint It Black

BONFIRES
Bonfires • Crocus

CANDY MAN
Candy Man • Bitter Taffy
Lollipop • Tart and Sweet

DREAMSPUN DESIRES
THE MANNIES
#25 – The Virgin Manny
#37 – Manny Get Your Guy
#57 – Stand by Your Manny
#62 – A Fool and His Manny
SEARCH AND RESCUE
#86 – Warm Heart

Published by DREAMSPINNER PRESS
www.dreamspinnerpress.com

By AMY LANE (CONT.)

FAMILIAR LOVE
Familiar Angel • Familiar Demon

FISH OUT OF WATER
Fish Out of Water
Red Fish, Dead Fish
A Few Good Fish
Hiding the Moon

KEEPING PROMISE ROCK
Keeping Promise Rock
Making Promises
Living Promises
Forever Promised

JOHNNIES
Chase in Shadow • Dex in Blue
Ethan in Gold • Black John
Bobby Green
Super Sock Man

GRANBY KNITTING
The Winter Courtship Rituals
of Fur-Bearing Critters
How to Raise an Honest Rabbit
Knitter in His Natural Habitat
Blackbird Knitting in a Bunny's Lair
The Granby Knitting Menagerie
Anthology

TALKER
Talker • Talker's Redemption
Talker's Graduation
The Talker Collection Anthology

WINTER BALL
Winter Ball • Summer Lessons

Published by Harmony Ink Press
BITTER MOON SAGA
Triane's Son Rising
Triane's Son Learning
Triane's Son Fighting
Triane's Son Reigning

Published by DREAMSPINNER PRESS
www.dreamspinnerpress.com

PAINT IT BLACK

AMY LANE

Published by
DREAMSPINNER PRESS

5032 Capital Circle SW, Suite 2, PMB# 279, Tallahassee, FL 32305-7886 USA
www.dreamspinnerpress.com

This is a work of fiction. Names, characters, places, and incidents either are the product of author imagination or are used fictitiously, and any resemblance to actual persons, living or dead, business establishments, events, or locales is entirely coincidental.

Paint It Black
© 2019 Amy Lane

Cover Art
© 2019 Reese Dante
http://www.reesedante.com
Cover content is for illustrative purposes only and any person depicted on the cover is a model.

Mass Market Paperback ISBN: 978-1-64108-141-2
Trade Paperback ISBN: 978-1-64080-843-0
Digital ISBN: 978-1-64080-842-3
Library of Congress Control Number: 2018948433
Trade Paperback published August 2019
v. 1.0

Printed in the United States of America
(∞)
This paper meets the requirements of
ANSI/NISO Z39.48-1992 (Permanence of Paper).

To my Mate and to my bestie.
And to my dad, who will never read this,
because you taught me to love rock and roll.

Shattered

BLAKE MANNING *loved* playing with his band, and Outbreak Monkey was on a roll tonight. Blake played second lead guitar, which meant that in some ways, he was superfluous—but not when he was onstage, soaked in sweat, singing backup harmonies he'd helped write, making music with the men he considered his brothers.

Mackey Sanders, the lead singer, was on fire. His bleached-blond hair teased big around his gamine face, his eyeliner extending to a mask around his eyes, Mackey looked naughty and sexy and wicked.

And it didn't hurt that he sang like a whiskey-soaked angel.

"So everybody out there feeling good?" Mackey whooped. The crowd roared, and Mackey turned to his band. "How about you, Kell—you feelin' good?"

Kell Sanders, Mackey's older brother and first lead guitar, played a rocking riff, preplanned, as his answer.

Blake played up his guitar riff and winked at Kell, knowing the big screen would take the bro-flirt for what it was when Kell winked back. Once upon a time, Blake might have interpreted that look as hopeful, but Kell had been married for eight years now and had two kids. Blake's long-buried crush on his bandmate had since morphed into what it always should have been—brotherhood.

The venue wasn't too big—about ten thousand seats, when they often played twenty-five—but the stadium was packed.

Behind Blake and Kell, Jefferson Sanders played bass guitar and Stevie Harris played the drums. And while the only serious talent in the whole ensemble was Mackey, the rest of them loved playing so much, worked so hard at it—at new songs, at being better every time out of the gate—that they'd managed to be on Billboard's Top Ten more weeks than not in the last nine years.

It hadn't come easy, still didn't, Blake thought, attuning his body to take the cues from Jefferson and Stevie as they finished their introductions.

But as Mackey took the crowd from the introduction into the bridge of "The I'm Sorry Song"—one of their oldest, most loved hits—Blake felt the adrenaline surge of making music, and making it well. So much work, so much pain under the bridge, but here, now, Blake Manning and his brothers-in-band were flying so high, nothing could bring them down.

It's all he'd ever wanted to do with his life. He'd tried it on his own, his solo album, and it had all but disappeared. But here, with his brothers, being a smaller part of a bigger whole? He was a rock star in the best kind of way, the kind that took people on a trip and helped them fly. Not bad for a kid from a trailer park in Lancaster, right?

He and Kell moved toward each other on the stage, doing that thing where Kell moved forward while Blake rocked back, and together they watched as Mackey clambered on top of the giant speakers on either side of the stage. Mackey was little and spry and hella fit—they all were, especially since Mackey and Blake had gotten out of rehab nine years before. The little monster seemed able to do everything. He'd been making this running-along-the-speakers thing part of the gig this tour, and the first time he'd done it, he'd scared the shit out of their manager.

Of course, Trav Ford was Mackey's husband, married in a quiet ceremony in upstate New York five years ago, so Trav got to freak out about Mackey as much as he wanted.

Still, they were tight. All of them. They lived together in a big-ass house with too many rooms. They ran together, they practiced together, they split off into groups and went on vacations together. Kell's wife, Briony, was working their soundboard, and Stevie and Jefferson's, uh, wife, Shelia, was back at the hotel room, watching Kell and Briony's children as well as hers and the boys'.

In a way, it was claustrophobic—Blake could see that.

But for the first few years, it had kept Blake and Mackey clean, because nothing made you as accountable as family up in your face 24-7. In the last few years, though, it had been more than that. It had been comfort and protection from a world Blake had seen the worst of.

For Blake Manning's first twenty years, he hadn't had a soul he could trust, and for the last twelve, he'd had a family.

He wasn't going to shit on that. In fact, he'd die to take care of it.

And like everybody else in the world, his heart lodged in his throat and tried to choke him when he saw Mackey Sanders scampering along the top of the giant amplifier.

But when he saw Mackey fall off, it threatened to stop.

BECAUSE MACKEY was a rock star and his family had money now, he got a hospital suite bigger than the trailer Blake had grown up in. And since it was bigger than the two-bedroom apartment most of the band had grown up in, he figured everybody got to enjoy the fruit platter and give Mackey shit for being laid up.

"Yeah, Kell," Kell Sanders mocked. "Not a problem. It's real smooth up there. Any idiot could run on top of it. Even you."

Mackey guffawed and then fell back against the pillows, grimacing in pain. He'd broken his leg, his wrist, and sprained his back. The doctors had offered to give him a continuous IV of good drugs, but Mackey was going over-the-counter only. He'd made eye contact with Blake when he said this, and Blake had nodded.

They'd both worked damned hard to kick coke, booze, and pills early on in their careers. They'd been such screwed-up kids when they'd started touring, and their first manager, before Trav, had been a junkie on his way down.

Finding his body hadn't made either one of them want to slow up none.

Mackey'd had demons too, big, scary ones that nobody his age should have carried. So he'd shared his demons by flogging Blake with them, and Blake had spent more than a year hoping Mackey Sanders died of crotch rot, slow and painful like—and being as bitchy as possible to Mackey Sanders at every waking moment.

They'd spent the last eight years trying to make up for that animosity, and Blake figured he loved Mackey like a brother now—except more, because he was their leader, and everything he did was for the good of the band, the brotherhood, and the motherfucking music.

Blake thought those priorities were about the closest thing to religion he ever wanted to find. He worshipped at the altar of Mackey James Sanders, like the rest of the world, and made no apologies for it.

That wasn't going to stop just because Mackey was laid up now.

"Wasn't my fuckin' fault," Mackey growled through gritted teeth.

God, maybe he should have just a little bit of Demerol to take the edge off of whatever his body was going through.

"Road crew was supposed to put a piece of plywood up there so I could walk between those two big ones. It wasn't there—I tried to jump."

"Woulda made it too," Kell agreed, holding his brother's hand as the pain wracked him again. "If the mic cord hadn't wrapped around your foot."

"Goddammit." Mackey breathed in hard through his nose. "God fucking dammit—Trav, no!"

Trav was ushering in a nurse with a syringe in her hand.

"I understand you're a former addict—"

"Always an addict," Mackey growled. "Don't make that mistake—"

"I understand," she soothed. "But there's so much swelling now, and you're in so much pain, you can't heal. This is a nonaddictive drug. I get that you're afraid of it being a crutch, so we're going to give you some until tomorrow and reassess. But right now, you can't get better, you understand?"

"Fuck...." Mackey scowled at the defeat, and Trav—six-foot plus of him, with auburn hair, angry brown eyes, and a body like a Sherman tank but not as soft—looked over his shoulder and gestured everybody to the family room of the suite.

Briony and Shelia were there with the kids, including Mackey's namesake, his first boyfriend's daughter, Katy. At first, Blake imagined Grant's idea to name the girl Katy—after Mackey's given name, McKay—would have been like a blow to the nads for Mackey. Grant had broken up with Mackey and sent him on tour because his girlfriend had told him she was pregnant. When she gave birth to Katy, ten months after the breakup, that had probably sent Mackey screaming for the pills and booze even harder. But now, leading the pack of family on the road, Katy was everybody's comfort, and as worried about Mackey as only a daughter could be.

For a moment, the boys were surrounded in a babble of confusion, until Kell took over and told everybody that Uncle Mackey was going to be just fine.

Briony Sanders was a pretty woman, with a waist-length braid of strawberry blond hair and a round, freckled face. She smiled weakly at Kell as he was talking.

Blake caught her eye, though. Something was wrong beyond Mackey, and she was trying not to bring it up now.

She nodded at Blake and moved through the knot of kids, past all the brothers and Shelia, and jerked her chin to the exit.

Oh, not even in the suite, then.

Blake followed her out of the room and into the subdued colors of the VIP hallway of Seattle's best hospital. God, they weren't even home. Why did all the bad shit on the tour seem to happen right when they hit the West Coast?

"'Sup?" he asked, keeping his voice down.

"Shelia told me that right before Mackey fell off the fuckin' stage, Heather called."

Blake's eyebrows went up. Heather Sanders was a lovely woman. Tiny and tough, she'd raised Mackey, Kell, Jefferson, and her youngest, Cheever, on a pittance. They hadn't had much, but they'd had food, clothing, and one another, even if it had all been in a two-room apartment that had been razed in the eight years since they'd last visited their hometown. Even more, she'd taken in Stevie, Jefferson's, uh, boyfriend? She'd treated him as a son, and Grant as well, back when he was Kell's best friend. And ever since rehab, she'd shown Blake that not all mothers were shitty, and that sometimes, someone could love you just for being you.

"How's she doing?" Heather and Cheever had moved to LA eight years ago, but they'd opted not to stay in the big family house. Cheever had been going to art schools since the boys started making money, and Heather had moved to be near him. Since Cheever had graduated from high school and gone off to college, she'd come to LA to live in an apartment near the beach. Close enough to live near her boys, she said, but far enough away to let them be men.

They all had dinner once a week—unless the band was on tour.

"*She's* fine," Briony murmured. "It's Cheever she's worried about."

Blake grimaced. The youngest Sanders was about eight years younger than Mackey—and he'd had a chip on his shoulder the size of the world ever since Blake had known him.

"What's the little shit done now?" Blake growled. God, he got it. The older boys had raised that kid, babysat for him, sacrificed for him. He got that they wouldn't see what a using piece of shit he was. When Blake had met the kid, he'd seemed like a decent human being. He'd even been kind of sweet, once he let go of some of his defensiveness and talked like a person.

Once he'd been a laughing boy who would ride a roller coaster until he puked and who had looked at Mackey and his brothers like the good men they were. Once he'd shown Blake a vulnerable face, and Blake had tried to be kind.

He remembered the first Christmas he'd spent with the band, the one right after Mackey and Blake had gotten out of rehab, when Mackey hadn't felt up to going home, but hadn't told anybody until they were all on the plane and he was in a cab heading back to the house. The band had gotten to Sacramento, told Heather Sanders what happened, and she had loaded them all in the SUV and driven them back to LA. Blake and Cheever had sat in the back of the car, and at first, Cheever had been sullen, angry, pissed-off because his brother had disrupted all his Christmas plans. To him, it looked as if once again, the entire world was changing on its axis for Mackey.

But by the end of the car ride, Cheever had opened up to Blake and Kell, talking about his art, talking about school. Blake'd had the feeling it was hard for Cheever to fit in, and Mackey coming out to the press hadn't made things any easier. Of course, Blake and Kell had started off pissed too. Cheever had talked to the press on his own, and he'd been a right shitty little prick about it. But during that six-hour ride to LA in the middle of the night, Blake and Kell had forgotten their resentment, and Blake remembered thinking wistfully that he might just be able to add one more brother to his growing made-family.

But that was once upon a time. Ever since Cheever and Heather had come to LA, that sweet kid disappeared. Nowadays Cheever ran around in the best cars, in the best clothes, doing the best girls and the best blow. He attended family affairs for the minimal possible time, barely spoke to any of them, smiled briefly at the kids, then bailed.

At least once a month, someone—Kell, Mackey, Jefferson, even Stevie and the girls—would make an overture, invite him somewhere, ask him out to lunch—and at least once a month the family waited breathlessly to see if Cheever would show up and try to be part of the tight group of those who lived in the big house.

Blake's stomach was knotted and sick with the naked hurt Cheever's brothers suffered, every fucking time. He'd learned, in his ten years with the brothers. Learned to not get angry, learned patience, how to be that guy who was there for the family. Not being a bitchy pain in the ass in order to take care of the people he loved had become Blake's driving goal. But Cheever—Cheever was pissing him off.

Blake loved Heather, and he loved the Sanders family. But once upon a time, he'd had hope for that kid.

For the last eight years, he'd been waiting for Cheever Sanders to take a fall, if for no other reason than so his brothers could pick up the pieces and show him what he'd been missing. So he could see that sweet, funny, amazing kid who'd drawn doodles and made Blake and Kell laugh all the way from Sacramento to LA.

"He ran through all his college money in a week," Briony muttered, pulling his attention back to the unhappy present. "She can't get hold of him on the phone. She thinks he's having one hell of a party, and she's worried about him."

Blake tilted his head back. "Fuuuuuuuckkkk...."

God.

It would be so easy to hate this kid.

So easy to just blow him off as an overdose waiting to happen.

But once upon a time, Blake had seen something in that kid, something hurt and needy. Something that nobody seemed to be addressing. Something that nobody else seemed to see.

Blake and Mackey had been just like him once, and Trav had given enough of a shit to save their sorry asses.

Of course, Trav and Mackey had been falling in love, but there hadn't been a rule that said Trav needed to make sure Blake cleaned up his act too. There were plenty of mediocre guitarists a shit-ton better than Blake Manning, and he knew it.

But Trav had cared for the Sanders *family*, and Blake had been included then, just like he was included now.

"Tell her to text me the address and shit," he said, looking at the knot of family in the center of the suite. His brothers had children, spouses, people who needed them. Mackey's red-haired, green-eyed brother was *not* going to fuck that up for them.

Blake just had this family. And Cheever fucking Sanders was going to clean up his act if Blake had to drag him through bleach.

Schoolboy Blues

Nine years before...

CHEEVER'S MOM'S new boyfriend was a bit of a prick. But his son, Aubrey, was...

Well, pretty.

He had a thick fringe of dark lashes and really intense blue eyes.

Something about that combination of colors in Aubrey's fair-skinned face made Cheever a little stupid.

He must have been, because Aubrey was something of a prick too, and he got away with more shit while batting those big blue eyes. Like right now.

Right now, Aubrey was taking a hit of weed right in the middle of the empty locker room. Cheever had seen him do this before. He'd blame it on the high school students and totally get away with it.

Aubrey exhaled, grinning wickedly, and tried to pass the joint to Cheever, but Cheever held up his hands. "Naw, man. My mom would kill me."

Aubrey rolled his eyes and pinched off the end, then hid half the blunt in a baggie in the bottom of his gym bag. "Baby."

Cheever shrugged. The thing was, his mom showed up for dinner every night at the expensive boarding school his brothers paid for. He wasn't sure why she was so damned excited about being there all the time—it had been Cheever and his brothers on their own while she worked her ass off, until a little more than a year ago, and that had been just fine. But Heather May Sanders would spot the red eyes and bad breath that went with pot in under a second. The only reason his brothers had gotten away with so much shit was that they'd been unsupervised. His mom had always been working.

"I like my free time," he said mildly, and Aubrey batted those blue eyes at him again.

"You like to draw your little cartoons," he teased. "Yeah, I know."

Well, that was the whole reason Cheever was going to boarding school.

"Is this all we're doing?" he asked, reluctance in his voice. If all he was going to do was watch Aubrey get halfway stoned, he should probably go to gym.

Aubrey smirked. "Wanna make out?" he asked.

Cheever's heartbeat sped up, and his palms started to sweat.

Oh shit.

Yes. *Yes*, he wanted to make out. He'd wanted to make out since he and Aubrey had met last year, when he'd started going to Tyson/Hepzibah Prep!

But Aubrey had never said anything like that before, and God, if he was just joking and Cheever said yes, he would be *toast.*

"Your party," Cheever managed to say, trying to sound bored. "I'm just saying, we should probably get to—"

Aubrey's lips on his were sweet.

Cheever inhaled, and Aubrey kissed him again, this time adding a little bit of tongue. Oh wow. Oh wow, he was *kissing Cheever*, and that's all Cheever had ever wanted and—

Cheever brought his hand up to Aubrey's shoulder, just to steady himself, when the sound of the door opening split them apart.

"Sanders! Cooper! Are you two still in here!"

"Yes, coach!" Aubrey sputtered.

"Sorry, coach!" Cheever managed to croak, thanking God they'd both changed into their gym clothes before Aubrey had pulled him aside.

Coach Richards strode in, blue polyester tracksuit only stretched a little over his forty-something belly, white-blond hair thinning enough to reveal the way his head flushed patchily when he was in a hurry. "Why aren't you two out—you know, never mind. You're both wanted in the office."

Cheever blinked in surprise. "Because—"

"Well, Sanders, your mother's here. Apparently she needs to blow town and was signing the weekend stay-over paperwork. Cooper, you've got a note from your father." Coach Richards grimaced; he wasn't a bad guy, really. Just clueless. "Whatever it is, it must be totally messed up, because the secretary did *not* like taking that. So anyway, both of you, go to the office and figure shi—erm, stuff out, then come back to class. And Cooper!"

"Yes, coach!"

"If I search your locker, is there anything you don't want me to find?"

Aubrey shook his head. "No, coach!"

"Good! Take your track bag with you, dump whatever is making that stench out at the trash cans, and make that a true thing!"

"Yes, coach," Aubrey said, looking a little bit green, like he'd had a close call.

"Now both of you, vamoose!"

They managed to get out the door without making eye contact, but as soon as it swung behind them, they both let out a chuff of air.

"Oh my God," Aubrey rasped, digging through his gym bag, then disposing of the incriminating baggie in the nearest trash can that wasn't overflowing with juice boxes and french fry trays.

"That was close," Cheever muttered, not even sure if they were talking about the same thing. *Aubrey's tongue had been in his mouth!*

"I know, right?" Aubrey winked at him. "But we can always pick up where we left off!"

Cheever didn't even know where that was. Literally, where did they pick up from Aubrey's tongue in his mouth?

Oh my God, Cheever was *dying* to find out.

But first he had to go talk to his mom and figure out what had brought her out of the tiny town of Tyson.

He found her in the counselor's conference cubicle, filling out the paperwork in tears.

"Mom?" For a moment, he was terrified. God. His brothers. He hadn't seen them in a year. There'd been cards from them, texts, but they'd been on tour during Christmas last year. Mackey had been beat up—that's what he'd thought, anyway. Everyone said "attacked"—but that had been a month ago, and he hadn't thought of it since. Which was weird. For his entire life, they'd been his everything, but for the last year, they'd completely disappeared. Were they hurt? Was that why they hadn't come?

Heather Sanders shook her head and grabbed a tissue. "Cheever, honey, we're going to have to have a real important talk, really quick, okay? Because your brothers live public lives, and when this hits the press, everybody in your school's going to be talking about it. So you're gonna need to be strong, okay?"

Oh God. "Are they hurt?"

She grimaced. "Yes, and no. Mackey—he's not doing so well right now. He's apparently been doing coke to get up in the morning and pills to go to sleep. Right now he's in a world of hurt."

Cheever knew he was gaping. "He's a... a druggie—"

His mother grabbed his shoulder and shook it, hard. She was tiny, and at thirteen, he was about two inches taller than her, but he was still young and small enough to be intimidated by her.

"He's an addict," she said simply. "But he's recovering. He just bared his soul to me. Do you understand? He was so worried about me not loving him—of course I still love him, but that's not gonna be the hard part."

Oh God. All the kids were gonna be talking about it. This boarding school, with all these rich kids outside these two tiny towns.... They chewed over gossip like old gum!

"What's the hard part?" He was damned afraid to ask.

"He's gay, honey. And it shouldn't be hard. It shouldn't be hard for anybody, and it shouldn't hurt anybody, but it hurt him. And it's been eating him up inside, and I gotta go make it right."

Cheever gaped at her, the vision of Aubrey's mouth on his flashing before his eyes.

His brother was gay. Dimly he remembered being about five years old, walking in on Mackey and Grant Adams—Kell's best friend—making out on his mom's bed when they were supposed to be watching him.

Wait, aren't I gay?

His brother was gay, and it was eating him up inside.

Is there something wrong with me?

His mother had to go make it right.

Aren't you supposed to stay with me?

He thought of all the times he'd rolled his eyes when she'd shown up to have dinner with him.

How would she know that, dumbass?

His mother loved him, though. She patted his cheek softly. "Oh, honey. Don't look so panicked. Mackey's going to be fine." Her lower lip wobbled, making a lie of her words. "I worry about what your school will say when it gets out." She shrugged. "It's never been easy on you boys...."

Well, four boys, four different fathers. It was a small town. Word spread. Everybody knew Jefferson's dad was Willis Jefferson, who'd moved up to Oregon after Heather had broken up with him. And Cheever's dad, Enos Cheever, had been given a restraining order. He'd moved to Redding, just to stay far away.

There weren't many people who didn't know about Cheever's family—including the way the three older boys plus Stevie Harris had gone on to make a big name for themselves as Outbreak Monkey.

But still.... "Can I come with you?" he asked plaintively, and she patted his cheek again.

"I love you for asking," she told him, kissing his forehead. "But you'd be missing school, and I'd be concentrating on the bigger boys. Everybody's gonna be talking about grown-up stuff, hon, and you'd be bored shitless. But I should be back in a week, okay? I'll text or call you every night, but I gotta hurry. Their manager is having a plane come to our little airstrip, and it's gonna be here in—oh my God! An hour!" She grimaced. "You'll have to stay here for the weekend, but I promise, you'll come home for the next one." She managed a little smile. "I'll be back in time to make your Halloween costume, okay?"

His class was dressing up as old movie actors from the '30s and '40s—he'd actually been sort of looking forward to it because it made Halloween, which he should have been too old for, into something grown-up and sophisticated. It was like they knew all these actors that the babies in the sixth grade didn't.

"Okay," he whispered. For the first time, he realized how much he looked forward to his mother visiting. His brothers had left him, but she hadn't, and he'd forgotten how much that meant.

But she kissed his cheek and left, giving a little wave behind her as she did. Cheever walked out of the conference room and went looking for Aubrey, who he was pretty sure would have waited for him after he got his note from home.

Aubrey wasn't in the office waiting room, so Cheever ventured to the outside hallway, calling his name softly. "Aubrey? Aubrey? What was your thing about? You will not believe—oof!"

"See this?" Aubrey snarled, shoving Cheever up against the brick wall of the school. "Do you see this?" He waved one of those little yellow attendance slips in front of Cheever's nose, the kind they used for messages.

"What the—"

"It says we can't be friends anymore!" Aubrey's voice quaked for a moment, then firmed up. "Your brother's a druggie faggot, and my dad threw your mom out on her ass!"

Cheever somehow doubted that. "My mom didn't care enough about your dad to even mention it," he snapped.

Aubrey's slap, hard across his nose, his lips, his teeth, was a complete surprise. Cheever had never been in a fight in his life.

"Fuck! Aubrey!" Cheever's voice escalated to a whine.

"Shut up!" Aubrey sputtered. He was crying. "My dad says I'm not supposed to have anything to do with you!" He slapped Cheever again. "Shut up! Dammit, I hate you! I hate you! My fuckin' dad—"

"Your dad who's dating my mom?" Cheever asked, baffled.

"Not any fucking more!" Aubrey snarled. "Your brother's a fag, and she dropped his sorry ass, and now we can't talk no more!"

He broke off and let go of Cheever's collar, turning his head to wipe off the tears and the snot.

Cheever's face ached, and his heart ached. And all he understood—really understood—was that his brothers, who hadn't been home for a year, and who sent him and his mom presents and cards and flowers but never any company, had apparently just fucked up his life.

Aubrey ran off, leaving Cheever trying to pull his shit together outside the principal's office. By the time he'd gotten a towel from the bathroom to staunch the bleeding in his nose and got back to gym class, the entire school knew.

Not that Aubrey and Cheever had kissed.

Not that Aubrey had hit Cheever and screamed at him and cried.

No, the entire school knew that Cheever's brother, Mackey, was a druggie and a faggot.

Cheever *really* missed his mom that next week. He spent breakfast, lunch, and dinner sitting at his own goddamned table in the cafeteria, wondering who was going to dump a tray of food on him next.

His mother showed up at the school the following Sunday to take him home for a little while and to tell him how things had gone.

"He's going to come out to the press," she told him, sighing.

"That sucks." Cheever shuddered. He couldn't think of anything worse than this last week—but then, he hadn't been trying hard.

"No," she said firmly, piloting their new SUV. "It does not. Cheever, your brother looked like a good stiff wind could blow him away. Kell and Jeff and Stevie were—well, they were worried. I couldn't get much out of Kell, but Jefferson told me that it got bad. Like, 'being afraid to check in his room' bad. If coming out to the press helps him live his life so he's not that unhappy, then it's going to be a good thing."

"Yeah, that's 'cause he doesn't have to fucking live here!" Cheever snarled, about done with his brothers' feelings. "They're out there, living the high life, and we're supposed to feel sorry for them because they fucked up—Mom!"

Heather had veered off the road and onto the shoulder. The face she turned toward him was tearstained and furious.

"Your brothers...." She shook her head and shuddered. "Your brother was nineteen years old when he signed that contract. The first thing he did was buy us a *house*. And a car. And your school tuition—"

"I fucking hate it there!"

"I don't care!" she shouted back. "Because you didn't have to go to the other middle school, so you don't know how many fights those boys got into. You think it's bad now, because the kids give you shit? Mackey wasn't the only one who came home with bruises. Kell, Jefferson, Stevie—God help me, even Grant Adams—they spent their lives trying not to get beat the hell up. I'm not going to let that happen to you!"

"Well, it would be a damned sight better than what they're doing now," he muttered.

His mom sniffled and wiped her face on her shoulder, just like Aubrey did. "I'm sorry about that," she said, her voice muffled. "You have no idea how much. And I'm sorry you couldn't have been born rich, like all these kids who knew each other from the cradle. I'm sorry me and Aubrey's dad aren't seeing each other anymore. I know you liked him, and I'm sure that makes things awkward."

Cheever rolled his eyes—but he didn't say anything because he couldn't.

"Or worse," she added. "But don't you see? Whatever you're going through now? It would be about a thousand times worse at the local school. And if I took you down to LA, us rednecks wouldn't stand a chance."

Cheever let out a groan and thudded his head back against the seat. "Mom!"

"Honey, it's like... it's like Mackey and Blake in rehab. They look like hell. Blake practically cried when I hugged him. I think they had to make an effort to shower, they both looked so tore up. But they're sticking with it because they know it will be worth it in the long run. You've got to eat some shit, and I'm sorry. There's nothing I can say that will make it taste better. But when this meal is done, you know oatmeal won't taste half bad."

Cheever grunted, done with the conversation, and his mother started the car again. He went home and sat down to a meal in peace, and thought she might be right.

This was going to suck. But in first grade, his mom's car had broken down, and Kell had given him a ride to school every day in his shitty pickup truck. Kids had laughed at Cheever because getting out of that thing had been a laugh riot—he'd slid down the seat, off the runner boards, and onto his ass every damned time.

And it hadn't been a picnic.

But it hadn't been walking the two miles to school either.

So Cheever would tell himself it was like that.

Couldn't be *that* bad, right?

AUBREY'S SHOULDER hit Cheever hard in the back, and he went slamming into the bank of lockers with a bang.

"Watch where you're going, faggot!"

Cheever could have—oh God, he could have said, "You're the one who shoved his tongue down my throat, motherfucker!"

But he didn't.

"What the hell's your problem?" he demanded, tired of just taking this shit. It didn't get any better tasting—not after the last week.

"Your fucking brother, flashing his little twink bod on TV. You think I want to be associated with that shit?"

Cheever scowled. His mother had told him the press conference was coming, but he just hadn't put two and two together. "Man, what in the fuck does my brother have to do with me? I have not seen him in over a *year*, do you get that? I show up here, and I'm thinking I get to start brand-new. It is not my *fault* he's doing whatever he's doing!"

"Your whole fucking family is out there, telling him he's okay! Why the hell should you be any different?"

Cheever's brows knit together. "Even Kell?" Because Kell was the oldest, and he hadn't seemed that liberal when he'd lived in Tyson. Cheever couldn't imagine how that had changed.

"He was standing there, looking all tough and all, but your brother just came out, wearing some fag getup like it was all good."

Cheever thought he'd try for reason. "But he's not hurting *you*, is he?"

Aubrey had *kissed him*!

And Aubrey's eyes grew shiny, like he remembered that.

"Fags breathing my air hurts me," he said. Was Cheever the only one who heard how automatic that sounded?

But Aubrey was getting a crowd.

"Sure," he said, turning away. "You are that weak."

He walked away, his back straight, his heart turned to ashes in his chest.

That night, when he was walking from the cafeteria to the dorms in the chill of late October, he heard a voice behind him. He whirled, scared for the first time in his life, and was surprised when a young man with a scruffy beard and a hipster sweater held up his hands, looking around surreptitiously.

"Hey, little man—no worries. I'm not gonna hurt you."

"Who the hell are you?" Cheever snapped, blood roaring in his ears.

"I'm just, you know, spreading the word. I'm Rob Kirkman. I work for Celebratation—you've heard of us?"

Cheever regarded him with unfriendly eyes. "No. No, I have not."

The man smiled, an ingratiating flash of teeth under his scruff. "Well, we're a celebration of celebrity," he enunciated, so Cheever would get it. *Heh-heh. Right? Celebratation?*

Cheever stopped short. "You're paparazzi?"

"Yeah! We were wondering if you'd give us a quote?"

Cheever's heart burned in his chest. Oh God. Here was his chance. His chance to get these assholes off his back, to let people know exactly how he felt.

Rob held up his phone with a nod, letting Cheever know he was on record. Cheever stared straight into the little flashing light and threw his brother under the bus.

His MOTHER was so pissed, she pulled him out of school to yell at him.

For an entire day.

Which was still better than being at school.

"Cheever, I just wish you appreciated what your brothers have done for you—"

"My brothers don't give a shit about me!" he shouted back, and his mother—his mother slapped him.

Not hard.

Not for blood, like Aubrey had.

But like he was being hysterical and she was trying to get his attention.

"You will live to take that back," she said.

"Why rehab?" he snarled back. "Why aren't they coming home?"

"Because if we want to keep the house, they've got to get back out on tour," she said, eyes fierce. "You think they've been out there, having a big party? They're out there *working*. Mackey has been *working*. Do you know his manager told me he'd organized his entire CD, and the one after it, when he was struggling with drug addiction and close to dying? Trav was stunned, said he'd never seen a bunch of kids with a better work ethic. Because they know what's at stake for us if they fuck this up. So yeah. Now that they're not a mess, they're gonna see us more. They're coming here for Christmas for two weeks. I've got the house all ready. But what they're doing, they're doing for all of us—even you, if you'd see it. And you just thanked them by stabbing them in the back."

Cheever swallowed, remorse hitting him like a freight train to the chest, adolescent pride the brick wall at his back.

"I'll believe it when I see it," he muttered. His mother just shook her head.

"You know, Cheever Sanders, even if they broke that promise, it has nothing to do with you talking to the press. You know that, right? Their sins aren't yours, but selling your brothers out? That's all on you."

Great. Cheever felt like shit.

And the weekend had only begun.

B<small>Y THE</small> time Christmas rolled around, Cheever had lost twenty pounds and gained a shit-ton of bruises.

It didn't matter that he'd talked to the press. His class had forgiven him, but Aubrey hadn't. Aubrey's attacks had become less public, though. Less violent.

And more disturbing.

Right before Christmas, Cheever was packing to go stay with his mom, because he and his mom were going to pick up his brothers in Sacramento the next day, when there was a knock on his door.

Before Cheever could even open the door himself, it flew open and Aubrey stormed in, kicking it shut behind him.

"What the—"

Aubrey shoved him, face-first, against the wall. "You gonna spend your time with your faggot brother over Christmas break?"

"Yeah." Cheever tried to take a breath but couldn't. "So?"

Aubrey leaned close enough that Cheever could feel his quickening breath against Cheever's ear. Right when he expected Aubrey to speak, Cheever felt something wet and sloppy along his cheek, dragging up to his temple, and his stomach turned. Aubrey had *licked* him.

"Ew! Gro—"

Aubrey elbowed him in the back, then whipped his foot around Cheever's, bringing him down to one knee.

Cheever pushed up against the wall, only to have Aubrey grab him by the hair and shove his face in his crotch.

"Get used to that view," Aubrey growled.

And then he was gone.

It took an hour in the bathroom for Cheever to calm down enough to finish packing.

All that, and the next evening, after a two-hour drive to the airport to greet the plane, Mackey didn't even get off. Jefferson, Stevie, Kell—even Kell's best friend, Blake, and some girl Jefferson and Stevie had sort of co-opted as, like, their mutual girlfriend. But not Mackey.

No. They were going to have to go all the way back to Tyson, get clothes for Cheever and Heather, and drive all the way down to LA so poor fucking Mackey didn't have to be alone with his faggot boyfriend for Christmas.

By the time they got there, Cheever was pissed off enough to spit nails. He'd been shoved to the back corner of the SUV, listening to his brothers go on and on about tattoos and rehab and exercising and clubs and shit—and oh my God! Every half an hour, one of them would turn to him and go, "Hey, Cheever, how you doin', man? You're so quiet!"

Like he was going to spill his soul right there?

The only bright spot had been, unexpectedly, Blake Manning. During the quiet parts of the trip, Blake would turn to him and ask him about his drawing, about his school. Blake had seemed human, and he'd managed to pull Kell into their quiet little bubble for part of the trip too, but it didn't outweigh the resentment in Cheever's heart that they had to do this at all.

Fuck. Them. Fuck them all.

Mackey and his giant orangutan of a manager were stumbling about in their boxers in this ginormous house when they arrived, and God, he tried to piss them off. He dropped the *F* word—not the cool one that meant fuck, either—in every goddamned sentence, a sort of bitter satisfaction washing over him when he saw Mackey's big gray eyes get damp and shiny.

And then the orangutan grabbed him by the throat and took him outside for a little glory hallelujah.

Travis Ford had served in the military with distinction as an MP for eight years. He'd gotten out of the service and gone to college on his own dime, and then he'd earned a living in a hard fucking occupation.

All that, and he put up with Cheever's asshole brothers.

In his entire life, Cheever had never felt so small.

Yet.

Cheever let Trav's words sink in, then walked back into the house and made up with Mackey and the guys. For two weeks, they made him the king of their house, took him to every amusement park known to man, tried hard to show him a world beyond Tyson/Hepzibah, which they all seemed to loathe as much as he did, and worked *really* hard to show him he mattered, right up to taking him on amusement park rides until he puked.

And Blake Manning had held his head while he threw up. Plain, quiet, with a slow smile and a sly wit, Blake seemed like he was happy being the guy nobody noticed. Cheever tried to learn from him.

He held on to that feeling for as long as he could when he went back to school. His brothers loved him. They would do anything for him. He had to remind himself of that again and again, because they were going on tour for nine months and he wouldn't see them again until the fall.

And in the meantime, Aubrey only got worse.

It had been bad enough when Cheever expected violence, but what Aubrey was doing was horrific.

A random hand on his ass, one on his crotch, a tongue on the back of his neck when he wasn't expecting it.

Any moment alone was a moment to be afraid of having his person touched without his consent.

At the end of the school year in May, when Kellogg and Jefferson and Mackey were nothing more than texts and postcards from Europe, and his mom was an uneasy, fidgeting presence at dinner every night, Cheever was studying in his dorm when he heard the doorknob turn.

His heart froze in his chest. He'd forgotten to lock it. Holy God, he'd forgotten to lock the goddamned door. He'd remembered—ever since Aubrey had come in before Christmas—to lock the goddamned door, but not this time. Not this night.

By the time he'd stood and rushed toward the door, Aubrey had slid in and kicked it closed behind him.

Then he locked it.

"Get out!" Cheever told him, but there was a quaver in his voice. Here, at school, was the only place he'd had his own room. He'd been waiting for two years to find out it was a mistake and he'd be sharing this space with three people in one bunk bed.

"Make me," Aubrey taunted, voice low. "Make me."

Cheever had seen his brothers wrestle, had always told himself he was too civilized to fight. But being here, locked in his room with his antagonist—the guy he still had tortured wet dreams about—left him in a cold sweat.

He made a clumsy rush at Aubrey, unsurprised when Aubrey put him in a headlock and flipped him to his back.

"Get out!" Cheever panted, winded. Aubrey had grown this last year, in height and breadth, and Cheever was taller but still slender, like his mother.

Aubrey responded by throwing himself on top of Cheever, his knee at Cheever's groin, his hands pinning Cheever's above his head.

Cheever's vision went a little gray at the graze to his balls, and the scream he had planned turned into a whimper.

"Get out," he whispered.

"I said make me."

"I'll tell. I'll tell every—"

Aubrey bit him in the neck, sucking hard, hard enough to leave a hickey, and no amount of squirming could dislodge him.

"You're mine now, bitch," Aubrey taunted. He moved his knee so he could grab Cheever's crotch, and Cheever made one final desperate bid to dislodge him.

Aubrey cracked him hard across the face and put his mouth low to Cheever's ear. "Stop it," he hissed. "Stop it. You're mine. You let me do what I want, and I'll let you back into the class next year. You're already my bitch—just let me own you, and there'll be no more getting tripped in gym. No more shit dumped on you at lunch. Just take the 'be-my-bitch' package, Cheever Sanders, and your life'll be gold."

Oh God.

Cheever didn't even know what else Aubrey could do. All the ways he could be hurt. All he knew was that every day at school since October had been one long horrible sinkhole of loneliness, and Cheever was so fucking done.

He didn't say yes. In the following years, he'd remember that. He never once said, "Yes. You have my permission. Use me."

This time he just closed his eyes and let his body go limp.

And tried to pretend that what happened next was happening to somebody else.

WHEN IT was over, after Aubrey had left him whimpering on the floor, and he'd rinsed his mouth and wiped the come off his face and showered for an hour, he thought he should be thankful.

His pants had stayed on.

He had bruises on his nipples, his throat felt bruised and swollen, and he was going to have to sit on a pillow because his balls ached from that first graze, but his pants had stayed on.

They wouldn't always.

Aubrey had promised him that. He was going to have to come back to school at Tyson/Hepzibah Prep with his ass prelubed, because next year, Aubrey was going to expect an all-access pass to Cheever's room.

And Cheever's body.

Cheever was owned now.

There was no way out.

SUMMER WENT by in a blur of his mother's helpless worry and his own helpless misery. Three days after he was back in the dorms, it happened. He prepared for it—no tearing, no ripping, just some pain and Aubrey's harsh breaths behind him.

When it was done, Aubrey patted him on the head and told him he'd see him tomorrow.

Cheever cried all night, but by God, he sat with Aubrey's friends the next day.

A month later, he could face those boys and talk, laugh like they had before Mackey had come out.

Which was not always a free ticket out of hell.

"Yeah, Cheever. We'll stop calling you a fag when you lose your V-card!" Roger Gilchrist chortled.

Cheever looked up from his mashed potatoes and sighed. His mom had apparently taken the hint of all his rolled eyes and cold silences, and she'd started leaving him alone a couple nights a week. A part of him was relieved, but a bigger part of him was hurt. Shouldn't she have known he didn't mean it?

"I'm not sleeping with any of the girls here," he said shortly. Yeah, he'd heard about Grant Adams, his oldest brother's best friend. The guy should have gone with Outbreak Monkey, made it big, gotten the fuck out of the goddamned Tyson/Hepzibah area—but he hadn't. No, Grant had gone and knocked up his girlfriend. Cheever wasn't going out that way. For one thing, he didn't feel that way about any girls, but for another? He could think of nothing worse than to be stuck in this tiny area, married to a girl he didn't love and having to bend over for Aubrey Cooper for the rest of his fucking life.

The actual thought of it made him physically ill. He'd looked up suicide. He'd looked up the easiest way to do it. Right now he was thinking pills because he wanted something quiet, but he'd take a razor to his wrist if he had to.

"Then find a stranger," Roger said with a cavalier shrug. Unlike Aubrey, who was pretty and substantial, Roger was plain, with a thin face and limp brown hair, but he moved with a liquid grace that Cheever found unsettling. Aubrey had gotten fairly impersonal about what he did to Cheever a couple of nights a week. Roger just moved like he could hurt someone. "It's not like you gotta marry 'em."

"Right?" Tim Bronson rounded out Aubrey's little group of popular jocks. Tim had a broad, ruddy face, sandy blond hair, and sort of narrow, piggy blue eyes. He looked like Aubrey would, if Aubrey was a cartoon character that ran into a plate glass window. Just sort of smushed.

Of the three boys, Cheever suspected Tim was the one who had actually had contact with a girl.

"What do you mean?" Cheever asked, keeping his voice pitched at ingenue levels. The thing was, he knew what they were talking about, and he'd always thought it was sort of revolting. But God, he was desperate. Aubrey was bad enough. If Cheever didn't produce some sort of knowledge about being with a girl soon, he was afraid Aubrey wasn't going to be his only nighttime visitor. Those razor blades were looking better by the second.

"Man, don't even ask them," Tim sneered. "Just reach out and grab what you want. My dad says that's the only way to make a bitch mind."

Cheever stared at him, his brain blank. The thought of calling his mother a bitch just did not fucking compute.

"My dad says so too," Aubrey chimed in, looking at Cheever with pure possession in his eyes. "Once they're yours, they got no say. You can share 'em however you want, and they'll always come back to you."

Cheever gave up on his mashed potatoes, his blood running cold. He heard the message loud and clear.

God. He was going to have to grope a girl.

NOBODY WAS more surprised than he was when one dropped into his lap.

Apparently just thinking about Grant Adams and his brothers was enough to conjure a miracle. Of all things, Grant was dying of cancer, and Cheever had a brain cell to think that Grant was the luckiest sonuvabitch Tyson had ever seen.

The rest of him was just sort of excited that his brothers were going to be home.

He could talk to them, right? They seemed okay with Mackey coming out, and the ways he'd fucked up. They could be okay with Cheever and Aubrey Cooper's all-access pass to his ass, right?

Maybe just spending some time with them, like Christmas had been… maybe that would be enough.

But things were a mess when they got to the house.

Some girl who had been touring with them was sick, and the guys were all knotted up, because apparently, Grant Adams was someone they really fucking loved, unlike Cheever, who was someone who got in their fucking way all the time.

That wasn't entirely fair—Cheever knew that.

The morning Grant came to their house, Cheever saw him in the kitchen and went to hide in his room, feeling wretched.

Grant looked awful.

Cheever remembered how pretty he'd been when he'd been in high school, how his gold-brown eyes had practically glowed, looking at Mackey or Kell. Cheever remembered seeing him kissing Mackey when Cheever was supposed to be napping, and how he'd always hoped he'd end up with someone that beautiful, so pretty, it made his heart hurt.

There wasn't anything left of Grant now. Withered and wax-pale, he made Cheever rethink that "Yay for cancer!" idea. He was too tired to walk—Mackey's asshole manager/boyfriend had to carry him to the table, for fuck's sake.

And Cheever could tell, just from that first morning, that the guys, their visit, it wasn't going to be about him at all.

He tried not to be heartbroken. Tried not to feel alone.

But his mom's house was filled with people, most of whom he didn't know. When he realized one of them was a pretty girl—Briony, who apparently ran the light and soundboard for the band, even though she barely looked older than Cheever—Tim's words about just reaching out to take what he wanted started ringing through Cheever's brain.

When he stumbled to the bathroom to take a leak and she popped her head out of the shower to see who it was, it seemed like... well, an opportunity. Just... just... reach out and touch it. That's all. Reach out and touch it.

A boob. He could say he touched a boob.

If he'd had any idea what would happen next, he would have just taken the razor to his wrist right then.

MACKEY AND his mom had left—something about going to fetch Mackey's boyfriend—and Cheever was alone, sitting at the kitchen table, shell-shocked.

"Hey, you okay?"

Cheever barely glanced up.

It was Blake Manning again. Tall, thin, slouchy—like a cat—with a narrow, appealing face and sort of a scruffy goatee. He had dark brown hair that layered from his nice hazel eyes to his narrow jaw, and there was something... feral about him. Not quite tamed.

Sort of like Mackey, actually, but not mean. Just skittish.

He'd been part of the Greek chorus of male voices, the companionship Cheever had craved but didn't know how to unlock for himself, and now he was just... comfortable. Cheever still remembered that trip from Sacramento to LA, stuffed between Blake and Kell, and Blake's quiet attention.

"No," Cheever said shortly, not even able to lie.

"Want to talk about it?"

Cheever glanced up and saw nothing but honest concern on Blake's face. "Did that really happen?" he asked, not even able to put words to it.

"You touching Briony's boob, or us all sitting on your brother to keep him from losing his shit about it?"

Cheever ground his palms into his eyes, but it didn't stop the burning.

"The reason he got so pissed? Was it because his ass was for sale?"

Blake sat down, giving a neutral grunt. "Your brother's ass was never for sale," he corrected firmly. "Naw. Right after detox, but before rehab really stuck, you know? Some asshole roofied his beer—roofied it so fuckin' bad, he almost died. Trav got to him before he could OD, but not before the asshole could...."

"Have sex with—"

"Rape," Blake substituted, again, not judgy. Just no bullshit. "Your brother was raped. He did not want it, and he was unconscious, so he couldn't prevent it." Blake let out a sigh. "And then he almost died."

Cheever was silent then, appalled, because it sort of hit him. He was going through hell, but his brother had already been there. And his brother was mad because Cheever had gone and foisted *his* hell on somebody else.

How was Mackey supposed to know? How was anybody?

And here they were in the same house, and everybody's hell was so big, so all-encompassing. It was like there was no room for another person's hell in his brother's heart. His own hell was already more than he could handle.

"I was... I was not a nice person then," Blake said ruminatively into the silence. "I... you know. We've all got our own shit to sort."

Cheever actually looked at Blake, saw him as a person. Unassuming, in a way, although Cheever had seen the concert footage and knew Blake had it in him to be noticed.

"What's your shit like?" Cheever asked, suddenly so hungry to hear about someone whose hell did not begin and end in Tyson fucking Hepzibah, he couldn't hardly stand it.

Blake shrugged. "You know, Trav had to take a restraining order out on my mom. She kept hitting the band up for money. Threatened to tell the press about the shit I did to make rent after I bailed." He looked around Cheever's house then, at the sweetness with which Cheever's mother had decorated, once she had a place of her own and money to do it. "I... I would have bought her a place too, if she'd even given me a fuckin' minute to breathe after I signed the contract. Our old manager just kept paying her off. Trav was the one who put a lid on her and made her stop." He took a breath then, like he was shoring something up in his chest. "I sort of live in fear, you know?"

Cheever frowned. He couldn't fathom being afraid of his mother. "Of what?"

"Of her deciding it's not enough and coming back. Trav, he likes to protect us. I'm just going to hope he keeps doing that."

Cheever stared blankly. "I never thought of that as a blessing." Would Trav protect *him*? After last Christmas, Cheever was afraid to ask.

Blake didn't answer. He just looked around the house again and graced Cheever with a smile almost as sweet as Heather Sanders's pink drapes. "You're real lucky your mom loves you. She'd love you through just about anything. All the yelling she did at Mackey, at Kell and Jefferson— even Stevie. It wasn't yelling 'cause she thought they were useless, or 'cause she thought they owed her something when they didn't. She was just yelling 'cause she was worried."

"She doesn't worry about me," Cheever said glumly, and Blake's inelegant snort made him flinch. "What?"

"You're her baby. The way that woman looked at you, when she realized what you'd done—she might worry about you most of all."

Cheever swallowed. Oh God. She did. And he'd locked himself inside his hell and never even gave her the key.

Blake stood up then, stretched, and yawned. "God, I'm tired."

Cheever squinted up at him and realized that he sported a black eye and a swollen nose. In fact, *all* of the Outbreak Monkey guys had gotten in at asscrack in the morning, looking like they'd been hit by Satan's hammer.

"What in the hell happened to you all, anyway?"

Blake yawned again and then tried to widen his eyes against it. "Lessee… we finished off an exhaustive tour and took a plane to this flea-shit town—no offense."

Cheever found a smile somewhere in his shame. "None taken."

"And then Briony was sick, so Mackey and Trav were in the hospital all night with her."

Cheever groaned. "I… I did not know that. I got here the afternoon after you all got back."

Blake nodded and wrinkled his nose. "A quiet apology might be in order. She had walking pneumonia and a sinus infection and is taking enough antibiotics to kill a horse. That girl had a rough two weeks, if you know what I mean."

At school, with Aubrey and the gang, Cheever would have expected that to mean sex, but the girl Cheever had violated—oh my God, he *had!*—had apparently been recovering from the mother of all bugs. *Fuck.*

"Yeah," Cheever rasped, wanting to die a little.

"And then we met Grant." Blake's voice dropped some.

"Yeah." So did Cheever's. God. So many hell universes, all under this one fucking roof.

"And then last night we played in some dump called the Nugget, and your brother played two love songs. And the first one was okay, I guess, because it was about keeping things a secret. But the second one was for Trav, and I guess there's no keeping that shit a secret, because that almost started a motherfuckin' riot."

Cheever's mouth dropped open. "He just… just told everybody? He was in love? With a man?"

Blake shrugged. "No sin in loving someone." He flashed a self-deprecating smile. "No matter what these assholes say. Anyway, there was a helluva fight, our boys held our own, and we all ended up in jail. Guy who pays our checks showed up to take a picture of Trav 'cause they're best buds and he thought it was hysterical, and then he bailed us all out, and we got home. And then you grabbed Briony's boob. There we go. We're all caught up."

Cheever let out a laugh, because Blake was dry and sort of funny, and then it hit him.

How he'd thought his misery was the center of the world, when really, he'd just been making the people around him even more miserable, and they had more than enough sadness to share.

Mackey had reamed him—reamed him good—on his way out the door, and Cheever had sat there, resentful and angry, wishing he'd go fuck off.

Wishing he'd go to hell.

Remorse hit him. Hard. In the gut where it counted, and his next breath wasn't even or free.

"Hey," Blake said softly. "Cheever, look at me."

Cheever met his eyes, plain and hazel, feeling foolish because he was well on his way to a full-fledged pity party, but Blake didn't laugh.

"I cannot count the number of ways I have fucked up as an adult. Or the number of second chances I've gotten, in the last two years alone. You're a kid. You're gonna fuck up. Did you learn anything from all the fuckin' drama that went down here on your mama's kitchen floor?"

He was going to do it—be a facetious little fucker and say, "Don't grab a girl's boob," but he couldn't.

"Don't share your hell," he said miserably. But Blake's sigh let him know that was wrong too.

"You can share your hell, little man, if that's gonna make you feel better. But don't foist it on someone else. If someone out there is making you feel like a piece of meat so you think what you did was okay, that's bad. That's not just bad for what you did, that's bad because someone's out there teaching you the wrong fucking lesson, and it's hurting you as much as you hurt Briony today. So maybe share your hell, if that's what's going on with you. But don't take it out on an innocent bystander. Maybe we can go with that, okay?"

Cheever took a breath and wiped his face on his shoulder.

"Yeah," he muttered. "Yeah. Fine. Whatever."

"I'm going to just leave you alone," Blake said, sounding weary. "I hear you. Good talk, kid. Don't grab people no more."

Cheever couldn't look at him, but he nodded. "Sums it up."

He went to his room then, pretty much for the rest of the day. His brothers mooched about, all of them as tired as Blake had been, as ready to play video games or nap and snack as the next guy with a hangover, but Cheever didn't want to participate.

He didn't feel *worthy* to participate.

His mother got home and knocked on his door. "Cheever, can I come in?"

His heart hitched in his chest because he realized he could say no. *Oh my God. I can say no!*

And that's when he realized he had to say yes.

"Sure."

He'd been lying on his bed, staring moodily at the burgundy walls she'd painted at his direction, at the sci-fi posters hanging at the foot of his bed.

At the window that went nowhere.

He'd been pulled out of school for the guys' visit. Somewhere in his mess of expectations and the stupid thing he'd done that morning, he'd forgotten that little fact.

Aubrey didn't have an all-access pass to his ass here.

He was free in his mother's home.

"Cheever, how you doing?"

He gave her a small smile. "Feeling dumb."

"You should," she told him, and his small smile turned to a bitter laugh.
He turned his face to the wall. "I'm sorry, Mama."

Her weight on the bed was welcome, and her fingers through his
hair.... He sighed, easing the weight on his shoulders.

"Cheever, are you happy? At that school? With those kids—
whoever they are—who let you think all that in the bathroom was okay?"

He thought about telling her then. About Aubrey Cooper. About the
visits to his room. About being a piece of meat for the taking, trading his
self-respect for a chance to walk down the hall unmolested.

Hell, about being gay.

Thought about it.

Didn't.

"No."

"When all this is over and your brothers go back to LA, what do
you want to do?"

He had his face turned from her, so she didn't see the way the
tears just seemed to slide from the corners of his eyes into the comforter.
"Anything," he whispered. "Anything but go back there."

"So you won't," she told him. "I'm not sure what we'll do. Home
study, maybe for the year. Maybe we'll move to LA.... I was afraid of being
there last year, but now? I'm thinking it might be a good idea. Would you
like that?"

No. Yes. He had no idea. None. He didn't answer her, but just stared
into space and let her smooth his hair back, like she had when he'd been
a little kid.

"Think about it," she said, standing so she could kiss his temple.
"We'll make a plan."

She left, but he couldn't think about it. Couldn't make a plan. All
he could do at that exact moment was lie there and cry, feeling empty and
blank and uncertain.

His brothers all had matching tattoos. They had the band. They had
this friend who was going to die and bind them all together in grief.

Cheever just lay there on his bed and wondered what defined him.

He had his art, sort of. It was the whole reason he was going to this
special magnet school, right? Because he could paint a pretty picture,
draw a cartoon, use crayons like a pro.

His brothers had their band; he had his art.

He remembered his brothers, bringing him home penny crayons, stealing copy paper from school, anything so he'd have something to draw on besides the walls.

He hadn't taken an art class this semester.

Had gotten too caught up in what Aubrey and them were taking.

His mother—God bless her—was going to give him a do-over. Was going to give him another chance to become that other person. He'd been Cheever Sanders, nobody at his old grammar school. He'd been Mackey Sanders's little brother—and Aubrey Cooper's bitch—at Tyson/Hepzibah Prep.

She was offering him a chance to go somewhere else, *be* someone else.

He would be Cheever Justin Sanders, artist.

A part of himself—the part that hadn't stopped howling when Aubrey had first hit him, first groped him, first assaulted him—amped the howling up a notch. *You think you can forget me?* it said. *You think you can just forget you were that sniveling piece of meat on the fucking floor letting that bastard use you?*

But that voice was drowned out now by the rush of relief.

He'd been a little fucker that morning, trying to touch another human being like she had no feelings, no say.

He could fix that person. He could fix himself.

He was sure of it.

His mom was right.

He had a plan.

One week before Mackey fell from the sky....

"No, MAN. I'm not scoring this weekend." Cheever shrugged at Connor Gilroy gamely. He wasn't a choirboy, no—he did some weed, some X, when he was destressing from finals. But ever since his mom had taken him away from Tyson/Hepzibah, he'd been damned conscious of that whole second-chance thing.

He had an allowance, and he stayed within his limits, and he paid his school bills and didn't worry his mother.

He showed up for family gatherings, was respectful to his brothers, played with the kids, left before he could be a pain in the ass or make anybody uncomfortable.

He didn't make himself a bother, but just worked damned hard on his art.

That was it.

There was no depending on his family for too much—not attention, not affection. He'd seen it, that long-ago afternoon. Everybody had their own hell. His job was not to inflict his on anybody else, right?

Cheever was getting good at that. Not inflicting himself on people. Staying clear of drama. Hanging with his brothers was loud and messy and people up in people's business. Cheever watched Mackey about lose his fucking mind when Briony got pregnant the second time. The first pregnancy had been particularly difficult. Kell had been a wreck because he really did love that woman, and since she'd forgiven Cheever—or at least, she hadn't been awful to him—Cheever didn't blame him.

The second one was worse, and Mackey—Mackey had been messy and high-strung and freaked-out almost as bad as Kell.

It had boggled Cheever, caring for someone that much. He'd almost—*almost*—cared for Aubrey Cooper, and that betrayal had nearly destroyed him.

Caring for a friend—just a friend, not a lover—as much as Mackey cared for Briony, or hell, as much as Kell cared for Blake Manning, that was just too… too….

Messy.

Painful.

Cheever went to school, socialized with a few friends, and basically that was it. He kept things light. Skimmed the surface. Didn't get involved.

But he woke up in a cold sweat most nights, afraid someone was coming in through his door. Which was why he slept alone. Always.

It was so much easier that way.

He didn't have to think about the last way he'd been touched, Aubrey's hands on his skin, the stink of adolescent sweat and cologne. Didn't have to worry that he hadn't come out, his family didn't know, didn't seem to care.

They saw him with girls a lot—maybe that was it.

Girls liked him. He had party drugs, he didn't try to get in their pants, he didn't obsess about boyfriends. A party girl in his car was like family-repellent. He knew a few.

And once his mom had gotten him here, to this place where everybody's brother or mom or dad or sister was rich and famous, and nobody gave a shit that his brother was gay, he could just fade into the scene.

It was awesome.

And, like he was trying to explain to Connor right now, he just didn't like being too deep.

"Dude, no. I'm not partying. I've got my portfolio review in three days. I need three more pieces—and they're not easy—or I don't make it to the graduate program, okay?"

Connor was a good-looking surfer boy—rich kid, red Mustang, C student at CalArts in animation. Dealing party poppers was Cheever's equivalent of working a fast-food job in high school. He didn't really *need* the money, but he liked having something to do and a way to meet people.

"Aw, come on, Cheever! That girl—Marcy?"

Cheever grimaced. "Marcia."

"Whatever. She likes you. You come to that rave in Resita tonight with some X, and she'll give me the time of day!"

"She's in rehab," Cheever said flatly. "I took her there. No more party drugs for her." No more heroin either. God, he'd been the one to find her with a needle in her arm, knocking on her door asking for a spare toothbrush for his sculpture, for fuck's sake.

He hadn't realized she'd broken up with her boyfriend, or that the habit that Cheever indulged in, maybe twice a year, had become a hands-down need for her, something she'd rather die than not have.

Cheever didn't really see the point of these kids doing all the fucking drugs. A little, well, who didn't? Doing smack until your heart stopped or coke until your brain ran out your nose?

It was like love or hate or family or other people.

Just too damned much work.

And Cheever had his goal. Graduation was in a month, and most of his classes were a lock—but this one in mixed media arts was the most important. He had decent grades, but this class, this class he needed an *A* in.

He wanted to work in the master's program, figuring he'd get an MA in Fine Arts, and then he could start building a collection and selling pieces, maybe even start a studio of his own.

He liked oil paints and watercolors, but he recognized the use of computers in what he was doing. It was just that art—painting, drawing, whatever—was the one place he liked to get his hands dirty, that was all.

But this professor—Tierce, Raven Tierce—she was just so damned hard to please. And she *really* didn't seem to like Cheever *or* his art.

How perfectly balanced, Mr. Sanders. Did you do pixel math to make sure no emotion actually showed through?

What a subtle use of... beige, Mr. Sanders. Way to go big.

No sculptures in your portfolio yet? No, that would require a commitment, wouldn't it?

Which was where he was now.

Three days, three pieces. Mixed media—he needed one sculpture of clay, which he had to do first so it could get fired, one papier mâché that felt like a little kid's art project, and one comic book.

The comic book was his own idea. He'd already drafted most of the book and even gotten story pointers from a friend in animation— Marcia, actually—who had been happy to talk to him from rehab because apparently, she was bored shitless. He just needed to put the finishing touches on it and print it out.

Three days. He didn't need drugs—just hard work. The guitar Mackey had given him for his fourteenth birthday called a soft siren song in the corner of his room, but he ignored it. The hours of covert practice, when nobody could hear him and compare him to his brothers, were one of his biggest comforts and his secret shame. That guitar sang to him more than color, more than lines or balance and proportion—but art, dammit. *Art* was where he was going to make his mark.

Who needed inspiration? Who needed the big all-encompassing love of creation?

Cheever had elbow grease and willpower.

Cheever had this locked.

THREE DAYS later, he arranged his portfolio on the display table on top of a cool white tablecloth. Much of his work was done in subtle, neutral colors, so the white served as a foil, he hoped, and made the display eye-catching.

Please let this work. Please let this work.

He'd done his best. Everything he'd learned in the last ten years about color, balance, proportion, aesthetics, politics—all of it was here, on display, for his professor to assess.

He wanted in the master's program. He wanted it so badly, he could taste it.

But Professor Tierce didn't seem impressed.

He'd seen her go to other students and interact with their displays. Even when a piece was an obvious mistake, she'd laugh and talk gaily about how screwing up big was just proof of a big heart. Cheever *knew*— knew with every cell in his brain—that he was a much more capable artist than most of the students in his class.

He just didn't know, couldn't even fathom, why Tierce seemed to hate him so much.

"Hm," she murmured, coming up behind him. He startled so badly, he almost knocked his abstract spiral off the table. It had been his clay project, and he'd had more fun with it than he'd expected, because it had become a sort of puzzle—how to get the thing to spiral up and still balance on the table.

"Yes, Professor?" He smiled prettily and batted his eyelashes. Objectively he knew his eyes were a pleasing feature—big and green in his naturally tan complexion over a small freckled nose, they contrasted nicely with his curly auburn hair that he grew to his collar in ringlets.

He'd had offers, male and female, but always, always, the sound of Aubrey Cooper's harsh breaths echoed in the back of his mind.

"I see you took the same risks you always take," she said with a sigh. She was a midsized woman, in her fifties, with mixed genetics. Her hair was a shower of graying spiral curls sprouting from her crown, and her skin was only a few shades darker than Cheever's. Her eyes—dark brown—were frequently laughing or warm.

Just never, ever when she looked at Cheever's art.

Seeming bored, she picked up the comic book, frowning as she looked through it.

"So, a superhero who... who rescues kittens from trees?" she asked, frowning at him. "Is that all?"

"He's... you know. A grade-school hero. Saves kids from bullies. Helps them with their homework. That sort of—"

"Have you not read *Captain Underpants*?" she asked in disbelief.

Cheever swallowed. "No, ma'am." His first school had been too poor to have it, and his second had expected him to be reading *Animal Farm* by the time he got there.

"*Diary of a Wimpy Kid*? Any of that modern YA stuff with the pictures inside it?"

He shook his head, not sure where this was going. "No...."

"Well, you need to. The art's not as pretty, but it's a damned sight better than this."

Cheever swallowed. "Uhm, sorry. I'll... if you want me to study some young adult literature and—"

"Don't bother." Tierce sighed. "I mean, it's not like you did, anyway."

"That's not fair!" he burst out, rubbing his chest. "That's not fair. Professor, I worked my ass off for this—I read all the descriptions, I planned, I ran computer simulations, I—"

"Oh my God! Mr. Sanders, you're an art student! Don't you know what art is?"

"Which definition do you want?" he asked, his voice cracking. "I've got Foucoult, Pyncheon, Gardner—there's all sorts of definitions of art—"

"I don't believe this!" She pulled her hair back in a bunch and then released it, allowing it to leap out over her head again. "Cheever! Do you know how I feel when I see your art?"

He looked at his carefully assembled items, from the comic book in her hands to the seven pieces he'd done of Northern California landscapes. "Uh... pleased?"

"*Nothing*! Your art is all balance and proportion and no *emotion*! How did you *feel* when you produced all this?" She made a sweeping motion with her arm, and Cheever bit his lip.

"Happy," he said tentatively. "I... I loved doing this. It made me... happy—"

She shook her head. "No. No, it didn't. It might have been pleasant, working on this stuff, but I gotta tell you, I am *not* feeling happy from your portfolio. That's the point. I'm not feeling anything."

Cheever swallowed. "But... but I worked so hard! I... I dedicated my whole education to this. I—"

"Aren't you Mackey Sanders's little brother?"

Cheever gasped like his professor had swung a pickaxe made of ice at his chest. "Uh.... Yeah. My brothers are—"

"Do you know why people like his music? Do you have any idea?"

"It's good?" Because Cheever had listened to every goddamned CD—and damn. Damn if his brothers couldn't do their thing exactly right.

"Because the songs that don't make the listener feel like barbed wire is ripping through their chest make them feel like someone's stitching up the wound with a rusty needle and a bottle of scotch for the pain. It's not always happy, but God, those songs make you *feel*. That's art, Cheever.

This? This is… craft work. You could make a pretty bowl and get a lot of money for it, but nothing on this table is going to make someone relive the best or the worst moment of their life. *That's* what art is all about, and that's why you fail every time you come out of the gate!"

"Fail?" Cheever asked in a small voice. "I'm… I'm failing?"

"No," she said, voice almost kind. "But you're not getting an *A*. This work isn't bad, and it doesn't offend. But it doesn't inspire either. We're calling this a *C*."

"*C*?" He wasn't sure he'd heard right.

"Look, Mr. Sanders, you want to impress me? Give me art that makes me feel that look on your face right now."

In an instant, he was that beleaguered little kid at the kitchen table. "But nobody wants to share my hell!" he shouted. "What good is that? To force your hell on someone else? Art's supposed to be a cure for hell—not a bridge to it."

She gave him a look that was pure pity. "There is no cure for hell," she said softly. "There's only showing it to other people so they can share the burden."

Cheever gaped at her, at a loss, disappointment like a shiv in his gut.

A *C*?

And a directive to be more like his brothers.

A *C*—and no graduate course?

He got a *C*?

Cheever stumbled out of the portfolio exhibition and into the quad at CalArts, blind with pain and disillusionment, his plan shattered at his feet.

He'd failed. Everything he'd tried to build for himself, every grade he'd ever earned, all of it, in shambles.

He had his phone in his hand before he even knew what he was doing. His art wasn't any good. No good. He'd failed. No art for Cheever.

He could only think of one thing that would ease the pain.

Fumbling with his phone, he called up Connor Gilroy. "Connor? Yeah, it's me. I need a party package. Cheever Sanders, party for one."

Or ten.

Or a hundred.

Maybe he'd be like Marcia, except they wouldn't find him until his heart stopped.

That worked for Cheever.

It really fuckin' did.

Let It Bleed

LATER IT would hit Blake how close they'd come.

A matter of minutes, maybe?

Maybe an hour.

Blake took the first flight out of Seattle he could find and took a Lyft to the house in Laurel Canyon so he could get his truck. From there, it was two hours in traffic to the college. God, it was a fucking eternity, right?

If Cheever hadn't been so stoned, he might have been able to cut deeper, and then it would have been over.

Blake made his way to the CalArt's dorm in Valencia, the hilly Los Angeles topography as familiar to him as his own breath in his ears. The dorm itself was empty. He could see signs of the boy—sort of. High-end clothes scattered around like they'd been hit by a whirlwind. An acoustic guitar, which surprised Blake, 'cause he thought the kid had pretty much turned his back on all the things his brothers loved, sat alone in the corner on a pile of music books.

But those things were incidental. The important thing was the litter of artifacts that sat in the center of the room. They looked like projects, or they had been once.

Someone had jumped up and down on them and then set them on fire.

One of them, a picture in what looked to be a series of landscapes, depicted the raw open acreage all the way up Five, toward Redding—toward Tyson/Hepzibah. Something about the picture left Blake… chilled. His stomach cold, his bowels colder.

It could have been the way Blake felt about Lancaster—and the way all the guys in the band felt about Tyson/Hepzibah—but there was something wrong with that landscape. There was something horrible about the color of the sky and the color of the bleached farmland.

Too much gray?

He didn't know jack about art, but something about that picture reminded him of those pictures of dead animals that turned to rot. Sure, there was fur and a body at the beginning and earth at the end, but in the middle, there were maggots and putrefaction, and Blake could see that just under the surface.

That was the vibe he was getting from that picture, and it curdled his stomach. He looked around the room and cringed. There were a couple of those pictures there, and each one made Blake queasier than the last. Oh God. Apparently you could take Tyson/Hepzibah out of the boy, but part of the boy was definitely stuck in that suck-ass town.

"He's not here," said a voice behind him.

He turned and found a young woman, tiny—underweight, actually, as though she did more drugs than food. She had almond-shaped eyes and tawny skin, marking Asian ancestry, and long, thick black hair in a messy braid.

She was wearing what looked to be gray knit pajamas—very, very comfortable pajamas.

"Do you know where he is?" he asked, keeping his voice gentle. Something about this girl was delicate—peaked and sad and fragile.

She bit her lip and shook her head. "No. He was texting me at rehab every day, right? Like, I lived for his texts. And about three days ago, he called me, and he was... he was so upset. He'd gotten a *C* on a project, and it really tore him up."

"Like a grade?" Blake asked, wrinkling his nose. Trav had made Blake get his GED, and like the Sanders kids, he'd gotten an online degree since then—but to be this upset about a grade? Blake had trouble with that.

"It was his *whole life!*" she cried, tears starting in her eyes. "He practically became a hermit, working on it. And she gave him a *C*, and he was... he was losing it. He said he called Connor, that he was going out like a rock star...."

Blake's blood froze. For a moment, the world refracted around him, like a broken crystal, and he had to *make* himself breathe again.

"I'm sorry?" *Inhale. Exhale. Do* not *think of what Mackey looked like after their last rock-star party.* "Could you repeat that? And who's Connor?"

She wiped her eyes with the back of her hand. "He's our dealer. Cheever didn't use—like maybe at parties after finals, but it wasn't a habit... but everybody knows Connor. Cheever said he was going to call the guy, and I told him to call me back because I know that's a bad move, right? And he texted me a couple of times. But I could tell he was really stoned, and...." She wiped her eyes again. "He missed all his finals. He... four years in this place, he kept a 4.0, and he missed all his finals, and—"

Blake's blood wasn't moving any faster. "Darlin'," he said, trying to keep his voice even. "Do you have *any* idea where he might be?"

The girl nodded. "There's a hotel—it's downtown, we go party there sometimes."

Blake nodded. "Can you take me there?" he asked, his pulse beating a sluggish tattoo in his ear.

"Can you take me back to rehab after we make sure he's okay?" She wiped her face again. "I... I had to use a Lyft, and my parents aren't sending me any more money until I'm clean, and—"

She took another deep breath, and Blake nodded, remembering everything he'd ever learned about being a decent human in the last ten years. When he'd been an addict, selling his ass for rent and coke, he'd have been able to walk away from this moment. But not now. Not when this little girl was looking like she could shatter into a million pieces. Not when Kell's little brother was missing and in trouble. Oh man. He'd learned to help people since then, and he needed to do his best now.

"Darlin', I will not only take you back to rehab, I'll stop and get you a big shake and a burger on the way in. If I remember anything about rehab, it was that I craved the fuck out of carbs."

She smiled a little. "I just want to find Cheever. He's the only friend that didn't ghost me after I went in, you know?"

Blake nodded and took her elbow gently, guiding her to the parking garage where he'd left his truck. "Those are the kind of friends you keep," he said firmly. "What's your name, sweetheart?"

"Marcia. Marcia Lin." She sniffled. "Cheever's the only one who calls me that, though. Everyone else calls me Marcy."

"I like Marcia. I'm Blake. Blake Manning. Now, hon, how about you start telling me about this hotel, okay? I need to figure out the quickest way there."

BLAKE HAD grown up looking down on LA from up the hill, in Lancaster. The nearby Tehachapi Mountains were often cold as fuck, if beautiful, but Lancaster was a whole lot of desert. There was often nothing to do but look out at the sky and see the light pollution of Los-fucking-Angeles, looming over the horizon.

It seemed like everything in the world must be happening there, while not fucking much was going on in Blake's mama's trailer park.

Blake had figured that getting to LA was the thing that would change his life the most.

It wasn't until he started playing dive bars that he realized despair had the same acidic taste in every part of the world.

The road Marcia took him down was one of those roads that used to mean something before the freeways became the lifeblood of the area. As it was, it sat a few blocks off the 405 in a nest of dive bars, strip clubs, and equally shitty hotels. This one, the Trident, featured a killer-clown merman on the front, with neon blue skin, scales shaped like pendulum blades, and nipples that were oddly disproportional.

Blake figured that merman on the sign was for the kids who accidentally smoked oregano instead of weed, so they could look at that thing and *think* they were getting high.

"This the place?" he asked doubtfully. Peeling paint, mold under the eaves, cracked windows, and pavement that looked like hamburger. He'd stayed in better places than this when he was selling his ass for rent.

But Marcia nodded, her peaked little face going even paler, her skin stretched so taut across her wide cheekbones it looked like her apple cheeks would burst through her skin.

"I don't get it," he muttered, swinging from the Dodge Ram and moving around to help her out. He'd all but tossed her in the front seat to begin with, because she was short and wearing Eeyore slippers, for sweet Christ's sake, and he was in a fucking hurry.

"Don't get what?" She weighed less than Kell's oldest, Kyrie, who was seven years old.

"You kids got money. I mean, you got cars, you got school. What the fuck you people doing in this dump? I stayed in places like this because I had to—but you guys?"

"I don't know, Mr. Manning," she said, her voice wobbly as fuck. "You ever felt so ugly on the inside, you didn't want to be someplace pretty?"

Blake shivered. He had—after running away from home, he'd felt like that for a couple of years. But he hated thinking about Cheever Sanders, who had been cool and removed and beautiful and arrogant ever since he'd had the money and the privilege his brothers gave him, feeling that way.

Had he felt this ugly all along?

Blake was heading for the manager's cubicle, sweating in the humid late-spring air, when one of the doors opened and a couple of boys staggered out, laughing.

They were rich boys—he could tell by the high-end Calvin Klein underwear, which was the *only* thing they were wearing, and the cocaine that dusted their faces like talcum.

"What's so funny?" he asked sharply, mostly to cut through their high.

"That kid in there—he was, like, giving away blow, man. Couldn't fuckin' do it all himself."

"Oh God," Marcia moaned.

"Cheever Sanders?" Blake asked, to make sure.

"Man, who the fuck cares!" The taller one—blond and pretty, or he would be if he was cleaned up and not covered in coke and come and God, was that blood? "Best piece of ass I've ever had!"

The other guy guffawed. Shorter, built a little more brutally than his buddy, his laugh was an ugly donkey sort of sound. "You only say that 'cause he didn't fuckin' move! Just lay there and cried like a pus—"

Blake hit him so hard, square in the nose, the boy sat down, looking stunned.

"Dude," his friend said reproachfully, so Blake hit him too. He and the boys had been in their share of fights, but he'd been a scrapper long before he had backup.

"Oh my God!" Marcia squeaked, but Blake grabbed her arm before she could start doing lines off their faces and hauled her into whatever nightmare waited for them in the room.

The two idiots outside hadn't closed the door completely, which was a blessing, but that meant Blake got a good look as the California sun streamed in. And that was not a blessing in any way, shape, or form.

Coke mirrors were everywhere, and so were syringes and spoons and dirty fucking needles. The two beds were a mess, covered pretty much in what had covered the guys outside—coke and come and blood.

Marcia looked around and moaned. "I'm going to have to reup another thirty days just for standing here," she whispered, but Blake ignored her.

Where was Cheever?

Then he remembered Mackey, and that year or so they'd toured together before Trav, when everybody knew Mackey didn't sleep on a fucking bed. He made his way to the far corner of the room and peered between the bed and the wall.

Cheever was there, face iced in cocaine like a cake with frosting, blood streaming from his nose. His eyes were wide and dilated, and his knees were drawn up to his chin. He was naked, and Blake's heart cracked as he realized Cheever's nose wasn't the only thing that was bloody.

Those fuckers. Those fucked-up raping little assholes. Blake should have used their faces to clean the cement.

And then Blake saw what Cheever was doing and even the violation ceased to matter. Cheever had a razor blade, and he was cutting deeper, steadily deeper, into his own wrist.

"*Cheever fucking Sanders, you stop right now!*" Blake shouted, and Cheever dropped the razor blade in surprise. Then he took one look at Blake and began to cry.

BLAKE GRABBED one of the top sheets from the floor, figuring it would be the cleanest thing in the place, and wrapped it around Cheever's long, slender body. The boy was pipe-cleaner thin most days, but now he was just skin and bone.

"Marcia, don't touch nothing!" he snapped. "Follow me!"

She was still frozen in the center of the room as far as he could tell, but his nose was tingling just from the amount of product in the air.

He used the running board to put Cheever in the middle seat and then helped Marcia up, handing her the pocket knife he kept out of habit.

"Rip off some strips from the sheet, wouldya, darlin'? He missed most of his vein, but he's still bleeding quite a bit."

"Oh my God!" she squealed, probably getting a good look at the blood seeping through the sheet as Blake ran around the truck. But she had a strip ready for him as he slid into his spot. He went for Cheever's wrist first, tying the first strip pretty tight, then the second one too. He used the third one to wipe the boy's face, and then made a grim assessment.

His breathing was thready, and he'd lost some blood. And God knows if he'd need stitches or care for his backside.

He'd definitely need an AZT pack if he wasn't on PReP, and that alone was going to require a hospital stay.

"Marcia, honey, we're going to have to take him to the hospital before I get you back to rehab. I hope that's okay."

She nodded, stroking Cheever's hair back from his face with gentle little strokes. "Oh, baby," she whispered. "Why didn't you tell me it all hurt so bad?"

"'Cause that would mean he had to talk to someone," Blake snarled, feeling savage. "And his whole fucking family sucks balls at that."

He looked at Cheever again, his eyes closed, shivering, face a waxy sort of green, and figured they were twenty minutes from Cedars-Sinai.

Then he stepped on the accelerator and made it in fifteen.

HE CARRIED Cheever into the ER himself, screaming for a doctor like seven kinds of fool, but the nurses were quick to get the boy on a stretcher and take him past the big locking door, leaving Blake to give all the information to admitting.

When he was done, the woman—tall, blond, late forties and a real knockout—fixed him with a gimlet eye. "And who are you?"

"I'm a friend of the family. The boy disappeared from school, and his mama was worried. His brother just got hurt in Seattle. I came as soon as his mama let us know."

The woman raised her eyebrows. "And how long has the boy been using?"

Blake looked at Marcia, who was shaking hard enough to be in shock. "Ma'am, can we get a blanket for her? She wasn't exactly in prime condition to come on this ride, and I'm a little worried."

The woman blinked past his shoulder, and her expression softened. "Sure, sweetheart. In fact, let's get you a bed and a sedative—"

"I'm in rehab," Marcia said, like her words came automatically. She actually looked around her then and flushed. "I mean, I sort of broke out, but only because I was worried." She bit her lip then, looking earnest. "He's going to be okay, right?"

Blake looked at the admitting nurse, smiling tentatively. "Right?"

But the nurse didn't take the bait. "How long?" she asked.

Blake looked to Marcia. "He sort of used occasionally," she said softly. "I've never... never seen anything like this. This was... this was a breakdown. This... this wasn't like Cheever at all."

An orderly came out with a wheelchair and a blanket, and Marcia looked desperately at Blake.

"Can I come back there with her?" he asked. "You'll find us when you know about Cheever?"

He took two steps toward the girl as she sank into the wheelchair and grabbed his hand fiercely.

"Yes, that's fine," the nurse said, and her stolid, no-bullshit expression relaxed a tad. "We'll let you know as soon as we do, okay?"

Blake nodded and followed the orderly back, thinking furiously. This wasn't like Cheever—not the Cheever that Blake had known over the years.

Nope, this wasn't cool or reasoned. This wasn't measured or planned. Since that one day, way back in Tyson/Hepzibah, after Cheever had grabbed Briony and sat at the kitchen table looking puzzled and forsaken, Blake hadn't seen Cheever when he wasn't looking at the time. He was always, *always*, trying to measure exactly how long he had to be with his brothers, how long he should play with his nieces and nephews, how long until he had to go do homework, or had plans with friends.

Not girlfriends, apparently—and that was something else the family didn't know.

But no, going out on a bender, taking a razor to his wrist, that didn't seem like Cheever at all.

But it was for shit-sure exactly like Cheever's brothers, which made Blake wonder who had been showing up at holidays and summer vacation for the last goddamned eight years.

They gave Marcia a gentle sedative, and after asking if she wanted him to contact her parents—and getting a hard no—Blake sat by her bed and held her hand while she sort of whimpered her way to sleep.

Poor baby, he thought, smoothing the hair away from her eyes. He promised himself he'd visit her in rehab and text her too. If Cheever had been her lifeline, well, he was sort of out of fucking commission, wasn't he? And Blake thought this girl needed more of a family approach.

Given the way she'd shaken her head when he'd asked about her parents, Blake was wondering if maybe he should take her to the house in the hills after rehab. She could go running with them same as everybody else, right?

She was a stand-up kid. Cheever had been standing up for her—and he'd apparently been doing a really good job—but the boy had his own shit to sort.

And fuck. So did Blake. He needed to deal with the family *now*.

As soon as she was asleep and Blake could claim his hand back, he pulled out his phone.

"Blake?"

Travis Ford might have been out of the military for over fifteen years, but that snap to his voice wasn't ever going away.

"Yessir."

"How's Cheever?"

Blake took a deep breath. "Better and worse than we expected," he said honestly.

Trav's response was a waiting, unamused silence.

"Well, me and Kell, we thought the little bastard's been doing everybody's drugs through college, right?"

"He doesn't go through that much money," Travis said, his voice measured. "His grades are impeccable."

"Well, yeah. You would know that." Trav knew fucking everything. "He was a cold little asshole to us, and we were thinking it was rich kids and cocaine, but it wasn't. Anyway, he got a *C* on a project, and it, like, ended his world. Like... *ended* it. Like... like he bought a round of drugs for the whole school and did them until he couldn't do no fuckin' more." Blake's voice was rising, semi-hysterically, and he didn't think in a thousand years he would ever be able to explain the horror of seeing Cheever, crouched in the corner, trying to leave the rest of his blood on that mangy carpet.

"Oh my God." Trav's horror echoed Blake's own. "Is he okay?"

"No." Blake couldn't contain his shudder. "I mean, I think he's going to survive this round but... but it was like Mackey, right? If he didn't spill his guts to someone, he was never gonna be okay."

"Or you," Trav said gently. Well, Blake's problems had been garden-variety bullshit. Mackey's had just cut deeper.

"Well, now it's Cheever," Blake told him, his eyes burning. "I.... Look. He's got a friend who pretty much escaped her own rehab to come help me find him. He's not really an addict, I don't think. This was... this was—"

"Suicide by coke?" Trav asked, voice grim, and Blake broke.

"And the coke razor," he said, wiping his face on his shoulder. He just couldn't stop remembering that kid, the way his face had emptied out when he'd been a little shit at thirteen. Talking about not sharing his own hell. Blake had thought he had your normal garden-variety hell, nothing like Blake's own bullshit in rehab, right? But still—there wasn't anything special about Blake Manning's problems either—they were probably in every shrink textbook known to man.

Maybe Cheever's problems were special to *Cheever* and nobody had told him that was okay.

"Oh, dear Lord—"

"He couldn't find the vein," Blake said, needing to spill it now so it couldn't destroy his reason in the next few hours. "But... God, Trav. That was a bad fucking moment right there."

"Shit. Shit, shit, fuck. I'll tell his mother—"

"Not yet." God. Blake hated to interfere like this, but... but he remembered him and Mackey stuck in their own hells together like it was yesterday. "Look, me and Mackey, we got a chance to control it, okay? The boy needs his mom—I'm not gonna lie. But maybe right now, tell her we found him. I'll call back and tell you if... when... he can talk. But in the meantime, he needs... like rehab, but—"

"We'll call it a mental health retreat," Trav said. "We can even use the same doctor."

Blake brightened. "Doc Cambridge? I love that guy!"

"I'm sure he'll be thrilled to hear from us again." Trav's voice had that dry little sandpaper sound in it that meant he was being sarcastic as fuck.

"Well, Mackey was sort of a tough nut to crack," Blake admitted.

"Yeah, well, he told me he wanted the entire band in his office so he could shrink their heads. I told him Jefferson, Stevie, and Shelia would break him and that would be a shame."

Blake let out a badly needed laugh. At that moment, the nurse from admitting came in, looking at Marcia in question.

Blake held his finger to his lips and stood. "Trav, I'm putting you on speaker."

"Who's on the phone?" she asked.

"Cheever's brother's husband. He's sort of... well, he takes care of the lot of us. You'll be sending your bills to this guy."

The nurse's eyebrows climbed. "Okay, then. That doesn't sound weird at all. Anyway, your friend is ready for recovery. He nicked the artery on his wrist, so there are a couple of stitches there, a few in his, uh...." She looked at the phone and blushed.

"His other injuries," Blake supplied.

"Yes, sir. And we gave him a sedative to counteract the effects of the cocaine. Now, we require a seventy-two hour suicide watch after seeing injuries like that—"

And Trav's voice came from the little box. "Can I send an ambulance for him? I've got a room booked for him at a psychiatric center nearby. It's usually meant for rehab, but they're set up to take patients with depression and other problems as well."

"I need more information about this place, sir, and I need to consult with the doctors working on him, and—"

"Blake, give this nice woman your phone."

"Yessir." Blake handed it over. "You can bring Cheever here while we're waiting for the ambulance?" he asked the nurse, whose name badge proclaimed her to be Nurse Crandall.

"We were planning on that," she said.

"Oh, hey, Trav? Can you book another room for his friend? She's going through rehab, and she could sure use a buddy. I think she'll do Cheever good too. He can see how much he scared her, yeah?"

"I can do that. Nurse Crandall? You and I need to exchange insurance numbers."

With that, the nurse took off with Blake's phone. No sooner had she rounded the corner than Cheever was wheeled in.

He looked... young.

He was lying on his side, his cheek on the hand handcuffed to the bedrail. His vulpine features—a little longer in the jaw, but much like Mackey's—stood out in stark relief against his tanned skin, pointed and vulnerable.

Blake double-checked on Marcia and moved his chair, waiting for the nurse and the orderly to settle Cheever's monitors and medication before he got all cozy.

Cheever opened his eyes blearily as he heard the scrape of the chair across the floor.

"Blake?"

"Yeah, kid."

"Mom?"

"Do you want me to call her?"

He watched then, the struggle over Cheever's face, and his heart constricted in his chest. God, this boy wanted his mama so badly. But a room full of blow and his ass torn open for good measure—what kid wanted his mama to know that?

Not to mention that big incriminating bandage on his wrist.

Blake couldn't hardly look at it.

"No," Cheever whispered at last, his eyes filling.

Blake stood. He hadn't seen this much emotion in the kid since the day Mackey had lost his shit at him for grabbing Briony's boob. He came near the bed and smoothed Cheever's hair back from his forehead like he had for Marcia.

"That there is the biggest fucking lie I've ever heard in my life," he said mildly, as Cheever's shoulders started to shake.

"Not like this," Cheever sobbed.

"Son, that woman loves you—"

"Not like this!" he begged. "God, please. Not like…." More sobs filled the room, big and loud and noisy. He kept trying to cover his mouth so nobody could hear, but hey, he was handcuffed to the bed because he'd tried to hurt himself, so there they were, his messy emotions, pouring into the empty air.

Blake just stood there, smoothing that curly red hair back, and thought it was about fucking time.

The sobs died eventually, and Blake brought the chair close to the bed—and grabbed a box of Kleenex too, so he could clean the boy up.

"Blow," he murmured automatically. He hadn't known kids until Mackey brought Grant Adams's little girl home. But first with Katy and then Kell and Briony's kids, Kyrie and Kansas, and the triplets' kids, Kyla and Kale—Blake had spent the last eight years becoming everybody's favorite uncle, and loving every kid as the blessing he'd never been.

He knew how to get a kid to blow into a Kleenex, and how to clean up traces of tears, and even how to sing a kid to sleep if he was too keyed up to let his brain relax.

"I am not this person," Cheever said, his voice lost, like a kitten in the rain. "I don't cry. I don't…. Oh God, I don't do what…." His body started to tense up again, like he was going to lose it, and Blake wasn't sure he had anything left in him to lose.

"Sweetheart, I need you to take a deep breath, okay?"

Cheever did, bless him, and nodded.

"'Kay. Now I'm going to talk, and if I bore you to sleep, that's fine. But you start out listening, okay?"

A small nod, and Cheever's enormous green eyes focused on Blake's face like he held the magic keys to the kingdom.

"Good. Now here's the thing. In eight years, we been seeing a stranger show up where Cheever Sanders was supposed to be. He said all the right things, and he did all the right things, but he never seemed like he wanted to be with us. So in eight years, I ain't ever known who you were, Cheever. But today, I know you're the kind of person that would make that little girl break out of rehab in her Eeyore slippers and stand in the middle of a cocaine tornado because she missed you and was worried. I know you're so hurt inside, you don't want to show your mama, when you want her here more than you want anything in the world. And I know there is shit in your heart—probably ugly, festering shit—that you ain't shown nobody, not your brothers, who would lay down and die for you, and not your mama, who would bring you back to life. So now, I'm real fucking curious. Who in the hell *is* Cheever Sanders, and why was he hiding behind that shitty rich kid for the last eight years?"

"He's nobody," Cheever whispered. "He's a sniveling baby, crying on the floor, just letting shit happen to him that nobody wants to know."

Blake made a hurt sound. "I've been that kid," he said softly. "That kid can grow into a decent person. You just gotta let him cry a little, let him know he's heard."

Cheever's breath was long and shaky, and his eyes kept leaking tears, but that terrifying storm of weeping seemed to be kept at bay. "Who wants to listen to that kid?" Cheever asked after that long breath. "I sure don't."

"I do," Blake said, surprising himself. "I've been waiting for that kid to talk to me for eight long goddamned years."

Cheever's eyes fastened hungrily on his face. "I wanted to not be a fuckup," he moaned. "I wanted to be someone worth listening to."

So needy. This kid—all his coolness, all his arrogance—he'd been trying to earn their approval?

Blake cupped his cheek. "Aw, kid. You wanted to not be a fuckup? You were born into the wrong damned family. We are fuckup city here. We just make that work for us. Welcome to Outbreak Monkey, right?"

That got a smile from Cheever, surprisingly enough. He used his free hand, the one not cuffed to the rail, to capture Blake's palm against his cheek.

"I'm glad it was you," he said, which surprised the hell out of Blake, "who found me."

He didn't say why, but his eyes fluttered closed, and Blake breathed a sigh of relief. That rot was still there, festering, needing to be bled out, but maybe Cheever's heart could rest for a little bit before it did.

Shelter

CHEEVER CHECKED out after that storm of weeping, letting the procession of nurses and doctors and directions wash over him. He understood three things at this point.

One of them was that if he ever did coke again, especially in quantity, he would probably suffer a brain aneurism and die.

The other was that he'd needed a pint of blood and fluids after his failure with the razor blade, and that people were not going to stop looking at him as if he might try to jump off a bridge again any time soon.

The last thing was that he'd somehow acquired Blake Manning as his own personal guardian angel in the past few hours, and the part of him that wasn't positively wilting in shame was pathetically grateful.

Cheever couldn't define the emotion when he'd opened his eyes to see Blake's narrow, average face over his bed. He'd forsaken his scruffy beard for a handlebar mustache for the past few years, but he'd shaved even that over this last tour, and what was left was surprisingly appealing. He looked like a businessman or a shopkeeper, and the only rock star thing about him was his dark brown hair, slicked back from his brow and hanging in loose curls at his nape.

But his eyes—plain hazel, ordinary—had held so much compassion, it was like transmutation. Blake's average features, as everyday as river rock, were suddenly transformed into gold.

Cheever wondered if he could ever see the man as ordinary again.

As the doctors consulted and Blake signed the papers and talked to the nurses and made sixty-dozen arrangements that had Cheever's head spinning, all he could feel was the heat of Blake's callused hand against his cheek.

It was like the only thing he'd really felt since Aubrey Cooper had violated his space, his trust, and his person.

Even as he closed his eyes in exhaustion and felt himself being carted off to another hospital with different doctors, he held on to that heat and began to hope.

HE CAME to in what looked like a really nice hotel room, with personally chosen artwork and an in-room basin and flowers on a small table at the foot of his bed.

Blake was there too, asleep in an armchair by the bed, his head tilted back, snoring softly. The fluorescent light wasn't flattering—Cheever could see the acne scars on Blake's cheeks from when he'd been a kid, and the crookedness of his nose. He'd had his teeth fixed sometime in the last few years—but Cheever remembered.

It was one of the reasons Cheever's brothers had trusted Blake, he guessed. Because Blake had come from a shitty background, just like theirs.

Cheever couldn't seem to remember being hungry or hating his clothes or being crowded into a two-bedroom apartment, like they did. He just remembered his brothers, all around him, until suddenly they weren't.

"Do my brothers know?" he asked into the silence.

Blake choked on a snore and flailed, looking around. "Wha'? You okay? You feeling okay? They said to watch for tingling in places."

Cheever stared at him, nonplussed. "Tingling?"

Blake grimaced. "They were worried. About bubbles in your brain. But you haven't stroked out in the last twelve hours, so I think you're safe."

Cheever groaned, not even wanting to think about all those chemicals buzzing through his body. "Safe?" Then he remembered... oh God. Not just his body. How many? How many guys had taken him while he'd been rolling around on that shitty bed? He closed his eyes and swallowed. "Never safe," he whispered. But he didn't want to go there. Not now. Not here. Not with Blake looking at him with those oh-so-sympathetic eyes.

Too late. Blake was squinting at him a little.

"What did you ask me?"

Cheever turned away, his wrist still clanging on the bedrail. Shit. He remembered someone taking him to the bathroom the night before and handcuffing him again when he got back. So much for a room full of flowers.

"My brothers," he said, his chest feeling thick. "Do they know?"

"I told Trav," Blake said softly. "He will probably tell the others this morning. But not Mackey."

Cheever looked at him, frowning. "Why not?"

"'Cause Mackey fell off an amp right before you had your little adventure, Cheever. He's probably still in the hospital, in traction, trying not to take any painkillers and driving the staff batshit."

"Aw God-fucking-dammit!" Cheever tried to sit up. "My brother got hurt and nobody fucking told me—"

"Well, we were *going* to tell you, but before we could even call you, your mom called *us*, panicking because the school wouldn't give her a fucking answer. So how's that?"

Cheever scrubbed his face with his free hand. "Well, great. So you *should* be in Seattle; that's what you're telling me. You *should* be with my brother, making sure the family is okay, but instead, you're here, cleaning up *my* fuckup. Goddammit!" He banged the bedrail with his fist. It was like his worst nightmare. His own bullshit coming back to hurt his family.

"Now wait up there," Blake said, standing up and stretching before coming to the bed. "You got that wrong. I am *exactly* where I should be, and I gotta tell you, running along the top of those amps was not the best idea Mackey ever came up with." Blake grimaced. "But the road crew was supposed to leave a plank up there, and they fucked up and didn't. He was going to make a leap and his foot got tangled in the mic wire, and... well, let's just say that for once, it wasn't Mackey's fault."

Cheever let out a strangled laugh. "Jesus fuck, Blake. Is he going to be okay?"

"Yeah. *Yeah!*" Blake pulled out his phone and checked, smiling tiredly. "He's gonna be fine, see?"

He held the phone out, and Cheever checked the messages, his eyebrows going up when he realized it was a group text, and his brothers bitched at each other in text like they did in person.

Mackey: I know you're checking on my little brother, Blake. How the fuck is he?

Kell: Stop bothering Blake, Mackey. He's doing his best and you're gonna hurt yourself.

Mackey: I'm fine. I'm peachy. I'll run a goddamned marathon tomorrow. HOW'S FUCKING CHEEVER, MAN, TRAV WON'T TELL ME SHIT!

Stefferson: Trav won't tell you shit because he's trying to keep you from struggling in traction, dumbass!

Jeevie: Somebody text Trav and tell him to take Mackey's goddamned phone!

And then, from Trav to everybody involved: *You assholes could always fucking TALK to each other and get off the goddamned phones!*

Kell: What's wrong with Cheever? Goddammit, how come nobody tells me shit?

Trav: FAMILY MEETING MACKEY'S HOSPITAL ROOM NOW! Except you, Blake. Keep us posted. Tell Cheever we love him. Out.

Cheever laughed a little, chewing on his lower lip and reaching out to touch the screen of the phone. "God, they're a fucking circus."

"Yeah, they are," Blake said, taking his phone back. "But they're our monkeys, and we love them. Did you notice the subtext there?"

Cheever nodded. "They love me," he said a little sadly. "I don't want to worry—"

"Well, tough shit. You want to know the truth? They've been worried about you for a lot longer than the last three days."

Cheever couldn't look at him. "What do you mean?"

Blake wasn't having any of it, though. He caught Cheever's chin in his fingers, and Cheever found he had to meet those average hazel eyes again.

Except they weren't average anymore. They were gorgeous and kind, and Cheever couldn't figure out how to make them go back to being ordinary.

"Remember last Christmas? You and your mom came, and you were supposed to stay for two weeks? Your brother planned for those weeks, you know. Trips to Disneyland for the kids and for you, concerts, art shows. Mackey got on the internet and found fucking breakout artists—had a whole wine-tasting thing arranged for you, 'cause you'd turned twenty-one."

Cheever grimaced. "Mackey hates that shit."

"He does. But these last years, you being all cool and bullshit—they've missed you. Mackey had this grand plan, how he was going to go mix it up in your world. Then maybe you wouldn't think they were too fucked-up to play with, right?"

Aw hell. "That wasn't—"

"But you left—two days after Christmas. Got a car, grabbed your bag, said you had friends out at the beach. Fuckin' broke your brother's heart, you know that?"

His family, so close, just like that round of texts. They were in each other's shit, the kids a big swirly mess, and Cheever didn't know them, and he felt like he was fucking contaminated, like if they knew him, he'd fuck them up somehow, like a curse. If Cheever was their friend, they too could have school bullies sneaking into their rooms to… to….

"That wasn't the plan," he rasped.

"Then why'd you leave?"

Cheever closed his eyes. "I… just didn't belong there—"

"You didn't even give them a chance!"

"I'm just…. It's just nice that they worried, that's all," he said, trying to get back to that shaft of goodness that the text had given him. "They… they don't need to, you know—"

"To know you?" Blake said softly. "That's a great idea, Cheever. You can show up, judge them, and run away before they get to know you. I mean, I know I've only known them for ten years, but I gotta tell you, that's a shitty way to be a part of the family."

Cheever tugged at the handcuff on the bed and grunted, tilting his head back against the mattress. "I'm not worth knowing," he said, his voice clogged. "I just flunked out of art school. Did you know that?"

"I know you got a C!" And there was a sort of baffled judgment in Blake's voice that finally, *finally* gave Cheever something he could be pissed off at.

"Is that all you see?" he yelled. "The grade? I put my *life* into that art. All I wanted to do was be an artist. I was so excited, right? Everybody loved that professor, said she really knew her shit. And she looked at me, and she saw my art, and she *hated* me. She hated my art—no. Worse. She was *indifferent* to my art. If she'd hated me, she would have given me an *F*, but she was *unimpressed*, so I got a C. That's all I am—oatmeal. Milquetoast. And then she has the nerve to tell me I needed to make art like… like my fuckin' brothers! Like I'm not even making *music*, right? And I'm *still* expected to live up to their fuckin' names!"

To his surprise, Blake laughed.

"What!"

"That's you in there," he said, sounding surprised. "Like, that's a fuckin' Sanders kid. Dang, boy—you had me worried there for a second."

Cheever gaped at him, suddenly ashamed of himself. "That was not very nice of me!"

And Blake sobered. "No. But you want to not live in your brothers' shadow? I get that. That's fuckin' human. It's the most human thing I've seen from you besides, you know, the last twenty-four hours or so."

Cheever fell back against the pillows, feeling suddenly weak. "You stayed," he said quietly.

"You needed me," Blake replied, just as quietly.

Cheever nodded. "I... I do. Do... do my brothers know... do they know everything?"

Blake pursed his lips. "Trav knows some of it. He knows about the drugs and the hotel—he had to hire someone to go clean that up. He knows about the grade and the professor, and is currently talking to CalArts administration. Apparently there's a nervous breakdown clause somewhere, so you might be able to make up your finals—"

"Gah!" Cheever ground the palm of his free hand into his eyes. "God, how fucking embarrassing." And then his voice dropped, as the other thing, the truly embarrassing, humiliating thing, battered insistently at his consciousness. And his aching netherparts.

"Does he know about them... those—" All of them, rough hands, laughing voices, that heaving breathing that sounded just like Aubrey, like they were pounding meat. "—those guys?"

"He knows you were assaulted," Blake said quietly. "But given the amount of drugs in the room, Cheever—"

"No charges." Cheever closed his eyes and shuddered. "I deserved it."

He was unprepared for the rage suffusing Blake's mild features. "Now *that* is total bullshit and the second biggest lie you've spoken today, Cheever Sanders—"

"Justin!" Cheever taunted, maybe to distract him and maybe because dammit, if this man was going to know who he was, he should *by fucking God* know who he was.

"Cheever *Justin* Sanders! You didn't deserve that! You didn't deserve any of that. Maybe not even the fucking *C* in God who gives a shit! But nobody deserves to get their ass reamed like that—no poetry, no fucking consent. What in the *hell* makes you think that's the way things should be?"

"Gay, ain't I?" Cheever whispered, wondering if it would feel better just to say it out loud.

"Are you?" Blake asked, the words barbed.

Cheever cut his eyes to Blake's face and saw bitterness—and, yes, hurt. "Yeah, so? Who gives a shit."

"Well, apparently not *you*, since you don't even have a boyfriend, or have never had a boyfriend, or have never even told your mother, who, you should know very fucking well by now, would not begrudge you a single moment's happiness because you are gay just like your goddamned brother!"

"Yeah, well, he came out. Why should I?"

"Augh!" Blake turned around and kicked the chair he'd been sitting in, hard and again and again. "Fucking Sanders boys are gonna drive me back to the goddamned pills, I swear to fuckin' God!"

Something perverse awoke in Cheever then, something thrilled to make Blake, the most easygoing of the band members, the mildest, most laid-back, even-tempered man he'd ever met, lose his shit.

"You got an answer to that?" he taunted. "Why should I? Who gives a shit if little Cheever Sanders is gay? Who *cares*!"

"*I* care, and *you* should too, because it's a part of you!" Blake roared, turning on him and kicking the bed with a clang. "It's a part of you, and not one you felt you *had* to hide, but some big secret you *wanted* to hide! Would it be so goddamned hard for you to just fuckin' let us *know who you are*!"

Cheever's breath caught, and he remembered who he was again, and how he'd ended up here. "Nobody wants to know who I am," he said again, but this time, he was broken. The fight had gone out of him. Aubrey. Those guys. Gay was not the problem. "Too ugly inside to know."

"You're not ugly, Cheever *Justin* Sanders, but God, you are driving me fucking crazy."

Cheever locked eyes with him then, wanting to see… something. Something angry, something wild, something to convince Cheever he was lying.

What he saw was hurt.

Hurt and tenderness.

And worry.

He opened his mouth to say something. Anything. But a dry, sarcastic voice interrupted anything his brain was putting together.

"Judging by the racket, I'd say one of the Sanders boys is in town."

Blake swung around, a look of such profound relief on his face that Cheever actually felt comforted. "Doc Cambridge!" he said, laughing a little. Cheever saw him swipe at his eyes, and a new wave of self-loathing smacked him in the gut. Blake had stayed—he'd stayed and been kind—and Cheever had repaid him by… by being a shitty adolescent, all over again.

Wow. Cheever was starting to see the boy who'd bought a hotel room full of drugs and let himself be used and tossed aside like an old coke spoon.

Same ugly little shit who'd foisted his hell on his brothers when he was in middle school.

"Blake." There was such a wealth of kindness in that one word, and Cheever looked to see an older man—maybe edging toward retirement age—giving Blake a warm, familiar hug.

"Doc Cambridge!" Blake said, lowering his voice like someone would for a parent. "Good to see you here."

"Surprised to see *you*," Cambridge said frankly. "I saw the footage of Mackey falling off that speaker. How is he?"

Blake grimaced. "Hurting and pissed off and worried about getting hooked on painkillers and making life fucking insane for everyone in the hospital."

Cambridge's exasperated chuckle told Cheever all he needed to know about how well this man knew his family. "I wish them all luck," he said cheerfully. He sobered. "As long as he knows he can always come here if he needs to, okay?"

Blake nodded and gave a weary smile. "We appreciate it. That's why…." His eyes sought out Cheever's. "We brought you a hard case, sir," he said, his eyes moving restlessly like he was trying to see inside Cheever for a word to put to what had brought him here. "He's not an addict, I don't think, but…."

The doctor turned toward Cheever and took in the bandage on his wrist, the handcuffs, and Cheever's appearance.

Cheever wagered he looked like he'd climbed out of hell to speak of horrors, judging by the kindness he saw in Cambridge's eyes.

"Troubled," Cambridge finished gently, walking toward the bed. He extended his hand, and shook Cheever's free one. "Pleased to meet you, Cheever. How are you feeling today?"

"Tired," Cheever said, which was nothing but the truth, because that thing he'd been doing with Blake had about exhausted him. Being honest was brutal. "I'm sorry to trouble you. I… you know, this isn't really me." He looked at the bandage on his wrist as if he hadn't been planning that move for eight years. "I was stoned out of my head—never been on a bender like that, you know? Maybe, maybe if I detox a little, you can let me go home, you think?" He smiled winningly, the smile that had always worked on his mother when she seemed about to fuss, or to worry, or to insist he stay at the family thing when he was ready to run screaming with repressed rage.

Cambridge regarded him with an expression of stone. "Oh, he's cute," he said to Blake. "He thinks that's going to work with me."

Blake gave Cheever a sour look. "'Course he does. It's been working on his mama for eight years now. He's had practice."

"Yeah, these Sanders kids—art and emotional repression. It's like their best things." Cambridge turned back toward Cheever, his eyes narrowed and his jaw clenched. "Do we want to try that again?"

Cheever closed his eyes. "After my nap?" he begged.

"Sure. Mr. Manning and I will just take our lea—"

"Not Blake!" Cheever's eyes popped open, and he searched wildly for Blake. "He said he'd stay. He promised." He tried to still his breathing, his panic, and Cambridge's eyes opened wide.

He looked at Blake as if for explanation, and Blake shrugged and looked away.

"I ain't broken a promise to him yet," he said, his self-deprecation so strong Cheever wanted to smack him until he... what? Coughed up to being a knight in shining armor? Admitted that Cheever's brothers loved him like family? It didn't matter. Blake's ability to "aw shucks, I ain't nothin', folks" was making Cheever every bit as crazy as... as....

As Cheever was making Blake.

Cambridge turned his attention back to Cheever, just as Cheever swallowed and fell back against the bed. "Your family is going to break me," he said pleasantly. "But at least I won't be bored. Very well, then, I'll leave you in Mr. Manning's capable hands for the night. You two try not to kill each other, yeah?"

Cheever glared at Blake, who rolled his eyes.

"No promises," Blake said sullenly.

"I hate my job," Cambridge retorted. "I'll have the orderlies bring you both some food. Mr. Manning, we can get you a cot, but tomorrow you may want to go home and get some clean clothes—and maybe some for Cheever, as well. I suspect he's going to be here longer than he expects."

"Unless he's like Mackey and tries to leave fifty-dozen times," Blake muttered.

"So much. I hate my job so much. Have a good evening, Blake."

"You too, sir."

And Cambridge left.

"Are you happy, kid?" Blake asked, throwing himself into the chair and lifting his foot over his knee.

"I tried to slit my wrist," Cheever retorted. "Apparently not."

"Good. Because you just pissed off the best shrink in Los Angeles, and I might have broken my toe."

And that—that right there—was when Cheever realized he might be in some serious trouble. Because that mattered.

"I'm sorry about your toe," he said, feeling like shit.

"I'm sorry about your heart," Blake said back softly. "Because whatever's going on inside you, it's gotta hurt a damned sight worse than this."

Cheever closed his eyes and hoped for sleep.

THEY ATE dinner quietly, without much conversation, until Blake took a message on his phone. "Marcia's all done being admitted," he said. "Maybe she can keep you company tomorrow while I go pack up your dorm room and bring you both some clothes."

Cheever stopped in the middle of pushing his vegetables around on his tray. "Why is she here? Wasn't she in some place by the school?"

Blake shrugged. "She was a stand-up kid. You don't remember, but she was there when I found you—took me to the hotel and everything." His face grew bleak. "She got me there just in time."

Cheever bit his lip and shoved his tray aside. "Why'd she do that?"

"Because you were her lifeline and she was worried about you," Blake said softly. "Because you matter. And she... she needed someone. A friend. So I thought you two might want to do your time together. It made brothers out of Mackey and me, you know. Doing rehab together."

Cheever remembered Marcia, that terror of finding her unconscious, his grief that she'd felt so bad she thought that was the only way.

"We were... coffee buddies," he said roughly. "That's what I thought. I didn't realize... you know...."

"You were friends," Blake finished. "It's a big deal, having a friend."

Cheever's eyes flashed to him. "Mackey?"

Blake snorted. "As. If. No—Mackey and me are brothers, but Kell's my best friend." He grew pensive for a moment, and Cheever looked closer.

"Did you... did you love my brother?"

"I love all of them," Blake replied smartly, and then let out a sigh. He muttered to himself, something like, "I'm supposed to be mature...." And then spoke out loud again. "I did have me a hell of a crush on Kell, back before he and Briony got together. But he doesn't swing that way, and I swing both ways, so I kept it to myself so shit didn't get awkward."

Cheever regarded him, thoughtful. "Why'd you tell me that?"

"'Cause.... 'Cause you're going to be expected to shed all your secrets here. And it's going to feel invasive and painful and fucking infuriating. And I told the guys I was bi—once I figured it out, because for a while, I was that asshole who protested too much about gay porn, right? 'Good for you guys, but not for me....' I even came out to the press, but it didn't blow up because Mackey did it first. But I didn't tell anybody how I felt about Kell, although I'm sure Mackey figured it out. So here we are. Now you know something about me that I ain't—didn't—tell anybody else in the world. And you can see it didn't break me. So now, when you have to talk to the doc, you know it can be done."

Cheever nodded and swallowed, thinking about Marcia's surprisingly sly sense of humor, and the way she liked silences when two people were working, and her secret love of all things kawaii—cute, like Hello Kitty and Pokémon Go.

And how Blake had just told him something special so Cheever wouldn't feel alone.

"Thank you," he said softly. "You're... you're kind. You're so kind. I... I hope my brothers know how kind you can be."

"I wasn't always," Blake said, shoving his own half-finished food away from him on the little porta tray. "Sometimes I think you have to have a reserve, you know? When your soul is stretched thin, you don't have kindness to give. Lotta years there, my soul was tight as a drum. No give."

"I'm glad you got your soul back, then," Cheever said. He wanted to ask then, what had sucked so much out of a man who seemed to have so much to give. But he was tired, and Blake was right. He had just enough strength to worry about himself right now. "You put it to good use."

"Eat, kid," Blake said gruffly. "Food isn't half-bad here."

"You first." Cheever had noticed.

Blake sighed and pulled his tray back. "Fine. On count of three, both of us will eat. One, two—"

Cheever took a bite of potato buds and gravy and gave a small smile. Blake swallowed a forkful of chicken.

Three.

Can't You Hear Me Knocking?

SOMEONE GOT Blake a blanket and a cot. He dozed, watching over Cheever's sleep, and he pulled that soft blanket close as dawn crept around the blinds drawn over the windows.

Restless and exhausted, Blake stood and worked the blinds, opening the room up to some sunlight and not that grim fluorescent crap.

Cheever looked young. So young. Pretty—God. The only Sanders boy who'd missed out on "pretty" was Kell, and he knew it. It didn't matter once Briony saw through his caveman exterior, though. His wedding picture—Briony with a six-month baby bump, Kell with a look of utter besottedness and bafflement—was one of the most beautiful things Blake had ever seen.

But Cheever had the pretty gene that Kell missed out on. Delicate bone structure, that striking coloring. When his eyes were open, he looked like an anime character, and when they were closed, with those long red lashes fanning his cheeks, he looked like a sleeping prince.

His lower lip had a sort of fullness, a ripeness to it that left Blake feeling uncomfortable and awkward about being in the same room while he was sleeping.

But dammit, the kid had begged.

Blake wasn't sure how he felt about telling Cheever about his long-ago crush on Kell. It was almost laughable now, because Blake wouldn't have deprived Kell of his life with Briony for anything. Not even those half-imagined kisses he'd yearned for.

But it was such a small thing, that crush, compared to the big thing, whatever the big thing was, that had sent Cheever looking for a razor blade. Yeah, sure, he might never have gone for it if he hadn't been a screaming tornado inside from all that coke, but still.

That urge had been inside him, somewhere, just waiting for a chance to cut its way out.

Blake wondered if he was going to have to tell the kid more, about the times he couldn't make rent, or the times he'd needed a hit of something, anything, to make him forget the shit that happened after he ran away from home.

Or the reasons he'd run away in the first place.

He'd come clean about most of it, at one time or another—to Mackey, to Doc Cambridge, to Kell. It wasn't any big secret. Blake Manning had been young and desperate and addicted and sad. His ass had been for sale, and he'd learned to give a mighty fine, tip-worthy blowjob to boot.

But dammit.

That kid… that kid looked at him like he was something.

He hated to admit it, even to himself, but the way Cheever looked at him, talked to him, called him kind—that shit meant a lot to Blake, who, for most of his life, had never been really worth all that much.

To have a kid—pretty, smart, hurting—think Blake was important made his chest tight and his eyes burn.

God, it would be something, wouldn't it? To be that kind of man?

For a moment, Blake's hands shook, and like that horrible room full of sex and drugs and despair hadn't done, the thought made him crave his first hit in nine years.

Closing his eyes against the sunshine coming into the room, against the craving in his gut, he asked himself why. Why now?

I could let him down.

Blake took a deep breath against the want.

I could. But I'll definitely let him down if I go that way. I know that. The only way to let him down is not to even fucking try.

Another deep breath and the craving subsided, a gentle snarl and it was gone. Blake turned back to the room and found Cheever's eyes on him.

"What just happened?" he asked softly.

Honesty. That needs to work for us. "I got scared," he said. "Your family's in Seattle—"

"Not yet!" Cheever begged hoarsely.

"I know. Right now, I'm it. I might not be enough, kid. But I'll definitely fuck it up if I run away now." Blake yawned and walked toward the bed, folding up his blanket as he went. "I'm going to take off, visit Marcia and get permission to get her stuff. I'll be back, okay?"

Cheever's eyes were dark and shadowed, and Blake sighed. "Kid, you're still recovering. You'll probably sleep all day, but I'll make sure Marcia's in here before I leave. How's that?"

Cheever nodded. "You won't leave—I mean, not permanent, will you?"

Blake rested his hands on the bed rail and was unsurprised when Cheever grabbed the one nearest his handcuff. Absently, Blake soothed the skin underneath the padded cuff and used his other hand to smooth the hair back that had fallen in Cheever's eyes.

"I been in your life for nine years. I ain't—*haven't*—left yet." Goddammit. He had a BA in humanities—he did. Yes, it had been mostly online courses, but he had a diploma that said he was more than a trailer park kid from Lancaster. And Cheever, with his 4.0 at CalArts, needed to see him as something other than a dumb-fuck hick.

Why is that important?

Fuck off, little voice, I don't got no answer to that.

"Good," Cheever said softly. His mouth twisted. "I can tell when you're upset, you know. Your grammar slips. Me and Mackey do it too."

"Can't take the trailer park out of the boy," Blake said, his voice still tense. He was going to leave then—going to back away and go back to the house and get a shower and then start what looked to be a busy day, but Cheever... Cheever raised his face a little, expecting something, and Blake wasn't sure what happened next.

He smoothed Cheever's hair back one more time and lowered his head to kiss Cheever's forehead, but he saw the disappointment in the boy's eyes, and....

And he brushed his lips instead.

Cheever arched his neck and parted his lips, and Blake lingered. A breath. A heartbeat. He used his tongue to barely tease the seam of Cheever's mouth, taste his skin, and Cheever opened on the inhale and brushed his tongue along Blake's own.

Blake pulled away, his heart hammering in his ears.

"What was that?" he whispered. Cheever's breath was awful—and he imagined his own wasn't arctic cool either—but that touch of lips, of tongues, of breath, that was... so damned....

Sweet.

"I just...." Cheever's brow knitted unhappily. "I coulda died. I ain't—haven't ever been kissed as a grown-up. Wanted to see if it's worth living for."

Blake grunted. "God, kid, don't judge life or death on *me*, on *my*—"

"It was perfect," Cheever said, and it was like the sunlight hit his eyes then, those remarkable shadowed green eyes. "I can stick around waiting for a kiss like that."

Blake's skin ran hot and cold, and he had trouble catching his breath. "I... I...."

Cheever nodded toward the door. "You got shit to do. Don't worry, Blake. I'll be here when you get back."

Blake had no answer to that. He turned and fled, making it to the front desk by sheer accident, and making arrangements for Marcia to visit Cheever on automatic.

It wasn't until he got out to the parking lot that he remembered he'd sat in the ambulance with Cheever on the way there and his truck was at the hospital, twenty minutes away.

Gah!

He was so fucking undone by one goddamned kiss!

THREE HOURS later, after he'd showered and changed—thank God, because those other clothes had been in his pits since Seattle!—he was looking at Cheever's room, at a loss again.

Someone had cleaned up the little bonfire, and the mostly intact stuff was stacked in a box. Blake figured he'd start with clothes and the computer, and maybe some books and art supplies.

He was halfway through packing when a woman appeared in the doorway.

"Oh," she said, sounding surprised. "I guess they're right. He's gone."

Blake turned toward her, scowling. She wasn't a student—being around fifty or so—and had a head full of gray corkscrew curls and skin the color of fired clay. Blake wondered if she was a teacher.

"He's... at a retreat," Blake said with dignity. Was it easier to say "rehab" because he'd been or because it was such a thing in LA?

"What... what happened?" she asked, staring at the burned art and flinching.

Blake felt a little bit of his own rage and confusion boiling up. "I don't know, lady. You tell me. The kid wanted to be an artist, so his brothers sent him to art school. He poured his soul into it. I know he did, because there wasn't that much soul left for the rest of us. Then someone told him he wasn't good enough—and worse than that, that he was *mediocre*. I've been a mediocre musician my entire life, and I have to tell you, it takes a certain amount of steel in your balls to live with something like that. Anyway, the kid had other wounds to heal, so he had to take a *fucking breath.*" Blake took his own fucking breath. "I'm only guessing about some of this, so you'll have to excuse the fuck out of me if I'm wrong."

The woman took *her own* deep breath, and Blake watched her eyes get red and spill over. "He did this because I gave him a *C* in Mixed Media?" she asked, sounding stunned. "I… I didn't see that much passion in his art. I could have sworn he didn't have any to—"

Something in Blake snapped, and he lunged for one of the pictures of Tyson/Hepzibah, with the off colors, the bleak sky, and held it up to her. "No passion?" he snarled. "You thought he had no passion? What do you see here, lady?"

She gaped at him.

"What do you *see*? Because I'll tell you right now, I'm not an artist, but when I look at this picture, I get a whole fucking lot of rage and death. Now I'm just a mediocre musician and an ex-junkie, but I think, I see a kid painting—what? *Seven* of these little masterpieces? Seven pictures that look like rage and death? I see a kid painting fucking rage and fucking death and you know what I *don't* do?"

Her skin had gone gray. "Humiliate him in front of his classmates and tell him his art has no passion?" she asked, self-recrimination in every syllable.

"*No, I fucking don't!*"

She flinched from his voice and wiped her face with the back of her hand. "Where is he?" she asked, keeping her back straight. "I'd like to apologi—"

Blake shook his head. "No. No. You want to apologize, fine. But the cuts in his wrist haven't healed, and all it would take is one big pity party to blow a hole in his brain. You're goddamned right some of this is yours to fix, but you'll have to wait until he's strong enough to talk to you again. Do you hear me?"

She wiped her face again. "Believe it or not, I do," she said, her voice rough. "I'm sorry, Mr. Manning—I wanted him to find his art. I didn't expect him to break."

"We're people, Professor," he said, not sure how she knew his name. "We're all broken inside a little. You step on us in the right places, we're gonna fucking shatter."

"I've listened to your CD a thousand times," she whispered. "I should know that by now, you know?"

"You should—Mackey's got a knack—"

"Not just Outbreak Monkey," she said, surprising him. "Your solo album. You know what they say about karma, how it's a real bitch?"

Blake stared at her. "Yeah."

"Trust me. She's barking now. Excuse me. I need to…." She looked around Cheever's room, then closed her eyes and shuddered. "I need to find a way to make this right."

Blake remembered something from his and Mackey's stint in rehab. "A letter," he said, throwing clothes into a suitcase again. "Those seem to be the thing to do."

"Sure." And then she hurried away.

IT TOOK him two trips to get Cheever's stuff into the back of his truck, and when he was done, he moved on to Marcia's rehab place, which was not anything like the place that had changed him and Mackey. This rehab was small and depressing and stank of cigarette smoke. The tile was chipped, and the inside felt more like a prison than a retreat.

Blake looked around and felt grateful that when he'd done his bit, he'd been at the good place with Mackey, on Outbreak Monkey's dime.

Money. He'd found quickly that it couldn't buy everything, but some of the stuff it *could* buy wasn't bad.

An orderly helped him gather her stuff, including a tablet and some books, and he got it into the back of the truck, rested his aching toe, and took stock.

Between the two kids, it was such a pathetic reminder of home.

He couldn't go to Cheever's mom and ask her for some mementos, and he wasn't sure how Trav had managed to get ahold of Marcia's parents, but he didn't know them from Adam.

He gnawed his lower lip for a moment and thought, and then pulled out his phone. Handy little computer here—it could give you the location of about any store you wanted between where you were and where you wanted to go.

Trav called when he was in the middle of Target, getting adorable pajamas for Marcia instead of plain gray ones. At first, he thought he'd have to go to the kid's section because she was so tiny, but it turned out they had tiny adorable pj's for grown-up girls too. Blake had to wonder when the last time he'd actually been with a girl had been, because this was something he did not know.

There he was, holding up some fluffy pajama pants with little banana people on them, trying to remember the last time he got laid, when his pocket buzzed.

He picked it up and said, "September, last year."

"We were taking a break in the middle of the tour and you got laid. Twice."

Blink. "Oh my God, Trav? How in the hell would you even know what I was—"

"Once by a girl and once by a boy," Trav continued relentlessly. "The girl was sweet—we were rooting for her, until you brought the boy to the hotel room. He was amazingly hot, and the girls were rooting for *him*, but you left them both in Dublin, so nobody was happy. Why are you thinking about this?"

"How did you even—"

"How's Cheever?" Trav asked, seemingly out of the blue.

"He's... he's fragile," Blake said, throwing the banana-people pajamas into the cart, along with a couple of T-shirts with Hello Kitty on them. And a pair of jeans with some flowers. That girl, in her gray pajamas, with her gray-and-beige clothes in rehab, sort of broke his heart.

He moved on to men's pajamas for Cheever, throwing in a couple of pairs of boxer-briefs for good measure.

Superhero pj's in fleece—score!

On the other end of the line, Trav waited patiently.

"What made you call?" Blake asked after a moment. "Is Mackey okay?"

"He's in pain and he's worried. Same shit, different day. Is Cheever settled into the rehab center yet?"

"Yeah." Blake blew out a breath. "I don't think drugs are really his problem," he said after a moment. "He... I think they were a way out this once. He was trying to get high enough to...."

He couldn't even say it.

"To follow through." Trav spared him the dirty work, as he did so often for the boys. "I get it. What... do you know what's eating at him?"

Blake thought of those horrible, nauseating paintings. *I haven't been kissed as a grown-up.* Considering that Marcia said he lived like a monk, it seemed odd that he thought he'd had that painful assault coming.

But Blake didn't want to say it. It was part of Cheever's story. One thing Mackey had taught him had been respect for a person's story.

"I have an idea?" It came out as a question because it was really only something gut-level. "Not something I can share right now. But… but he doesn't want me to leave him alone. Especially at night."

Trav sucked in a breath. "Shit. Are you okay with being his human woobie?"

"Were you okay with being Mackey's?" Blake retorted and fumbled the T-shirt he'd been grabbing with the Avengers on the front.

Mackey and Trav had a very adult relationship now.

The silence on the other end of the line was deafening.

"You wanted to know how I knew that's what you were thinking," Trav said.

"Yeah."

"You haven't been with anyone for a long time."

"I figured that out."

"This kid's looking at you like a hero."

Blake swallowed. "Doesn't happen that often."

"You're wondering if you're responding to that or to the celibacy I just mentioned or to the fact that you're suddenly intimate with someone, but not sexually."

Blake squeezed his eyes shut, remembering Trav and Mackey in the early days. "It's like you've been here."

"Yes."

"Yes, you've been here?"

"Yes, you're responding to all of it. Now see, if this had come up with the brothers, they might have lost their minds. But it's come up with me, and I know you wouldn't do anything to hurt this family, and I'm not crazy like everybody else."

Blake smirked, glad Trav couldn't see him. Sure, Trav *claimed* to not be crazy, but they'd all been there when Trav showed how protective he was over the guys. All the guys—Blake, Kell, the twins. Hell, even Shelia, Briony, all the kids.

Trav was no one to fuck with, and that went double for his family.

"Absolutely, sir," he said, hoping he kept his voice in line.

"Don't be an asshole." Trav let out a breath. "And I know that's hard with this family, so I'll go you one better. We will still love you even if you are an asshole. I know you wouldn't deliberately hurt Cheever. Do what you have to, but make sure you're both okay inside. How's that?"

"That sounds like I should keep my distance until he's fixed up a little."

"It's not always as easy as it sounds," Trav said, sounding baffled. Blake took in the contents of his cart and grimaced.

"No, sir, it is not." He wasn't putting any of this shit back. In fact, he was going to a nearby art store and getting more.

"I'll tell everyone to cool their jets."

"That is probably a good idea."

"You got three days to get him ready to see his mother. She's almost hysterical."

Blake knew Heather, and knew that was probably true. "I'll talk to her if you need—"

"No. In fact, don't answer any phone calls from her either. That woman's been your mother for ten damned years. You think it's going to be easy for you to tell her no? Even in Cheever's best interest? Let me deal with the family. You take care of your end. What are you doing, anyway?"

"Buying adorable pajamas, a fuck ton of Oreos, a sack full of paperback books, and some art."

Trav's low chuckle was worth more to him than gold. "You're a good brother and a good friend. Carry on, Blake." His voice lowered. "Be easy on your own heart here, okay? Take it from someone who's been there."

"Like you said, not as easy as it sounds."

Trav grunted and hung up, and Blake finished shopping. As care packages went, it wasn't high-end and it wasn't fancy, but he was going for comfort here.

Besides, sleeping in Cheever's room until Cheever could sleep by himself, this was as good as it got.

THEY'D TAKEN off Cheever's handcuff by the time Blake got back and had moved him to a double room with Marcia installed as his roommate.

"Girls and boys happen a lot here?" he asked Doc Cambridge on his first of many trips in with boxes of crap. He struggled a little with the guitar because he was also carrying the box of books. Cambridge took pity on him and grabbed the guitar.

"Not ever. But Cheever is gay, and they seem to have a rapport." Cambridge grimaced. "And frankly, you caught us by surprise. We're actually full up. I had to do some juggling to allow them both in."

"Well, I dropped by that other place where the girl was at. Better she have a room with Cheever here than her own room there."

"Believe it or not, I volunteer at other places. I wish all my patients could be here."

Blake heard the weariness and hoped the doc could take one more Sanders kid and his friend before he retired.

"You're a good guy," he said ruminatively. "Wish more people in the world could be you."

Cambridge grunted. "I wish Cheever would talk. Right now, he and Marcia seem content to sit and watch movies on their phones."

Blake grinned. "No worries there, Doc. I'm bringing in shit that'll have them bitching for days."

"*STARRY NIGHT*?" Cheever asked, looking at the cheap reproduction print. "Doesn't everybody—"

"*Water Lilies*?" Marcia was much less judgmental. "I love Monet!"

"And Lautrec." Apparently, Cheever approved of Lautrec. *Good for him.*

"Chagall—ooh, I like!"

Blake smiled at Marcia. She seemed easy to please.

He'd pretty much bought one of each painting that looked famous and figured they could decorate their room like they wanted. He picked up one print—not someone famous—of a gaggle of kids at the ocean, and ran his finger along the beveled edge of the matting. This one he'd grabbed because it made him happy. He figured when Cheever and Marcia put it in the discard pile, he could put it up in his room somewhere.

"Thank you, Mr. Manning!" Marcia threw herself into Blake's arms, and he gave her a surprised hug. "Thank you! This—the pj's and T-shirts— this is just so much... so much happier than the last place." She looked shyly at Cheever. "I mean, I know it's gonna sort of suck being here, but trust me, Cheever, putting this up will make us feel better."

"Seems like a shame to decorate for just a month," Cheever said. But he was grabbing some of that mounting putty too, and dammit, the picture of the kids at the ocean that Blake had set down.

"I wish I'd done it when I stayed here," Blake admitted. "But me and the guys were so used to living on the road, in hotels at that point, bringing in our own stuff and making the place home didn't even occur to us."

Cheever grunted and looked at the box of projects Blake had brought in last. "You can throw that shit away," he said brutally, ignoring Marcia's little gasp.

"I will not," Blake said, his voice mild. "You worked hard on that. If you don't want it here, I'll send it to the big house. You can go through it when you're done here."

"That's not where I live!" Cheever protested, because it was true— he stayed with his mother during vacations. But Blake was done with that noise.

"It is now," he said, not argumentative, just like that's how it was. "Family's staying out of your grill now, Cheever, but don't expect that to last. In fact, I think it's long past time. You're gonna be with us in the big house until you remember whose kid you are."

"If my brothers wanted that much to do with me, they wouldn't have left," Cheever snapped, and then clapped his hand over his mouth like a guilty child.

Blake's eyebrows lifted. "Oh, now we're getting somewhere."

"That was dumb," Cheever mumbled. "That's not what happened—"

"But it's what it felt like to you," Blake said, hating the reason in his voice. "Be honest. You were a kid, your brothers were your world, and they left. Hell yes, it hurt. We didn't say it shouldn't. We asked that you not be an asshole about it, but being hurt is just fine."

"See? I'm fine!"

Cheever had changed and showered once Blake brought clothes— directly into the new superhero pajamas. He'd needed help putting plastic around the bandages on his wrists, and at the moment, he looked like a sneeze would blow him through the window. He had bags under his eyes, a face almost shock white, and eyes that didn't track.

Blake just stared at him, until he sat down heavily on the bed behind him. "Maybe fine is an overstatement," Cheever admitted.

"Fine is a lie," Blake said flatly. "And I don't blame you for telling it—the family's been buying that lie for eight goddamned years. But we're not gonna swallow it anymore." His pocket buzzed, and he grimaced, hitting Ignore without even looking to see who it was.

"Mackey?" Cheever hazarded a guess.

"Or Kell. Or your mom. Probably your mom. Trav said he could buy me three days, which means you got three days to figure out why you're not fucking fine before I tell that woman where you are so she doesn't gut me like a flounder."

Cheever scowled. "My mother loves you."

"Maybe." She'd been the only real mother he'd ever had. He'd die for her. "But she loves you too, and right now, I'm the asshole who isn't giving her info on her baby boy. I know you think you've been an island all these years, 'baby boy,' but you've been fooling yourself. You're no more an island than I am an artist, so suck it up and sort out your shit."

They glared at each other, the tension in the air thick as dust, and then Marcia said, in a small voice, "You are too an artist, Mr. Manning. Me and Cheever listened to your solo album. It was real nice."

Blake closed his eyes. God, he kept trying to forget about putting his heart into that, and how the pitiful sales had made him feel like he'd let his brothers down. "Thanks, darlin'. That was a bad metaphor. Suffice it to say no man's an island, and neither is Cheever. How's that?"

"That's true," she said, considering. "Islands get drowned and covered by the sea."

Blake managed a small smile her way. "You and Mackey need to talk. He likes poetry too." He shifted to Cheever. "But did you hear that? You're not a fucking island. You're going to need to talk to her."

Cheever looked away.

"Just talk to somebody," Blake said softly. "Someone, baby boy." Cheever wasn't a baby—Blake hadn't been seeing him that way. But the endearment gave him power somehow, like he could pretend to be old enough or wise enough to tell this man what to do. "They left because they had to. Because they wanted to get their whole family out. They didn't get you out in time. That's not on them, but it doesn't mean you don't got scars."

"How would you know that?" Cheever asked sullenly, and Blake's bitter laughter surprised them all.

"Because I saw your fucking art, Cheever. Because I knew you eight years ago—not well, but you were going through something. The boys were going through something too. I wasn't your person then. I am now."

"Maybe it's too late," Cheever said, and he was trying to be spiteful, but what came out was pathetic. "Maybe I'm just broken. Nothing can fix me. Might as well bleed out."

"*You ain't even fuckin' tried!*" Blake screamed, the sound so raw that if his throat didn't suddenly ache, he wouldn't have been sure he made it.

Cheever and Marcia both stared at him, and Marcia made a little "buh-bye" wave before scurrying out of the room.

Blake found himself kneeling before Cheever as he sat on the bed. Cheever's enormous eyes were bright and shiny and filling with tears. Without even thinking about it, Blake took Cheever's hands in his, and realized his own hands were clammy and shaking.

"Boy, you don't know it, but you really are still a baby. You're amazingly fucking young. Don't write off the rest of your life like that, okay? There's some stunning, gorgeous moments waiting for you. Don't make a plan that'll make you miss out on them."

Cheever swallowed and nodded, looking away like he always did, redirecting whatever roil was beating his heart to pulp under that cool reserve.

It would never fool Blake again.

"Look at me!" Blake demanded. "You fucking look at me, Cheever *Justin* Sanders. You ain't even tried yet. How do you know you can't fix what's broken if you ain't tried? And nothing fixes without scars—you hear me? You think my insides aren't a mass of scars trying to make way for the good parts of me? But you won't know if you can heal if you can't take off the old bad patches on the wound and clean it out!"

Cheever nodded, and turned his head to wipe his face on his shoulder.

"*Look at me!*" Blake roared, not sure where the rage came from, fully aware that never in his life had he had the power to compel someone through sheer force of will.

When Cheever's gaze, miserable, swollen, and whipped, met Blake's fevered searching one, it felt like a miracle.

"I'm looking," he whispered.

Blake pushed up and kissed his forehead. "Don't give up," he begged, hoping that strange ability he suddenly had to make Cheever do what he wanted would stay with him. "C'mon, kid. It took Mackey three tries before rehab took. You ain't even tried yet."

Cheever bit his lip. "Three tries?"

"Yeah. I think Trav literally beat some sense into him, because the third time, he came back with a swollen jaw."

"He *beat*—"

Blake wrinkled his nose. "Cool your jets. Your brother has made it his life's mission to piss people off. Trav was probably...." Blake swallowed, thinking about that time, about how close they'd come to losing their center, the guy—the brother—who kept the whole family together. "He was probably just as scared for him as I am for you. You talk about bleeding out one more time, I will lock you back to that bed, you hear me?"

Cheever nodded, and a few more tears ran down his cheeks and down the long column of his throat.

Blake's knees ached, and he gave in, sitting down next to Cheever on the bed.

To his surprise, Cheever leaned against him, resting his head on Blake's chest, and Blake, so desperate for some reassurance that this kid wouldn't gouge his artery in with a paintbrush, wrapped his arm around Cheever's slender shoulders in return.

"C'mon, baby boy," Blake crooned. "You can talk to us. We'll still love you. That's a promise."

He felt Cheever's suppressed sobs, rocking his narrow chest, and held him tighter. He wasn't sure where the storm came from, but he was damned sure he'd be Cheever's port so they could weather it together.

19th Nervous Breakdown

"So, to be honest, Doc, I'm not really sure what I'm doing here."

Doc Cambridge examined his fingernails, picking delicately at a cuticle, and Cheever soldiered bravely on.

"I mean, it was, you know, a bad reaction. I'd just worked so hard, and the professor sort of hit me where I lived. I mean, I can see that you're worried, but I can only flunk out of school once, right?"

The older man widened his eyes and raised his eyebrows, as if he was trying to stay awake.

"I mean, I can't ever do coke again—the doc said I'm lucky I didn't get an embolism as it was. And that other thing, I mean, I'll only ever do that again if I'm stoned, and, you know, that's not going to happen, so maybe you could, you know, let me go home? Blake's there. He'll watch me."

Blake had, in fact, spent the night in Cheever and Marcia's room, against all protocol. He hadn't even had a bed because Marcia's bed had taken the place of his cot. He'd just sat at the foot of Cheever's bed after lights out, reading his phone like he belonged there, one warm hand on Cheever's calf.

They'd asked him to leave that morning, citing their regimen and protocols, but so far, all Cheever could see was a lot of PT that he got out of because he still felt like shit from the blood transfusion and the stitches in his ass.

"So, Doc," Cheever said, smiling and working on his anime eyes. "What do you say? Can I go home? What do you think?"

Finally the doctor that Blake and Mackey seemed to think so much of looked up and pinned Cheever with an unamused gaze. "What do I think?"

"Yeah!" Cheever put extra winning excitement in his voice. "What do you think?"

"I think I'm too old for this shit, Cheever Sanders. Jesus Christ—do I *look* like an idiot? Do I *look* gullible? Holy shitballs, kid, do I *look* like I want your blood on my hands?"

Uh-oh. He could swear the anime eyes thing usually worked. "Uh, no, not at all. I just thought, you know, since I'm not an addict, we'd have an understand—"

"Oh, we have an understanding, all right," Cambridge snapped. "I understand that you think I'm an idiot, and you understand that if you can talk me into letting you out of here, you're going to walk into traffic or jump off a bridge or rip a hole in your veins with a shiv, *that's* our understanding. Now how about you stop wasting my time trying to get me to let you kill yourself and start telling me why you wanted to do it in the first place."

It was Cheever's turn to check his cuticles. "I, uh, you know. Stoned."

"And why was that again?" Oh wow. Was this guy hard to impress.

"Professor. You know. Didn't like my art."

Cambridge nodded. "Are you aware of how often art gets panned?"

Well, yeah. "I mean, well sometimes—"

"Picasso, Lautrec, the Fauve—all of these artists were panned by the people who came before them."

"I mean, the cutting-edge people—"

"Ralph Waldo Emerson threw Walt Whitman's first edition of *Leaves of Grass* in the fireplace."

"He *was* pretty cutting edge—"

"Queen's 'Bohemian Rhapsody' was panned by every major music critic in the business—"

"See what I mean by cutting edge?"

"Would you describe yourself as 'cutting edge,' Cheever?"

Cheever swallowed, thought about all of the classic art forms he'd followed—yeah, sure, they'd been cutting edge in the 1800s, but landscapes and perspectives were sort of small potatoes now.

"No," he said softly.

"And there's nothing wrong with that. Nothing wrong with a classic approach to life. Just don't expect everybody to like it, right?"

Cheever took a deep breath. "Yeah," he whispered. "I guess I wasn't prepared."

Doc Cambridge's expression softened, but his eyes stayed level. "Do you still want to be an artist?"

Cheever thought of all the art supplies Blake had brought, stacking them in the corner. Paints, palette, watercolors, *(palette knife?)*, colored pencils *(pencil sharpener?)*, paint brushes *(metal edges?)*—he smiled dreamily.

"Yes," he said.

Cambridge grimaced and pulled out his phone, making a quick text. Then he took a deep breath.

"Don't you think you're going to have to get used to criticism?" he asked.

"Well, what? I'm supposed to run screaming to a shrink every time someone shits on my art?" Cheever demanded. *I'd rather die.* He actually frowned at that. *Why is that my only fallback?*

"Some people do." Cambridge glared at him, and Cheever sat back, surprised.

"Really?"

"Yes, really. Why does that shock you?"

Cheever had to think about it a moment. "I mean... Doc. Mackey may be the only person from our hometown who's ever been to a shrink. And it's okay for him, 'cause, you know, he's gay."

"So are you," Cambridge added.

"Who told?" Cheever covered his face with his hand because he actually sounded thirteen years old all over again.

"If you want it to be a secret, don't look so happy whenever Mr. Manning walks in the room. If he wasn't completely oblivious to you, I'd have us a private ass chewing because, at the moment, the relationship is totally inappropriate."

Oh no! "You won't, will you?" Cheever asked, biting his lip. "He, like, *reveres* you, and right now, he's the only thing keeping me from losing my shit!"

Cambridge let out a long cleansing breath. "Okay. I will make a deal with you."

"Yessir."

"Blake Manning can come visit you for an hour a day and longer on weekends if—and only if—you tell me why you are losing your shit."

Oh hell. Oh hell, oh hell. "You're right," Cheever said in wonder. "That first fifteen minutes here was really a waste of time."

"I need chocolate," Cambridge muttered. "Now shoot."

"I... I don't really know where to start," Cheever said, feeling empty. One go. It only took one go with this guy and half his excuses were blown to shit. No wonder Mackey and Blake respected him. That was damned impressive.

"How about we start with the way you thought you were going to take criticism?"

Cheever thought carefully. "I guess... I guess I thought I could take anonymous criticism," he said after a moment. "Like, like you said.

Journals and critics and blogs. That all feels... not quite real. This was someone I...." He shifted and tried not to wince. He'd been working overtime to not remind Cambridge about that portion of his whole "nervous breakdown" experience. "I respected," he finished. "I respected her, and when she didn't like my art... I felt like a fool."

Cambridge nodded. "That's an honest answer, son. Good. We'll talk about how to deal with criticism later—after the medical staff checks your art supplies for sharp objects."

Cheever resisted the urge to say "Who told?" again, mostly because it was redundant. "Fair enough," he muttered. "Are we done for today?"

"Why art?" Cambridge asked—so apparently no, they were not done for the day. "Your brothers picked music. Why art?"

Cheever thought about it. "I don't know. I was too young, I guess, when they started playing. But I'd draw on walls and stuff, and they'd bring home paper, and that made me feel special—'cause we didn't have *anything*. So I'd use the paper. And then they'd bring me crayons and told me how good I was, and... I guess, at the beginning, art made me feel good because they made me feel good about it."

Cambridge nodded. "That's sweet. I mean, it is. I know those boys. Their worry about you drove them through their first years down here in LA—keeping you fed, clothed, housed, safe. They wanted a lot for you. Sounds like you all thought art was the way to get it."

Cheever nodded. "And the more I did it, the more I... I just got lost in it. I loved everything about it, you know? Color, form—making it. It was like getting credit for playing, after I got serious about it."

"And when was that?" He had a deceptively mild voice, this doctor, when he wasn't being a sarcastic asshole.

"Middle school, I guess," Cheever said, remembering that moment on his bed, after his mom had left.

Then he remembered what had prompted that moment.

Oh, sneaky doctor.

"What made you decide then?"

Oh yeah, Cheever had seen that one coming. "My brothers' friend died," Cheever said, because that sounded good, right?

"Grant Adams?"

"Yeah. He and Mackey... they'd been, uh, boyfriends—"

"Secret lovers," Cambridge supplied grimly. "It almost destroyed your brother."

Cheever thought about that. "It's weird that everybody thinks it was a secret. I saw them making out when I was a little kid. I just thought everybody knew and it was okay."

Cambridge tilted his head, looking *truly* curious for the first time since they'd started talking. "Did anything happen to change your mind? That being gay might not be okay?"

Cheever shrugged and shifted on his seat again, this time not suppressing his wince.

"Son, do you need another painkiller? Garden-variety ibuprofen, right?"

"Yeah, that would be great."

Another quick text, and Cheever wondered how many people the doc had on speed dial.

"Cheever, we're running out of time here, and I'm sure that breaks your heart. But I want you to think about some things before we talk tomorrow."

Cheever waited, not even bothering to make his eyes big and limpid—that seemed to be happening all on its own. "Yeah, sure. Not running anywhere in the next few."

"Wait until PT kicks in." You could sand a deck with this guy's voice. "Here are some things I know about you. You're an artist, but you don't want your art to be noticed. You're gay, but you don't want anybody to know. You were sexually assaulted in a hotel room two days ago, and you won't even mention that your netherparts are uncomfortable. And you want to kill yourself in the worst way, but you don't want to tell anybody why. Have I about summed it up?"

Oh God. The tears weren't supposed to.... He'd planned to charm his way through this. How hard could it be, right? He sucked in a gulp of air through the tears running down his face.

"I don't really want to die, you know," he said, proud that he could breathe through that. "I just don't want to... don't want to... don't want to...."

Cambridge passed him a box of Kleenex. "Hurt anymore."

"Yeah." Cheever took a tissue and heard a warm, kind voice telling him to blow. He did, and the memory sustained him. "Will Blake really be allowed to come eat here?"

"Yeah, Cheever. You know—you can't live just for him, right?"

"I know." Cheever did. On a fundamental level, he knew he wasn't "living" for Blake. He was learning to appreciate him. "He'll just make me feel better for now."

"Good."

Augh! So much gentleness. Cheever dreaded tomorrow's session already.

"Blake... Blake is a good man. One of the best, although he doesn't think so. I worry about... about what you could do to his heart too."

Cheever sucked in a breath, because of all things, this hadn't occurred to him. "I... I wouldn't ever want to hurt Blake."

Cambridge nodded. "Good. But I want you to think about what... what you would have done to him if he'd found you after you'd bled out."

His teeth began to chatter. "Oh God." He wrapped his arms around his knees and buried his face against them, thinking about Blake, losing his mind the day before, yelling when Cheever had *never* heard him yell. Thought about the kiss—ah! That fragile, wonderful sunrise of a kiss, and the stunned look on Blake's face when he'd pulled away. Oh God!

Cheever started rocking back and forth, shaking, and Cambridge made an unhappy little sound. "Oh, son. Pain makes you selfish, did you not know that?"

"I do *now!*" Cheever wailed, unable to breathe, and while he was vaguely aware of Cambridge talking on the phone briefly before he came to sit next to Cheever and wrap an arm around his shoulder, Cheever wasn't really aware of anything else until an orderly pulled out his arm and gave him a sedative. After that, the world was a watercolor blur.

HE CAME to in his bed again, and, oh joy, the rail had been pulled up and the handcuff put on. "Fuck," he mumbled.

His response was a comforting hand on his calf, and he realized Blake was sitting at the foot of the bed again, his legs crossed, Cheever's guitar in his hands.

"You awake?"

"Yeah," Cheever rasped. He could taste the sedative in the back of his throat. "My mouth tastes like ass."

Blake snorted. "As if you would know. Let me get you some mouthwash."

Cheever pulled fruitlessly on the handcuff. "Is this really necessary?"

Blake just shook his head, like he couldn't talk about it yet, and he returned with the mouthwash and a spit cup and a bottle of water. Cheever rinsed and spat and waited for cleanup, moving his bed upright and sipping at the water. Blake looked... strained. There were bags under his eyes, his cheeks were stubbled, and he was pale, like he hadn't had enough sleep.

He's worried about you.

The thought popped into Cheever's head like a balloon, and he couldn't get rid of it.

"I'm sorry," he said as Blake returned.

"For what?" Blake dragged the room chair to Cheever's bedside and looked to Marcia's bed. "She was out when they brought you in— PT and a group therapy session and then dinner. They'll bring us some dinner in a bit."

Cheever nodded and kept his eyes on Blake's face, troubled.

"I'm sorry I worried you," he said, the words feeling weighted, painful, like he learned something just saying them.

"Yeah, well...." Blake shrugged like it was no big deal, but Cheever reached out with his free hand and snagged Blake's wrist.

"No—this is important. You're... you're worried about me. I... I hurt you, hurting myself. I'm sorry."

Blake tried a weak smile, but his lower lip trembled. "I was waiting here, and the orderlies came to search your art supplies. They took the palette knives and the pencil sharpeners and some of the paintbrushes that were too sharp on the end. They got a text, I guess, that your stuff might be dangerous, and I thought...."

Oooh—that Doc Cambridge was tricky.

And right.

"I didn't even know I was thinking about it until Cambridge said something," Cheever admitted, leaning his head back but keeping hold of Blake's wrist.

"Why?" Blake asked, and he took Cheever's hand and squeezed it, rubbed his thumb along the knuckles. He didn't let go, not even after he sat down.

"I think...." He closed his eyes, and what showed up behind them was his art, the paintings of Tyson/Hepzibah, the feeling he had in his stomach when he thought of himself as a punk-ass kid.

The way that feeling had spread, eating away at him like a cancer.

Until all that was left was the sickness, the feeling of being rotten to the marrow.

Of not even being able to be clean again.

"What?" Blake's motion with his thumb along the back of his knuckles never stopped.

"I just felt ugly inside," he breathed, amazed that the words could come out.

"I'm sorry about that," Blake told him. "I know how that feels."

Cheever opened his eyes and focused on Blake's plain, thin face, and how it seemed to grow more luminous every time they touched.

"I can't imagine you any way but beautiful," he said softly. He was expecting Blake's self-deprecating smile, so it didn't hurt.

"You ain't—aren't trying, which is kind." Without seeming to realize he was doing it, Blake raised Cheever's knuckles to his lips and rubbed. Deep under the sedative, the layers of pain, Cheever felt a little frisson of excitement—such a romantic gesture from such an everyday man.

"You keep trying to tell me you did all sorts of bad things," Cheever said, although his mind couldn't focus on what those were right now. "But you've never been anything but nice to me."

Blake's mouth twisted. "I don't even know where to start," he said frankly. "How's this? You know that shitty hotel room you were in?"

Cheever nodded, not picturing it, just knowing it had existed.

"I've been in that room a couple of times—not that exact one, but one just like it. There's a million hotel rooms just like it. I've been in that room doing lines, selling my ass for food, for coke, for a place to sleep. I've been hiding in a corner, ignoring the shit going on so I can catch a nap, and I've been on the bed, hoping it would be all over soon so I could take my cash or my snort and go. I've been the party and I've been the party favor, and...." He closed his eyes. "It doesn't go away, being in a room like that. The things you do there. The things that're done to you. It doesn't ever go away."

Something about the sedative let the tears come easy, and Cheever let them.

"How do you live with that?" he asked. In his head, he was picturing a boy's dorm—plain white walls, his favorite band posters the only decoration, and a quilt his mom had paid one of their old neighbors to make him so he'd have something special, living away from home. His guitar had been in the corner, in case his brothers ever asked him to play, and a rag rug had lain at the foot of the bed, because his mother had time now and could make things.

Aubrey Cooper, his stink, his breath, the smell of his feet in sweaty socks, was behind him, and his body was inside Cheever's, and it didn't hurt because Cheever had prepped, and it even felt a little good, because it was moving, moving, moving. But Cheever didn't want it, didn't want him, and in his head, he had a picture of a pretty young boy like an angel, exploding into a monster that was all cock, impaling Cheever's body like a fish on a fork.

"Being in that room?" Blake asked, his voice a lifeline out of that picture, and Cheever followed it to the door of his mind, clutching the frame with brittle white fingers.

"Yeah."

"You walk out," Blake said, his voice breaking a little. "You put one foot in front of the other and you just keep walking out."

"I can't," Cheever wept, feeling the strain in his arms as the Aubrey-monster threatened to pull him back inside. He couldn't even see what was outside of the room, but he heard Blake's voice there, so it had to be better than what was inside.

"Yes, you can, Cheever." Blake's voice sounded thick. "I know you can, kid. It's hard, but I wasn't ever loved like you were. You can come out of there because you know you were loved."

Oh God. The Aubrey-monster behind him didn't love him—but outside that room…. If he could just get outside that room, his mother was there. And his brothers. And he knew they loved him. He knew it. He might not have felt it in his heart for a long time, but he knew it in his head.

The monster roared and plunged back inside his body again, trying to claim him for that eternity in hell.

"No! God, please, no!" he cried, screaming in this bed, in this pretty room, like he'd never screamed as a kid. "Please stop. Please. I don't want to do this anymore. Please."

"Cheever! Cheever, come back here, boy! Come back!"

Blake's hand, squeezing his own to the point of pain, jerked his eyes open, and Blake stared at him as they locked hands. Blake gasped, white-faced, red-eyed, his free hand shaking as he scrubbed it over his mouth.

"Where were you?" That voice—warm and kind—sounded broken and scared, and Cheever was sorry, so sorry he'd hurt Blake, scared him.

But he'd seen the monster now, felt its breath on his neck, and he realized it had been there his whole adult life, and he'd been pretending it didn't exist.

Cheever was never sure how he had the courage to say it. "In the dorm, at my old prep school...."

In his mind, he took one step—just one—past the threshold, into the turbulent void beyond.

As Tears Go By

CHEEVER LOOKED... lost.

Terribly, terribly lost, and Blake felt exactly the same way.

"What happened there?" Blake asked, almost not wanting to hear the answer. His prep school.

Blake had expected Cheever to have been in a gas station, or in LA or at home alone or in a locker room when whatever had caused this had happened—anywhere but in his dorm room in a school where he was supposed to be safe.

Cheever shook his head and shrugged. "I can't," he said, shaking. "Not now. Not...." He clenched Blake's hand so hard. "I don't want you to see me like that," he mewled, and Blake didn't ask himself why it was so important that he not see Cheever like that—he didn't care what *he* saw. What was Cheever seeing that made him shake so goddamned hard?

"Do you think I want you to see me like that?" Blake asked instead, the shame of his time in that fucking hotel room—all those fucking hotel rooms—cutting so damned deep, he was surprised he didn't have a strip of flesh carved out of his ribs. "I keep showing you so you know I'm not perfect. So you know you got nothing to be ashamed of. And even if you do, you'll still be loved."

Cheever's hand came up to Blake's cheek, and Blake captured it there, closing his eyes and holding it.

This isn't how friends and little brothers act, dumbass. He's trying to tell you something.

So what if he is? You're going to cut and run now, when it's getting real? You fucking promised and you're that guy now, since the band got together. You're not the kid trapped in the shitty hotel room anymore, or Mackey's dealer, desperate for attention. You're the guy who keeps his promises and stays.

"You tell me stuff like that and all I can think is, thank God you got out."

"Don't you think we want you to get out, baby boy?"

Oh, he needed the authority that "baby boy" gave him—needed the distance. The hand on Blake's cheek wasn't a child's hand. It was long-fingered and callused and rough from working with art supplies and astringent cleaners. The nails were torn to the quick and the cuticles were bloody, but it was the hand of an adult, one with problems, sure, but not a kid's.

This kid is not thinking about sex—you know that more than anybody.

"I took a step today," Cheever said, sighing, his body relaxing, everywhere but that hand. "But I don't know what's beyond that room."

"You are," Blake told him. "Whatever you want to be. A kind you. One who plays with his brothers and fights with them like an equal. A you that gets to know your nieces and nephews and stays for family gatherings. A you that can court a man, be gentle, kiss a man like an adult, maybe getting your heart broken, maybe finding true love. A you that can paint pictures, ugly pictures and beautiful pictures, and know that whatever you put on the canvas, it's in your heart and it's worth something."

Cheever made a whimper, not scared so much as needy.

"You are what's beyond that room, Cheever Sanders. You've got so much potential out here. You just got to keep taking the steps, you hear me?"

"Yeah," Cheever whispered. "Yeah. I'll take the steps. But you gotta keep holding my hand, okay, Blake? 'Cause right now, I'm lost without you."

"I'm here," Blake promised. "I'm right here. I'll pull you back every time."

Cheever nodded again, eyes closed, and those slow tears just kept creeping down his cheeks. Finally his hand went limp, and Blake lowered it to the bed, resting his head against the rail.

God, if the kid was going to sleep through dinner, Blake could join him.

Last time he'd been this exhausted, he'd been on the other side of the shrink's chair, and he hadn't ever wanted to go back.

He was dozing lightly, his head still on the rail, when there was a gentle knock at the door. An orderly came in, bearing two trays of food, and Doc Cambridge was right behind him.

Blake turned and shook his head, thinking he couldn't eat. Since Cheever was asleep, there was no need for dinner tonight, right?

"Set the trays down," Cambridge insisted to the orderly. "Blake, see me outside, please?"

Blake stumbled outside, surprised by how drained he was and how much he needed his own nap. "I'll catch something on the way home," he said, trying to apologize.

"This has vegetables," Cambridge said, the "dad" in his voice sort of comforting at the same time Blake thought he was being a dick. "How is he?"

Blake's throat seized up, and he passed his hand over his chest a few times. "Sore," he managed to say.

Cambridge nodded. "How are you?"

Blake's mouth pushed up in the corner, and he rubbed his chest again. "Sore," he repeated softly.

Cambridge's mouth did the same thing. "I'm worried about his dependence on you," he said bluntly.

"Just until he's stronger," Blake reassured. "When he feels more able to talk, he won't need me so much—"

"I'm worried for *you*," Cambridge reiterated, rolling his eyes. "You're not Trav Ford, fifteen years older than Mackey, autocratic as hell. You may be a little older than this kid but... you had it a lot rougher, Blake."

Blake grimaced, thinking about what it must have been like to have been taken in the safety of your own room, when you'd been protected all your life. "Ten years," he said, ignoring the way Cambridge snorted. "And everyone's damage hurts," he said, trying to keep his dignity.

"Yeah. But you don't deserve to be this kid's human teddy bear because you were nearby when he had the worst moment of his life—"

"I wanted to be there," Blake interjected, his voice hardening. "I've known this kid a while, Doc. He's part of Kell and Mackey's family. I used to think he was a stuck-up little shit—but I still had hope, you know? And even if I didn't, he was still part of their family."

"Did you two have a rapport?" Cambridge asked. "Before this?"

Blake remembered that long-ago afternoon, after Mackey had lost his shit, with all the brothers dog piling him on the floor because Trav hadn't been there.

He thought about Cheever, looking young and defensive, and the way he'd talked about not sharing his hell with the rest of the world.

"We had a moment," he said. "When he was in middle school. Back when we went to visit Grant Adams before he died. Cheever was being an out and out little asshole, and he and Mackey got into it, and... well, it peeled the scab off a lot of Mackey's old business. And when it was over, Cheever was open. Vulnerable. And I sat down to talk to him, because... he sort of tugged at my heart, right? But he closed down like a fuckin' steel trap, and... I mean, me and the guys were wrecked. We'd gotten off a tour to go say goodbye to their friend, and the night before, we'd gotten bailed out of jail for a bar fight, and.... I keep thinking of the things I could have said then. What I could have done. To let this kid trust me more. But... I thought there'd be more chances, you know? I mean, he was just a kid. But he shut down after that. No more chances with any of the family. It was like he didn't even want us to try."

Cambridge frowned and searched Blake's face for a moment. "He's not a kid anymore."

Blake thought of that kiss, the way the kid lit up when he'd brought those battered knuckles to his lips.

"I... I guess not."

"He might develop feelings for you."

Blake waved his hand. "For a battered old coke whore? Once he gets his shit together, he'll have better people to love, Doc. Don't worry. You should have seen his school—Trav says he was getting straight *A*'s. Think of all those kids there to choose from. He'll forget about me when this is over, don't worry."

Cambridge had closed his eyes and was pushing really hard at that point between the bridge of his nose and his eyebrows with one finger. "I could retire," he said, as though to himself. "That would be good. I could retire, and the wife and I could move to a desert island, and—"

"Doc?"

"You're a good person, Blake Manning. Don't underestimate how attractive a good person who genuinely cares for you can be."

"If he gets a little crush, I'll be gentle," Blake said, although his heart died some at the thought of someone else taking his place by Cheever's bedside.

"And if he crushes your heart, I'll be here," Cambridge said with a sigh. "Go eat, Blake. Stay in the room until Marcia gets there—"

"Can't I just sleep there again tonight? Like I've done before?" Marcia had awakened with a little whimper the night before, and Blake had told her to hush, she was okay. She'd gone back to sleep, hugging one of the stupid stuffed animals Blake had brought her, and he thought that maybe she needed someone to protect her as she slept, just like Cheever.

Cambridge started rubbing the back of his own neck. "Sure. Because I have no idea why I even try."

"Because you're the best!" Blake said in surprise. "You saved my life! You saved Mackey's. We're not stupid, Doc. We listen to everything you say."

"You do," Cambridge said, nodding grimly. "I'm just not sure you hear it the way I mean it."

"But if the way we hear it unfucks our lives, that's still a good thing, right?"

Cambridge's stare was… unnerving.

"What?"

"I need to go reread about half of my graduate-level texts. And take a Motrin and some antacid for dinner."

Blake knew he was being kind of funny but wasn't sure how. "Make sure you have some dinner with that," he said, his mouth twisting. "You're gonna need some vegetables."

Cambridge laughed, but he still looked sad. "Blake, if you need to talk to me about anything, please do. Make an appointment if you can, but if you need to, I'll talk to you in my car getting takeout. In a thousand years, I could not have asked for boys who tried harder than you and Mackey. I see a lot of people working so hard not to fix themselves. I'd really like to keep the people trying in a good place."

Blake nodded. "Yessir. Will do. So, uh, that's a go on the sleeping here tonight?"

"As long as Ms. Lin is fine with it, so am I." He sighed and turned away, walking slower than Blake remembered.

Well, hurt people were hard on everybody.

Blake went back into the room and looked unhappily at the dinner trays. Well, shit. Might as well set a good example, right?

AN HOUR later, Cheever was still napping, and Blake was bored. His phone was charging, and he didn't feel like turning on the TV in the quiet—but Cheever's guitar? That beckoned to him.

He picked it up and started to play absently, going to that perennial favorite, "Stairway to Heaven" first, then shifting to "Ruby Tuesday," and then, on a whim, to "Wild Horses." He went randomly to a Gordon Lightfoot tune, singing gently about reading a lover's mind when a relationship was over, and then going back to "Heaven," because he hated to leave that one unfinished.

"Play your stuff," Cheever said quietly from his corner.

Blake looked up and smiled slightly. "Eat your dinner."

Cheever grunted. "Deal. But I draw the line at vegetables."

"Do that and you'll get Taylor Swift and like it."

Cheever's chuckle made him feel better, and he pulled the tray over to his bed. "How do you know I don't like Taylor Swift?"

Blake kept playing, but thought about it. "The music books in your room, I guess. Same shit me and the boys play. Was sort of... nice."

Cheever took a bite and chewed thoughtfully. "The music was always around me," he said, like he was thinking. "Even after my brothers left, it was like... at least I had their music."

"Mm." Blake tuned a recalcitrant string—the guitar was a good one, and nicely broken in. "You should tell them that. I think... you know. They're a little hurt."

"Yeah. They tried, you know? After Grant died. After we moved to LA, I was just not listening."

Blake smiled at him. "Listening's a good thing."

And then he launched into the only song on his solo album that had gotten any airtime.

"I heard the door close behind you
I heard the end of the dream
I heard you laughing with your lover
And you never heard me scream
Was never gonna be your lover
Never gonna be your guy
You never needed my hand in yours
Not your job to help me fly
I get to see you happy now
That's a promise I did keep
You get to think I'm happy now
And you'll never hear me weep
Such a smalltime hopeless crush on you
Not a lover, just a friend
You never knew I cried for you
And I never lost my friend."

THERE WAS a quiet riff at the end, something Mackey had helped him with, truth be known, because Mackey had helped engineer and record the album and hired the backup musicians so they could give new guys a boost. He played it, delicate, lilting, and let the final chord sound, and was surprised when Marcia started clapping from her side of the bedroom.

"You liked that?" he asked. He'd never even heard her come in.

"It was gorgeous," she said, at the same time Cheever said, "It hurts more now."

Blake stared at him, suddenly uncomfortable. What had he told the boy in the last two days that would make that song different?

"Why?" Marcia asked, and Cheever locked eyes with Blake.

"Because I know who it was for."

Oh. Blake had told him that, hadn't he?

"Wasn't for anyone," he lied. "It's just a song. You're not always the singer, you know. Sometimes it's a persona."

Cheever rolled his eyes much like Doc Cambridge had, and suddenly Blake felt naked. "And I painted those pictures of my hometown because I loved it."

Yup. Totally naked.

Blake couldn't look at him. "So, uh, any requests before I turn on the TV and we watch movies?"

"'Coffee Shop,'" they both said in tandem, and Blake stared at them.

"That wasn't even a B side." It had been his favorite song on the whole album. Mackey had insisted he include it because Mackey and Kell loved it too. But Heath, their producer, had told them it wouldn't get played, and while disappointed, Blake had just been so happy everybody had let him produce his little solo album in spite of how little it would probably sell.

"It's my favorite," Marcia said, hugging her Hello Kitty even closer. "It's... it's fun and it's sad and it's every dumb breakup ever. You should write more songs like that for Outbreak Monkey. Will Mackey let you?"

Mackey had, in fact, encouraged him. He'd put his backing behind Blake's solo effort had offered help when Blake had asked—and had told him, repeatedly, that he was proud. It was Blake's embarrassment, really, that had put an end to his songwriting. The album had a modest success, but nothing compared to Outbreak Monkey, and Blake had felt... inadequate. As though he'd let his brothers down.

"Yeah," he said, his mouth twisting as he found the beat on the guitar. "He likes my stuff."

"Then why haven't you written any more?" Cheever asked, and Blake grunted.

"'Cause your brother's too generous with his time, and I don't need more of it than I already take," he said, winking in case that sounded harsh. He launched into the song then, letting the quirkiness of the breakup in the coffee shop make the two sad young people smile. Marcia started chiming in first, and then Cheever, and they had a rousing chorus by the time Blake strummed the final chords.

The song faded, and Blake stood and set the guitar aside, then moved to take Cheever's half-eaten tray of food away from his bed and set it with his own by the door.

"They should be by in an hour or so," Blake said with a yawn. "Will you need to use the bathroom before then?"

"Maybe," Cheever conceded. "I'd like to brush my teeth before I go to bed." He pulled fitfully at the handcuff.

"Aw, Cheever, again?" Marcia commiserated. "What's it going to take?"

"I don't know," Cheever said, meeting Blake's eyes bleakly. "What's it going to take?"

"Honesty," Blake responded. "I've poured my heart out to you, boy. You need to return the favor to the doc."

Cheever sighed. "That's fair. Here—you call for an orderly, Marcia, you pick a movie, and we can settle down for the night." Yeah. "Baby boys" gave orders like that all the time. The kid had Mackey's organization and leadership when he was chained to a bed. Terrifying.

When the orderly got there to supervise his bathroom time, Marcia curled up on her side and looked at Blake from across the room.

"Is he gonna make it?" she asked, and Blake saw her own struggles written plainly on her face. He'd been helping his brothers raise their children for years now. It was a role that suited him, because apparently when not coked up or pissed off, he tended to be quiet and kind and shy. He knew when you gave a child hope instead of pure truth. Sometimes hope kept the dark at bay, when truth—even "I don't really know," sort of truth, would let it come surging in.

"We all are," he said with a reassuring smile. "Even you, darlin'. Don't think I can't see you hurting tonight."

She sniffled. "I really loved the concert. Wish you could stay the night every night."

Blake came to her bedside and kissed her temple, remembering how badly he'd wanted someone to do that for him. "Well, if I did that, you'd be dependent on me. Don't worry—you're strong enough to rely on yourself. You just need some training up."

"Thanks, Mr. Manning. How about a rom-com tonight? God, something funny, yeah?"

"Oh my God, yes!"

Marcia laughed a little, and Blake settled into their little family routine with a sigh.

Cheever wasn't out of the woods, but Doc was letting Blake help him out, and for this night, things might be okay.

BLAKE SLEPT near the foot of Cheever's bed again, this time in the chair he'd dragged to the side of it because Cheever wanted to hold Blake's hand as he slept.

He'd asked for that, with words, and Blake hadn't missed the knowing look from Marcia as he'd settled down to what looked to be a truly uncomfortable night.

"I saw that," Cheever murmured, after the orderly came to turn out the lights.

"What?"

"You rolled your eyes, like this doesn't mean anything."

Blake let out a breath. "It means you have people in your life that care," he said, laying his head down on the side of the bed.

"That can't be comfortable," Cheever told him. And then he pushed Blake's hair back from his eyes.

"It's not. Doc's gonna make me go home tomorrow."

"Then I'll just have to live," Cheever said, surprising him.

"Why's that?"

"Because I want to see you sleep sometime when you're comfortable and everybody's safe and you don't have this." Cheever used his forefinger to smooth the line between Blake's eyebrows, and a relief so acute it was almost painful flooded Blake, from his tightened face to the back of his shoulders.

"You should jump on tour with us sometime," Blake told him, melting a little. God, he hadn't even been aware of how tense he'd been. "Feels like all we do is sleep on the bus."

"I used to be jealous," Cheever said softly. "I think I still am. You guys, all together."

"Driving each other batshit," Blake laughed, remembering how Trav had made the bus stop in the middle of Bakersfield one year so he could break out the boxing gloves and let all the guys take swings at each other with padding and some rules. Otherwise, he'd said, they were going to snipe each other to death—if Trav didn't kill them all first.

"Y'all fight?" Cheever was drowsy enough to drop the rich kid voice, and as hard as Blake worked to drop his own trailer-park twang, he found that when Cheever used it, the effect was… charming.

"Lots," Blake told him. "We started carrying around boxing equipment so we could go after each other in the ring when shit got too real."

Cheever frowned, his eyes closed. "That's sort of… you know. Caveman."

"Yeah, that's 'cause you didn't see Briony and Shelia go after each other when Briony made Shelia's kids start washing their hands before dinner."

Cheever's eyes popped open. "They did not!"

"Sure they did. And we told your mother all about it last Christmas." Blake felt that line come back between his eyes.

"After I left," Cheever said sadly.

"Yeah."

"I wish I could be like you. Like a brother."

"So do they," Blake told him. He reached out with his own finger and smoothed the lines between Cheever's eyebrows. Seeing that full mouth turn up at the corners was enough to make Blake smile in return. "That's something worth living for."

"So's watching you sleep."

Blake was so tired. "Nothing to see here," he said, closing his own eyes with a yawn. "Trailer park boy who got incredibly lucky, that's all."

"Got out of the trailer park," Cheever mumbled, obviously close to sleep himself. "You got out of the trailer park. I can get out of that room."

"Good," Blake said back, almost done. He didn't realize how much he was hoping for that to be real, though, until he felt Cheever's thumb, wiping across the bridge of his nose, taking away the moisture he was prepared to deny existed until the day he died.

Emotional Rescue

"YOU READY?" Marcia asked, and Cheever checked his appearance in the bathroom mirror one more time.

"No."

"Tough. We both look like crap. I've got judgy parents to talk to. You've got your mother, who is trying not to lose her shit."

"And Blake." Because that was what had gotten Cheever through, this far. It had been four days since Doc Cambridge had allowed Blake to sleep in their room—four days marked by Marcia waking him up once a night with a soft, "Cheever, you're dreaming again," when he was well aware he'd been screaming—at least inside his head.

"That'll be nice," Marcia admitted sweetly. "I mean, he comes every day as it is, but only for a little while. This will be like my parents are meeting him."

Cheever gave her a guarded look. "Like a boyfriend?" he asked, and she rolled her eyes.

"Oh, Cheever—I wouldn't do that to you. I just mean…." She had such a tiny smile, the kind that made her cheeks and chin point. "He told me I could come stay with you when this was over. Live in a big house with too many people, all up in my business. Kids. Like, five of them, he said. Do you know I like kids? I have two cousins that we see, like, twice a year, and they're the best part of Thanksgiving and Easter. I can spend my summer vacation playing with kids, and Blake will be a part of that. It's…." She looked away shyly. "It's such a lovely dream. So much better than heroin. Just so… so noisy and crowded and awesome. My whole life, I've felt like I've been screaming in an empty room. Anyway. You know. He's part of that. I want them to see."

Cheever was not a hugger. His mother always hugged him when she saw him, and he spent a lot of time wishing he could crawl out of his skin before she absorbed something from him he didn't want her to see. But right now, Marcia was so hopeful—not overboard hopeful, like this dream could topple on her head and crush her, but tentatively hopeful, like maybe, even if some stuff wasn't awesome, it would still be a decent dream.

He turned to her awkwardly and gave her an impulsive hug, which she returned.

"What?" she asked when he pulled up in a hurry. "I did that wrong?"

He shook his head, embarrassed. "I'm so bad at it!"

"I know! Me too! My whole life, I've been embarrassed that somebody would hug me in case I screwed it up, but...." She bit her lip. "We should do it more often," she said. "So we get better. You're a good friend—you saved my life. I should be able to hug you."

"You saved my life too," he said, and he thought about Blake, and hugging Blake—maybe even today. "And I think you're right. We should practice on each other. So we can do this right."

They both caught each other's eyes nervously. Cheever had made some progress. He'd admitted to the doc that he'd been bullied, had even used that same word to Blake. But they'd both looked sad when he said it, like they were very aware of the word he was hiding behind the easy one. He wasn't planning ways to hurt himself anymore—but he wasn't finding out who he was outside of that miserable fucking room either.

So, some progress. But today they had to visit their parents, and some progress wasn't cured. It wasn't a promise. It was just a start, and that didn't always feel good enough.

He swallowed. "I have to tell my mother what I did," he said, because that had been looming over his head since he'd woken up in the hospital, feeling like shit and looking at the stitches on the inside of his wrist, like somebody else had held the razor.

"Use the word," Marcia said. He'd noticed she'd gotten pushy here—maybe because people were always pushing their way into Marcia and Cheever's business, she was picking up some skills.

"Suicidal," he said, surprised that it just popped out. "I was suicidal."

She nodded, pressing her lips together. "I'm a recovering drug addict."

Okay. They were doing this.

Without knowing he was going to do it, he fumbled for her hand. "Let's get it done."

MARCIA'S PARENTS were... reserved. Her mother—a blonde woman in a white suit, even on a Saturday, looked like a stiff wind would shatter her makeup and break her hair in half. Her father, a stocky man with

Marcia's almond-shaped eyes and slight build, said very little as her mother made brittle conversation.

Cheever's mother was quite a contrast.

Heather Sanders had spent twenty-three years of her life working her ass off so her kids could have food, clothes, and a place to sleep.

The minute Outbreak Monkey made it big, Cheever's brothers had bought her a house and clothes and a big shiny SUV.

The first thing Heather had done was open a tiny hair salon in the basement of her new home so she could still see her old clients.

After moving to LA—into a modest house by the beach so Cheever could go to a high school in which surfing was part of the curriculum— she'd done exactly the same thing. She didn't work a lot, maybe two days a week, but she liked to keep busy. And once her sons started giving her grandbabies, she was in her glory. Spoiling her grandchildren was her favorite thing to do.

Cheever couldn't count the number of times she'd looked at him wistfully and told him her one regret was the time she didn't get to spend with her boys when they were growing up.

In high school, Cheever had been mortified, but as he'd grown up— and seen the sort of benign neglect his peers had grown up with—he'd made an amazing discovery. His mother wasn't *embarrassing*. His mother was *awesome*. But by then, he'd devoted so much of his time to convincing himself he didn't need her as a mother, or as a friend, or as anybody substantial in his life, that he didn't know how to let her back in again.

Today, as he and Marcia made it into the tastefully decorated dining room—it had carpet and heavy wooden furniture and flowers at the tables, live ones—he saw his mom sitting in her spot, demure and nervous, and realized that maybe she was fifty, but she was also beautiful and vulnerable and about the most amazing woman he could possibly imagine in his life.

And she was worried about him. He owed her better.

She saw him, and her face—a little vulpine fox's face, like Cheever's and Mackey's—lit up, and she rushed across the dining room and into his arms.

For once, he couldn't let her down.

He opened his arms wide and hefted her up in the air, because he was five ten to her five-foot-nothing, and she gave a little squeal and held tighter.

"Oh, baby," she whispered, "why didn't you tell me? Why didn't you tell me you hurt so bad?"

He closed his eyes and held her closer. "I didn't have words, Mama. I'm so sorry. I didn't have words."

No pretenses, not here, with his mother. He'd tried to commit suicide. Whether it was suicide by coke or suicide with a razor, that had been him. He'd done that. He'd scared her, made her cry, made Blake—oh God, Blake had aged in the past week—made Blake exhausted and sad.

I need to tell Doc Cambridge that. I need to tell him I didn't know I mattered.

He had to put her down, sooner rather than later. People thought that losing blood was just a matter of getting it replaced, but he'd felt like an old man all week. Besides the antidepressants making him sleep, the thing he'd done to his body had been brutal and damaging.

It had never felt so brutal as it did when he stumbled a little and set down his mother.

Blake was at his elbow to catch him. "Oopsy daisy." Such a child's term from this grown man. Cheever's heart warmed a little, and he allowed Blake to escort him to their table before turning.

"Wait." He turned while Blake still had his elbow. "I didn't get my hug from you."

Blake stuttered, staring at him. "Uh—"

But Cheever had broken the ice with his mother and with Marcia; he could be brave now. He wanted to feel Blake's body up against his own, wanted to see what someone warm and kind felt like, on his terms.

He didn't hug hard, like a child. He rested his head on Blake's shoulder and clasped his hands loosely around his waist.

And waited.

Blake's arms rose up uncertainly around his shoulders, and then Cheever melted into him, firmly. Blake hugged Cheever's brothers all the time. Cheever had seen him hug the children—even Cheever's mom.

But this—this was special.

Blake leaned his cheek on the top of Cheever's head and the two of them eased into each other's space.

Ah!

Cheever felt safe. He couldn't remember feeling this safe since he was thirteen years old, and Blake pulled him tighter, and Cheever's entire body fluttered, like his libido was batting its eyelashes and saying, "Oh, yeah! I live here!"

Blake shuddered hard, and Cheever felt his lips rub Cheever's temple for a blissful moment, and then it was time to let go.

Blake settled down into one of the chairs at the table, and Cheever settled next to him and scooted the chair closer, carefully not looking at his mother's raised eyebrows.

"How you doing, Cheever?" Mom was leaning on her arms and not smiling. "I… I gotta admit, you had us all fooled. Mackey fell off that amp, and we were thinking, 'Yeah, well, Mackey would do that.' But you—you caught us by surprise."

Cheever cast an unhappy look at Blake, and Blake gave a sympathetic shrug. He'd tried to warn Cheever, but nothing could prepare you for telling your mother the truth after lying for eight years, could it?

"I…. Mama, remember when you asked me if I wanted to go back to that school?" He'd taken his step out. He had. And he didn't have a superclear vision of who he was out of that room, but he knew part of it involved being honest with his family.

"Yeah, honey." She took one of his hands in hers. "I remember. You were… so unhappy. Acting out with Briony. Saying things, doing things—we were worried."

Cheever nodded. "Well—wait. Did anybody tell you I'm gay?" He honestly couldn't remember, but his mother's eyebrows didn't even flex.

"No, sweetheart, but just like Mackey, nobody had to tell me. I was just waiting for you to get around to it yourself."

Blake's hand, warm and kind, on his knee, gave him heart. "Good," he said, grimacing. "I, uh… you know. There's one thing I don't have to mention."

His mother's eyes were blue, but she didn't look innocent or easily fooled. "I'm getting the feeling maybe you do." She flicked a sympathetic glance at Blake. "For various reasons. What happened in middle school, honey? What happened that got you so tied up in knots you couldn't even untie them enough to tell me you were in pain?"

"There were… there was someone in middle school who… you know. Wasn't nice. And… well, he sort of knew I was gay, and he was…. Uh… it got bad." Blake squeezed his knee, but when he looked up, he saw grim acceptance rather than approval.

Blake knew he was understating things. Maybe he even knew Cheever was hiding behind words that sounded like the truth but weren't.

Cheever took a deep breath and captured Blake's fingers with his own, and then met his gaze and shook his head. He couldn't do that now. He couldn't talk about how he'd been Aubrey Cooper's meat baby, just waiting, sweat dripping between his shoulder blades, hands clammy and shaking, to see if Aubrey would violate his space and his safety and his body.

Blake surprised him then, pulling his knuckles up to his lips like he had before and placing a sweet kiss on the back.

"In your own time," he said, and Cheever closed his eyes tight, which didn't help the aching in his throat or chest at all.

"That's.... I can't talk about it now," he said, because he knew he'd fly completely apart if he did. "But I'll tell Doc Cambridge, and Blake, I promise—"

"Not me?" she asked, hurt.

He searched her face then, for some realization that her boyfriend's son had raped him—and saw only concern for Cheever himself.

"Yeah," he said. "Someday, Mama. But... but right now, I'm getting out of bed in the morning and thinking about running or working out or listening to music. I'm not thinking about ways to kill myself in the shower."

She whimpered, and he knew he'd been cruel, but those were the only words he had.

"It's a big improvement," he said, nodding at Blake, who nodded back sadly. "I... I want to keep working toward that, okay? Just.... It got bad. It got so bad. And I let it."

"You were a kid," Blake snapped, and Cheever realized he was shaking.

"I'm sorry," he said. "This hurts you too—"

"I'm a big boy," Blake told him bluntly. "But I care about you—"

"Good," Cheever said, holding that knowledge to his heart. "Then you'll let me tell you and Doc and Mama in my own time, okay?"

Blake's chin dropped to his chest. "Ah... God, Cheever. I need—"

Cheever kissed him quickly, on the mouth, in front of his mother, and when he pulled back, he saw his mother hiding her amusement behind her hand. Blake was... well, poleaxed was a good word.

"I promise you, Blake Manning, I'm working to be the guy outside the room. And I want him to be good for you. Because you deserve good. Can you trust me?"

Blake nodded dumbly—well, he'd had a shock, it was clear.

"You trust me, right?" Cheever reiterated.

"Yeah," Blake said, sounding out of it. "Why did you do that?"

"Because he's the guy outside the room," Cheever told him. "And you can reject me when I get there, or you can say yes, but you need to know I'm coming. I *will* get my shit together, and you and me are going to have a chance."

Blake's mouth opened and closed, his hazel eyes wandering around the room like a lost child's.

"Blake?" Cheever said, trying not to let his heart sink.

Blake looked at him with shiny, red-rimmed eyes. "That's a big promise, baby boy," he whispered. "I might not be the guy you want to make that promise to."

Oh. This. "You are," Cheever said, recovered a little. "But don't worry. I'll have my shit together first."

Blake nodded and gave part of a smile, and Cheever's mother said desperately, "Blake, honey, is that girl waving at you? Cheever's friend?"

"Marcia!" Blake stood up then, and Cheever missed his heat, but appreciated that Blake needed a moment to himself. "I promised her," he apologized.

"Bring her over in a minute," Cheever's mom said. She looked at Cheever with meaning. "After Cheever and I have a little talk."

Blake nodded, distracted, and left. Cheever didn't miss the way Marcia's pointed features relaxed as he strode across the room.

"Cheever," Mama said, voice tough, "you had better not hurt him."

Cheever looked away from that stiff tableau of Marcia's parents and Blake, trying to be nonthreatening and charming, and turned back to his mother's eyes.

"Mama, you know how if you do something stupid you should learn from it?" Oh, he meant this.

"Yeah."

"If I learned anything from the last two weeks, it's not to take Blake Manning for granted ever again."

But she shook her head. "Honey, you do not understand. This is not my first visit to this particular facility, you know that, right?"

Cheever rolled his eyes. "I'm seeing Mackey and Blake's shrink, Mom. I am aware."

But she didn't laugh. "The first time I saw that boy when he wasn't a magazine clipping or click bait, it was when he was sitting where you are now. He was going to fade into the background when Mackey grabbed him by the scruff of the neck and said, 'Here, son, you're a brother now, meet Mom.'"

Cheever bit his lip. God, if nothing else, he was getting an education as to what made Mackey James Sanders such an undeniable force in the universe.

"That was nice of him."

Mama rolled her eyes. "He wasn't even trying to be nice. It just was. But I hugged that boy, and I swear, he'd never been hugged before—not by a mom. Watching him become everybody's favorite uncle these past years has been great—but it's been frustrating as fuck."

"*Mama*!"

She shook her head. "You don't understand. He's *hurt* inside. He's been down here taking care of you and your friend, and all his wounds were freshly peeled open. He'd been crying when he picked me up today. Crying. He won't even admit it, though, but he is *worried*. So it's all brave of you to offer him something when you're feeling better, but if you don't mean it, you will hurt him in ways he will not recover from. Our family is his life. Be careful with him, Cheever. I want you to get better. God knows…." She took a deep breath and wiped her face with shaking hands. "I'd give anything to know you were okay. But it's not fair to ask us to sacrifice that boy so you can heal. Do you understand?"

Cheever bit his lip and nodded. Oh, he did. "I've been selfish," he said, remembering Doc Cambridge's words. "I think when you're in pain, you get that way. And I get why you're afraid. But I'm not dicking with Blake. Please believe me. Have you ever looked at something every day and not thought about it? Like a painting on a wall or a view or a particular color that you used to see and it was just part of the background?"

"And then you look at it and it's beautiful?" she finished, surprising him.

"Yeah."

"That's fine, honey. Just don't break the painting or mix the color with black." She sighed and dragged her fingers through her hair. "And don't look at me like that," she said, giving a little laugh. "I… I hate thinking of you in pain. I just…." She looked over her shoulder at Blake and bit her lip, then turned back to Cheever.

"He took my place—" Cheever said, finally seeing what his actions had done to his family.

"No!"

He shook his head. "No. I get it. I was… unavailable." He was a *dick*. "Blake needed a mother."

"So do you," she said, taking his hand and stroking it. Her lips— still full, no cosmetics needed—twisted up. "And now that you're going to let me mother you, that's no-holds-barred."

Uh-oh. "That may take getting used to—"

"You're moving in with the guys when you're done here."

Cheever allowed himself a small smile. "You know that fits in with my nefarious plan—"

She shook her head. "You only say that because you haven't lived there. I've been there when they get into their routine—son, you have no idea. I pretty much just gave you to a commune."

Cheever thought about it—all those kids, places to go, serious moms doing serious mom stuff, Outbreak Monkey writing music and practicing. Mackey had apparently leased the house next door and turned part of it into a recording studio. Music, 24-7.

"Well, if it's too much, I can find a place to paint," he said, and then gaped at himself.

"What?"

"I want to paint…." The thought surprised him. He hadn't wanted to since… well, since his disastrous finals presentation. When Blake was sad, he picked up his guitar. When Cheever was sad, what did he do? A sneaky little voice urged him to go pick up the guitar in the corner of his room like he did when nobody could see—and that bothered him. His entire life, for eight years, had revolved around him picking up a paintbrush or a pencil or some other media every goddamned day. But only now was he thinking about using his… well, it wasn't a gift. It wasn't even a talent. It was something he'd worked at. Something that hadn't come naturally to him, but that he'd fostered. His skill? His occupation?

For the first time in a long time, he was urged to use something he'd trained himself to do as though he enjoyed it.

"I… I thought that was gone," he said, stunned. "Mackey wrote *music* in this place. Why don't I want to make art?"

Heather sighed, and for a moment, the lines of worry etched themselves into her face and she looked every day of her fifty years. "Honey, the school contacted me—or Blake, rather. They have a sort of nervous breakdown policy. When you're done here, you can go visit your professors and talk about your finals—two of your classes pretty much gave you the grade you'd earned before the test, 'cause you're a smart boy and got *A*'s in the first place. The other two professors say they'll take your final essay when you're ready—"

"Blake got my laptop. Can I send them?" His degree. He'd worked four years for that damned degree, and he was going to be the first Sanders to get that stupid piece of paper at a school, not online. Kell had made a big deal out of that.

Spending the last two weeks with Blake—who had gotten his degree online, between touring and making music—had made Cheever realize what pretentious bullshit that thought was.

His brothers knew so much more than he did.

"Yeah," his mother said, nodding. "Blake's got the information on his phone. But you've got one teacher, though—Dr. Tierce?"

Cheever's heart sank. "Oh God."

"She wanted to work with you for all next semester. She said she wanted you to get an *A* in the class, but you had to work for it."

Cheever groaned again, lacing his fingers behind his neck. "Augh! Really?"

"Is there something wrong?"

She's only the woman who drove me to a nervous breakdown. Nothing to see here!

"Do I really *need* that degree?" he asked, feeling pathetic.

"No, Cheever, but you're almost finished. She sounded really excited about working with you."

"Of course she did." Probably looking forward to seeing him lose his shit all over again. Wonderful.

"Think about it, honey," Mama was saying. She squeezed his hand. "Cheever?"

"Yeah?"

"You're at a crossroads here. I mean, you were going to be anyway— you were going to need to decide what your life was going to be like after graduation. But you're at a bigger one now, you see? Not just what your life is going to be like, but what *you* are going to be like. Are you someone who takes the easy way out and drags the people who care down with you? Or are you someone who does the grown-up thing, even if it's not always easy. Doc Cambridge isn't ready to spring you yet, and I think that's good. I think... I think you need to take this time to do some figuring out."

Cheever nodded, suddenly exhausted. Blake came by the table, holding Marcia by the hand. She looked about done in too.

"Sorry." She wobbled, leaning on Blake. "Sorry. Didn't mean to get all weird and emo on you. Just… they kept saying 'when this is over,' and they weren't seeing—"

"You were unhappy before," Blake said softly. "I heard it, though. You know it. The doc knows it. Here, come meet Cheever's mama. She cheers about anybody up."

Cheever met his mother's eyes and nodded, and his mom turned mom and hugged Marcia like she was made for hugs. Blake disentangled himself from them and came to sit by Cheever like it was the most natural thing in the world.

"Honey, I don't know about you, but I get lost looking for the bathroom here. You wouldn't want to show me, and then we can stop and get the boys some ice cream on the way back," Mama said, and the way Marcia smiled, so relaxed, made Cheever proud.

"You look cooked and done," Blake said kindly, his eyes crinkling in the corners in one of the few reminders that he was older than Cheever by ten years.

"Mama doesn't pull any punches," Cheever said, lacing his hands behind his neck again. He turned his head and gave Blake a good once-over, seeing again the bags beneath his eyes and the paleness. "This isn't easy on you, either," he said, feeling bad.

"I can take it," Blake told him mildly, and Cheever sighed.

"Yeah, but you wouldn't tell me if you couldn't."

Blake yawned then, and instead of leaning back in his seat, he put his head on his fist on top of the table. "Cheever?"

"Yeah?"

"I liked that kiss. Don't second-guess that, okay? I mean, don't focus on me instead of on getting better, but don't… you know. Make yourself crazy wondering if you did the right thing."

Cheever smiled and echoed his pose so they were side by side, thighs touching, triceps touching, chins resting on their hands. "Okay. I may do it again. Promise to tell me if you want me to stop."

"I'm an addict, Cheever. Knowing when to stop is pretty much my worst thing."

"I have never, ever had sex with someone I wanted to be with," Cheever told him, and then blinked, because that was a confession he maybe should have made to his shrink, but it seemed like Blake needed to hear it more. "If I want to touch you or kiss you like that, it's important to me. I want it to mean something to you."

Blake let out a little sigh. "It does. My brain's all muddled now, though. It means something—I just don't have words for what."

Cheever smiled softly and leaned closer, taking his heat all through the side of his body. "We'll start with it means something."

"That's fine."

They just sat there, almost dozing, until Heather and Marcia got back with ice cream. When Blake and his mom left, Cheever hugged his mama and then let Marcia get in to hug her too, and then he moved to Blake.

"You look tired, rock star," Cheever said softly. He captured Blake's chin with his fingers then and kissed him again, closing his eyes when Blake opened his mouth and let him in.

The kiss grew deeper, fuller, and Cheever pulled away. "See you tomorrow?"

"Yeah."

"Get some sleep, Blake. Maybe your brain won't be muddled tomorrow."

"Brain's always muddled around you, boy."

And with that, Blake and Heather walked out of the visitor's area, leaving Marcia and Cheever to wander back to their own room, where they both admitted they were looking for a nap.

"Your parents seemed nice." Cheever yawned, hoping she'd forgive him for the social lie.

"They barely said hi to you," Marcia said with a yawn of her own. "Don't worry, Cheever. I'm a little disappointed. Remember when you were a kid and you thought, 'Hey, I wish I could be sick just long enough to get everybody's attention'?"

"No," Cheever said, feeling dumb. "If I was sick, one of my brothers had to take care of me, somebody didn't get to work, and that was one day more of ramen noodles and one day I didn't get hamburger or something for dinner."

Marcia stared at him. "I honestly forget. I mean, I know the bio and the backstory, but that was a real thing for you. Okay so, when food and rent aren't a consideration, sometimes, you think, 'If I could get sick, my parents would stay home and play games with me and make me feel like the prettiest princess and the most special and important thing in their lives.'"

Cheever couldn't even imagine. "Did that happen?"

"No," Marcia said, sounding grumpy. "No, it didn't. Because my parents were pretty sure my raising was done once I turned seven and could dress myself and make my own cereal for breakfast. Anyway, I had one of those fantasies about my parents coming to rehab to see their darling daughter and how unhappy she was, and do you know how that turned out?"

"About the same?" Cheever hazarded a guess, feeling bad. His mother had shown up with life advice and a way for Cheever to fix his education and the promise to be there for him as much as she possibly could and the very credible, real threat to throw him into the midst of his family and make him grow up, but with love and acceptance and support.

He *did* get to be the prettiest princess for the day.

"Oh, it was worse," Marcia said grimly. "I got a lecture about being a fuckup and embarrassing the family and about how my degree was going to waste and—"

Cheever looped an awkward arm around her shoulder. "And you're coming to my brothers' big dumb house and playing with children. And they can go to hell."

"Did your mom say that was okay?" she asked, sounding defeated.

"Blake said it, and since he lives there, he gets say." Cheever remembered something. "I understand that's how Kell's wife started living there, anyway. She was Mackey's friend. He dragged her home and said, 'Here, she's good. We'll keep her.' And she and Kell fell in love."

"It's like a fairy tale, you realize that, right?"

Poor Marcia. "Well, I think we all need a fairy tale once in a while."

Cheever wanted Blake. Blake was his fairy tale. Now Cheever had to make it come true.

THE NEXT day Cheever woke up with the urge to paint. He participated in morning PT—light, yes, but he could run a mile now, so that was good. He spent time after breakfast in a class that dealt with positive visualization, and he took his hour after lunch to himself.

He went straight to his room and broke out his charcoal and sketchbooks, determined to do something, anything, artistic before he went to see Doc Cambridge.

For a few panicked moments, he stared at the blank page, looming like a brick wall in front of a train, and then he did what he always did when he was stuck.

He closed his eyes and cleared his head and made a few passes over the page with the charcoal.

He opened his eyes and gasped, horrified.

He'd been expecting to see Blake—he'd been thinking about Blake, hoping for him.

But what he saw was… was a monster, a monster with a giant phallus pinning a poor man to a wall with his mighty weapon.

Cheever's breath caught in his chest, and his vision went dark. For a full five minutes, he had to fight actively not to visualize a thousand ways to end himself.

Lazy thinking. There are other alternatives.

Then his phone went off for therapy, and he stood up.

He took a few steps toward the door and then grabbed his sketchbook with resolve.

Well, the doc wanted to know what was on his mind? Turned out Cheever had a picture that would do the job just fine.

Dandelion

BLAKE FELT the oppression the moment he walked into Cheever and Marcia's room, even over the strains of his CD, which was coming from someone's phone.

Cheever was in bed, lying on his side, handcuff still in place. Marcia was sitting at the foot of the bed, and Doc Cambridge was in Blake's chair. All of them had closed eyes, as though from exhaustion.

What happened?

Marcia saw him first, and she pushed off the bed tiredly and came in for a hug without saying anything.

"What—"

"He'll tell you," she said. She pulled a piece of paper out of her pocket that had been balled up at one point in time and folded many times over after that. She pressed it into his hand.

"Doc?"

Cambridge startled. "Oh," he said softly. "Blake. We've been waiting for you."

"What happened?" Blake asked, lost.

"A good thing, I think," Cambridge said, touching Cheever's hand in the cuff. "This is just a precaution." He grimaced. "It was a rough day, and let's just say, I've learned not to trust the lot of you when you say you're all right."

"I'm not Mackey." Blake and Cheever both said it in tandem, and Cambridge's acidic laugh told Blake more than he needed to know about his own problems.

And Cheever's.

"You boys...." Cambridge shook his head. "That kid is not taller than a spit on a plate. If you get nothing else from Cheever's time here, I hope you get that you cast your own damned shadows." He turned to Marcia before either of them could respond. "Let's go see about dinner. Or ice cream. Or cake. What time is it?"

"Three in the afternoon," Blake said, his throat aching.

"Ice cream," Marcia said decisively. "And then funny movies. All the goddamned funny movies."

"That there is the best drug known to man." Cambridge paused at the door. "Maybe plan to stay tonight, Blake. It'll probably be the last night we have to do this."

And then they were gone, leaving Blake holding on to the much-abused piece of paper. He sank into the familiar chair.

Without thinking about it, he smoothed Cheever's hair back from his forehead and caught the boy's shadowed green eyes on his face.

"You look tired," Cheever said, his voice rough from what sounded like suppressed screaming.

"Your mama kept me up last night," Blake confessed. "Do you know she's kept pictures of one form or another since Kell was born?"

Cheever frowned. "I guess—"

"She had all the phone ones put on paper, and she made books for all of you. They were supposed to be Christmas presents this year. She's been working on it for… I don't know. Since you graduated from high school."

"Oh God. I was so *ugly* in high school."

"You were *not*," Blake argued passionately. "God, you were such a pretty kid. Unusual coloring, you know? I mean, we got redheads—we got Trav and Briony. But your color hair, your skin tone, the shape of your face. Your eyes." *Oh, how embarrassing.* "You're just… pretty."

Trav had needed him to set up the house for Mackey—a special chair up the stairs, special equipment in the workout room, a special orthopedic bed in the bedroom, even a rail in the pool, because Mackey was going to be doing a lot more laps than running. He had apologized profusely to Blake about the trouble, and had asked about Cheever kindly, which was not a word Blake would have used to describe the big man when they'd first met. Blake had been happy to do it, but thinking about Mackey's long road to recovery had left Blake sad and raw, and walking with a tearful Heather through the rough, painful beginnings of the guys he loved had left him sore and bloody.

He had no barriers. No defenses now against the giant tsunami that had hit Cheever while he was gone. Anything of strength, of wisdom, of "We can deal with this" had been scoured from his soul over the past week, and he didn't know where to reach to find a way to comfort the lost boy in the bed.

"You really think I'm pretty?" Cheever asked plaintively.

"I always have." Blake smiled to take the sting out of the next words. "Didn't always like you, but I thought you were gonna grow up pretty when you were a kid. You grew up... damn. Like the sun. Like autumn or the ocean. Pretty."

"Do you like me now?" Cheever asked, capturing his hand.

Blake was too naked to fuck around. "Yeah. You're hurt, kid. But all the ways you could have acted out, you picked the one that would hurt the family the least—at least until it all blew up in your head. Marcia thinks you're a saint. That tells me something too. And... and you've been real respectful of me."

Cheever nodded. "I was raped when I was a kid."

Blake sucked in a breath, thinking he was ready to hear that, but it wasn't any easier to bear. "I.... To be honest, I sort of figured."

"Wh.... When I was away at school, me and Aubrey Cooper kissed. And it was great. But his dad was trying to get in Mama's pants. Mackey... well, he sent his letter home, and Aubrey's dad... I guess he fucking overreacted."

Blake knew his eyes opened really wide. "I did not know—"

"I don't think Mom's dated anybody since," Cheever said, his voice clogged. "And Aubrey—he started... like, groping me and touching me. And the whole class hated me because I was the poor kid anyway, and because...."

"Mackey had come out," Blake said, horrified.

"I talked to the press, you remember?"

Oh God, yeah. The guys had been so pissed. "I remember."

"And it got a little better, but Aubrey.... And then he started coming to my room. And he warned me, right? So I was... ready. Like, I used Vaseline so I didn't rip, because I was so afraid of pain. And he kept coming. And I told myself I was just... just getting a break. 'Cause people were talking to me again, as long as I didn't tell about what he did to me in my room, and...."

"Oh God... baby. I'm so sorr—"

"Don't you see?" Cheever managed between sobs. "I'm a *whore*!"

"*The hell you are!*" Blake couldn't breathe. Oh God, he knew it was bad. He *knew* it was bad. But this was the kind of bad he wasn't ready for. "I've been a whore, boy. I lubed myself up and bent over and dropped to my knees and cleaned it up, and I took that dime bag and that rent money and I said, 'Thank you, sir, you can come back any time.' I *know* what being a whore is, and what you were doing was just trying to survive."

"But I let him... I let him... I—"

"You didn't feel like you had a choice," Blake told him. "You think I don't know that? Where if you scream or cry or complain, your life is just gonna get a fuck-ton worse? So you just pull back in your own head and you walk away from the shit that hurts. *I've been there*, Cheever. But I got away from being used to offering my shit up for cash. You didn't do that. You walked away. You walked away and tried to fix yourself. You know what? There wasn't anything wrong with you. You needed to be heard, that's all. You didn't 'let' him—he forced you. Coercion is coercion, man. It's not your fault."

"It's not yours, either," Cheever whispered.

"I was strung out—"

"And hungry. And sad." Cheever closed his eyes tight and carried Blake's knuckles to his lips. "You haven't told me any of it. You just let pieces drop when you think it will help. But I know you were hurt, Blake. As much as I was. And you've been peeling off your armor so I can see that I'm going to be fine. But you're walking around without your armor, just for me, and I've got to get better or you're not going to make it."

Blake's hands were shaking too bad to even take them from Cheever's grasp and use them to wipe his eyes. "I can make it, baby boy." He was the grown-up here. He was the grown-up, and he was falling apart. "As long as you can make it, I'll be just fine."

"I'm going to make it," Cheever promised him. And Blake had needed to hear that so bad, he almost slid out of the chair. "I'm going to make it. I'm not that little kid anymore, trapped in that room. You gotta know that. You gotta know that so you can stop worrying so hard about me. So you can be okay too."

"You're gonna be fine." Blake couldn't breathe. "You're okay. You're gonna be okay." Oh God. He couldn't breathe. This boy—this beautiful boy, who kissed him out of the blue and smiled and made sure he was okay when neither of them were okay, when everything hurt and Blake felt like an open nerve dancing with sandpaper—he was going to be all right.

"Breathe, baby boy," Cheever whispered. "C'mon, breathe—"

The first sob felt like it was going to rip him apart. The second sob shook him from his groin to his throat with an extra punch to the stomach.

The third one tore through his throat like a grappling hook, and Blake was done. He rested his head next to Cheever's and let go, naked, squalling, as hurt and needy in this moment as he'd ever been in rehab.

Cheever was stroking his hair back from his forehead, whispering comfort words in his ear, and Blake drank them in and believed them, like a child believed promises of warmth, of safety, of love, because he had no choice. And his heart—so seasoned to the matter of betrayal, of disappointment, of being alone—was soft and young now, and he had no way else to be.

The sobs subsided, leaving him clean and empty.

Cheever said, "You still got the picture. The one I drew."

Blake fumbled with the little paper pellet and started to very carefully disengage it from the folds. "Oh my God," he muttered when he saw the monster with surprisingly wide and limpid eyes in the middle of raping a boy with curly hair. "That's... that's—"

Cheever took it from his hands and folded it gently, the handcuff rattling on the bedrail. "It's awful," he said, his voice tender. "Don't worry, Blake. It's not yours to worry about. That's mine."

Blake wanted to argue—but it *was* Cheever's. Blake could help him get out of the room, but Cheever had been there. That monster breathing over his shoulder had been Cheever's reality. It wasn't Blake's to keep, as much as he might want to shield Cheever from the pain.

"Can't say it's boring," he managed to say, his voice rough and broken and not hardly his own.

"Nope. Here—put it next to my bed, would you? I have the feeling me and the doc are gonna hash out that little piece of paper until it falls apart in sympathy."

Blake did that for him and then turned back, unsure of what to do or even where they were now.

"Come here," Cheever commanded softly. "Take off your shoes and climb in bed with me. I need to be held."

Blake wondered if Doc Cambridge would approve, but he didn't have anything in him to do more than wonder. He kicked off his boots, shed his denim jacket on the chair, and scrambled up awkwardly behind Cheever, pulling that long, slender body along the front of his own. He didn't wrap his arm over Cheever's shoulder at first—that picture had been so damning.

"Full hug," Cheever whispered. "Don't worry. Not feeling trapped. Just alone."

Blake moved his bottom arm so it was under Cheever's head and the top arm so his hand spanned Cheever's stomach. Cheever covered his hand and laced their fingers together, and Blake closed his eyes, letting Cheever's closeness seep into his body.

This implies that we're lovers. Or that we will be when this is done.

"Who was your first?" Cheever asked softly. "That you wanted?"

This was actually such a lovely memory, it gave comfort when he shared. "A girl named Cindy Crosby. She had a reputation for being easy, but really, she was just lonely. Afraid of being rejected. Like me."

"What was she like?"

Blake thought about it, remembering that first furtive, quiet grope, the way she'd guided his hands and touched his face. Cheever complained about being ugly in high school—Blake still had scars from where acne had pitted his cheeks. He'd gotten his teeth fixed in the last eight years, but there'd been no braces then to fix his crooked overbite, and shitty nutrition gave you shitty bone structure.

But he remembered that she'd closed her eyes and enjoyed his touch, smiling and even laughing when he'd said something self-deprecating like 'damn, that was a quick ride.' And then she had slowed the whole thing down and made it sweet.

"She was kind," he said now. He'd learned then that "easy" often meant kind and gentle, when the rest of the world could be a real shithole. "We were together right up until I ran away."

"Tell me why."

Blake groaned, burying his face against the back of Cheever's neck. "Boy—"

"Say my name."

"I know who you—"

"You call me baby boy to be the grown-up so you've got control. I don't need you in control. I just need you. Say my name again."

"Bossy little shit."

Cheever laughed. "That's not on my driver's license."

"Cheever Justin Sanders."

"Mm." Cheever closed his eyes. "I used to hate my first name. Named after a daddy not good enough to stay. But I figured later that she was trying to give us the best parts of our fathers. Sure, the relationship didn't last, but at one point, she saw something good about this person. That's who she wanted us to see when we looked in the mirror."

"Your mother's a good woman," Blake said, meaning it. It wasn't fair, her being alone. She deserved someone.

"She's the best. But you skipped out on the question."

Blake's temples were throbbing, and he gave a little whimper. "My mom's boyfriend," he muttered. "Lots of groping. Then there was one shitty night where he did all the drugs, and I needed some painkillers for my ass in the morning. I took off before he woke up. Didn't finish high school, just grabbed my guitar and my iPod—" He laughed. "'Cause it was that long ago. I didn't even have a fucking phone. Just music, a backpack full of clothes, and some street savvy. I eventually found some clubs, was backup for a couple of outfits, worked a day job flipping burgers. Then I saw the ad for tryouts for Outbreak Monkey." That memory was still fresh. He'd had to run from his day job to the studio because he couldn't even find a bus. By the time it was his turn to go, he'd been sweaty, tired, pissed off, and so fucking desperate.

And they'd liked him.

Suddenly he was surrounded by people who liked him, wanted him in their group.

Everybody but the guy he admired most.

"You know the rest," he finished, and Cheever grunted.

"No. No, I don't. But I don't want to hurt you any more right now, so I won't ask."

Oh, thank God. "Good."

"Tell me about your first guy."

"Why?" He scrambled to find the moment in his head.

"I… I've been sort of… sexless, the last few years. I know you all think I was hiding that I was gay, but that wasn't it."

"What was it, then?" Blake had been honestly curious. "Mackey was afraid his brothers wouldn't love him anymore, or his mother—"

"But they did." Cheever shrugged, his body snugging against Blake's some more. "It was never a question of that. It was that… that I felt dirty. Contaminated by… what happened at school with Aubrey. I didn't want to share myself because I didn't want anyone to see that filth—"

"No…," Blake whimpered, and Cheever petted his hand.

"Shh. I need to hear good memories about sex. I don't have any. Please, Blake? Let me hear yours?"

Okay. This really was a good one. "He was pretty," Blake said, remembering. "We were on tour, and we had some time off. We were all in a little club, listening to local talent—we like to do that, you know?" He and

Kell had made some good discoveries, kids like they had been that they'd been able to give a hand up. Made them proud when they did that.

"I didn't," Cheever murmured. "That's good. And important. Good to know."

"Whatever. So this guy played this old Damien Jurado song—and he was sort of short and slender, and he had that giant gruff workingman's voice and these big brown eyes. He came to sit with us when the set was over, and… and sat right next to me. Touched my shoulder. Touched my thigh. And I… I let him. It felt good. The attention felt good. I… I was beyond that whole 'I'm not gay' bullshit by then, but hadn't really admitted I was bi. And then the party was breaking up, and he just grabbed my hand. So I told them all I'd meet them there in the morning. And…."

"And?" Cheever sounded hungry for the details, but Blake wasn't going to tell him what went where.

"Was a lot like Cindy, truth be told. Seamus laughed and was tender. Kind. I realized that for me, it was the way someone made me feel, not the parts."

"Mm." Cheever took their laced hands and kissed his knuckles. "I want that," he said after a moment. "I want someone who will make me feel kindness. Laugh when I'm dumb. Touch me gentle."

Blake thought about his last lover, the boy Trav remembered. He'd been superhot—Blake thought he might have been a porn model—and aggressive as hell.

"Rough can be sweet too," he said with dignity, and Cheever's laugh was a reward.

"I'm not an addict," Cheever said softly.

"I know."

"I don't want cocaine or any other drug. That's not why I'm here."

"I know."

"I'm depressed and in pain. But I'm making that better."

A bubble of hysteria squeaked past Blake's throat. "I'm so glad."

"Do you see where this is going, Blake?"

Blake did. But he was older, and a friend of the family, and this bright and shining young man—

"I'm twenty-two."

"*Stop reading my mind!*" He hid his face against Cheever's back in embarrassment.

"Do you see where this is going?" he repeated.

"No." The lie tasted peevish, like juice and Cheerios.

"Tell the truth, Blake Manning. Do you see where this is going?"

"Yes." Blake tried to unlace their fingers, but Cheever captured his hand firmly. "I should—"

"Do you like holding me?"

Oh God, yes. He felt so right. "That's not—"

"That's the only point. Stay. Don't lie to me about it being wrong. Don't lie to yourself. Not now. We've been nothing but honest, Blake. Don't stop now."

Blake stopped struggling. "I don't have much fight in me today," he confessed, and pulled Cheever tighter. "I just…. You feel so good."

"You too. Just stay. Just… stay."

"Your family," Blake breathed, thinking about the night he'd just spent with Heather, looking at those pictures, having his heart ripped out. "There's not much I wouldn't do for any of you."

"I want me to mean the most," Cheever told him. "But we'll get there."

Yeah. Fine. Whatever.

"Sleep, baby," Cheever told him. "Tomorrow we can start again. I needed a picture, you see? What pretty looked like. What it should feel like when someone touches you. I needed to know you had a picture."

"What if I didn't?"

"We would have looked together." Cheever let out a sigh. "We'll still look. For one that looks like us. But right now, you know what it looks like when it's sweet. We'll work toward that."

Blake was falling asleep, hard. "You Sanders boys," he mumbled. "Looking for art, for poetry, for story, for music. Like meteors, carving light through the sky. How'm I supposed to be in that picture?"

"We need the sweetness," Cheever said. "You're real good at that. Now sleep."

Bossy little shit.

Blake's heart, tender and sore, curled in on itself and pulled him under.

HE WOKE up alone, about two hours later. Cheever's spot was still warm, and panic shot him upright. He heard the sound of water in the bathroom and, surprisingly enough, Cheever's pleasant baritone, humming.

One of Blake's songs.

Weird.

"How you feeling?" Marcia asked from her side of the room. She was sitting cross-legged on her bed, doing something on a tablet.

"Like I needed the nap." He yawned. "How about you?"

She looked up and smiled slightly. "Like I miss art, but not as much as I should."

Blake frowned. "You should miss art?"

"I OD'd the month before I got my degree as an animator," she said, matter-of-fact, like you got in rehab. "And even Cheever picked up a pencil when he was feeling good enough. And I don't even think he *likes* art that much."

Blake thought about it. "Mackey and me went to music," he said. At first it had been Mackey mostly, but the more he drove Blake about practicing, becoming the best musician he could be, the more Blake remembered how a song, or lyric, or just a bar of melody, had saved him, pulled him out of that hotel room and back to trying one more time. It had become his joy again too.

"You're good at it," Marcia agreed. "But me, you know where I went?"

"Not art?"

"Your promise of children in the house." She looked at him, her face pinched and a little desperate. "That promise still stands, doesn't it?"

Blake nodded. "I talked to Shelia and Briony about it." He remembered the relief in Shelia's voice. "Shelia was like, 'Oh my God! You found us a nanny!' and I was like, 'I found you help, not an employee, just a friend—'"

Marcia's face lit up. "I can take classes," she said in wonder. "I can take classes and *be* a nanny."

Blake held out a hand. "How about just spend a week with them and make sure it doesn't drive you batshit!"

Marcia's low laugh reassured him. "How about CPR and early childhood education," she said. "I can start some of those classes from here." Her face fell. "Cheever said he'd stay as long as I was here, but he shouldn't have to."

Blake thought about it. "Maybe he wants to, darlin'. You know, Cheever needs to rethink how he's been living too."

"Cheever wants you—"

"I'm on tour six to nine months out of the year," he said, hating himself for that. "Cheever might not want to spend all that time on the road."

"Why don't you ask Cheever," Cheever said, coming out of the bathroom toweling his hair. It hung in ringlets around his eyes, and for a moment, Blake was distracted by the pale skin revealed under a fluffy white bathrobe, the few strands of cinnamon hair down his lightly defined chest, the freckles that appeared to be sprinkled on his shoulders.

"I… uh…. You showered." He wanted to slide his hand underneath that robe and see if the freckles really did cover his shoulders.

"I did. The doc let me out of the handcuff."

"I'll, uh, go outside while you change."

Cheever and Marcia exchanged glances, and Cheever's gaze hooded.

"I'll go," Marcia said mildly.

"No!" Blake said, a little panicked, but he couldn't seem to stop staring at Cheever's chest. "I need to… uh…. I can't…." His mouth was so dry, his tongue stuck to the roof.

"Go ahead and go outside," Cheever purred. "I'll get dressed, and we can go for a walk."

"That's a great idea." Marcia looked from Cheever's smug expression back to Blake, who was feeling panicked and probably looking that way, as well. "I like that idea. Go wait outside."

Oh Lord. "You two are so not as cute as you think you are," he muttered, but it allowed him to close his eyes so he didn't see Cheever's *almost* naked body and slide outside the door.

He was leaning against the frame when Doc Cambridge sauntered down the hall. "Hey, you're up."

"Yeah. I, uh… didn't mean to sleep—"

"Cheever said the family's running you pretty ragged. You looked like you needed it." The hallway had big plate windows that overlooked the grounds, and Blake glanced outside at the lowering afternoon sun.

"Yeah, but it's getting pretty late. I… I think he's feeling better. He really doesn't need me to spend the night."

Cambridge's lips twisted, and he rolled his eyes. "He got you on the run?"

"I used to hope—*pray*—that Kell would turn his sights on me. Did you know that?"

Cambridge cocked his head. "You never said that in so many words, but I got that impression."

"Now… God. Those boys don't fuck around when they get an idea in their heads, do they?"

"No, they do not," Cambridge said mildly. "Does that scare you?"

"Yes." Blake leaned back against the doorframe and closed his eyes against the pretty golden shadows. "You gotta tell me why this won't work. I'm good at doing what you ask. You give me a reason this is bad for him, a reason he could be hurt, I can hook on to that. Like quitting coke and pills, right?"

"Cheever's not an addict, Blake. He's troubled, yes, but people with depression, in therapy, they have relationships, get married, start families. He's ready to do the work. You need to be ready to see him as something other than helpless while he's doing it."

Blake glared at him. "That's shitty advice. No offense, but you may be the worst shrink in Beverly fucking Hills. Can't you see I'm not good enough for him?"

Cambridge let out a slow breath. "No, son. That's what you see. And for the record? It's not true. Now you can run away from this relationship and tell yourself you're protecting him, protecting your family, doing all sorts of noble bullshit, but it'll be just that."

"Bullshit?" Blake's voice cracked.

"Grade A. Now, do you not see him that way?"

"As a lover?" His voice went up two octaves.

"Asked and answered." Cambridge rolled his eyes. "Then you can run away, tail tucked firmly between your legs, and avoid him at all the family meetings—"

"That's an option?"

"Or you can lie to him and say you don't see him that way—"

"That has not worked so far."

"Or you can—"

Cheever popped his head out of the room, his hair hastily slicked back, a button-down shirt and cargo shorts firmly in place. He was wearing tennis shoes, not slippers, and Blake sort of gaped at him. "You ready to go for a walk before dinner? That's okay, right, Doc? You said so, when Blake was still sleeping."

Cambridge looked Blake in the eyes. "Or you can take this young man's hand and see where he leads you," he finished mildly, like it was not the most terrifying choice on the list.

"You're a terrible person," Blake said, deeply sincere about that.

"Let's just say I have my ways to get petty revenge. Now go." Cambridge made shooing motions. "Scoot. Watching you two get out of this building will actually be the happiest part of my day."

"Come on," Cheever said, grabbing Blake's hand and tugging. "We have about a half an hour before they stop serving dinner."

Blake followed him, for no good reason other than he smelled good, like fresh bodywash and aftershave, and he was so damned pretty when he smiled. Together they slid out a side door and onto grounds that looked like a movie shot of an English country garden—except it was in California, so there was the general scent of Joshua pine and dust.

"There's walkways around the back," Cheever said, pulling Blake until he fell in step. "And some trees and places to sit. You can see the sunset—or so I'm told."

"You can," Blake said, remembering sitting with Mackey one evening and playing until the sun set and they both missed dinner. It wasn't that his memories of rehab were fond, exactly, but he did treasure those moments when he and Mackey had become brothers.

"I forget, sometimes." Cheever sighed. "I feel like sort of a special snowflake, since I'm not like most of the people here. Addiction is a terrible thing. It's like they wake up every morning and know that their whole day is uphill. Every fucking day. And I know…. Well, I guess I just have a different promise of better, you know?"

"Yeah?"

"Yeah. I woke up this morning and wanted to paint. It was all I could think about, all day. And I was so excited. And then I drew that picture and ran into the doc's office, and it all poured out—and it was awful, like having my chest dragged on broken glass. Like, anguish— that's what it felt like. And you came, and talked to me, and it was painful, but it was… better. Like, I'd been all cleaned out by the anguish, and the talk with you reminded me that sometimes pain was good for you. And now, now I'm happy. And the sadness is there, waiting for me, and I know I'll have to battle with it, maybe for a long time. Maybe forever. But I also know I'll have days when I wake up and the world is bright and shiny like it is…."

They rounded the corner to the back, where the grounds dropped off, and they were at the crest of a gentle green hill. The sun cut through the clouds, blinding them both for a moment and then settling, casting a molten sheen on everything before them.

"Now," Cheever said, squinting against the light but smiling too. The sunset brought him joy.

Blake stared at him, his heart thudding in his throat, and thought about those times when he would have given his soul for a bump of coke, for a Percocet, for a body in the dark or a fifth of anything, including radiator fluid.

This moment here, seeing Cheever's eyes closed, his face lifted toward the sun, was worth not doing it, every time.

"Pretty," he said, his voice thin. Cheever opened his eyes and looked at him slyly.

"You think I'm pretty," he said with a winsome smile.

"I told you that." Blake tugged at their hands, but Cheever didn't let go.

"I think you're pretty too," he said, dead seriously, and this time Blake managed to yank his hand free.

"What antidepressants are you on? Xanax? Zoloft? 'Cause when you break my heart and I hit the pill bottle again, I want to know what you're taking."

"That was mean," Cheever told him, eyebrows knitted. "What did I say?"

Blake shook his head. "Just... you can't look at me like I'm a fantasy and offer me something real."

Cheever's mouth parted, and his fingertips came up to graze Blake's cheeks. Blake knew what he looked like, knew the scars of youth on his face, and he tried to jerk away.

Cheever grasped his chin. "I see who you are, Blake Manning. I see the scars. I even knew you before you got your teeth fixed and you were still growing the chia-beard. I could paint a completely accurate picture of you, right down to that spot on your chin you miss shaving, because it's indented. And people would still look at it and think you're beautiful, because that's what art does. You wouldn't see the scars or the shadows or the calluses on your fingers. You'd see what...." He stopped, his eyes wide. "Goddammit," he muttered, as if to somebody else, and then he focused completely on Blake. "You'd see what I feel," he said. And then, like he'd made a realization that sort of pissed him off, he added, "That's how art works."

Blake managed to quirk an eyebrow at him, because admitting Cheever's words moved him was just too hard today. "You don't sound too happy about that," he said.

"I just realized why Professor Tierce gave me a *C*," he said, irritated. "Because anything I felt strongly about, I tried to hide."

Blake shuddered. "You didn't hide those fuckin' landscapes, Cheever. I'm sayin'—"

"Yeah, but you're the first person to look at them and say, 'Oh, hey, that looks like the boy's planning to bury his own body there.'"

Ugh. "They were not pleasing." He managed to turn away from Cheever and watch the crown of the sun shooting spears over the horizon. Cheever grabbed his hand again, and Blake allowed him to lace their fingers together.

"You are," Cheever whispered. "I'm going to paint such a picture of you—"

"No...." Blake heard the pleading in his voice. He and the boys stayed away from pictures on their album covers, stayed away from having their face in the trades. Mackey was the pretty one, but he didn't really give a shit unless he was planning his wardrobe for the band. But as a whole, they all knew what they looked like and knew where they were from. A bunch of anonymous redneck white boys. They weren't much to look at. They were just there for the music, thanks.

"Just for me," Cheever soothed. "So you can see what I see. See why it's so important to me. See why... why I'd crawl out of hell for you."

Like he just had. Blake shrugged, trying to shove all his internal organs back to where they belonged. "I can't tell you what to paint," he said mildly, and Cheever's frustrated sigh was about what he'd expected.

The sun disappeared completely, and Cheever moved between Blake and the sunset, smiling slightly. "Like what you see? Or are you blind now from looking at the sun?"

What he saw was Cheever, playful, luminous, relieved of the terrible burden that had removed him emotionally from everyone he knew.

"Still blind," Blake said breathily.

Cheever leaned forward and kissed him, taking charge this time, teasing the seam of Blake's lips with his tongue.

Blake opened his mouth, undone and unguarded, and let him in.

Ah... it felt so right. Cheever kissed softly, sweetly, every brush of his tongue an exploration, every reaction from Blake a glorious reward.

Oh man—it had been so long since anybody had treated Blake special.

Blake took it, accepted every foray into his mouth, accepted Cheever's hands on his hips, accepted their bodies, pressing close together along the front. He wrapped his arms around Cheever's shoulders and stroked his back, cupped the back of his neck under his hair, held him close—and kissed him some more.

Cheever gave a happy, breathless little moan and ground up against Blake, pulling him forcibly back to the present, where they were in public and Cheever was very young and very new.

He pulled back, panting, and rested his forehead against Cheever's. "You're going to miss—" Deep breath. "—your dinner."

Cheever nodded, but he didn't buy it. "This isn't over."

No.

"We can't finish it here," Blake said simply. "Wait until your time is up, until the doc gives you the all clear. Then you can come to the house." He winced. "We'll see each other there."

"What? What was that look?"

Well, hell. "You and Marcia will have your own rooms," Blake said, worrying his lip. "But Mackey needs all sorts of equipment. He's in a bad way, and even after the casts come off, he's gonna need PT shit, and it's gonna be all over the house. The studio house is only in use on the ground floor. I had the movers take my bedroom stuff over there—"

"Then have them put mine there too!" Cheever burst out, taking a step back.

"No, sir, you are there to reconnect with your family."

Cheever glowered. "That was pretty fuckin' tricky, Blake. You planning on being home a lot this summer?"

"Actually yes." Dammit. "Me and the guys were going to replace a lot of the studio equipment and the instruments. Mackey usually runs around trying to do everything his damned self, but I have the feeling he's going to be sitting and we're going to be doing all the work. So don't worry. I'm not planning to be on the other side of the state. Just next door."

Cheever nodded, wrinkling his pert little nose. Augh, yes, Blake had noticed. Mackey's nose was small and pointed, Kell's was large and square, and Jefferson (and Stevie's) was perfectly normal, if a little aquiline.

Cheever's was a perfect button.

Fucking adorable, that's what it was. Blake wanted to smack him.

"You'd be on the other side of the state if you could be," Cheever muttered.

"Well… yes! Sort of!" The kid looked at him with honest hurt, and he relented. "Just because you could hurt me, Cheever. And you could hurt yourself. But… but I get to be your first lover… I mean, you know. That is, if we make it till then without killing each other. That's okay. That'll be—"

"If you say nice, I'm out of here."

Blake closed his eyes and squeezed the bridge of his nose. He didn't know why people did that. It never fuckin' helped.

"I… I might not survive it," he said with dignity. "And hopefully, it won't be awful for you, because you've had enough of that. Great. But… but you are in a place to move on. I'm your… your stepladder lover, until you find the great guy you really care about."

"And you?" Cheever had moved forward again, and was searching Blake's face avidly. Blake couldn't stand that sort of scrutiny. He took a step back and then turned around, heading for the mess hall because Cheever really could stand to eat more.

"You didn't answer me," Cheever said, skipping to keep up.

"I don't do casual anymore," Blake said. That weird and wonderful week that he and Trav had talked about, when Blake couldn't seem to lose in the hookup department, that had seemed like a sign. And he was tired of hookups on the road—he really was. He was tired of meeting someone and thinking "relationship" when they were thinking "fling." He wanted permanent. He'd been thinking that way before the week of two hot hookups, and he hadn't had a lover since, because he hadn't been willing to settle. Not when he saw what his brothers were doing. Not when he wanted what they had too.

"I do… I do serious," he proclaimed, the first time he'd said it out loud. "So, you and me make it to bed, and I'm doing serious, and you're doing the healing kama sutra, and I'm…." Where he always was— second first guitar. Last guy anybody saw. Which had always seemed good enough, better than Blake Manning deserved, actually. But looking at Cheever in the purple light of a summer night, it seemed like the final cut that would let Blake bleed out of the heart.

"You're what?" Cheever challenged.

"I'm nobody important," Blake told him. "Which is who I am, anyway. Go ahead and do what you have to, Cheever. I obviously don't have the spine to stop you."

Cheever let go of his hand then and watched him walk away.

HE CAUGHT up with Blake in the dining room as Blake was trying to wheedle two trays of food from the attendant, who had obviously been doing the last of the cleanup.

"Aw, come on, darlin', we're sorry we were late." Blake tried his best smile. "We were just walking outside to see the sunset. I mean, it sure is a beaut, right?"

The woman serving—fiftyish, dyed chestnut hair, a kind, if worn, face—sighed. "You are being incredibly charming. I'll see what we can do. Any food allergies?"

Blake shook his head and managed to gesture to Cheever without actually looking at him. "Cheever?"

"No. Anything you can manage would be welcome."

"Fine, boys." She reached under her counter and handed them both plastic tumblers. "Go get some soda. I'll be back."

Blake took the tumblers. "Preference?"

"Root beer," Cheever said promptly, and Blake nodded, still not looking at him. He couldn't stand to see hurt, if that's what he'd put there, or sadness, or the "You're right, we shouldn't do this" that he knew was coming.

Blake got them both drinks, and they settled at a table. Cheever picked one by the window, still overlooking the grounds.

"You ever going to look at me again?" Cheever asked pleasantly.

Blake managed to raise his gaze to Cheever's chin before he looked down again, and Cheever swore.

And then he moved so they were no longer across from each other, but kitty corner, close enough for Cheever to grab his hand.

"God, you're stubborn," he said, sounding like it was a big discovery or something. "I mean, you seem so mild mannered. 'Yes, Cheever, yes, Trav, yes, Doc Cambridge. I'll do whatever you want. I'm just here to help.' But one relationship gets deeper than you planned and boy, you don't give us any help at all, do you."

Blake glared at him. "I am doing what you want," he said, but the words grated like tinfoil on his teeth.

"No, you're not. Because I want you to hope!"

Blake took a big gulp of his root beer and then belched because that's what you did when you ingested too much gas in one swallow. Cheever held his fingers in front of his lips and tried not to giggle. God, he was unsettled.

"Cheever—I'm thirty-two this year, you know that right?"

"Blake, can't you even try? I mean...." He waited—Blake had to give him that. Waited until Blake looked up and saw that his eyes were kind, and he was biting his lip provocatively, and he didn't *look* like somebody who would dick with Blake's heart like that.

"Mean what?" Blake asked, fighting his own smile.

"It was a pretty good kiss, wasn't it? You're the only person I've ever kissed that I wanted—but that was a pretty good kiss."

"You got a lot to learn kid," Blake said, and then, before Cheever could deflate, he added, "and that was a *great* kiss."

Cheever's eyes crinkled in the corners again. "So why the gloom and doom? C'mon, Blake, let's at least plan to date."

Dating. Okay. Fine. Blake could date. "Okay. Good. I can take you to dinner, we can go to clubs and museums—that sounds fun." It's what he did with the guys anyway, and what he'd done with the few relationships he'd had since he'd gotten out of rehab. Dating was nonthreatening. It was neutral. It was neither good nor bad; it was just an experiment.

"We can kiss some more," Cheever said, unrelenting. "We can make love."

Blake sighed. "If that's where it goes."

"You could sound more excited about that," Cheever said mildly. "I mean, it's a pretty big deal to *me*."

"It should be a big deal to anybody," Blake said. "Even if it's just for a night. It's when you don't remember the person's name, or what they were doing there with you, that you know you were doing it wrong."

"I didn't phrase that right," Cheever said, and his shoulders drooped just a little. Blake suddenly remembered Cheever'd had a truly, truly awful day, and Blake wasn't making it any easier for him.

"Don't worry about it," he told Cheever, being kind, he thought. "Look, we've got time to do it right, you know? You've got a few weeks here—" He frowned. "You do, right? You were going to stay with Marcia?"

Cheever grimaced. "I'll be honest. I'd love to just come visit the doc once a week, starting next week. He said that was an option. But...." He looked behind him, as if his waifish, lonely friend would suddenly appear in time to hear him talk about her. "But yeah. I don't want to leave her here by herself. She was so alone in the last place. We texted every day, and… and I don't think she would have made it if things hadn't.…" He blew out a breath. "I didn't think it was true, when people said something was a mixed blessing. On the one hand, it seems like it's taking a helluva time to recover from practically blowing a gasket. But on the other.…"

"You realized you have a true friend and you want to do right by her," Blake filled in.

"Yeah. So, yeah. If you guys don't mind footing the bill—"

"We don't." Blake winked. "In case you missed it, we're making rock star money. We're good."

"Ha-ha." Cheever looked around at the vaulted ceiling, the nice carpet, the heavy-duty furniture, the flowers on the table. "You know, we started having money when I was a kid, and it didn't really occur to me how much easier it could make life. All I could think of was my brothers went away. But… but if I'd done what I did back in Tyson/Hepzibah—"

Blake shuddered. "Please don't," he said, his voice hard. "I just.… Please don't."

"Yeah. I know." Cheever caught his gaze then, made sure it held. "You too. If you hadn't made the money, and then stopped doing the drugs—"

Blake's stomach went cold, and he thought that maybe eating was going to be a work of optimism. "I'd be dead in a shitty trailer in Lancaster," he said. He knew it. "It's like that sunset, maybe. I'm grateful, grateful for every day I've been given."

Cheever kept eye contact. "Me too. Can you believe that I'm grateful for the days I've been given with you? All that time, you were sort of this orbital part of my life, and I never saw you. But now I do. And you're really beautiful. And I really want to keep you right here, front and center. Can we have that kind of faith, Blake? Please?"

"Yeah. Sure."

That head tilt—the one that called bullshit, pure and simple, was going to be his undoing.

"Yeah," he said again, in good faith. "Yeah, Cheever. Let's call it a thing. Let's treat it like it's real. You get out of here, we're dating."

Cheever nodded. "When'll we tell my family?"

Blake had to laugh at that. "You know, Trav and Mackey just moved in together.…" But then he saw the hope on Cheever's face and shut that down, right quick. "We're going to dinner," he insisted. "We're going to do stuff. Maybe we're better off as brothers—"

"I don't want to kiss my brothers like I want to kiss you!"

"But if we don't work out, we still gotta be brothers, do you understand?"

Cheever rolled his eyes in what was probably the youngest expression Blake had seen on him that day. "That sounds gross."

"Well, take it like it's meant, not like it sounds," he muttered, feeling grumpy. At that moment, their friend the dining room attendant came in with chicken fried steak and green beans.

Blake stared at the food, surprised and touched. "Darlin', this is some seriously good karma here. I cannot thank you enough."

She winked girlishly. "My kids and I just love Outbreak Monkey," she gushed. "Just wait until I tell them I saw you today—they'll be so excited!"

"Tell them he was here to see his boyfriend," Cheever said, a gleam in his eye, and the woman didn't bat an eyelash.

"Well, my fifteen-year-old will be a little crushed. He's always had sort of a thing for you, Mr. Manning, but it's good to see you're dating Mackey's little brother. He'll think that's the most romantic thing ever."

She giggled—honest to God giggled—and then gave a little wave and disappeared, probably to finish cleaning up.

Blake took a bite of his steak to fortify him for whatever havoc that "Mackey's little brother" bombshell was going to wreak and then looked at Cheever—who was eating his own meal and not looking much put out.

"What?" Cheever said after he swallowed.

"Nothing."

"I've lived in Mackey's shadow my whole life," Cheever said. "First time ever it's something good. Don't crap on my parade. I've got a boyfriend and dinner. Like you said, it's the little things in life. They just keep looking better and better."

Blake shrugged. Okay. Fine. That's what they were doing.

He could think of worse ways to break his heart.

Get Off My Cloud

"OH GEE," Marcia said, her voice dry as the dust motes in the sunlight. "Let me guess. It's... oh wait... *Blake*."

Cheever looked up from his sketch and rolled his eyes. "No, smartass.... Look again."

"Oh." Marcia's arid voice warmed a little. "That's pretty. Thank you, Cheever. It's nice that you see me that way."

"Not every picture I've done has been of Blake," Cheever said, but he sounded defensive and he knew it. In the two weeks since their first "date" watching the sunset and eating chicken fried steak, he'd started a campaign to draw Blake as Cheever saw him—not as Blake obviously saw himself.

The results had been some of the shittiest art Cheever had ever made. He'd actually ripped up most of the sketches because he thought if Blake ever saw them, that would be it. It would be over. No more Blake coming by in the evening and going for walks—and kisses—and no more texts during the day.

No more promise of going home next week, no more laconic banter. Blake would take one look at those sketches and think Cheever was like... like everybody else. Every person who had ever made him feel second. Every person who had made him feel less. Blake Manning's life had made him feel like he was backup and nothing more, and it was Cheever's job to make him realize he was *Cheever's* star attraction. Those pictures weren't going to do it.

"No, honey, not *every* picture has been Blake, but it has been sort of a thing."

Cheever looked at the sketch of Marcia, done as she listened to music in the room, and smiled a little. "Apparently, I'm better off drawing you," he said, ripping it off the pad and handing it to her. "Here."

"Thank you," she said primly. Then, ever perceptive, she added, "You need to actually finish a drawing of him, first. You haven't let me see any of them before you rip them up."

"They're crappy," he grumbled.

She grimaced. "Maybe they're really good, Cheever. Even the best picture, drawn with the best heart, isn't going to see what you see. He's not a movie star. Objectively, he's sort of plain—"

"He is not!"

"I'm an animator!" she protested. "Or at least, I was gonna be. But I know those features—they're not beautiful. But that doesn't mean we wouldn't rather look at him or listen to him talk more than almost anybody else in the world. Maybe the problem is, you have to see him warts and all. Maybe he'll be even more beautiful if you draw him as he actually is."

Cheever tilted back his head, bumping it gently against the wall. "Why am I so shitty at this?" Well, besides the fact that he was starting to see Professor Tierce's point, really.

She regarded him levelly. "Because you've kept your heart in a glass jar since middle school. It has some growing up to do."

He opened his mouth to tell her that he couldn't afford for his heart to keep growing up—Blake had to see him as an adult *now*—when they both heard a clatter down the hallway and Doc Cambridge's exasperated voice raised in admonition.

"Look, I know you boys mean well, but we have regular visitor hours and—oh hell. Whatever. I'm retiring next year anyway."

The door to Cheever's room crashed open, and Cheever gaped.

"Hello Outbreak Monkey."

"You look okay," Kell said, the scowl perfectly at home on his blunt features. "Blake's been going on about how you need food and color. I thought you were dying."

"Hug him, idiot." Stevie Harris was not technically their brother— but he and Jefferson had been friends since kindergarten, and Cheever had never not known him as one. He and Jefferson had sandy hair and the same anonymous white-boy features and could pretty much pass as twins in any company.

"I'm hugging him," Jefferson said. Except Jefferson was the family truth teller, the one quietly unafraid of emotion, and Cheever found himself in his big brother's embrace and happy about it.

"Good to see you," he said, comforted beyond measure by his brother's warmth. Suddenly his eyes burned. "Good to see all of you," he said, in wonder. "God, guys, I missed you."

And then it was Stevie's turn and then Kell's, and Cheever was crying because this was what he'd missed when his heart had been in the glass jar, and God, it was more than he'd ever imagined.

The hugging ended, and Cheever introduced Marcia, and then asked the obvious question.

"How's Mackey?"

The looks his brothers traded could be described, at best, as grim exasperation. "In a lot of pain!" "Stubborn as fuck!" "A complete pain in the ass!" came the chorus, and then they all took a deep breath and calmed down.

"He's trying to do it without painkillers," Kell said, then looked around himself and grimaced. "And it's not that I blame him. It's just that...." His face fell. "It's hard to see him suffer." And then, with a perceptiveness Cheever wouldn't have credited him with, he added, "It was hard to know you were in pain, little brother. Why didn't you... I don't know. Say something?"

Cheever pulled back and sat on his bed, and the guys—oh God, the guys gathered around him like they used to do with Mackey. This was story time.

"I.... You guys left," he said baldly, and when they merely looked back and nodded and didn't get defensive, he realized... they loved him. That they'd missed him too.

"We're sorry," Kell said, his voice soft. "I know that doesn't make up for—"

"It wasn't your fault." God. Cheever remembered when Kell's good opinion could make or break his day. "You guys were trying to get out—trying to help *us*. It just happened sort of sudden. And Mom put me in that school because she didn't want me fighting, like you guys had to, and...." He let out a frustrated sigh. "Rich people are mean," he said sullenly, and Marcia's smothered laugh made him realize how childish that sounded. "I mean... those kids in that school, they were... they were bullies. And at first, I was friends with one of them, and then Mackey came out, and...." This should have been old—*would* have been old, he realized, if he hadn't "put his heart in a jar."

"Cheever?"

He'd been quiet for a really long time.

"He raped me," Cheever said, and then swallowed what felt like a golf ball. "For a couple of months. It was my... pass. All of his friends let me into their group because he did. I... I... anyway. It was awful. It was awful, and I decided I wasn't going to be that person anymore. But... but I turned off all the... all the good stuff in my heart."

Oh, he had to make amends for this somehow. He looked up at each of them in turn. "I was a dick," he said, grimacing. "I just... I didn't want to bother you guys with the bad, so I didn't let you see anything at all."

Kell regarded him sorrowfully. "We really missed you," he said, and Cheever nodded.

"Me too, but I didn't realize it." He rubbed his chest. "It was all just so... so cold." He took a deep breath before he could get derailed. "Anyway, something stupid happened at school, and I... I just remembered feeling helpless, the way I did before. All the parts where I was supposed to be a grown-up felt like a fraud. And that's when I did what I did."

"All the drugs and the permanent bracelet," Kell said, glaring at the last of the stitches on Cheever's wrist.

"Yeah."

His brothers nodded grimly.

"We're sorry," Kell said, talking for them all. Well, he *was* the oldest. "We're so sorry we didn't see it, didn't know it—"

"You guys were in pain too." Cheever bit his lip, remembering. "So much pain. It was like all these little worlds, all of us. And every one was hell."

"But we could have done something about your hell," Jefferson said softly. He and Stevie were clasping hands, and not for the first time—or probably the last—Cheever wondered what their relationship really was. "You need to tell us, okay?"

Stevie nodded soberly next to him, and Cheever smiled, all gentleness.

"Okay, guys. I promise." Then, not sure how far family gossip would extend, he added, "You guys know I'm gay too, right?"

Kell rolled his eyes. "That is the *one* thing you didn't have to worry about. Jesus, this family is so far beyond gay, I probably should have come out as straight."

"Your wife keeps getting pregnant," Jefferson said dryly. "It's an indicator."

"So does yours," Kell responded like this was an old argument. "As far as I can tell, that doesn't mean shit."

Stevie and Jefferson just laughed, in sync, their chests rising and falling at the same time.

"I declare myself too young for those details," Cheever said, grateful, *so* grateful, for his brothers.

Kell snorted and then looked at the twins. "Yeah—so the drugs thing. You doing that anymore?"

Cheever shook his head vehemently. "God no. I…." He remembered the terrible buzzing in his head, the racing of his heart, the fear he'd never come down from that rush. "Guys, that was a one-time deal—"

"The hurting yourself too?" Kell demanded. "Because I get that doing the big party was just to let loose, but that other thing had to have been building in you for a long time."

Cheever nodded. Kell had grown up a lot from when he used to yell at Cheever to get out of the goddamned truck. It occurred to Cheever that Kell had been young then—eighteen? Nineteen? Working a dead-end job to help his mom pay the rent. Sure—God, probably so damned sure—that he was never getting out of Tyson/Hepzibah, and he'd die there, as sure as he lived there.

"It was," he confessed. "I'll be seeing Doc Cambridge regularly and taking antidepressants for a while too." Right now, they seemed to give him peace, and he was good with that. But he was alert for when that went away and left him with anxiety or bled away all his joy. "Mostly, I just needed… need to get out of that room. It was like I got stuck there, in my head. It kept me away from my family, away from relationships, away from my friends." He looked over at Marcia, who bit her lip in sympathy. He'd been so close to losing her because he didn't want to commit to the friendship that was saving her life.

"Good." Kell let out a breath. "I mean, we don't really *believe* you're all okay, so, you know, you're moving in with us and shit. Because, dude, that was a close fuckin' call. Man, you don't even want to know the look on Trav's face when he had to tell us that shit. And Mackey—Mackey almost sprained all the things in his body again trying to get out of bed. So yeah. You're coming to live with us—and Blake said your friend is coming too, which is fine." Kell nodded at Marcia, who smiled sweetly back. "Although it sucks because he had to move next door—"

"He can move back," Stevie said. "We can take over the top floor of the studio house."

"After we get back in November," Jefferson finished.

"Yeah. Don't want to do it over the summer. Just gotta pick up and go again."

"You're leaving?" Cheever hated the anxiety in his voice. "The band's touring again?"

"We're finishing up our missed dates," Kell told him. "The earliest Mackey's on his feet is August, so we'll leave in mid-September. Finish the West Coast tour and add another year of studio work before our next one." He gave a sudden, cavernous yawn. "God... we got in last night—"

"Night before," the twins said in unison.

"Slept for sixteen hours," Jefferson told Cheever while Kell stared into space and counted on his fingers, obviously too tired to do basic math. "God. And we thought we were tired. Then we got home and saw Blake."

"Boy looks like shit," Stevie agreed.

Then both of them. "What'd you do to him?"

Cheever bit his lip and shrugged. "He's just been real helpful here," he evaded. "He visits every day, and I guess Mama's been giving him an earful—"

"And Trav had him run ragged to set up the house," Kell said, coming back from how many days he'd been out of it. "He did a great job, but like I said, it sucks that he had to move out. I mean, it's dumb, but Briony usually has the kids up super early, and we get up and work out and shit. I'll miss him over orange juice."

A sudden vision of Blake, in pajama bottoms, drinking orange juice in a white-tiled kitchen, washed behind Cheever's eyes. He was so lean, so muscled. Would he have hair on his chest? Did he wax? Cheever had never actually touched a bare chest—that seemed like the pinnacle of his adulthood, right there.

"I'm sure you'll still work out," he placated, but he was suddenly seeing some of the advantages to Blake having his own space.

"I just don't like shit changing." Kell yawned.

"Says the man who's trying to get his wife pregnant again."

"Shut up." Kell glared at Jefferson. "That's all her idea. She's sick as a dog when she's pregnant. I hate it. I mean, I love the kids, wouldn't mind a hundred, but she's sick and that sucks."

"You could adopt," Cheever said, sort of throwing it out there, because, really, who did that? But Kell's face went blank.

Stevie and Jefferson laughed softly and stood up from their story-time circle. "Go, Cheever. You just reminded the boy he makes that kind of money," Stevie said.

"Which means we don't have to hear them bitching at each other," Jefferson added. "Now come on out of this room. Let's get some soda, and you can show us the grounds—"

"And you can tell us why you get moony-eyed every time Blake's name is mentioned. Did somebody tell you he's bi?"

"*Blake* did," Cheever retorted, getting up too. "And he's been really awesome. Me and Marcia wouldn't have made it without him. I'm not even shitting around."

"Cheever—" Marcia said warningly.

Cheever shot Marcia a glare, and he noted that Jefferson and Stevie caught the look and made their own eye contact, but Kell did not.

"He's been wonderful, right?"

She knew. She'd watched the two of them together, had even walked in on them kissing once, much to Blake's embarrassment. But Blake was afraid to tell the guys, and for good reason. They *were* up in his business, and if whatever this was with Cheever didn't work out, they *would* be upset, probably at both of them.

"He's been great," Marcia said, glaring at Cheever with narrowed eyes. "I don't imagine we would have gotten this far without him."

"Well, we're here now," Kell told them, stomping ahead, because that's what he did. "He's not your only family here now. You can give him a rest."

"He'll still come," Stevie said, under the ungodly racket Kell made as he barreled down the hall. "We'll make sure of it."

"Thanks," Cheever said. The guys didn't ask anything else as they sat down for sodas and ice cream, and Cheever was grateful. They left after an hour, bringing Cheever and Marcia back to the room with lots of hugs and lots of "Love you, little brother." Marcia was on him as soon as the door closed behind them.

"And you didn't tell them because...?"

"Because Blake didn't want to tell them, and until they were all here, I thought it was bullshit."

"What happened to change your mind? They seemed nice!" She put her hands on her hips and actually stomped her foot.

"They *are* nice!" he replied, laughing. "But they're also in everybody's business. Blake... Blake doesn't just *love* my brothers. He *reveres* them. If we get together and, God help me, I fuck it up, he's the one who has to face the music. He has to face them in his grill, has to face that he was almost really their brother and it didn't pan out. I'll get the 'Oh, poor Cheever, he got his heart broken!' card, but Blake's older. Blake'll get the 'Blake, what did you do to our little brother!' card, and that will *destroy* him!"

She folded her arms, still glaring. "Every sitcom I've ever seen says this is the wrong move," she told him earnestly. "Every book I've read, every TV show, every movie—"

Cheever scrubbed his palms over his eyes. "Yeah, yeah, me too, okay? But has it ever occurred to you that this shows up so much in those places for a reason?"

"Sure. Because people are stupid. *That's* why it shows up there. Because people are dumb as shit. But fine. You and Blake try to keep this a secret. I'm telling you, the first time he looks at you, the jig is up."

"Do people even say that anymore?"

"I have a therapy circle to attend," she said loftily. "And you are officially too stupid to talk to. Now draw your damned boyfriend while you remember him happy, because the rest of this shit can only end in tears."

She walked out, her head held high. Cheever watched her go, and then after a minute, he went back to his bed and picked up his sketchbook.

He thought of Blake in the morning, with orange juice. Thought of his hair—not curly unless it was long—mussed from sleep, from lovemaking. Of a bit of sandy stubble along his jawline and the way he seemed to be built under the T-shirts and denim jacket he wore.

He thought of his self-deprecating smile, and the way he still tilted his head like he was hiding his teeth. Of the way he hid his solo work, like it was not good enough.

Thought of all the things he wanted to hide as marks of shame but that Cheever was just so damned glad he'd survived.

Not perfect.

He was right—Blake wasn't a supermodel and didn't have aspirations to be.

But he was beautiful.

Thoughtfully, Cheever began to draw. Not the idealized Blake, the one he wanted Blake to see from his heart, but a real Blake.

One he wanted to see in his bed.

TWO WEEKS later, it was his own bed he was surveying. He and Marcia shared a bathroom, and he could hear her, oohing and ahhing in appreciation in her room on the other side of it. Briony and Shelia—super excited that a *girl* was finally getting recruited to their midst—had gone all-out on Marcia's room. They'd stopped by the center and visited and gotten her preferences, although she'd insisted on the posters Blake had brought for them, and Cheever thought that was only right.

He'd brought the one of the kids playing on the beach. He couldn't say why it was his favorite—certainly the art was ordinary—but something about it… something beautiful… made him keep it.

The rest of the room had been put together by Blake, one element at a time.

He'd painted one wall the exact blue of *Starry Night* and one wall the gold of the stars. He'd found paintings from Renoir and Chagall and Le Fauve and put one on each wall, and bought the bed set to match the walls.

It was simple—almost childlike in its simplicity—but there were no flowers and no flounces. The area rug under the bed was a simple black, and the desk and bed were done in dark wood.

Blake had brought in a music stand and an easel as well. As Cheever looked at the newly painted wall, he made a discovery.

"You had work done here," he said, surprised. The wall was put together oddly, as though it had been extended. Blake had made the window much larger than it probably had been originally, and had other windows installed above it.

"Light," Blake said with a shrug. "So you can draw or paint. There's some other open rooms in the two houses—the studio house has some nice areas on the top floor. If you stay for a while, we can set up a work room for you there."

"Stevie and Jefferson were talking about relocating there," Cheever said with a shrug. "This is great—you took real good care of me."

He'd been worried about coming. He and Marcia had barely been able to sleep the night before, but as soon as they got out of the car, the family had been there, surrounding them. And suddenly there was nothing to worry about.

Cheever tilted his head as the voices in Marcia's room reached a high pitch. "That's going well."

Blake shrugged, smiling a little. "I think Shelia brought in the kids—they bought her some stuffed animals. They get really excited about guests."

Cheever bit his lip. The kids hadn't been all that excited to see him. Grant's daughter, Katy, had been the worst. She'd taken one look at Cheever, scrunched her little brow together, and said, "Wait—do I have to call him 'Uncle Cheever'? Or do I just call him Cheever, like I call Uncle Blake Blake?"

"I… I don't know how to fix that," he mumbled, partly to himself. God. He'd spent so many years being Uncle Cheever, too busy to bother with the kids. So much of it was bullshit. He'd been a spoiled diva princess for his entire life. It was time to pay it forward.

Blake moved a little closer, and a feral, animal part of Cheever relaxed. They needed to be closer. Such a simple answer to making the world better.

"Don't worry. Hang out with Marcia. Make kid jokes. Watch movies with them. Play with their toys. Hell, draw them in pictures—you'll be their favorite in no time."

Cheever closed the gap between them even further, lacing their fingers together and touching Blake's temple with his lips. "What do you do with them?"

Blake grinned. "Play music. Mackey told them how he started a rock band, and we have piano and guitar lessons daily. Stevie gets in there with drums and bells—they're getting pretty good."

Cheever laughed softly and breathed in the scent of his hair, nipping softly on Blake's earlobe. Blake leaned into his space and made a pleased sound.

"Someone's going to see," he said, his reluctance obvious.

"That's not a problem for me," Cheever whispered.

"Maybe… you know. Let's go on a date fir—"

Cheever took his mouth, because he and Marcia had been having that discussion for two weeks and Cheever was over it. Blake was standing here, looking proud and pleased, having literally *knocked down a wall* to make Cheever happy.

Cheever had to taste him, pull him inside, make him real after the weeks of visits and sunset kisses and holding hands. Blake answered, turning in his arms, cupping his face, plundering. Ah! He tasted good—so good—warmth and home and kindness.

And passion.

That's what this is. Passion. Damn!

Cheever upped the ante, pushing back, rucking up Blake's shirt, palming the smooth skin above his belt. They hadn't gotten this far in the facility—every time Cheever had tried, Blake had pulled away. No sex in rehab. And even though Cheever had been doing something different there, it was a caveat Blake wouldn't break.

Blake moaned and took his own liberties, moving his hands so they spanned Cheever's middle, kissing along Cheever's jawline and going for his neck. He nibbled there for a moment, and Cheever slid his hands forward, taking in Blake's chest and... oh damn. Under his shirt it was just as hard, just as impressive as he'd imagined, with a little patch of silky hair. He found a nipple with his thumb and rubbed softly, getting a rush as it hardened. Blake's teeth sank into his shoulder, just under the shirt line, and Cheever whimpered, arching against Blake's leg. He was hard and growing harder under his jeans.

Blake rested his forehead on Cheever's shoulder then, pulling back and panting with the suddenness of the storm.

"That's different than it was in the rehab place," he mumbled.

"God yeah. *So* different." Cheever slid his fingers through Blake's hair and tugged until Blake looked at him. "Dating? Still?"

Blake stood straight, which sucked, but then he pulled Cheever against his chest, which totally made up for it. "Yes, dating. For all I know, I'm the only guy you've looked at since you were a little kid."

"Not looked at," Cheever told him, thinking about distant crushes, subtle attractions. "Just dreamed about." For the last week, he'd woken up with an aching erection that made rooming with Marcia awkward in a way he hadn't thought possible when they'd started.

"That's almost worse!" Blake groaned, but his arms tightened around Cheever's shoulders, not loosened. "God. So, get settled, dinner with the family tonight—"

"You'll be there?" *Please, Blake, please, still be family.*

"Yeah, yeah, don't worry. Briony and Shelia have been planning this one. We don't always do the whole family thing—I mean, in case you haven't noticed, we've got three family groups living here. Mackey and Trav eat in Trav's study a lot, unless Katy's here."

Cheever nodded and studied Blake intently. "The house next door's big. The twins could move their family there, and you'd probably still—"

"Have a room and a sitting room and a bathroom," Blake confirmed. He looked around him. "This house—man, when Trav first got it, it seemed impossibly big. I mean, Mackey moved Briony in here as a friend, and she just disappeared, you know? But now… it's small. And that's not bad. Just, you know."

"Shit's changing."

Blake's eyes were faraway and not altogether happy. "Bound to do that," he confirmed. "Just… I didn't realize until I moved, how much it had changed without me."

Cheever grazed Blake's cheek with his knuckles. "Maybe it's both of us," he said. "Both of us living with our hearts in jars."

Blake stepped away. "I… yeah. So tonight, big family meal. Tomorrow night, uh, you, me, the movies. You like the shoot-'em-up stuff or the stuff with the subtitles?"

Cheever thought about it. "Lots of special effects," he decided. "The more alien life-forms, the better."

His reward was Blake's smile, and he felt like he'd won the lottery.

I Wanna Be Your Man

THE TRIP home had been rough on Mackey—they'd taken the bus so he could have a full-fledged bed to stretch out on. He wasn't cleared to walk for another two weeks and was going out of his mind.

Blake spent the family meal with him, while Trav checked up on everybody, sort of a habit leftover from the days when Trav had taken a bunch of shiftless fuckups and helped to make them men.

"Briony can cook," Mackey muttered, taking a chicken-sized bite of the beans she'd sent up. "Man, I miss home cooking."

Blake looked woefully at the barely touched plate on Mackey's lap.

"You're not eating," he said bluntly, and Mackey grimaced.

"I can't fuckin' move, Blake. I'm not hungry. And if I *did* eat, I'd gain weight and that would make moving harder." He grunted and ate another bean. "You don't have to stay up here, by the way. I mean, that was bitchy, what I said just now, and I'm telling you, it's not getting better than that."

Blake smiled. "I've taken worse."

Mackey rolled his eyes. "But you shouldn't have to. Jesus, I know I was a dick to you way back, but I thought we were past when you thought you'd earned that."

"I'm just saying—if you need to cut loose, I'm good for it."

Mackey set his plate aside. "As sweet as that is, no. Trav's already offered himself up there. I take him up on it sometimes, but mostly? Mostly I don't feel like ripping people's heads off. I just feel... sad. Like I'm missing out. I mean, Katy's downstairs and I barely saw her all day. *Cheever* hasn't come to visit me yet, and...."

It was hard for him to move, but he managed to swing his head around to meet Blake's eyes. "How's he doing?"

"Good," Blake said, happy to settle Mackey's mind about this, at least. He'd had Cheever's permission to tell Mackey everything, once Kell and the others had heard the story, and Mackey hadn't taken it well. "He... you know. I mean, you remember, right? Once you actually said the thing that was wrong, once you got it out in the air, you could breathe again."

"But Cheever's thing...." Mackey shook his head. "Mama cried on me all day yesterday, you know that, right? She fell asleep in that chair, just wrecked. I keep asking myself, how could we not know?"

"Don't," Blake said, his voice sharp. "'Cause that's all of us. And the truth was, we could barely wipe our own asses back then. It's... Cheever talks about not wanting to share his hell. Like we all have our own world, right? And he didn't want to trap you on it. We didn't know—you and me, we were barely learning back then that letting someone see your world is what sets you free."

"Pretty," Mackey grunted, trying not to yawn. The pain was exhausting, and they'd had the physical therapist in there for over two hours, trying to work Mackey's back out so he could walk with the cast. Even more than that, Mackey hated being helpless. Struggling to just accept he was stuck there was probably the most exhausting thing of all. "Why don't you write more, Blake?"

Blake startled. "Cheever been saying something to you?"

"No." Mackey settled back against the pillows. "I told you, haven't seen him. No—I just missed you on the bus ride back. Listened to your CD a couple of times. It did decent, Blake. You should try again."

Blake remembered when Mackey couldn't say a good word about Blake with a knife to his balls. This was way fuckin' better—but embarrassing.

"I've... you know, been writing songs."

"Mmm. Well, while we're sort of in limbo before we go back out on tour, maybe you should work those up. I mean, you used studio musicians last time, and I got your reasons. But you really love playing with the guys. Maybe that'll make it fun."

"As long as it doesn't cut into—"

"Blake, brother. I am *laid the fuck up.* I can barely pick up a guitar. It would fucking do me good to know you could make this your chance to shine. You do surely deserve it. We got the studio—after we replace the equipment, it should definitely get some use, right?"

"What about Cheever?" Blake hated himself for asking.

"He's crazy about your CD. Let him help. Hell, ask him for cover art suggestions—maybe some sketches of you guys practicing. It would be great if he could be part of it." Mackey grunted. "It would be great if *I* could be part of it. Jesus, I'd play backup guitar for you if I could just get out of bed." He brightened fractionally. "Maybe I could produce. That's fun."

"But we're going back on tour in September—"

"Well, yeah. But maybe we could use some of the songs this time, sort of pimp it up. I mean, last time, you did it all yourself, and you wouldn't let us talk it up or anything. Let your brothers help you, 'kay?"

Blake sighed. "Yeah. Okay. I'm not sure how excited Cheever'll be, but—"

Mackey frowned at him. "You and Cheever got really tight the last few weeks, didn't you?"

Blake could feel the burn of embarrassment as it washed his face. "Uh, yeah. I was… you know. The only family besides your mom and—"

"Blake."

Mackey's gray eyes were searching his face, and Blake wanted to hide. He remembered when Mackey hated him—*really* hated him, because Blake hadn't been Grant Adams—and when Blake pretty much wanted Mackey dead.

God, he'd give anything not to go back to that. But would he give up Cheever?

"What?"

"My family has done this before, remember?"

"I have no idea—"

"Except I was the younger brother in love with Kell's best friend."

"There's been nothing about lo—"

"And the thing is, it wouldn't have been a bad thing, really. But it was back when *gay* was a bad word and Kell was a fucking Neanderthal—"

"Your brother's chan—"

"But what cut Kell up the most was that nobody told him."

"Fuck." Blake buried his face in his hands. "It's not even… we haven't even gone on a date yet, Mackey! Don't make me come out to your brother when we haven't even gone out on a date yet!"

"You kissed?"

Blake peeked at him between his fingers.

"Was it good?"

Oh geez. That kiss in Cheever's room had been the closest to God Blake had been since that one time he and Mackey had tried heroin, right before Trav showed up and cleaned their sorry whoring asses the fuck up.

"Life changing," he muttered, because for once, Mackey was shutting up and waiting for an answer.

To his surprise, Mackey reached out and pulled on his hand. "Look at me, brother."

Blake dropped his hands and his pretenses. "I won't hurt him. I mean, I'll do my best to not—"

"Don't let him hurt you," Mackey said softly. "And tell Kell as soon as you feel it. Don't be afraid. Kell won't hurt you. Cheever might—he's young. You remember us at that age. We weren't great at considering other people's feelings."

"Cheever's better."

Mackey nodded and dropped his hand, wincing. "Good. Because if I could set you up with someone, I'd set you up with someone older. Someone who'd be kind."

Blake realized it then, that Mackey only had memories of Cheever—cool, aloof, breaking Mackey's heart when Mackey was trying to get to know him.

"Mackey, you think I've changed these last years?"

"Both of us have."

"Your brother has changed the same way. Don't worry about—"

"I always worry." Mackey yawned again. "Shut up with that noise. Always worry."

"Like I'm worried that you're not eating," Blake said pointedly.

Mackey didn't even open his eyes, but he smiled.

"Yeah, but I'm not worried about stupid shit. Go downstairs, Blake. Make him feel good. Tell him you've got a summer project he can help with. Introduce him to the kids." He took a deep breath, then another, and Blake knew he was done.

He stood and kissed Mackey on the forehead. "Get some sleep, brother. You'll be running us off our asses soon enough."

Blake met Trav on the way down, and Trav grimaced when he saw the plate. "Goddammit."

"He's worried about getting fat."

"I'm worried about him, period."

Blake hated to ask, but he'd been gone for the last three and a half weeks. "What does the doctor say?"

"He says… says he's in a lot of pain. And the thing with pain is that it can bring on depression. Mackey doesn't do drugs, period, but…." Trav shook his head. "Except what he's doing is *just like* drugs. He's so damned stubborn about accepting help of any kind…. Augh! It's good to know he can still make me crazy, right?"

"Runs in the family," Blake said weakly, and Trav gave him a sharp look.

"You about done with Cheever?" he asked.

"No! No. Just… the making crazy. I mean, we been doing it for what? Ten years?"

"Yeah. You have. I been here nine."

"We didn't count before you," Blake said loyally, although his crush on Kell had been going strong for that first year.

"How *are* you and Cheever?"

Blake had to remind himself that Trav knew—had known almost from the beginning. "Going on a date tomorrow," he said with dignity.

"Movie?"

"Yeah."

"You're done for then. Movies will either make you hate each other or make you fall in love. Gotta say, I don't see you hating him—not with the way he's talking about you like you're the Second Coming."

Blake shrugged. "I don't want to talk about it," he said, his throat clogging. "Too much…."

"Too much rests on the outcome." Trav nodded. "I hear you. Anything else I should know before I go up there?"

"He wants me to put out another CD, this time with the guys backing me. He thinks we can do it this summer, before he's ready to go out on tour. What do you think?"

Trav brightened. "Hey, he can help produce it. He won't have to move around so much—it'll be great. Good idea!"

"All Mackey," Blake muttered. God. All these people and their fucking faith in him.

"What's wrong? Heath's been asking about you. He thinks you could have a little solo career when the guys are off-season. Is that bad?"

"Heath knows my name?" Blake joked weakly. He sometimes thought the only reason their producer had let Blake put out a solo album was that he and Trav knew each other from way back in the military.

"Shut up. Are you worried about that whole band-breakup thing? I don't think so. The bomb could go off and you guys would form radioactive dust that would get back together and play. What's wrong with you doing your thing?"

"It's… I mean, I'm not Mackey. He gets on the stage and plays on his own and…. Never mind."

Trav let out a sigh. "Blake, you have your own talents. Mackey can do that for a stadium of twenty thousand people. We both know it. But you can do it for an intimate club, and that's a different sound. Not a worse one. Don't… don't put yourself down because you're not Mackey. I think we've established you're Blake."

Blake nodded. "Let me put this in the kitchen," he said, gesturing to the plates in his hands. Truth was, he didn't want to talk about it anymore. The reasons that doing the solo album made him feel naked and vulnerable and completely inadequate were his own.

"Blake—we'll talk tomorrow. In fact, we'll meet in the studio. Tell the guys. Eleven o'clock, after everyone's gone running and worked out. We'll have a band meeting. Ask Cheever if he can stay with Mackey. It's a thing."

"Great," Blake muttered, and not even he could tell if he was being sarcastic or enthusiastic.

"Jesus," Trav muttered back, starting up the stairs again. "This shit never fucking ends."

DOWNSTAIRS, CHEEVER and Marcia had already finished eating. They were in the family room, Cheever with a tablet of paper and some special pens, Marcia with her tablet, and they were taking Blake's advice.

They were drawing.

"Blake!" Kyrie, Briony's oldest, was a sturdy little girl with bright red hair and brown eyes, who was hell on the soccer field and heaven in a pink dress pretty much all the other times. "Look! Cheever is drawing us in a characterater—"

"Caricature," Katy corrected gently. Grant's daughter was beautiful—golden, with wide-set eyes, Grant's unique, straight-bridged nose, and an oval face—but the most beautiful thing about her was her joy in her cousins. "Cheever just told me it's a special kind of drawing."

"Yeah!" Kyrie kept going, undaunted. "Anyway, Cheever makes 'em, and Marcia scans 'em and makes 'em move. It's *great*!"

Oh! One better than drawing pictures. A multimedia production—just the thought made Blake smile.

"I'll come back in and watch in a sec," he said. "I gotta put the plates in the kitchen."

Cheever looked up from drawing and winked at him. He managed a smile back, but he also managed to flee the room before anything else happened.

Briony was waiting for him when he got there, arms crossed, staring from the plates in Blake's hand to Blake and back.

"What?" he asked, feeling defensive. He moved to the sink to scrape the plates into the garbage disposal.

"Don't you fuckin' dare," she told him. "Which one of those plates is Mackey's?"

Blake stared at them both. "I, uh, honestly can't remember."

"I thought so. Sit down." She pointed imperiously to the kitchen table and took the plates from him. "This one's yours. You like avocado on your burger, and he thinks it's from Satan. Now I'm going to cut this burger up, like I do with the kids—"

"Briony, you don't need to—"

"And then I'm going to add some fries right out of the oil, because they're delicious and bad for you—"

"I'm fine, sweetheart—"

"And then add some bacon beans. And *then* you're going to sit at that table and eat. And then maybe tell me what's got you so fuckin' weird you wouldn't eat my cooking."

"This family really *is* fucking extra," he muttered. "Seriously, darlin'—"

"I am completely immune to any charm you ever possessed." She ignored him for a moment, getting to work on his plate and minding the big vat of homemade chips on the stove. "Shelia!" she called. "Shelia! Do we have any more burgers out there?"

"We got some brats!" Shelia called, wandering into the kitchen barefoot, wearing shorts, a tank top, and a giant apron to protect her from the grill. Where Briony was tall and strong, with a sweet round face and a lithe, athletic body, Shelia was tiny and buxom, sort of everybody's idea of a brainless blond bimbo. Except Shelia had a kind of sweet good sense about her. She was never going to write a novel, but she might write a cookbook or a child's picture book, and she'd do a good job at it and charm everybody's socks off. She was an amazing, if slightly flaky mother, and Jefferson and Stevie worshipped her.

She presented Briony with the plate of brats, and Briony wrinkled her nose. "Any burgers working?"

"Yeah, done in five. Last batch."

"Good, this burger's a little rare. I'm gonna toss it and make Blake eat sides until it's done."

Shelia looked at the two plates and frowned. "Him and Mackey not eating?"

"Oh dear God," Blake muttered.

"Mackey's sad," Shelia continued. "I get that. But Blake and Cheever are in love. He should be fine."

Blake put his head in his arms and groaned. "Oh dear God."

"He's all worried," Briony told her. "You heard Marcia—he's worried because Cheever's so young and he's got that 'tragic dark past.'"

"I hate you," Blake said.

"It's no darker than ours." Shelia looked down at her brightly painted red toenails and then grinned at Blake. "I mean, I'm practicing poly… poly…. Goddammit, what's that word again, Briony?"

"Polyandry," Briony said, grinning.

"It's a fancy word for slut," Shelia said winsomely, peeping to see if Blake would take the bait. He'd learned not to even question the three of them about their ambiguous and strangely perfect relationship because they were all so good about yanking the family's chain when questioned. When he merely rolled his eyes, she continued, "The only one here who wasn't doing all the drugs and all the sex was Briony. Well, and Trav."

"I was six months pregnant at my own wedding." It was as though Briony was clinging to that to make her a "bad girl."

"La-de-fuckin'-da," Shelia teased. "Alert the news—Pollyanna here had a baby bump."

"Well, polyandry here has another one," Briony snapped back, and Shelia laughed.

"Hush! The boys don't know yet. They just think the titty fairy showed up for shits and giggles. Blake, eat. I'll go get your burger." She wandered back outside, taking some of the sunshine with her, leaving Blake with his mouth open.

"What?" Briony asked, bailing a batch of chips out of the grease.

"Is she really pregnant again?"

"Yup. I'm pretty sure it happened that first week after Mackey got hurt. The twins got clingy then, and there wasn't a lot else to do except worry."

Blake sighed. "I hate to ask, but does she ever have any idea which—"

"No." Briony shrugged. "She told me once that their come even tastes the same."

Blake started to choke, and Briony poured him a glass of milk. "Speaking of which, when are you and Cheever getting to it?"

"Oh dear God!"

"You can't just keep saying that, Blake. I'm not sure if you noticed here, but this family isn't so good on the boundary thing. Here, have some chips. They're really good with french onion dip. Just saying."

Blake took a chip because he was helpless and stupid against her. "Mm...." Oh yes. So much better warm.

"Good. Finish that stack there. Let me fix your burger and then we'll talk."

By the time she was back with his burger, he was actually hungry. He ate one of the pieces she'd cut up and sighed.

"So...." She cocked an eyebrow.

"I'm too old and I have a tragic past." Well, Shelia had put it out there.

"So does he. So does Mackey, and Kell, and the twins, and everybody but Trav and me, mostly."

"What if it doesn't work?"

"What if Kell walks into the bedroom tonight and decides he wants a twenty-two-year-old virgin instead?"

Blake raised his eyebrows and played the no-boundary game. "It's my understanding he already had him one of those, darlin'. After you knock one up, you don't get a do-over."

"Ooh, that was impressive. What's the problem really?"

He will eventually see the real me. I like the way he's looking at me now.

"I'm—"

A crash and a squeal came from the living room.

"Never mind. Whatever you tell me right now in the kitchen, with the kids raising holy hell in the other room, is a total and complete lie. Does he make you happy?"

He swallowed and went to push his plate away.

"Don't you dare. Of course he makes you happy. You wouldn't be so freaked out about losing him if he didn't make you happy. Jesus fuckin' Christ, Blake. You have done your goddamned time. You think I haven't heard the 'Oh my God, you're so young and innocent!' speech before? It was sweet when Kell gave it, but really unnecessary. It's even more unnecessary now."

"Why, because Cheever's a boy?"

Paint It Black | 151

"No, because he knows what he's doing! He's an adult!"

"Yeah, but he's already had one scumbag ruin his life. Does he really need another?"

She smacked him on the top of the head, hard enough to bring tears to his eyes.

"Jesus, Briony—"

"Shut up," she said thickly. "You'll just make me stabby. Eat your fuckin' burger. And for sweet fuck's sake, remember this whole family is up in your business, making you eat, jumping past your fucking boundaries because we fucking love you. I mean, I sort of hate you right now, but I love you. Now fucking eat and don't say another fucking word until you're done."

Blake finished his dinner in silence, and was just cleaning off the plate in the sink while Briony consolidated leftovers when Cheever came in.

"You eat two dinners?" he asked Blake, laughing.

Briony growled and shook her head. "All men suck." And with that, she flounced out.

Cheever watched her go, frowning, and then moved up behind Blake and leaned over his shoulder. "What was that about?"

It wasn't his fault Blake was having a quiet crisis, right? Blake kissed him on the cheek and went back to the dishes. "I was just unsettled. I'm telling you, Cheever, if you move in, there will be people so in your face about being happy, you won't even have a chance to second-guess yourself."

"What's got you going?"

"Your brother. He's not doing good. Actually—" Oh hey! Blake had almost forgotten he had a job to do. "Actually, we could use your help. We're having a band meeting at eleven, after we go running. I think your mama is going to be keeping him company in the morning, but could you go keep him company during the meeting? Odds are good he'll call in, which is fine, but, you know. It would be nice for him to have some company."

"I'll bring my sketch book," Cheever said, hesitant and proud. "I... I don't remember the last time he saw what I could do."

"I think he'd like that. He has some plans—wants to give you some work this summer, I think—"

"Doing what?"

"Well, you know. We got a project coming up. He wants you to do the cover art. It's no big deal. You can say no—"

"Are you kidding? He wants me to help?"

Oh God. There was so much excitement and validation in one little request. "It's what he said."

"But… he doesn't even know if I'm any good!"

"Your mom's been showing us your art since you were in grade school. We know you can make it pretty. Just…." Blake grimaced. "It's gonna be the guys as backup, so, you know, not too much of me, okay?"

"It's your next solo album." Cheever's voice had that same note in it that Briony's did.

"Yeah, whatever. Mackey's gonna produce the sound—whatever he okays, how's that?"

"I get to work on a project. With my brother."

"Yeah." Blake smiled, liking the way Cheever's whole face lit up. Then Cheever took Blake's chin and pulled him to face him, kissing him hard and deep. That tight band in Blake's chest, the one that cut off his hope and made him think every time he and Cheever touched, they were going faster into a brick wall, loosened up.

Blake closed his eyes and fell into the kiss, only pulling back when he heard a clatter of steps near the kitchen door.

"Cheever! Cheever! Marcia said we can watch a movie! She's gonna tell us how they do some of the stuff. Wanna watch with us?"

"Yeah," Cheever said, turning to look at Kyla and Kansas. The younger kids in the family were both chubby and looked surprisingly alike, with brown hair and hazel eyes. Like Stevie and Jefferson, they tended to travel together and were spooky about reading each other's minds. "Yeah, guys. You go pick the movie with Marcia. I'll be in there in a sec."

They ran off, and Cheever kissed him again. Blake's worries about being too old, too damaged, second best, deserted him as Cheever's taste filled him and Cheever's touch overwhelmed him, leaving him stupid and cow-eyed and not worried at all. "I like that look," Cheever teased, pulling away.

"Good. You sort of give it to me a lot." Blake pecked him on the lips. "I like that you're making an effort with the kids. You and Marcia made them really happy tonight."

Cheever looked behind him. "Are they always this easy?"

"Oh God, no. This is 'we have company' manners, right after the tour. They're still fighting exhaustion. Give them a week when they're bored and restless and still tired, and tired of being tired. The whole family snarls at each other like bears. It's great."

Cheever chuckled. "See, *that's* what I remember about kids. I'll be much more comfortable when they start doing that shit."

God, he was so young and so excited. "Go watch your movie," he said. "I've got to talk to your brothers, then I'm walking home."

"Can't I walk you—"

Blake rubbed his thumb over Cheever's lower lip, full and swollen from their earlier kiss. "Get to know your family. We go running in the morning at around eight. Everybody meets here in the kitchen. One person stays behind to get the kids cereal, and we usually take turns."

"I don't have running clothes," Cheever said regretfully. "I mean, I've got clothes I can run in, but no good shoes."

"We can shop for them tomorrow, maybe, before the movie?"

"Excellent. I'll be up to watch the kids. I'm helping!"

Blake chuckled. "We'll use and abuse you until you run screaming," he said. "Marcia too." He sobered. "But be honest if it gets overwhelming. Shelia and Briony have been talking about getting an actual nanny—or two—for the last two years. You're not free labor. We all know it. It's just, you know, easy to take advantage of family."

"Like you, keeping my mom calm and moving all of Mackey's stuff into the house and being there for me every night?" Cheever asked archly.

"That was a special circumstance," Blake said, shifting from foot to foot. "Nobody knew you and me were so… time intensive."

"Mmm…." Cheever rubbed Blake's cheekbone with a rough thumb. "Why didn't you tell people? Like you said, make boundaries."

Oh damn. Cheever was so pretty. And the look he was giving Blake wasn't childish at all. "I was so afraid you'd be out of bounds," he admitted breathily.

"I'm not," Cheever said. "I'm right here."

Blake kissed him again, ever mindful of the clatter outside the kitchen, and this time, when Cheever's hands slid down under the waistband of his jeans, he let himself arch against Cheever's hip. Hard. His cock was hard, and his hands shook as he cupped Cheever's neck. Pulling away this time was insanely difficult, and not grabbing Cheever by the hair and hauling him to his room to keep that kiss going was one of the hardest things he'd ever done.

"We gotta—" He broke off, panting, hating himself for needing so much, hating Cheever a little for making him need.

"Here's an idea," Cheever whispered. "My brother's out there with his kids, who love me. How about we tell him now, and then we can go have private grown-up time!"

Blake chuckled weakly and disengaged. "How about you go be with your family," he rasped. "But first, I'm going to... shit, finish the dishes, then go talk to the guys."

Cheever wrapped his hand around Blake's bicep, and Blake shuddered. For the first time, he wondered who would be the aggressor in bed. Yeah, Cheever might need to be taught a few things, but Blake had the feeling he'd be a very assertive lover.

The thought made his stomach clench.

A lover who would take care of him. It hadn't happened since Cindy.

"I'll finish the dishes," Cheever said in his ear. "You go do what you need to. But Blake, remember I'm the spoiled youngest son. I don't wait too long, and I don't wait patiently. You're the guy who helped take my heart out of the jar, and now my heart knows what it wants."

"You weren't spoiled," Blake said bitterly. "And maybe the guy who takes your heart out of the jar shouldn't be the one who gets to hold it."

"Maybe he's *exactly* the guy," Cheever snapped. "Go." He reached behind Blake and caressed his backside, setting up another howl of want thrumming through Blake's body. "Now go—go think about you and me, naked. I'll see you in the morning."

One more kiss, brutal, taking Blake's mouth hard and without compromise, and Blake was turned loose. The set of Cheever's shoulders told Blake he wasn't talking anymore, and it was time for Blake to leave the room.

THE NEXT day felt so normal, except for getting up and checking on the fish. Blake hadn't had time to set the tank up again, so he'd left it in Marcia's room, with her permission. The thing was, Blake wasn't really certain those fish were *his*.

One of the things he and Mackey had picked up in rehab was the idea of caring for something other than yourself. Mackey had tried plants. Blake had gone with fish.

But they'd both had pretty busy lives at the beginning, and Mackey confided in him once that the only reason the ficuses survived was that Astrid, their housekeeper, kept moving them to the sunshine whenever Mackey got too busy.

At first, Blake had worried. He'd thought, "Hey, Mackey's *cheating* at this one thing, so he might not make it!" Turned out, Mackey's one thing to keep alive was the band itself, and it probably wouldn't have worked with anyone else on the planet. But then, Mackey was special.

Blake had known he was not.

He had to keep those fuckin' fish alive.

He'd worked on it. He'd read books, watched videos, and thought, "Hey! It's working! They seem to be getting bigger... but don't they keep changing number?"

It wasn't until he got back from their first tour that he realized his tank had gotten bigger and all the fish had changed except for this one big scumsucker on the bottom that nobody paid any attention to until he just lunged out of the fuckin' castle for shits and giggles. Funny, he'd been worried about Mackey not being able to keep a ficus alive, and apparently Astrid had been the one keeping the fish and not Blake.

Except when Blake told Kell about it—feeling damned sad, because, hey, he couldn't even keep fuckin' fish alive—Kell sheepishly admitted that *he'd* been the one replacing the fish. So Blake had figured that if nothing else, he could keep his friendship with Kell alive, even after Kell and Briony had hooked up and their relationship should have all but disappeared.

That made having the fish, even if they were Astrid's fish and Kell's fish, sort of a badge of honor. Hey! Blake had symbolic fish for real relationships! He'd won at rehab—at least in the fish department.

And for the last few years, he felt like he'd been taking care of his actual fish himself. He knew that when he was not on tour, he lost a few every year, and he was the one who replaced them before Astrid or Kell ever got the chance.

So leaving the fish back at the main house felt odd, but meeting up with the guys in the morning felt perfectly normal.

"Me and the twins'll move your tank into your house tomorrow morning," Kell said, panting. They lived in a giant gated community, with paths that wound between houses and along canyons. On the one hand, they felt like they were running through a park, but they were all very aware of the walls and the security that kept out paparazzi. If it hadn't been for the walls, Kell might have stopped his running regime years ago out of embarrassment. He had a naturally thick body. Even though they tried to stay fit on the tour, he was the first one to put on weight and had to work the hardest to lose it. "Think the meeting itself'll take long? You got homework for us to do?"

Blake did indeed. Walking away from Cheever had left him feeling achy and restless, and—God help him—*horny*, so after talking to the guys he'd spent the rest of the night pulling out the songs he'd worked on in the two years since his solo album had been released. He even had three or so about Cheever, although he'd kept them gender neutral because that was the band's policy. Weaving the illusion of stars in the music web was all about letting the crowd think the stars were *their personal* stars. It was easier to do when they didn't have to fix the words.

"I got some shit for you guys to practice a little and play. I figure we take two days, everybody decides which ones we like best, then put a spin on them, and we go to the studio and see what shakes out."

"Sounds like a plan." Well, it was for Outbreak Monkey, anyway, and it had been how Blake had run his ship last time out. Back then, he'd thought that just once, he'd like his own voice to be heard. Now, he would just as soon his brothers drowned him out.

"I'll try not to work you too hard," Blake told him. Mackey was the slave driver, but then, that's probably why Outbreak Monkey would always be the bigger band.

"Good," Kell agreed. "But how long tonight? Briony wants to enroll the kids in actual school this year, which'll sort of suck because they won't be able to tour with us. But she figures we should give them at least until Christmas to see if they hate it, and if they do, then we'll use the homeschool curriculum. Anyway, there's paperwork and shit, and we gotta hassle that out tonight."

Blake looked up to see how far behind the rest of the guys they were, and realized that Trav, Jefferson, and Stevie were only a few feet ahead. So much for a quiet moment alone.

"Early," Blake said. "Got plans."

"Yeah? Doin' what?"

Well, honesty. With spin. "Taking Cheever shopping for shoes so he can come running with us."

"D'oh! Damn, Blake. It's a good thing he's got you for a brother. I just fell down on the job."

Blake nodded, and ahead of them, Trav kicked it into gear for their last two miles, as usual, so Blake didn't have any breath to tell his best friend that the things he and Cheever had in mind for each other weren't brotherly in the least.

Let's Spend the Night Together

CHEEVER'S MORNING with his brother was a revelation.

"Oh my God! You ain't played Fortnite before?" Mackey asked, almost at the beginning. "Because me and the guys saved it for after tour. They broke it out when I was in the hospital, and oh my God, we need to fuckin' beat them. If I have to hear Kell brag about it one more time, I'm gonna beat him to death with a controller."

Cheever had cracked up. "Wow. I mean, I'd sort of thought that whole sibling-rivalry thing had gone away—"

"That's 'cause you always take off after the first two days. We're *behavin'* then." Mackey snorted, and Cheever wondered if the twang was deeper in his voice because he was more passionate about *everything*.

"I... uh...." Cheever sighed. "I should have stuck around. This sounds like high entertainment."

Mackey's evil chuckle was all-forgiving. "Oh, you and me are gonna beat the crap out of the rest of them. And don't never let Jefferson and Stevie be on a team together. It's like the same fuckin' person. It's uncanny!"

"Understood." Cheever brought the remote controls over and let Mackey set up the game, explaining things like which characters there were and what strengths they had. His passion for the videogame was just as infectious as his passion for music, for his family, for anything else, and Cheever was a little overwhelmed. He'd spent his entire life trying to keep all his shit to himself—Mackey was the exact opposite.

And Mackey expected Cheever to share back.

"You just died, and you are too goddamned quiet. Can't trust a man who don't curse when they die onscreen. What's wrong?"

Cheever let out a little gasp. "I just... you know, didn't want to be a whiny asshole."

Mackey scowled, although he kept his guy in the action. "Video games were *made* to be your whiny asshole outlet. Jesus, if you can't whine about up and dying, how you gonna fuckin' talk about real shit as a human being?"

"I whined enough as a kid." Embarrassment flushed Cheever's whole body. Every time he'd ever complained—wanting something different for dinner, wanting dessert, wanting clothes someone else hadn't worn—came back to haunt him.

"You were a fuckin' kid—no, no, no, you little motherfucker. Goddammit, Cheever, why'd you have to fuckin' die. *Shit.*"

"Sorry, Mackey," Cheever said sheepishly.

"Well, you damned well should be," Mackey snapped. "That thing you fuckin' did—scared the shit out of all of us. We don't even know you, little brother. Don't fuckin' make us lose you."

"Not much to know," Cheever said quietly. Mackey's anger seemed to subside, thank God. "I was just a rich kid who couldn't cut it in school—"

"That's fuckin' bullshit, and we both know it." Mackey tossed his remote control aside and fell back against the cushions of the orthopedic bed that took up much of the otherwise masculine room. "Cheever, you know we know. You told the boys all about it, and they came back and told me. And even if they hadn't, Blake gave me the uncut version."

Cheever swallowed sickly, but Mackey barreled right ahead.

"Did you think we wouldn't get it? We all grew up in that town— we lost Grant to that town. You think we don't know what it's like to be powerless, with jackals trying to take us down like weak fuckin' antelopes?"

"Then why didn't you take me with you?" Cheever yelled, surprised when it came ripping out of his throat.

"'Cause for our first year, it was just as fuckin' bad!" Mackey yelled back. "My God, do you think Blake and I woulda ended up in rehab if we'd had any power besides how high we could get? Blake became my fuckin' dealer so he could have something, *anything*, he fuckin' owned himself. That guy who did that to you—you may think he just lives in Tyson, but I'm telling you, Cheever, he's fuckin' everywhere. He's got a dozen fuckin' names. And if you don't give it up to them, they take it, until you finally reach your limit and take 'em down by the throat. But you were our little brother; we thought you were somewhere safe."

"I wasn't! I was that weak fuckin' antelope without my goddamned herd, Mackey. I never knew how much you all protected me until you were gone!"

"*We're sorry about that*!" Mackey took a couple of choppy breaths and then a deeper one. "We're so fuckin' sorry. But we been tryin' to be your herd for a couple of years now. We wanted you back so goddamned bad."

He'd planned Christmas vacations around Cheever—ones Cheever had never stayed to take.

"I didn't want you to have to do this," Cheever said brokenly, feeling wrecked and purged and clean and hurt, all at the same time. "'Cause this fuckin' sucks."

Mackey extended the arm with the cast on it and gave Cheever an imperious look. "I can't get up and hug you, Cheever. You gotta fuckin' meet me halfway."

Cheever laid his head on his brother's chest and cried, his face mashed up against his brother's ragged T-shirt, smelling, up close and personal, the same fabric softener their mom had used since they were kids. Animal herd. Goddammit. Why didn't someone make him smell family sooner?

"Wow." Cheever took a ragged breath.

"Wow what?"

"I forgot how fuckin' real you can be."

"Yeah, well, I'm in pain. Makes everything more real." Mackey's almost continuous restless stroking of Cheever's hair stilled. "How real were the last eight years for you, Cheever?"

"They weren't," Cheever said, not moving. This—without the static electricity of attraction he felt from Blake—was so comforting. "My heart was in a jar."

To anybody else but his family, that would have sounded insane.

"What's it like, out of the fuckin' jar?"

"Better than I expected. Turns out I got people here."

Mackey heaved a sigh. "I'm glad you think so, because we're gonna stick sort of close. I mean, we gotta tour and shit, but I swear we might even steal you away for some of that. Ain't no rule says you gotta be anywhere after you finish school. We'll just drag you along with us."

Cheever let out a laugh. "As what? An entourage of one?"

"Learn an instrument," Mackey said bluntly. "I gave you a guitar when you were, what? Fourteen? Did you sell that?"

"I taught myself to play," he rasped, feeling absurdly proud. Mackey remembered. Cheever had looked up his guitar once, after he saw concert footage and realized Mackey's was much like it. His brother had bought him a guitar that cost more than a car. It had given him a little hope then. Mackey had given him something he loved. Something that meant something to him.

"You did?" Mackey's voice cracked. "Really? Like… how much?"

Cheever grunted. "I'm not Eddie Van Halen," he said glumly. "Not Kell or Blake—"

"Kell and Blake weren't Kell and Blake to start with. I mean, Blake was probably *better* than Kell when we picked him up, but they've been practicin' fierce since."

"Blake's solo album's really good."

"It is. I hope you told him that. He… I mean, it came out, and it did well, but it didn't do Outbreak Monkey good. He got embarrassed, I think. That's why I pushed him. Since I'm laid up, he should do another one. Just because we're better all together, that doesn't mean we can't be stars alone, right?"

Cheever sat up, squinting. "Is that what he's doing today? I just knew he had a meeting with the guys."

"Yeah. Doing a concept pitch, I think. Like, he's got all the songs, and he gives them to the guys and says, 'Hey, what do you think?' It's how I ran shit, so I think that's the reason he's doin' it. Why?"

The hurt was irrational. "I just didn't know, is all."

Mackey rolled his eyes and reached for Cheever's hand. Wow. His brother really must have learned to communicate in the last few years. "Little brother, you had Blake to yourself for a whole month. What do you think?"

"I think he's wonderful." Oh, it felt good to say, but it hurt too. What if Mackey said this was bad?

"He had a long journey to get to wonderful," Mackey told him. "Not an easy one. You ride that much rough road, you're only going to see the bruises, not what they taught you. You understand?"

Cheever sighed. "You're telling me to be careful with him." He swallowed. "Like… like *careful*, careful."

Mackey turned his head and searched Cheever's eyes. "That's what I'm saying. He needs someone who can keep his heart safe. You said you just got yours out of a jar. How you gonna make that work?"

Oh hell. "I… I'm going to not hurt myself, for one thing," he said. "And that's whether or not Blake and I work out." He closed his eyes, for once facing failure like a man. "He needs to know my life doesn't depend on the two of us getting together. I gotta make sure he knows that."

He could practically feel Mackey's sigh of relief through his palms, where they still touched. "You do indeed," Mackey said. "How you gonna do that?"

"Well, isn't that the sixty-four-thousand-dollar question?" Cheever snapped. Then he added, "Where do we get that expression, anyway?"

"I got no idea. I got it from Mama, but it *is* a big deal. What you wanna do with yourself, now that you found out where your heart is?"

"Art?" Cheever had brought his sketchbook, because he always brought his sketchbook. But instead of sketching his brother, he'd ended up talking to him instead.

"You love that?"

Cheever thought about it, maybe for the first time since he was twelve. "Yeah." He thought about Blake's fingers on his guitar strings, the lonely hours Cheever had spent in his room practicing, where there were no brothers to judge. "But it's not everything I love."

"Good." Mackey took a deep breath. "Cheever, nothing you got going on now is set in stone. And that's a good thing. You want to do art? You do art. You want to be our entourage? That's a go. We'd love to have you. Hell, Briony can teach you stagecraft, because a competent road crew—one that don't let you fall off a fuckin' speaker—would be a godsend, if you feel me."

Oh yeah. Cheever nodded vigorously, because seeing Mackey here, in pain, trying to help sort Cheever's life, was a serious lesson in how grown-ups handled the shit that fell out.

"You want to fall in love?" Mackey's voice lowered, and his no-bullshit expression softened. "I'm not gonna stop you. But I am gonna ask you, very nicely, that you not hurt a guy that your brothers love as if he was one of us. A guy who's been broken a lot. I know he's older—I married a guy fifteen years older'n me, so I'm not even gonna try to give you shit. But I am gonna tell you that this guy ain't Trav. It's in Trav's blood to try to fix things, to take care of things. He runs this family like a tight ship, and yeah, that includes the school the kids are going to.

"Blake is learning, but he ain't there yet. And he needs someone who'll take care of him. This album—I think it'll do great. But the market's a scary place. What if it tanks? Me and the guys'll be there to pick up the pieces. You gonna be there too?"

"Yes," Cheever whispered, before he even knew he'd say anything. "I… I mean, I know it's not that easy. And I know what you're asking. A month ago, I was a fuckup doing blow in a hotel room—"

"That wasn't your usual, Cheever. A month ago, you had a meltdown. Call it what it was, but don't paint it blacker. Go on."

"I want to take care of him," Cheever said, being as precise as he could be. "I'll figure it out. Art, music, being part of the family. But you're right. I may have needed Blake when I was at my lowest, but Mackey, he needs *me*. He needs someone to tell him he's good inside, someone he will believe."

Mackey nodded, a quiet smile on his face. "Okay, then. Good. We might all survive this." He tilted his head back and blew out a breath. "Look. One more thing. Don't keep this a secret from Kell. I'm pretty sure the twins know. The women *definitely* know. Blake told Trav all about it. That means Kell's the only one, and Blake's his best friend. If we do this to him one more time, it'll kill him."

Cheever thought about that. "How bad was it when he found out about Grant?"

Mackey grunted. "Well, since he didn't know until Trav and I had a knock-down-drag-out fight about going to see Grant before he died, I'd say it about ripped open his chest. Kell don't deserve that again. Don't treat it like a big deal. Just... you know. He's not a sitcom character. He's your brother."

The phone buzzed next to Mackey's bed, which saved Cheever from a reply. Mackey picked it up and hit speaker, then set it down again.

"Yeah, Trav. I'm here. You guys got a plan and shit? Do I get to play too?"

"Yeah, Mackey. You should be up and around by the time these guys have the songs worked up. We figure two weeks to start recording? That way, we can do a couple of tracks live when we finish up the tour."

Mackey smiled a little. "Blake, you lazy asshole, you know this means you gotta do solo work in front of a crowd, right?"

"Yeah, Mackey. You know this means you gotta do backup vocals behind me."

Mackey grinned. "We could hire someone—"

"You," Blake said gruffly. "I can't do this shit again without my guys."

"It'll do great," Mackey soothed. He closed his eyes, and his face tightened, as though he'd been fighting pain this whole time and it was finally catching up to him.

"How's he looking, Cheever?" Trav asked, and Cheever regarded his brother grimly.

"He's hurting, Trav. Is he ready for another painkiller?"

"When was his last one?"

Cheever looked at the clock. "I've been here about two hours and—"

"And that's an hour and a half over when he should have had it. Mackey, Cheever's getting you medication, you stubborn asshole. Take it."

"Sure, Trav," Mackey murmured, and Cheever's heart ached. That wasn't the voice he'd been using with Cheever or Blake. That was the voice of someone who was letting someone else care for him.

Cheever realized he hadn't heard Blake's "I'll let you care for me" voice yet.

He needed to. He wouldn't know they were for real until he did.

AN HOUR later, after Mackey was medicated and napping, Cheever went downstairs and told Briony he was going across the street. He figured the meeting in the studio should be winding down, and he had something he needed to do.

Briony nodded, and then chimed in with "Have fun on your date. Blake's looking forward to it."

Sure he was. "Blake's been looking forward to dodging it," Cheever told her. "But that's okay. He just needs to trust me a little."

Briony gave a noncommittal grunt. "Just remember, y'all gotta earn that shit."

Cheever was still pondering that on his way out the door.

Per Mackey's instructions, he didn't knock, but just opened the door and walked inside. Once past the kitchen and the stairs, the whole thing had been converted into a studio, complete with a recording room and a sound booth. But they'd left the front room as a lounge. Couches and lots of instrument and music stands as well as a couple of tablets littered the area.

When Cheever opened the door, he saw that Blake had his acoustic guitar out and was playing a rough riff, singing lowly. He finished up and set the instrument aside and looked at Kell.

"I was thinking that, with a soft percussion, cymbal swishing, and a counter-melody—something real delicate. Think you can do that?"

Kell gnawed his lip. "You may want to ask Mackey to do the counter-melody. You know he's got a softer touch."

Blake grimaced. "Yeah, maybe we should save that one—"

"We could put that one on the next Outbreak Monkey album," Stevie said, his enthusiasm breaking up the painful realization that Mackey probably wouldn't be able to hold a guitar for another month.

"I like that," Trav said decisively. "Put at least one of Blake's songs on the main album. It'll give this one some press, make Blake a bigger attraction for the band. You guys got any objection?" Trav's eyebrows went up. "Or, you know, any of your *own* songs to add?"

Stevie shook his head, but Jefferson looked down at his feet, and Kell sort of shrugged.

Cheever let out a snort, because, oh my God, apparently he wasn't the only one who had trouble growing up. Everybody turned their head at the sound.

"Cheever?" Trav was obviously surprised.

"Mackey fell asleep—I told Briony," he reported, and then, on impulse, he moved to stand next to Blake. "It's getting late, you know. I was hoping Blake and I could go on our date."

Jefferson, Stevie, and Trav all widened their eyes in surprise.

Blake blushed and studied his ankle boots.

Kell squinted at them.

"Date? I thought you two were going to buy shoes?"

Cheever gave Blake a droll look and gently grabbed his hand. "That was part of it," he said. Blake looked at him in resignation as Cheever pulled Blake's battered knuckles to his lips and kissed them softly.

The resignation disappeared, replaced by such terrible need.

Cheever leaned sideways over him and took his mouth in a brief kiss. "We'll have to see where the rest of it leads," he said, watching as Blake closed his eyes, as if he was savoring the moment.

"Well, peachy," Kell snapped. "Dammit, why didn't anybody—"

"I just did," Cheever said. "It was… was my job to tell you. Because Blake's been super responsible and super 'We shouldn't do this because blah blah blah age and blah blah blah Kell and blah blah blah recovery.' And I've been the one who pushed. So I had to be the one to tell you."

"Blah blah blah?" Blake asked, amusement twisting his lean mouth, and Cheever rubbed a thumb over his lower lip.

"How'm I gonna take care of you when you keep going on about why this is a bad idea?"

"I thought that was my job?" he asked.

Maybe a month ago, Cheever wouldn't have seen the darkness in his eyes for what it was.

But now he saw hurt and knew he was right.

"You need someone who can care for you," Cheever said with dignity. He looked back at his brothers. "You guys think?"

"Righteous," Jefferson said.

"Everyone needs someone." Stevie's smile, so insidious at the best of times, crept up to being diabolical. "Or several someones." He and Jeff did the fist bump of polyamory and turned to Kell.

Kell was pinching the bridge of his nose. "I hate being the last to know," he said simply. "But I appreciate you telling me." He stood and set his guitar on a nearby stand. "Guys, I'm gonna go take my butt-hurt self to the house so I can whine on my wife about this." He grimaced. "Does she know?"

"Oh God, yes," Blake said with such passion Cheever had to wonder what had been said.

"Well, marrying someone smarter than you are is a curse and a blessing." He graced the twins with an evil smile of his own. "Isn't that right, guys?"

"I know you're trying to start something," Jefferson said laconically, "but we both know you're talking about Shelia, so consider it finished." He and Stevie went in for the fist bump again, and then they stood, so fluidly, so close together, Cheever was forced to wonder whether the three of them didn't take turns being in the middle of the sandwich.

Stevie caught him staring and winked. "Whatever you're thinking, little man, add whips and chains and handcuffs, then double it."

Jefferson rolled his eyes. "He's messing with you. But yes."

They walked out together, laughing at their own private joke, and Trav and Kell shook their heads at each other. "Yes," Trav said, like it was a long-standing argument. "Yes, the boys *do* sleep together when they all sleep together."

"I don't think so," Kell retorted. "Because they would have said something. I mean…." He flailed. "Mackey and you been together, what? Nine years? I'm obviously not gonna lose my shit!"

"Yeah," Blake said, pushing himself up from the couch with an effort. "But it's so much fun to watch the rest of us try to figure it out."

"Oh my God. That is a hell of a long time not to kiss someone in public if you love them like that," Kell muttered. "We know they all sleep in the same bed! Nobody cares which one's the father of which kid! Who cares if they kiss? Are they looking for some sort of award? 'Cause I'll give it to them myself if we can just stop talking about this six times a year!"

Cheever claimed Blake's hand again, and to his relief, Blake laced their fingers together. "Really?" Cheever asked, fascinated. "You guys... I mean, this happens a lot?"

Kell gave a snort of disgust. "It's the dumbest fuckin' thing. The only one who isn't curious is Mackey."

"And Briony," Blake added. "Because I think the women tell each other *every*thing." For no apparent reason, his ears turned red.

Kell stared at him. "Explain that."

"Nope." Blake shook his head vehemently. "Nope, nope, nope. Just... you know, ask Briony."

Kell chuckled, his earlier irritation apparently dimmed. "Cheever, we're getting up at fuck-all in the morning, per usual. Don't break our second guitarist. We like him."

"I'll be gentle," Cheever said virtuously. And then, more soberly, he added, "Thanks for trusting me with him."

"You're grown," Kell said mildly. "Make sure your shoes fit good. Blake can show you how to put that moleskin stuff on so you won't get blisters."

And with that odd but sound advice, Kell and Trav turned and left, leaving Blake and Cheever together in the empty living room.

"Why'd you do that?" Blake asked.

"'Cause I meant what I said. It's my job." Cheever moved into Blake's space and cupped his cheeks. "Now kiss me, and then feed me. Apparently dinner, a movie, and shoes are going to determine the progress of my whole life."

Blake closed his eyes and kissed him, and as Cheever's eyes fluttered closed, he thought that maybe it wouldn't be the dinner, the movie, or the shoes.

Maybe the whole course of his life would be determined by this kiss.

BLAKE KNEW the town.

Shoe shopping went quickly, Blake telling the sales girl what terrain they'd be on, asking Cheever where his tender spots were, and then grabbing some socks that he said saved the guys a lot of blisters. Guilelessly, Cheever told him to grab some running clothes and special underwear while he was getting stuff, because bringing a backpack next door would have been too obvious. But Cheever had hopes for how this night would end—he just didn't want to scare Blake.

Blake had prepurchased tickets at the Regal Cinemas with 4DX—their seats buzzed; the theater had wind and scent effects *and* 3D—and Cheever had never enjoyed watching shit blow up over a field of flowers quite so much. They had reservations at a Korean barbecue place, where you cooked your own meat, and Blake knew the sides to order. He warned Cheever away from the kimchee because he said they made it authentic there and redneck white boys weren't smart enough to like it.

The meal took a long time because they had to cook their own stuff. They had time to talk, gentle-like, and if the conversation lulled, there was always, "Wait, do we cook the calamari or do we eat it raw?" which could occupy them until Cheever started to talk about the market for artists who could sketch for science books. Then they'd be on a roll again.

Toward the end of the meal, as they finished their sodas and waited for their chapssaal doughnuts, the kind filled with red bean paste, Blake looked down at his fingers as he toyed with his napkin.

"This was fun," he said softly. "This, being outside of the hospital. You're a fun date, Cheever. I could do this again."

"Me too." Cheever gave him a measuring look. "Do you do this a lot with people?"

Blake bit his lip and looked away, hiding a shy smile. "Not so much," he said. "Not after the rock-star thing."

"So maybe we could do it again," Cheever said, pleased. "That would make you and me sort of special."

"You think you're not special?" Blake turned his head and caught Cheever's eye, that shy smile on his lips Cheever's undoing.

"You think you're not?" Cheever asked, suddenly shy too.

Blake shook his head. "Lucky," he corrected. "You're special, Cheever boy. I'm lucky."

Cheever laughed softly. "Would you like to get lucky?" he asked, because *God*, his skin tingled from wanting Blake's touch.

For a moment, Blake's eyes got really big, and he worried his lip again with his teeth. Cheever could see a big red flag of *hell yes!* waving behind his eyes.

But then he closed those hazel eyes, the ones that seemed to glow for Cheever alone, and shook his head, his shy smile fading. "Not tonight, baby boy."

Ah, the "baby boy"—the words Blake used to remind himself that he was the grown-up when he was feeling vulnerable. Cheever wasn't buying it.

The waiter arrived with their doughnuts, and Blake picked up his fork. "Let's eat our dessert and go home."

But his cheeks were flushed, and he had trouble meeting Cheever's eyes for the rest of the conversation.

BLAKE HAD driven one of Kell's *many* cars on the date—this one a brand-new red Mustang Fastback that Cheever loved a lot.

"Yeah, it's okay," Blake judged, shifting smoothly as he took the 405 back into the hills. "I just wish he wouldn't buy shit in candy-apple red. Man, I'm going like five miles over the speed limit, maybe, and every cop for miles is sporting a chubby just because they know there's a red car going fast somewhere. I mean, in Lancaster, all you had to have was a red primer spot on your car and some asshole would pull you over for driving while white trash and ticket you." He shook his head. "The night I ran away from home, I took my mother's Toyota. It was made of primer spots. I swear to fuck, I went exactly one mile below the speed limit until I cleared the grapevine."

Cheever's breath caught.

"Did she report it stolen?" he asked.

"She woulda, but I left it at the bus station in Burbank and called her from a phone booth before I took a bus to Santa Monica Pier. Man, I had a plan to be a street musician and someone was gonna fuckin' discover me."

"Who discovered you?" Cheever asked, hearing the bitterness under the self-deprecation.

"My first trick," Blake said grimly. "But that was three days later, when my hands were shaking from hunger. It went all right. At least it was a choice."

Cheever reached across the console and touched his thigh gently, not wanting to shake his concentration on the road.

"Choice is important," he said. "I'd be a big choice for you, wouldn't I?"

"A scary one," Blake admitted. He captured Cheever's hand for a brief moment and squeezed. "It's all right. I can make that choice if you can."

I've made it. I'm in love with you.

"I can," Cheever replied mildly and then rolled down his window and let the wind blow away words for a while.

Blake parked in the big garage at the main house, which seemed overloaded with cars. "Your brother's got a passion for 'em," he admitted, after jockeying into exactly the right spot. "He'll buy old ones and fix 'em up and sell 'em to the Hollywood hotlist who want a car worked on by a rock star. But he likes new and hot for himself, and ones built like a fuckin' tank for Briony and the kids."

"I didn't know that," Cheever said, humbled. "Why'd he start doing that?"

Blake shrugged, killing the engine and the lights. "Trav sort of encouraged all of us to get a pursuit—something outside of the band. Kell picked cars, Jefferson and Stevie run kids' charities on the side, Mackey has a program gathering music equipment from spoiled rich people and donating it to schools."

"What do you do?"

Blake tilted his head back. "Book drives. We read on the bus almost constantly—everything we can find, since we all did school online. You know, my school had a shitty library. If I'd had somewhere, anywhere to escape to, I might have stayed home for a little while longer and figured out how to get a job before I started turning tricks on the pier, you know?"

"You're such a good man," Cheever said, his throat tight. All his brothers were. How could he not have known?

Blake gave him a sweet smile in the heated darkness of the garage. "I'll be a better one after I walk you to the door," he said, and then he got out. Cheever followed him, pausing to grab his bag of purchases. He was curious about how Blake thought he was going to just leave Cheever on the doorstep.

He stood waiting just outside the kitchen, smiling a little. "There's a button behind the door that'll shut the garage door. Wait till I'm out, okay?"

Cheever nodded. "I don't even get a kiss?" he teased.

"Oh, baby boy, I been waiting all night to give you a kiss."

Mmm. Cheever should have been used to Blake's kisses by now. Had it only been four weeks since their first one? That one had been instinctual, desperate, colored by sadness and shame.

This one was so much better—glorious, a seduction, Blake rubbing his mouth softly, sliding his hands down Cheever's sides, under his waistband, cupping his behind through his underwear. Cheever moaned deliciously, bucking up against Blake's hip. His own hands were wandering, none-too-subtly, and he shoved them under Blake's shirt and found his little male nipples surrounded by short strands of silky hair.

He squeezed gently at first, and then a little harder. Blake's hands on his backside got more aggressive, frantic, so Cheever gave a short, sharp pinch on each nipple.

Blake pulled away from him and moaned against his neck. "Okay," he panted. "Good night kiss achieved. Don't forget to hit that button and lock the garage."

He disengaged so fast, Cheever might have wondered if he'd grown a second head if he hadn't recognized the retreat for what it was.

Fear.

Fear of taking Cheever before Cheever knew his own heart. Fear of falling in too deep with Cheever and being brushed aside. What was it he'd said? A stepladder lover. God, Blake's whole life, he'd been an afterthought. Until he'd joined the band and Cheever's brothers had found him and inflicted their own wounds, completely by accident. Because Blake wasn't, and could never be, Grant Adams.

Cheever didn't give a shit about Grant Adams. All he'd ever want was Blake.

Cheever watched Blake hustling past the garage door. He glanced behind him and Cheever waved, then pretended like he was grabbing his stuff and going inside. Instead, he waited a few minutes, until Blake was crossing the yard to the other driveway. God, these houses were big, and the plots were big too, so Cheever waited. One, two, three….

He reached inside and hit the button that closed the door before grabbing his gear and hustling out. He ducked as the door came steadily down, getting out just in time to see Blake's front door close.

He knocked this time, and waited.

Blake looked confused when he opened the door—but not dismayed.

Cheever met his eyes in the light from the porch. "No," he said, reaching up to cup Blake's cheek.

"No, what?"

"No, that wasn't enough of a good-night kiss. Kiss me in the morning and ask me then."

With that, he hauled Blake's mouth on top of his own and shoved them both inside the house.

Wild Horses

BLAKE'S MIND shut down the minute he saw Cheever, looking determined and adult and so ready to take charge.

The kiss melted what little resistance was left rattling around in his skull.

Cheever's taste, his enthusiasm—God, his need—sent Blake reeling back into the house, and Cheever just kept kissing him. He dropped his bag of stuff just inside the door, and suddenly the little shit was made of hands. Blake's T-shirt, a new one, special for that night, got dragged over his head and dropped in the living room. His cargo shorts were pushed down his hips as they hit the stairs, and since he'd had just enough time to kick off his boots before the knock at the door, they stayed there as Cheever kept kissing, kept touching, and Blake just let him, allowing him access to his body, to his skin, to his soul, because he couldn't imagine anybody else as qualified for the job.

He fell back against the stairs midway up and sat down hard, but Cheever didn't slow down. Blake's ears, his chin, his neck—Cheever nibbled and bit, suckled and laved them all, as Blake panted, trying to keep up with every sensation as it fired across his nerve endings. Using the stairs as leverage, Cheever leaned down and took Blake's nipple into his mouth, suckling hard, and Blake cried out, suddenly so close to coming, it was embarrassing.

"Cheever! Not here!" Cheever pulled back, and Blake managed to find some dignity. "Please, baby boy. Let me at least give you a bed."

Cheever straightened and offered him a hand, which he took. But when he'd stood, Cheever came up even with him and spanned his midsection with his long-fingered artist's hands. "A bed is fine," he whispered, teasing his lips along Blake's jaw. "No more running, Blake. This'll be us, you understand?"

Blake nodded, because he had no choice. "Yeah."

"I mean it. I may make mistakes, say the wrong thing, but I'm not ever gonna willingly throw you away. You have to have some faith in me, in us. We're gonna make love and it's gonna be okay."

Blake closed his eyes, his heart pounding in his chest almost as hard as his cock was throbbing in his undershorts. "Okay," he whispered. "Okay. You got any ideas about the making love part? I… I got experience, but it seems like you got a vision."

"I want to touch all of you," Cheever whispered back. "And you can do the same to me. Let's see where that goes."

Blake swallowed, his throat almost too tight. "Cheever—"

His fingertips on Blake's face were a comfort. "I promise, Blake. I won't let you down."

"You could never let me down." This kid—this man—had only done his best. It was all Blake had ever wanted, someone who cared for him. "You don't have it in you to hurt me." Even when he moved on and flew away.

Cheever kissed him again, and then gave a gentle shove. "I don't even know where your bedroom is."

Blake turned and grabbed his hand, leaving the clothes where they'd fallen. He pulled Cheever past what looked to be two suites, one on either side of the hallway, complete with bathrooms and sitting rooms, and to a back room, a little smaller, but with the lights on. Cheever could see the rumpled bedclothes in burgundy and gold, and posters of rock legends on the walls.

Freddy Mercury and his cats, Bruce Springsteen and his children, Kurt Cobain holding Frances Bean, David Bowie with Iman and their son—Blake looked at the posters and saw them through Cheever's eyes and felt naked. Would he notice the theme of rock stars and their families, in the room of the only single member of the band?

But Cheever had eyes only for Blake. "You look worried."

With you? Always. But he responded with a kiss and allowed Cheever's response to wash away the worry, the anxiety of being seen for who he was, of being left for who he wasn't.

Cheever's hands at his hips burned with intensity, and moved with an assurance Blake couldn't imagine feeling at twenty-two with his first lover. Blake started to unbutton Cheever's skinny jeans with fingers that trembled, and Cheever covered his hands, soothing his knuckles with gentle thumbs.

"Easy."

Blake slowed down and took the fly button by button, then pushed down and helped Cheever out of his jeans and boxers with one fluid movement. They paused for a moment—Blake because he wanted to look, Cheever because he wanted to be seen.

"You like?" Cheever asked, a hint of smugness in the corners of his mouth. His body, long and pale, slender like a reed, had a dusting of cinnamon hair at his happy trail and a thicket of it at his unexpectedly large cock. His chest was almost completely hairless and his stomach concave, the skin soft to look at.

Blake reached out, his fingers shaking again.

Softer to touch.

And he couldn't stop touching. Up, down, drinking in the softness, the flutter of Cheever's breath as he moved toward his chest.

His chest was narrow, with light definition—slender, no fat, a little muscle. Blake took a step closer to feel his heat, and kept exploring. At Cheever's clavicle, prominent, delicate, Blake had to lower his head and nibble. Cheever let out a hiss of breath and skated his fingertips along Blake's shoulders and down the sides of his back. Blake drew his lips up, along Cheever's throat, pausing to nuzzle right behind his jaw, to nibble his earlobe, to breathe softly in the whorl of his ear.

He lowered one hand to Cheever's hip bone and was surprised when Cheever took it and wrapped it securely around his cock.

"In a hurry?" Blake asked, stroking that amazing erection. Thick and fat, long and curved upward, Blake had to marvel at it, how he was the first to touch it who knew what a treasure he had in the man behind it.

"You're stalling," Cheever sang breathlessly. "Had we but worlds enough and time…." He reached out with his other hand and pinched Blake's nipple assertively, hard enough to make Blake's knees wobble.

"Nungh!" Blake's grip on Cheever's erection tightened, and he stroked boldly. Apparently, Cheever had waited long enough to have caring hands touching him. Blake dropped his head to Cheever's own nipple and suckled on it, grazing with a hint of teeth.

"That's it," Cheever crooned. "Ah, God, yeah, the other one!"

Blake moved to that one, nibbling some more, still stroking, and a spurt of precome drenched his fist. Blake pulled away and raised his hand to Cheever's lips, wondering how bold Cheever was feeling.

Cheever pulled Blake's fingers into his mouth, sucking off his precome, then getting them wet, plying his tongue, making Blake shiver.

He released Blake's fingers with a pop and whispered, "Lie on the bed. Stretch yourself. I want to explore you before I come."

"We don't have to—" Blake had the speech prepared. Penetration didn't equal sex. They could pleasure each other without the butt thing. Blake had enjoyed it before, but Cheever might not be all that excited.

Cheever thrust Blake's fingers into his own mouth, and Blake shuddered.

"I...." Cheever leaned forward and nibbled on Blake's earlobe. "Want...." He trailed his lips down to Blake's clavicle. "To...." Lower, to suckle on Blake's nipple again. "Pleasure...." He moved lower, lower, until he was on his knees in front of Blake, pulling down his boxer-briefs, his breath dusting the wet head of Blake's cock. "You."

He stuck out his tongue and licked, and Blake's knees gave another wobble, and he pulled his fingers out of his mouth to massage Cheever's scalp through his hair. "C'mere...." He breathed. "Baby, there's a bed. Let me... let me...."

Cheever reached behind him, cupped his naked thighs, and walked him back until he felt the bed and sat down.

And then proceeded to treat Blake's body like his own personal amusement park. He started by licking Blake's cockhead, playing with the bell, the ridge, squeezing the shaft, and Blake sat up, fingers tangled in that long curly hair, trying to remember his own damned name.

"Oh... God, Cheever. I'm gonna come—maybe, you know, let me—"

Cheever looked up and stuck his tongue out, licking Blake's cockhead before sucking the precome off his tongue. "If you come," he murmured, "are you going to just roll over and go to sleep?"

"No! I'd take care of you, Cheever—I wouldn't leave you hang—nungh! Gah!"

Cheever sucked him to the back of his throat. Not all the way, but he was smart, using his fist to squeeze the bottom while his mouth did all the mouth things—lips, tongue, suction, pressure—that made Blake's balls swell and his nipples tingle and his ass clench and....

"Oh God, Cheever! You're good at this!"

"Been dreaming," Cheever confessed, sticking out his tongue and licking Blake from base to tip. "You been dreaming about me?"

"No...," Blake lied. "It'd be too hard if I didn't get you—augh! *Cheever!*" He took Blake even farther this time, until his fist didn't fit around the base, and he used that hand to tug gently on Blake's sac.

Oh God.... Oh God.... Blake fell back on the bed, and he drew his feet up and bent his knees so he could arch his hips. Cheever followed him, shoving gently at his thighs and fondling his balls some more, until Blake could feel the sap boiling in the pit of them.

"Please!" he begged. "Oh! Oh my God!"

Cheever let some spit trickle between his cheeks, and while he still had Blake's cock in his mouth, he parted them. One finger, long and delicate, spread the spit across his taint, and Blake whimpered.

Cheever sucked harder in response, and Blake almost felt like laughing. *He* was going to teach *Cheever* about sex?

And then Cheever's finger grew bolder, tapping at his entrance, and Blake arched his hips and tried not to thrash.

Cheever pulled back from his cock—but kept thrusting with that one finger. "Play with your nipples," he said, in the same voice Blake used to direct musicians to play a different chord in a song. "I think that'll get you there."

Then Blake *did* laugh, but he moved his fingers to his bare chest and pinched, just as Cheever drove his finger in deeper and sucked his cock back in again—

And Blake's world exploded.

Everything. Oh damn, *everything*. Light changed to dark and dark rearranged itself into objects and shadows became true things.

Cheever became a true thing. A real possibility. Someone who could be in his life for more than just an affair, or a few kisses, or long enough to unbalance the family Blake had worked so hard for.

Blake blew everything out his cock—come, his safety, his peace of mind.

Cheever's mouth worked him, not expertly, but like someone who'd been ready for it, who had mentally prepared himself. Blake stroked his cheek with one hand and threw the other over his eyes, trying to hide his helplessness, his complete submission to what this man had just done to him.

Cheever moved, letting go of Blake's cock, pulling away from his private parts altogether and pushing himself on the bed.

"How was that?" he asked, and Blake made himself look Cheever in the eyes. He sounded so proud.

"That was real good." He wanted to smile at the glaze around Cheever's mouth, the utter debauched look of his messy hair and his swollen lips, but even his voice was broken.

"Hey, what's the matter? You... Blake?" It wasn't until Cheever wiped the dampness trickling down his temple with his thumb that Blake realized moisture had slipped through.

"It was... just intense," Blake whispered, undone. He was defenseless, more than naked.

"Blake... Blake, look at me. Did I do something wrong?"

Blake shook his head. "You did it exactly right." He managed a smile. "Just exactly right. Just... when it's really good like that, I guess, you're afraid. You're just...."

"Vulnerable," Cheever said, kissing his temple, tasting the tears. "You're vulnerable."

"Yeah." Blake squeezed his eyes shut, and Cheever kissed him. In the dark, there was just the taste of his own spend in Cheever's mouth, Cheever's hands roaming his body again.

There were scars, Blake knew where. Fights, sports. His knees were a chaos of skin abrasions from riding skateboards, even into his twenties. His collarbone had been broken when he was a kid—one of his mother's boyfriends had gotten rough—and the bump was still there. A car wreck when he was fourteen had created scars where his wrist had been broken and needed to be reset. Cheever's whole body had been pale skin and freckles, the only scar the still recent one on his wrist. Blake's body told a different story, and Blake couldn't even hide from it in his mind.

But Cheever kept touching him, mapping his scars, his imperfections, kissing him, grinding against him. He positioned himself between Blake's thighs and slid their cocks together, his swollen and dripping pre, Blake's getting thick again, waking up from the terrible emotional upheaval Blake couldn't quite put behind him.

Blake reached down between them and gripped them both, giving Cheever some friction to grind against, and Cheever moaned gratefully. "It's good," he said, "but I want more."

Blake knew what he wanted—didn't have the defenses to tell him they didn't have to. He reached behind him, under his pillow, and pulled out his lubricant.

"I'm negative," he panted. "I know you are." Cheever had been tested twice in the hospital. Blake had been there when he'd gotten the second round of results. "Here—you know what goes where."

Cheever chuckled, the sound vibrating where their groins rested together, and Blake felt the first spurt of slickness, cool and sweet, drip on him as Cheever greased his own erection. For a heady moment, he gripped them both together like Blake had, squeezing and stroking until Blake was hard again, shaking with need all over again, stripped bare of pretense, nothing left but wanting.

"Let me in," Cheever whispered.

Blake had no choice. He spread his thighs and lifted his hips up, almost sighing in relief when Cheever fit himself in place and thrust forward.

Blake pushed out—he knew how to bottom, how to accept, how to take someone's flesh into his body. But with every inch Cheever slid in, he felt less and less of himself, his worry, his pain. Cheever left no room for anything but Cheever, and when he'd finally thrust all the way in, Blake was floating, happy with the stretch, the ache, thrilled with the pressure, his entire body tingling, waiting for Cheever to make his move.

"You okay?" Cheever asked, brushing his cheeks with careful lips.

"Perfect," Blake breathed. "You good?"

Cheever gave a little thrust. "I gotta move," he groaned. "Please tell me I can move."

"Yeah, fuck me. However you want. I'm yours."

"Oh, thank God."

Hard. Cheever pulled back and thrust forward *hard*, and Blake's floaty goodwill was replaced with *oh my God, wow!* Blake cried out, lifting his hips and holding his thighs spread, a blatant invitation to be plundered, which Cheever took him up on.

"C'mon, baby, more," Blake heard himself begging, and Cheever gave it to him. Hard. Fast. Deep. Total possession. With no hesitation, no half measures, Cheever took Blake's body and reshaped it, made it his from the inside out.

Oh wow. Oh damn, oh hell, oh shit. "Oh *fuck*!" Blake screamed as Cheever hit his sweet spot, again and again, until the fireworks behind Blake's eyes were bloodred and his dripping cock splatted on his abdomen with every thrust.

"I need," Cheever mewled plaintively. "I... help me! I need... I need, oh please...."

Blake squeezed as tight as he could, and Cheever groaned again. "More, Blake—*yes*!"

And that. The vulnerability. Cheever needed it, like Blake did. Blake could do this for him. He just had to... had to.... He grabbed his cock and stroked, his fist blurring, the sound of fapping and fucking filling the air.

This orgasm ripped him inside out, with Cheever buried in his ass and coming with him in a scalding rush.

Blake heard the sound he made, and it was barely human. But Cheever's groan, his shout of release, that was all Cheever, and it gave Blake a tether so he could pull himself back to his own body when he threatened to float away.

"*Gawd*...." Cheever collapsed on top of him, sweaty, as coated in Blake's spend as Blake was, still twitching. Blake wrapped his arms and legs around that slender, lovely body and clung tightly, another wave of emotion washing over him that he was helpless to control.

"Hey," Cheever whispered, as Blake squeezed his eyes shut tight. "Hey. I'm here. Look what we did! Wasn't that amazing?"

"Yeah," Blake told him, needing him not to be afraid, needing him not to regret. "It was so good. I... I...."

More kisses peppered his face. "Then what's wrong?"

"So lost," Blake whispered. "I was so lost. And everything I needed was right here."

"Yeah, I know." Cheever pushed his hair back from his face. "I'm as surprised as you are. It's pretty awesome, right?"

Blake closed his eyes and nodded, comforted by Cheever's weight, by his joy, by his words. But not comforted, not even a little, by the way his heart settled from chaos to joy with Cheever's body wedged completely inside his.

This boy was going to leave him. He was young and bright and so full of promise, and Blake was nobody's first choice. Cheever would leave him, and Blake would be lost all over again.

And this time, he'd never find his way home.

CHEEVER WASN'T a cleaner, and Blake was grateful. He'd had lovers whose first act was to go wipe all traces of sex off of and out of their bodies, and Blake had always felt a little slighted. Cheever slid to the side, and Blake moaned as he pulled out. Blake's ass felt stretched and used, and the rest of his body was loose, connected to his consciousness in the most tenuous of ways. When Cheever spooned him, stroking his chest, his stomach, nuzzling his neck, Blake melted into him, ignoring the mess and the sweat.

The shelter of Cheever's shoulders was the best home he could ever wish for.

"That was *tremendous*," Cheever murmured. "Is it always like that?"

"No." Blake dragged his floating brain for words. "Not for me. It's... sometimes it's more practical than that."

Cheever's voice seemed to have deepened, and he emitted a low and earthy chuckle. "Practical sex?"

"It's a need," Blake said with scant dignity.

"Hence the lubricant under the pillow?" Cheever mocked, and Blake buried his face against Cheever's arm.

"Better my own hand than someone I don't care about," he said.

"Even better." Cheever kissed the back of his neck again, and Blake shivered.

"You are going to get me started all over again," he cautioned.

"Good. I've waited my whole life for a night like this one. Don't want it to end so soon."

Blake could feel him, hardening against Blake's backside, and almost unconsciously he thrust back to see if Cheever meant it. Cheever ground against him, their bodies rocking gently, without urgency, but building.

Cheever draped his leg over Blake's hip in a proprietary way, and kept rocking. "How about you? You all done with me?"

"No," Blake whispered. "Not even close." Never. This kid—this man—was a part of Blake's topography now. If he ever had another lover, when they were looking for scars, they'd find Cheever written large across his heart.

"Good...." Cheever took advantage of Blake's entrance, dilated, sloppy, still slick, and thrust in again, and Blake rode him, rode the crest of the wave, clutching Cheever's hand to his chest, his body caught in the surf of another climax, crashing to earth with Cheever's low grown and a slow, painful orgasm that pretty much wrung him dry.

Blake slept a little after that, falling asleep with Cheever still inside him. He woke up when Cheever rolled out of bed, and flailed a little. "Going?" he asked fuzzily.

"No. Turning off the hall light and going to the bathroom."

"Oh." Blake closed his eyes again, and a moment later, he felt Cheever's warmth behind him and the nubbly invasion of a washcloth that usually signaled the end of sex.

"Did you want me to go?" Cheever asked.

"No." Self-protection was useless now. Artificial boundaries like, "Is it too soon to stay the night?" had been annihilated with Cheever's spectacular entrance, barreling through Blake's door and into his bed with single-minded purpose.

"Good." Cheever held him tighter, and Blake took the hand lying on top of his chest and kissed the fingertips.

Then he saw the scars on Cheever's wrist, pink and straight and still new.

"Oh my God," he said in wonder. "I almost lost you. I almost lost you before I even knew who you were."

And it was like the quiet *after* the storm. Because before he knew it was even coming, sobs wracked his body, and Cheever turned him into his chest and was whispering words of comfort in his hair.

THE HANGOVER he woke up with the next morning was so epic, it put some of his worst drug benders to shame. Someone was pounding on his front door, and then clattering across the hallway downstairs.

"Blake! Blake! Are you okay? Did your laundry basket explode? Jesus, dude! Get out here and tell us what to do with your fish!"

Blake shot upright in bed and then clapped his hand across his eyes. "Sunlight!" he croaked. His mouth tasted cummy. He wiped his face and felt the residue, remembered waking up again, late at night, voracious for the taste of Cheever's skin. He'd licked his chest, sucked his nipples, and when Cheever had tangled his fingers in Blake's hair, pushing gently, Blake had gone down, starving for the final taste of him.

His jaw still ached from Cheever's cock stretching his mouth, and Blake hadn't been able to swallow all of it, he'd been so overwhelmed.

He'd fallen asleep again, his face against Cheever's abdomen, barely conscious of Cheever pulling him up until their heads rested next to each other on the pillows.

"Oh shit. Ouch! Why is there sun?" And now it felt like twin white-hot spears were trying to ice-pick his brain.

"Oh, baby." Cheever stroked his back gently. "You got a crying headache. Those suck."

"Your brothers are here," Blake muttered, not sure about the sympathy and peeling himself off the sheets.

The despoiled sheets.

Blake was covered in *Cheever Sanders's come*, and his *brothers* were on their way up the stairs.

"Oh my fuckin' God, your brothers are here, and they're bringing fish!"

He ran naked to the door and stuck his head out. "Be down in a second!" he called. "Stay there. Right there. Don't come up." He slammed the door and winced. "Jesus God, my head hurts. And I'm naked. Shit! Pants!"

He looked around wildly for the shorts he'd been wearing the night before and then gave it up, grabbing clean underwear from the drawer to pull over his sticky body and a pair of sleep pants from the drawer next to it.

"Blake?" Cheever sounded remarkably calm.

"Your brothers are here!" But they could both hear the clatter up the stairs that meant Kell and the boys didn't mind any better than Mackey or Cheever.

"I'm not jumping out the window, sweetheart," Cheever said kindly. "We're adults, and if they didn't know this was coming—"

The door swung open.

"They weren't paying attention," he finished with a roll of his eyes. "Morning, Kell."

"You left Blake's clothes all over the front room, little brother."

"Fish," Blake mumbled. "I'm so sorry—I forgot to set my phone."

Kell held up Blake's cargo shorts, which were emitting a very pleasant vibrating tone. "Not sure forgot is the right word."

"Sorry. Oh God. I'm sorry." He looked over his shoulder at Cheever, who slid out of bed holding the sheet to his hips before the ringing of the phone pierced his skull worse than the light. "Augh! Make it stop!"

"Hey, what's the matter?" Kell squinted at him in concern and handed him his pants. Blake scrambled to make the noise stop and almost cried with relief when he hit the button.

"Kell, could you give us a minute?"

"Cheever, he looks awful. You didn't make him drink last night, did you?"

"No!" Blake snapped, then winced. *God. Painkillers. Now.*

"No," Cheever said softly, not defensive at all. "Kell, I wouldn't do that."

Kell held his hand to Blake's forehead and grimaced. "Cold. He's dehydrated. Shit. This happens sometimes after concerts with him. He doesn't drink enough water, does too much, and sleeps too little. It fucking levels him. Get him some water and some painkillers and don't let him outside today—it's going to be a scorcher."

Blake's stomach turned, and he thought about how he hadn't eaten the day before until dinner. Great.

"Okay, Dad," he said weakly. "Lemme shower first—"

"Oh my God, please do," Kell said, and he patted Blake's cheek gently. "You ain't smelled this bad since Houston."

Blake let out a strangled laugh. He and Kell, back in their cocaine days, had done a lot of fucking together in the same room. A couple of times, they'd even banged the same girls, and Houston—well, Houston had been the two of them and a king-sized bed and three women older than they were. They were too hung up to so much as look at each other naked, but when the girls had left, well, the two of them had needed a shower in the worst way.

"My head hurts worse today," he confessed weakly, and Kell winked.

"That's 'cause you're not medicating it with Jack already. Go, be a grown-up and take care of yourself." Then he looked up at Cheever. "You and me need to talk—"

"Let me take care of Blake first," Cheever said firmly.

Kell shrugged. "You have until the twins get up here with the tank." He held up a bag of bewildered fish, which he set inside the door. "We were gonna run the hose up the house through the window. No fuckin' till we're done."

Blake had turned toward the bathroom and was leaning on the wall to steady himself. "No fuckin' till I can stand," he corrected.

"Fair enough." Cheever followed him into the bathroom then and closed the door behind them.

Blake was rooting through the cupboards and finding nothing. "Goddammit, I think the ibuprofen is downstairs." He leaned his aching head against the mirror, not even wanting to see his own face after last night. Razor burn and love bites showed up on his skin in the worst ways. Behind him, he felt Cheever's warmth, and he watched, almost detached, as Cheever reached around him to fill the cup on the counter with water that he held up for Blake to take.

"Dehydration?" he asked, resting his chin on Blake's shoulder.

"Haven't eaten much in the last few days," Blake mumbled, taking a grateful sip. "Been fretting."

"About me?"

Blake finished off the water and turned in his arms, meaning to reassure him, but finding Cheever pushing Blake's head onto Cheever's shoulder instead.

It felt like he was supposed to be there.

"You feel wonderful," he said wistfully.

"Don't worry about me," Cheever said, touching his face with rough fingers. "I wouldn't trade last night for… for all the talent or money or lovers in the world, okay? I don't want to trade you in for a newer model. Why would I do that? You're everything I need."

"Old," Blake grunted. "Used. Second best."

Maybe if his head hadn't been pounding, his nerves so raw, his body so needy after the night before, he wouldn't have said the words.

Something hot plopped on his bare shoulder. And again. He looked up and saw slow hot tears coursing down Cheever's face.

"Baby—"

Cheever shook his head. "Don't call me baby—not after saying something like that. Don't open your mouth," he said gruffly. "You'll just say more bad shit about yourself. And none of it's true. Now get in the shower. I'll be back with some painkillers and more water."

He didn't move, though. Just squeezed Blake hard, those scalding tears not stopping.

"Cheever—"

"You're smart," Cheever said. "Kind. My first choice. Repeat that to yourself." He pulled away then and used the sheet barely hanging around his waist to wipe his face. "I'm gonna go change our sheets."

He was out the door, and Blake was standing under the pounding showerhead before he realized that Cheever had said "our" sheets, not "your" sheets.

And he smiled.

Jumpin' Jack Flash

"OH, JESUS," Stevie complained, steadying himself after Cheever's accidental bump. "Trav, could you make him stop that? Good fucking God, it's like having Mackey here, but Mackey's usually planning a record when he runs!"

"Sorry, Stevie," Cheever apologized and concentrated fiercely on the sidewalk. The family lived in a very wealthy gated community with its own security. He'd been told that at the beginning, they'd gone running off the property on occasion, but the bigger the band got, the less attractive that idea had been. Now they stuck to one of the many wandering paths that looped around the ginormous lots for the mansions in the settlement.

Very chichi—but also very convenient.

Unless Cheever was bouncing off people like a pinball.

"Cheever, drop back here and run with me!" Marcia complained from the end of the little group. "I'm dying!"

Cheever did what she asked, settling into the back of the pack, and tried not to be bitter. He'd been a little bit excited when Kell asked him to come running with them.

By the time Blake had gotten out of the shower, Cheever had changed the sheets and the guys had started to install the fish tank on a shelf obviously designed for it. They'd settled Blake down with a big glass of orange juice and a bottle of water, then went to work like pros. Stevie, Jefferson, and Kell finished the job, and by the time they'd put the chemicals in the tank and checked it for the right saline levels and shit, Blake was curled up in a little ball, sleeping. Then, and only then, did Cheever have a chance for his post-sex shower.

He'd finished just in time for Jefferson to throw his bag of running gear in his face and tell him to suit up.

He'd been so pleased.

They wanted him with them, even though Blake was out of commission.

And there he was, all that expensive running gear on, his phone tucked into a sleeve on his arm, a special little hat keeping his fair skin from burning, shoes that practically cushioned his feet in angel's jizz, only apparently, he'd forgotten one lousy fucking thing.

He couldn't run.

"Don't worry about it," Kell told him as he dropped back. "Mackey does the same fuckin' thing. Practice going in a straight line. Even Mackey can manage it sometimes."

And with that, Kell passed him completely, and Cheever fell into a semicomfortable rhythm next to Marcia. He sighted a spot on the sidewalk about six feet in front of him, a foot from the edge of the lawn, and told himself he was running right down that line.

Hopefully it would work.

"So," Marcia asked quietly as he found his rhythm, "how'd it go?"

"The date?"

"Yeah, the date! You were so excited! How'd it go?"

Cheever had to smile. "So good it didn't end until this morning," he said smugly, and Marcia giggled a little.

"So Briony said Blake is sick?" Briony had come by in running shorts and a tank top, muttering about getting her run in later after she made sure Blake was okay. She'd left Marcia, because apparently Shelia was with the kids, and she'd been a little irritated because she missed running.

Cheever hauled in the biggest breath he could and tried to grok that statement again.

Nope. Nothing. He couldn't imagine being irritated because he missed running. He might have been thinking about his brothers as his herd, but this was one antelope who preferred yoga and the pool.

"Yeah," he said, doggedly keeping one foot in front of the other. "Dehydration. I guess he's forgotten to eat the last few days."

"What's that like?"

Cheever's stomach gurgled. "I got no idea." Some of his bravado faded. "He woke up with a headache and…." And he'd cried. And called himself old and used and second best. "And he's really afraid of being hurt."

"Isn't everybody?"

Cheever looked up, saw his brothers and Trav but no Mackey and felt the absence. "How broken do you feel?" he asked, thinking about the way Blake had touched his scars and cried.

"Mm… I feel stupid," she said after a moment. "I… I think about heroin every day, and I get a low-grade craving. There were people in rehab who… who would break into an active sweat if you so much as—" She panted for a moment. "—said the word cocaine." For a moment their footfalls sounded abnormally loud. "Short-term addiction. Overdose. I was stupid."

Cheever pondered for a moment.

"Would you do it again?" he asked.

"Not if I'm busy. Not if I feel needed. Not if I'm loved. You?"

Blake's lips on his wrist, the feel of his skin under Cheever's palms, the way he'd turned his head so Cheever wouldn't see the need on his face….

"I've got way too much to live for," Cheever breathed, and looking back at his herd, he felt that double. "But I can't forget." Was that Blake's problem? He was afraid he'd forget, forget what drove him to excess, to drug use. Forget how far he could sink and go there again?

No.

Those things were etched into Blake's consciousness.

Blake was afraid of more basic things.

Afraid his heart would be broken and he wouldn't be able to deal.

Kell never did have a chance to have that talk with him after the fish, but suddenly Cheever knew what he'd been going to say, and why it was necessary.

"Me too," Marcia panted. "Today, we're taking the kids to the zoo. Want to come?"

On one hand, yes. Cheever had enjoyed his night being Uncle Cheever, the artist—that sounded fantastic. On the other hand….

"I'm on Mackey duty when the guys meet about the record again."

"I thought Blake was sick?"

"I don't think you could drag him away from this solo project with a backhoe and a semi," Cheever muttered. It was true—Cheever had been leaving, bending to kiss Blake on the forehead as he slept, when he mumbled, "Set my phone for ten."

"Kell?" Cheever asked, and Kell's mouth twisted.

"We'll check on him to make sure he's okay. If he's up to it, sure, we can talk some more."

Cheever was running back to Blake's house to make sure he could go to work. No one ever talked about the work ethic of a rock star, but they should.

"That's cool," Marcia said. "I mean, you know. More CD's for us, right?"

Cheever thought about it, about how he'd wanted his sketchbook or a notebook for poetry and some quiet that morning, because Blake, asleep, was one of the most vulnerable things he'd seen in his life. He thought about how the band couldn't seem to go a minute without music or rhythm infusing their senses. Even now, Jefferson and Stevie were starting a chorus of Doo-Wah-Diddy to keep everybody on pace.

"I think art is the family drug," he said after a moment.

"Better than heroin," Marcia said, and then both of them took a deep breath and shouted, "Doo-wah-diddy-diddy-dum-diddy-doo!" for all they were worth.

There was no more talking after that. They were lucky they didn't pass out.

CHEEVER FIGURED he and Blake were about the same size. Blake was a little taller, but he slouched, and he was longer in the waist than Cheever, so their jeans should be about the same length.

He didn't even go back to the main house for clothes, like Kell and the guys did.

Instead, he finished his run and ran back to the studio house, relieved to find Blake still sleeping, an empty plate of what had possibly been freezer waffles and fruit on the nightstand.

Go Briony.

Cheever took his time for the second shower of the day, checking for love bites, marks, any sign that he'd spent a glorious night inside and next to Blake Manning.

Besides a faint hickey on his neck—and stomach muscles that felt like he'd been doing crunches—all of the change appeared to come from inside, and he was vaguely disappointed.

He wanted the world to know he and Blake had made love. But at the same time, the things that had gone on in their bed had been unbearably private.

He remembered back when he was a kid, when he'd talked to that blogger about his brother's sexuality, and his face burned in mortification.

Now—*now*—he understood how someone would want those things about themselves to be secret. Not because they were embarrassed or ashamed or anything else, but because these wounds and vows and fears were *personal.*

It was the same reason Cheever wouldn't tell anybody about Blake seeing the scar on his wrist and weeping—that moment was *theirs.*

He came out dressed in the towel and sat down next to Blake on the bed, stroking his bicep as it bulged from his T-shirt, because on any other morning, he'd be still working out.

Blake's right bicep was decorated with a tattoo—Cheever had been so jealous of them, way back when. Mackey had one on his stomach, Jefferson and Stevie had one on opposite shoulders, and Kell had his on his chest. Cheever would place money that Trav had one, but it was somewhere hidden by clothes, and he was pretty sure he'd seen one on the small of Shelia's back. Briony probably had one too.

It was Outbreak Monkey's first album cover—a screaming monkey, shattered glass and all—and Cheever wondered, what? Did they all just decide to go out and mark themselves? "Hey, we're a secret little club and we're gonna show everybody how much we belong!"

"Run over?" Blake mumbled. "Time to get up?"

Cheever stopped tracing the tattoo and leaned forward to kiss his cheek. "Not yet. They were going to meet back at eleven. You still have an hour to sleep if you need it."

"I may," Blake said with dignity. He rolled over on his back and rubbed his arm, like it itched or tickled. "Whatcha looking at?"

"Everybody got one," Cheever said, not even thinking about saying, "Nothing" and sulking. "What made you all decide to get the same tattoo?"

Blake held his hand in front of his mouth as he yawned. "Mm. Mackey and me been outta rehab 'bout a month." He squeezed his eyes shut. "I have got to remember my fuckin' grammar. Anyway. We were out of rehab for about a month, and Trav went on a surprise business trip right before we gave this big benefit. And we were both... both so thrown. We used to do drugs just to cope with situations like that, you know? So Mackey looked up a decent tattoo place—because Kell had some ungodly shit put on his body, and I had a few that I have since removed. Anyway, we took him there, because we were all looking out for each other, and he got the tat, and we liked it…. We just… liked it. I was hurting too, so I got one, and then Kell got one, and Stevie and Jefferson got one, and then Shelia followed."

"Trav and Briony?" Well, he had been curious.

"Yeah. Trav's is on his hip. Briony's is where Shelia's is—the small of her back. She just doesn't wear shit that shows it unless she's at the pool. But it was just the band at first. We… we'd been through so much by then. It was like… you know, a promise we'd stick with it."

Cheever thought about their little running cult, and how they even ran in sync. "That's good," he said, prying away the jealousy, the possession, and flushing it down the crapper along with the part of him that thought going out in a big room full of blow was somehow a great idea. His brothers, his lover—this band was all of them. It was the families growing up close to each other. It was the running cult, and his friend, getting a chance to hang out with a noisy happy family for once.

"It's probably codependent and weird," Blake muttered. "But I'm not letting go."

Cheever laughed. "Scoot over," he ordered softly.

"Why?"

"Because I just want to hold you while you sleep."

"Now *that's* weird. Can't we have sex?"

"No!" Cheever let his towel fall and slid in naked, not embarrassed in the least. "You are under strict instructions to nap until your thing, then spend your day hydrating. I pretty much sexed you out anyway, old man."

Blake snorted and rolled so they were facing each other. His eyes were at half-mast, and Cheever knew if he was any sort of decent boyfriend at all, he'd let his lover sleep.

"You think you sexed me out?"

"I think I drained your balls dry," Cheever taunted, enjoying the way Blake's eyebrows tried to go up when he couldn't actually open his eyes.

"Let me nap now and we'll see whose balls are dry." Blake moaned then and buried his face in Cheever's shoulder. "That so did not come out right."

"No, it did not. But that's okay. I'll be back tonight after your meeting. I'll bring dinner."

"Briony left some stuff in the fridge already. Come after dinner."

"No, idiot. Jesus, you're stubborn. We'll eat dinner and watch TV and be a couple. Then we'll drain your balls again." Cheever chuckled again because ball jokes never grew old.

"We're a couple," Blake said, and although his eyes were closed, his voice sounded very lucid. "So, when the girl puts the microphone in my face and says, 'You seeing anybody, Blake?'"

"You tell 'em you're seeing Cheever Sanders," Cheever whispered. This was Blake's reality. He realized it was about to become his.

"Okay. Okay. Just…." Blake's sigh shook his body. "Don't tell no one the secret stuff, okay? I never told any other lover that stuff. Just… I just trust you 'cause you're Kell's brother."

Cheever stroked his hair back from his face. "Blake, go to sleep. I'll keep you safe. I promise."

Blake's breathing evened out, and Cheever lay there, watching him sleep, thinking that in all the years of living in Outbreak Monkey's shadow, he'd never felt so blessed at what that gave him. It gave him money and resources, his schooling and options.

And it gave him Blake Manning's trust, when it was obvious the only people Blake had trusted in his entire life were Cheever's brothers.

This man needed him—needed Cheever, specifically and particularly.

And Cheever wasn't going to let him down.

"I LEFT him food," Briony said, her voice unfriendly.

"I realize that." Cheever tried a smile, but her puckered, angry face didn't relax one iota.

"I brought an entire bag of groceries to that man's refrigerator. I checked with Trav, and he authorized Rosa's sister, Lily, to start working for us, specifically to take care of things in the studio house, and that includes Blake."

"Well, that is very organized, and I did *not* realize that," Cheever told her, taking a deep breath. Wow. Kell's wife was something extra. "But that is very good of you. Thank you."

"Why are you going through my refrigerator?" Briony asked, none of her unfriendliness going away.

"Because, uh, I wanted to make him dinner tonight. You brought him sandwich fixings, and I was hoping for… I don't know. A thing I could make."

"Do you even know how to cook?" She had a little line between her big brown eyes that was absolutely laser pointed in irritation.

"I can make pasta," he said. "I took a home ec class in college. I can—"

"Look, Cheever. You are starting to sweat, and that pleases me. But Shelia and I keep this refrigerator like the pantry of God. Grant's daughter, Katy? She's allergic to nuts. Shelia's kids? They get sick with milk products. My kids? They have gluten allergies. If you so much as move a container of leftovers from one side of the refrigerator to the other, you could kill somebody."

Cheever shut the refrigerator with a snap. "I'm so sorry."

"I have told Lily that you are fed for tonight. If you want to call in takeout, that's fine. If you want to leave Lily a shopping list, that's fine too. If you want to call the driver to come take you somewhere, you are shit out of luck, mister, because we are going to the zoo in five minutes and he is helping. If you want to borrow someone's car, well, you need to talk to them. Do you know how to drive? Do you know how to drive in LA? Do you even know where your car is?"

"Uh, yes, yes, and no." Cheever thought with a shock that he hadn't asked about his car. "I, uh…. Blake and Trav must have taken care of it."

"Then go upstairs and tend to Mackey. His stuff is in the drawer labeled 'Mackey and Trav' and in the cupboard to your right, also labeled 'Mackey and Trav.' You may have some of his crackers, but you can't eat 'em all. You may even have some of his food, or the food labeled 'Family Leftovers'—that is also acceptable."

"Thank you," he said, seriously dripping sweat down the middle of his back in the air-conditioned kitchen.

"What you can't do," she emphasized, poking him in the chest, "under *any circumstances*, is muck about in this refrigerator without knowing what the fuck you are doing."

Cheever nodded, pale. "Understood."

"You also can't"—poke—"break Kell's best friend again. Do you understand?"

And now Cheever was sweating even more, and his face and ears were prickling. "I do," he said. "I'm sorry. I'll bring bottled water and juice upstairs, I promise."

"Feed him."

"I was try—"

"I get that. I'm saying he's got food there, feed him. Water him. But *don't break him.*"

Cheever nodded, closing his eyes. "Look, I didn't know he'd get dehydrated. It was unintentional—"

"Everything that happens to Blake Manning needs to be intentional, and it needs to be intentionally good. Do you understand me?"

Cheever nodded, afraid, in awe and... and pretty much in love with Kell's sweet-faced, fearsome warrior wife. "Thank you," he said, kissing her unexpectedly on the cheek.

"For ripping you a new asshole?"

He shook his head. "For treating him like a brother. Let me get Mackey some foo—"

"I'll run it up before we leave. Go talk to him. Tell him how you sexed Blake out. It'll do him good."

Cheever wasn't going to gainsay her or second-guess her. He was simply going to flee.

"YOU LOOK scared," Mackey said, looking up from a tablet that seemed to be consuming his attention. "What did you do? The whole house could hear Briony chewing you out."

"I was going to put together a dinner to take to Blake—"

Mackey's eyes got big. "Are you insane? You don't tamper with that woman's kitchen. Her and Shelia, they've got that place dialed in. You stick to your own cupboard, you understand me?"

"What if you want an Oreo in the middle of the night?" Cheever complained. No wonder this place was good for Marcia—it was more intensely regulated than the mental health facility.

"You make sure she has it on the list!" Mackey rolled his eyes. "Jesus, man, I'm trying to save your skin here. Pay attention!"

Cheever flopped into the seat next to Mackey's bed, suddenly out of fight. "Mackey?"

"Yeah?"

"I'm in love with your second guitarist."

Mackey let out a breath. "Good. I'd hate to think you were throwing the family into this much confusion because you were dicking around with his heart."

Cheever laughed a little. "Okay. Good. As long as I know you're okay with it—"

Mackey waved the tablet in the air. "You should hear the songs he's written about you, little brother. I'm not really okay with it—but God. The poetry. I can't see any reason to break you two up when he's making such gorgeous fucking rock and roll in your honor." He set the tablet down and leaned back against the pillow with a sigh. "Best part of my day was getting those songs. Hope the guys do 'em justice."

"They will," Cheever said, breaking out his sketch book. "They love him too."

"What you drawing there?" Mackey asked, some of his depression lightening up.

"You. I want one of all the guys."

"Not here," Mackey muttered fretfully, picking at the blanket over his midsection, leaving his cast poking out. "Not in bed. Not when I can't fuckin' move—"

"I'll get you later too," Cheever said softly. Then, because he was starting to learn. "Trust me here, Mackey. In your good and your bad. Trust me. I won't do you wrong."

The look Mackey gave him was terribly young and terribly sad. "I'll take your word for it," he said bitterly. "It's like you and Blake. Not much I can do about it anyway."

Cheever was sketching already, gnawing on his lower lip and taking in the fox-pretty features of his older brother. "You could make us miserable about it," he said softly. "Thanks for trusting me not to."

"Augh!" Mackey fell back against the pillows and gazed listlessly at the television. "Please tell me we can play video games after this. Trav is no good at 'em, and you got some fuckin' hope to not suck."

"I promise."

"Good." Mackey closed his eyes, and the lines of pain etched his face. Cheever thought that if he could keep his brother from gnawing his own foot off while he was stuck in bed, he would have done his best goddamned deed ever.

THEY FOLLOWED the same routine—video games, bullshitting, followed by sitting in via Skype on the meeting at the studio. Cheever made sure Mackey had his pain pill this time, and Trav made sure Blake was drinking orange juice and water, and the guys... well, the guys did this sort of magic thing. Cheever figured Blake had been working on those songs a while—well, some of them—but the guys had apparently taken his music ideas, swished them around in their head a little, and come back with some solid riffs and instrumentals, which they played as they discussed. Any doubts Cheever'd had about them finishing the solo album before they had to go back on tour in September were erased by the amazing gestalt his brothers created just by loving what they did.

Cheever sketched Mackey while he was talking, just his face, with the sun coming in the window behind him, and when the meeting was done and the phone was off, he presented both sketches, the good and the bad, the happy and the sad, and the smile he got in return....

He had to swallow twice just to breathe.

"Those are so good, little brother. Those... you were going to do all the guys like this? Two sides of the coin? 'Cause that—*oh my God*, turn Skype back on!"

At that moment, they heard the door downstairs slam and the guys—all of them, including Blake—talking up a storm.

"Guys!" Mackey called, "Blake! I got your album title! Come on up!"

Blake came up, looking much better than he had that morning—even late in the morning, when Cheever had left him for his meeting.

"Jesus, Mackey, it's like you scream onstage for a living or something."

Mackey gave Blake a fuck-off-and-love-me grin, and Cheever had a sudden insight to just exactly what sort of power his brother must wield live. "You'd think I run a rock band or something instead of a bunch of broken monkeys, right? Now shut up and look at what Cheever did."

Blake glanced at Cheever and snorted softly. Cheever blushed, and Mackey rolled his eyes.

"If you two start talking about that shit when I can't even beat you, I will take out a hit. Do you hear me? Now look at his sketchbook—those two pictures."

Blake's hazel eyes softened, and he took the book from Cheever with a furtive little glance under his lashes. Cheever bit his lip and smiled, and their night came flooding back.

"Yeah?" Blake looked at the good one and his face lit up; then he looked at the bad one and it fell to sadness. "Those are real good, Cheever."

Cheever's smile was going to take over his entire body. "Thanks."

"They're the two sides of the coin," Mackey said with meaning. "Get it? *Two Sides of the Coin?*"

Blake's posture snapped straight and his eyes got big, as if he and Mackey had been hit with the same electric current. "Like the songs on the LP," he said, the thrill of excitement in his voice, and Cheever got it then. Blake's songs—the melancholy love songs and the snarky breakup songs that were his specialty—both sides of love.

"Yup. You got your concept, son." Mackey's grin was 100 percent Mackey-James-Sanders Grade A happy, and Cheever's breath caught in his chest. God, his brother was like a nova sun.

"And you get your producer credit, Dad." Blake's grin was quieter, not as showy but just as deep, and Cheever's heart ached. In any other company, Blake would be the star. But Blake didn't seem to mind.

Maybe because being around Mackey made them all better.

"That is a good day's work," Mackey said in satisfaction and then fell back against the bed. "And no offense, guys, but I need my nap."

"Still hurting?" Blake asked softly.

"Yeah. But at least I have the good sense not to break myself with sex." Mackey's chuckle was all dirty. "You two thought you'd get away without me even mentioning that? Oh my God. It's like you don't even know me."

Blake let out a guffaw. "Wait until you're up and around—you and Trav won't come out of this room for days, and then you'll be walking funny."

"Cocoa butter," Mackey said with satisfaction. "Hell on laundry, easy on the balls. Now go. Send Trav up." He swallowed, and his ebullience and larger-than-life attitude faded. "I... I kind of need him."

Blake squeezed his shoulder gently, and to Cheever's surprise, Mackey caught his hand.

"Like that?" Blake asked, and Mackey bit his lip and nodded.

"Let's just say it's a good thing I need help to pee," he muttered. "Can't get out of bed to get high."

Blake looked over his shoulder at Cheever. "The guys are downstairs getting dinner and planning a TV night. Go join them?"

Cheever's vision—him, Blake, alone, takeout—wafted away like smoke. "Yeah. I'll go get in their way."

Blake winked at him. "Just be there to get in my way. And send Trav up if you get the chance."

Cheever stood, and Blake took his seat, but he paused to squeeze Blake's shoulder, just as Blake had squeezed Mackey's. Blake surprised him then, took his hand and kissed it, and then turned his wrist out and kissed his scar. "Thanks."

Cheever bent and brushed his lips over Blake's temple. "Of course."

He left thinking he meant those words.

Of course. This was Blake's family in a way Cheever still had to fathom. Cheever was learning, but Blake knew their pulse, and it was up to him to call the shots.

As he went downstairs, Cheever hoped he could talk somebody into ordering pizza.

Sympathy for the Devil

THEY WATCHED TV with the guys—it was Kell's turn to pick, so they ended up watching reruns of *Sons of Anarchy*, but it was one of Blake's favorites too. Cheever leaned against Blake, sketching while he propped his feet up on one side of the love seat—a very Mackey thing to do, actually, even though Mackey and Trav's customary couch was left vacant, by habit or respect.

Like they did, they commented on the show—who was a badass, who shoulda done what, when. Cheever would look around, catching the conversation and smiling every now and then when someone said something pithy or funny. About an hour into it, the kids got home and they turned off the TV to go help with the great disembarking and bath time. Marcia was still bringing stuff in, so Cheever told Blake to stay there on the couch and pick his nose (exact quote) while he went to help.

Blake ignored that last bit and grabbed Katy, who was trailing in with her souvenirs and her sunhat. She was too big to swing up in his arms, so he took her hand and twirled her in a pirouette, because little girls going in circles were usually a good thing.

"How you doing, Katy-bug?"

She smiled, but a little sadly. "We had fun," she said, her voice clogged.

"Why the face?"

She swallowed, her nose scrunching. "'Cause we had to decide what else we're gonna do before I go visit Grandma and Grandpa. Only I don't *want* to visit Grandma and Grandpa."

Blake grimaced. Katy's original visiting stipulation was six weeks out of the year. The end. And then Briony and Shelia had their first kids, and they established a routine that involved kids, and they asked— nicely—for more time.

Grant's widow had balked at first, but then Trav had a talk with her. Blake didn't know what he'd said, but one minute it was "No, you can't have my baby!" and the next, Katy's mom, Sam, was in college and then law school. And Katy was living in LA during the year and living up in Tyson for much of summer vacation. She called and skyped her mom almost every day—she even had her own phone so Blake knew they were in contact a lot—and she spent most of her summer vacation with Sam.

But she spent the first two weeks with Grant Adams's parents, and that… that was the problem.

"They got horses," Blake said diplomatically, because when they'd been visiting the Adams ranch, giving Grant some peace before he died, that had been the main attraction. Blake had never seen horses, not up close and personal, and he and Jeff and Stevie had spent a lot of time showing Katy the horses while Mackey, Kell, and Grant had closed the books on a lot of shit that Blake would be forever glad he wasn't involved with.

Blake had learned to love the critters—enough so that he took the older kids on trail rides, using a local service, a couple of times a year.

But Grant Adams had sickened and died before he turned twenty-five years old, and most of it, from what Blake could see, was because of the poison that had existed in that painful, angry household.

His dying wish was for his daughter to spend as little time as possible there—and he hadn't been foolish about it either. Blake and Mackey had privately admitted that one of the things that had kept them clean in those first years was the knowledge that before Katy came to their home, the whole band was going to have to pee in a cup.

They still did, actually. But now raising kids, having them in their lives, was part of the fabric of the band's being. Unless something shitty and stupid happened, like Mackey falling off a giant speaker and being stuck in a room in his own head without any relief, neither of them had enough time, much less any inclination, to think about using.

"You take us to see horses," Katy said, her voice quavering. "And you're nice, and you never yell because I touched the wrong thing, and you're not dirty rock stars, and they're just so mean!"

She started crying, and Blake comforted her, taking her to her room and letting her cry on his shoulder until she fell asleep—prebath, of course! Blake hoped Briony wouldn't be too cross. Katy was nine, so she was almost too old for this, but the family rule of thumb was never wake a sleeping child. Sheets could be washed, a bath could wait, but the time lost comforting an overtired kid could never be regained. He took Katy's phone and her souvenirs and her hat and then her shoes, leaving her in her shorts and her pretty blouse while he tucked her in.

He caught Briony on the way out, when it was obvious she was looking for the girl.

"Sorry," he said, gesturing to Katy's room and closing the door behind him. They'd asked her if she wanted it done in all pink, but yellow and green had been her choices instead. Briony and Shelia had put butterfly decals on the walls, which she'd loved, and most of her stuffed animals were cats. Blake was under the impression that if staying put during the tour worked out, the kids would get pets, and he looked forward to coming home to that.

Briony grimaced. "Shit. Well, tomorrow's a pool day, so we can just skip the bath and play in the pool instead, right?"

Practical woman. Blake adored her. He and Kell had once had to lift her bodily and take her to safety because she was busy running their equipment while a riot boiled up around them. He'd never forget the terror in Kell's eyes as they realized that not only was the crowd getting ugly, but Briony was in the thick of it, running around at the foot of the stage.

"Yeah. She's… she's not excited about going to Grandma and Grandpa's."

Briony's eyes got tight at the corners. "Neither are we. I'll call Sam. Maybe she can be there for the visit."

Blake looked behind him and made sure the door was shut. "I… I don't like those people," he said, letting his raw loathing escape. "I… I know it's only two weeks, but she spends more time with the nanny than with them. And they talk shit about us." He felt stupid saying it. "I mean, we're expecting it, but Katy likes it here. When she goes with her mom, Sam takes time off and stuff and they have fun. I got no problem with that, but…."

"But that place killed Grant," Briony said softly.

"Yeah." Blake had walked in Grant's shadow for a long time—long enough to stop hating the shade and start loving the shelter. Grant had left them, left the brothers, left Mackey, and Blake had stayed. Anything he did, any fuckup he made, would forever be measured by the fact that he'd stayed.

He'd been there as the brothers had grieved, had seen the damage wreaked on someone who should have been young and beautiful, but who instead had wasted in the poison of his parents' garden.

Blake had lived in a poisoned garden once. Only he'd uprooted himself and gotten free. Helping the guys as they mourned their friend had made him realize something important about himself—he had enough compassion to feel for Grant Adams, to wish him happiness when his body let him go. He had enough self-respect not to hate Grant for coming first, and for being grateful he had a place in the lives of the men they'd both loved.

Katy had been the family's blessing in so many ways. If nothing else, Blake would fall on his knees and kiss the man's picture, just for moving hell and high water while on his deathbed to make sure his little girl got to belong to the Sanders' family and not the place they were sending her now.

"We have no choice," Briony said, deflating a little. "Kell has no choice. I'll talk to Trav—"

"Trav is right here, and we need to move before she wakes up."

Trav looked irritated, but then he often looked irritated. He'd looked irritated as fuck when he'd showed up at the hotel room to take over managing the band, and he'd looked fucking irritated as it became clear that the bunch of fuckups who'd been getting high and wandering lost for a year needed more than a manager—they'd needed a daddy figure.

And he'd looked irritated as fucking *ass* when he'd realized he was falling for Mackey Sanders and wanted nothing to do with being that man's daddy.

But through it all, he'd provided guidance, structure—hell, a road map—for a bunch of guys who'd never had someone show them what a man really did when he walked in the world.

One of the few times Trav Ford did *not* look irritated was when he was playing with Grant Adams's daughter. At first Blake had been unsure—Trav had spent most of Grant's dying time with Grant and Mackey, and he just wasn't that cuddly. But during Katy's first visit, it became clear that Trav was one of her safety people—maybe he just exuded calm in chaos—and Trav, stoic, capable, irritated Trav—melted around the little girl, as he seemed to melt around nobody else but the other children.

Kids were his soft spot. Who knew?

So if Trav was in on this conversation, that meant it was important.

"I'll call Sam Adams—"

Briony suddenly smirked, reminding Blake why she got best friend credit in Mackey's heart.

"Samantha," Trav corrected, giving Briony the kind of look any parent would give a recalcitrant twelve-year-old. "I'll call *Samantha* and ask if we can fix the visit with the grandparents." He grunted. "If nothing else, maybe we can put it off until Mackey's online. As it is, he's going to have to miss dropping her off, and that'll kill him."

"Maybe…." Blake chewed on his bottom lip. "Maybe, you know. Invite Sam out here instead? At least for a couple of weeks? Let her in on the summer fun or winter break." He gave Briony a smile that was all teeth, but Briony perked up.

"That's an awesome idea. Marcia is a great help, but…." She grimaced, and Blake remembered she had a secret.

"Shelia hasn't told them yet?" he said in a low voice, and Briony shrugged.

"She hasn't had time to take the test yet!"

Trav's expression went from speculative to blank. "Are you serious?"

Briony's sheepish look said it all. "So serious. We're gonna need Marcia's help full-time, Trav, like, we should pay the girl. She's competent, the kids like her, and we're gonna have…." She paused, and her eyes widened. "Oh, holy jebus. Yeah. Six. And if you all are taking off right when school starts…."

Trav rolled his eyes. "I expected this seven years ago," he said. "You guys are killing me. Any thought about moving half our little gang somewhere else?"

They started to hash things out, and Blake's eyes unfocused a little, the obvious solution presenting itself, but he didn't want to step up and say it.

He should move. He should find an apartment nearby, within running distance so he could still be part of the family. But he should give over the studio house to Stevie and Jefferson's family, and let Briony, Kell, and Mackey live here.

The whole reason they'd all moved into the big house in the first place was that the guys—none of them—could find their asses with both hands back then. But they were a different family now.

Blake didn't need his brothers with him 24-7 to not use. He could, in fact, have a place of his own and a quiet life of his own.

With Cheever.

Sure.

Somewhere the guys didn't have to see him fall apart if Cheever decided he didn't want Blake in his life like that.

As Trav and Briony tried to set the family firefly jar in stone, Blake resolved to talk to Trav quietly later.

He could find something nearby. In the same neighborhood, hopefully—although everything was so big there.

Someplace he could park his own car. Someplace he could come over and play with the kids or hang at the pool. Someplace he could have a practice room and a painting room for Cheever.

Or, you know, a guest room. An anything room.

A painting room for Cheever.

"Blake?" Trav said, as Briony went off to finish up the kids' baths.

"Yessir?"

"Don't look like that. I want you to stay in the studio house, and I'll look for something nearby for the twins."

Blake's mouth dropped open. "But—"

Trav shrugged. "Look, I know you like to think you're the least important guy in the group, but Kell would lose his shit without you, and the twins have each other. Also, with your solo career, it's convenient to have the studio so close. Just don't make any plans to move soon, if that's okay."

Trav turned around to go back to whatever cave he'd come from, and Blake watched him go with an open mouth.

Cheever took that opportunity to run by, chasing a naked Kansas, who was egging him on, his four-year-old buttcheeks wiggling as he ran. "C'mon, Cheever, you're the one with a towel."

"What's wrong?" Cheever asked, throwing the towel in a beautiful arc down the hallway.

"Nothing." Blake blinked and pulled himself back to the present. "I just didn't know Trav could read minds, that's all."

Cheever grimaced. "Damn, he's scary enough as it is."

"Uncle Cheever!" Kansas wailed, and Cheever took off again, leaving Blake to navigate the chaos on his own.

FINALLY ALL the kids were down, all the guys were with their significant others, and it was time for Blake to raid Mackey's cupboard for cookies and go back next door.

He found the package of cookies and grinned in triumph, heading for the exit, only to be caught with his hand on the door by Cheever, who carried a backpack over his shoulder.

"You're just going to leave me here?" he asked, not even hurt, but amused.

"Wasn't sure you wanted to—"

Cheever stopped him with a kiss. "Unless I say I need my space, assume I want to stay."

And all of the night before came flooding back. Of Blake, naked, body and soul, of Cheever turning him inside out and still claiming him.

And he wanted another night.

Blake was going to be blessed with another night in Cheever Sanders's bed.

"Unless I say not tonight, assume I *want* you to stay."

They'd be leaving on tour in September. How many more nights were there?

He wasn't even sure it was his voice.

Cheever's mouth claimed his again—he'd had a mint after dinner—and Blake devoured him greedily. Oh wow. How had Cheever been there, so close to him, all day, and they hadn't done this since this morning?

Cheever crushed Blake up against his body, lining them both up and arching against Blake's hip. "I want to stay," he whispered. "Now c'mon. If we get caught having sex in the front room, I will never live it down."

With that, he trotted out the door, Blake on his heels, the box of cookies in his hand all but forgotten.

They arrived at the house, and Cheever took the cookies from him, then found a cupboard that had apparently been filled with Blake's favorites already.

"Briony," he said smugly.

"She's diabolical," Blake agreed. Then he smiled sneakily. "But these are *Mackey's* favorites, and sometimes his cookies just taste better."

Cheever's low chuckle gave Blake a happy little buzz. "That's great! It's, like, I don't know, you guys are brothers!"

"Pretty much." Yeah, Kell was the brother Blake would have special ordered, but he'd realized that nobody got to special order *all* their family. "Anyway, I steal Mackey's cookies, he gets all competitive about 'nobody better take my fuckin' cookies!' and—"

"And all of a sudden, he's eating more," Cheever said, his eyes doing this sort of glowing thing that said he approved.

Blake nodded. "So, want a Chips Ahoy!?"

Cheever shook his head. "Nope. My favorites are E.L. Fudge."

"No! No! White chocolate covered Oreos!"

"You, sir, have champagne taste in cookies!" As he spoke, Cheever was moving closer, backing Blake up against the refrigerator, zeroing in on his mouth.

"Apparently, I have champagne taste in men too," Blake teased, thinking it was true. Something about Cheever—his intelligence, maybe? His sense of humor? Maybe it was just the God-given lines of his slender body—but *something* told Blake repeatedly that Cheever was an indulgence. Too rich for his blood, too good to be permanent.

But standing there in the darkened kitchen, Cheever's warmth permeating the air-conditioning, the smell of sweat and kids' shampoo seeping into Blake's senses, he felt the sudden craving for something sweet.

Cheever lowered his head, and Blake closed his eyes, anticipating the sweetness, and then Cheever jerked away.

"What were you all talking about, anyway?"

"Huh? What?" Blake opened his eyes and squinted.

"When I was chasing naked children through the house? What were you talking about?"

"About the twins getting a new house. I thought they'd move here and I'd get an apartment or something nearby—"

Cheever frowned. "But that doesn't make any sense. The studio's important, and what? The kids are going to live in the top part of the house only? That's silly. Trav said no, right?"

"Yeah. He said I should plan to stay here."

Cheever nodded, gnawing on his lip. "That's good. There's enough room. I can move a studio here, and we can make an art room in the big house for the kids."

Blake felt a little explosion right behind his eyes. "Why would you move in here?"

Cheever's eyes got big, and for a moment, Blake thought he'd made him mad. That's not what happened, though.

He shook his head and pursed his lips. "Because that's what couples do," he said with exaggerated patience. "But I'm starting to get that you've got a big blind spot about that for yourself, so I'm going to let that pass."

Blake thought about pushing him away and schooling him on the ill-conceived idea of becoming that close, that fast, after only one night together. Instead he just grazed Cheever's cheek with his knuckles.

"I see what you're saying, but I don't want you to feel obligated."

Cheever laughed, the sound so low and growly, Blake felt it where their stomachs touched. "I feel obligated to take you upstairs and make love again, if only to remind you how much you need me."

Blake bit his lip to keep in the low cry that wanted to escape. "I can't need you, boy. What happens when you leave?"

"Shut up," Cheever said gently. "Not gonna happen."

This time, the kiss landed, and Blake didn't crave him any less than he had before. He opened his mouth and let Cheever in at the same time he took over the kiss, keeping his lips firm and his tongue dominating so Cheever knew....

Cheever knew.... Oh hell, the boy's hands were in his pants and Blake couldn't say no. He was kneading Blake's backside, grazing his fingertips down the inside of Blake's cheeks, and Blake rutted up against Cheever's hip in need.

His fingertip sought out Blake's pucker, and just when Blake moaned, Cheever pulled his hands up and cupped Blake's waist.

Blake whimpered and ripped away from the kiss, resting his head against Cheever's shoulder.

"This is so not fair," he muttered, bucking against Cheever without restraint. "This is... this... oh God."

Cheever tickled his ear with soft lips. "Go upstairs and get naked."

"What?"

"I'll be there. Just go get naked." Cheever batted his eyelashes. "For me? I mean, I could blow you here—"

He made as though to squat on the kitchen floor, and Blake grabbed him by the bicep.

"No! Jesus, Cheever."

"Then go. Naked. Facedown on the bed. Turn off the lights if you need to—"

"But—"

"Just go." Cheever kissed him again, and Blake found himself running up the stairs, fully clothed this time, his cock aching and body tingling in anticipation.

He said hello to the fish—who appeared to all be alive, which was nice—and then stripped quickly and did what Cheever asked, not sure why he was doing it, other than the fact that Cheever made him feel good.

Cheever was up a few moments after he'd gotten situated, with a bottle of orange juice and some napkins... and two boxes of cookies, which made Blake laugh softly to himself.

"Not taking any chances tonight?"

"Are you kidding? I'm getting a mini-fridge up here just to take care of you." Cheever stopped for a moment and pulled the blinds over the bed up, then turned off the light.

"What?" Blake asked, turning slightly and resting his chin on his hand.

"You look...." Cheever ran his palm down Blake's back, sliding it across his shoulders, down his spine, framing his hips. Blake arched against the bed, thrusting into the sheets because Cheever's hands were hot and rough, and even when they were moving gently, they hinted at total possession.

"Look what?" Blake mumbled.

"Beautiful," Cheever told him. He bent and kissed the back of Blake's neck, adding a little teeth, a little tongue, and Blake moaned softly.

"So not—"

Cheever dragged his tongue down Blake's spine, the same path his palm had taken. "See," Cheever murmured, finishing off with a little nip at the small of Blake's back. "That's what you're not getting. You see...." He parted Blake's cheeks and blew softly, and Blake sucked in a breath that almost choked him. "You see...," Cheever repeated, suckling on Blake's buttock, hard enough to leave a mark. He let it go with a pop. "You see all the bad shit you told me, because you didn't want me to feel alone."

He licked the love bite, and Blake squirmed. He resisted the urge to pull his knees under his chest. Any more submission and he wouldn't be able look Cheever in the eye tomorrow.

"It's who I am," Blake said, trying for dignity, but it came out in a whine.

"No." Cheever parted him again, and this time swiped all the way down his crease with his wicked, terrible, wonderful tongue. Blake saw stars and buried his face in the sheets, not able to find any words.

"No?" he managed to say. Oh God, no ropes, no chains, and yet this kid had him naked and helpless and shaking.

"No," Cheever repeated. "It's shit you did to survive. Who you are is a guy who'd make himself naked to help a fucked-up kid get through the worst week of his life. You think I'm going to let you go?"

"I got no idea," Blake moaned, stretched out and needy. Cheever spat in his crease a couple of times, raw and animal, so erotic Blake writhed at the thought of it.

His finger at Blake's entrance was no surprise, slender, teasing, and Blake arched his back, sweating.

"Cheever, what are you—"

"Seeing you naked," Cheever said softly, thrusting in, pulling out. "Like I said, you're beautiful."

Blake pulled one knee underneath him, fully intending to roll over and sit up so he could explain why this was a bedroom thing and not a life-together thing... and then Cheever added another finger.

Blackness washed behind his eyes, and he gibbered into the pillow. "Oh my God.... Cheever—Cheever this isn't... *yes, more, bigger!*"

He was shaking with need, and unbidden, his other knee came up underneath him. There he was, as raw and vulnerable as he'd ever been, and Cheever kept thrusting, kissing the small of his back and tracing his spine with a wicked tongue.

"I won't leave you hanging," Cheever whispered. "Stay there. Spread yourself if you have to."

The fingers disappeared and Blake did as he'd suggested, the part of his brain wondering where his self-preservation had disappeared to, completely submerged by the part of his brain crying out to have Cheever's body in his.

Cheever made quick work of his clothes and then came to the head of the bed, where he rooted under Blake's pillow and came back with the lubricant. Blake stared at him with helpless eyes, and Cheever bent to take his mouth again.

"There are so many ways I want to do this," he whispered. "I want to have sex every way known to man twice, then again, then a hundred times more to see if it's always this good."

No. No, it can't possibly be. How could it always be this good when I feel like I'm going to explode when you touch me right now?

But Cheever had moved away by then and drizzled the slick down Blake's backside, rubbing it in with his thumb.

Blake was trembling so hard, he couldn't remember his own name.

But he remembered who was about to fuck him, sure enough.

"*Cheever!*"

One long, slick thrust and Cheever was inside him again, where he belonged, and Blake emitted a long, low howl that was barely human.

Cheever wasn't gentle this time, wasn't tentative. He pulled back fast and snapped forward hard, and all Blake could do was hide his face and scream.

Again and again, not too fast, slow enough that every thrust hit home. Blake wound tighter and tighter, like a watch about to bust its spring. He thought he might rocket into blue balls, except Cheever started... touching him.

Cheever gave him everything he didn't know he needed. Slow caresses to his flanks, his ass, his thighs. Gentle words about his body—strong back, tight ass, muscles that popped in the moonlight. Soft kisses against his shoulders in between thrusts.

Blake almost sobbed, he was so undone. And when Cheever said, "Okay, Blake, grab your cock and make yourself come," Blake wondered who the kid thought he was fucking.

But that's all it took. One long, hard, painful squeeze and Blake was coming like a fire hose, locked around Cheever's cock as Cheever groaned overhead and fell over his back, lost in his own orgasm, sweating with exertion and climax, and *face it Blake, fucking triumph*! Because the kid had won.

Blake was his. Cheever's course for their relationship was theirs. Blake had no recourse and no backbone—not in this.

Blake's knees went out from under him, and he was left flat on the bed in a puddle of his own come while Cheever finished stuttering inside him.

"Blake?" Cheever said, running tender fingertips along his shoulders.

"Yeah?"

"I want to move in and let Briony have my room, as brilliant as it is. That way I don't have to hide my paint supplies from the kids, and I can use the light in that empty room up here to paint in."

Blake wanted to laugh—as he was sure Cheever meant him to—but he could barely breathe because he was still rocked by orgasm and Cheever's *cock* was still *in his ass*.

"Sure," he managed to say. September. He'd leave in September, and Cheever would move out and he'd be alone. "Sounds great."

Cheever pulled out and shoved at Blake's shoulder. Blake rolled to his side and Cheever stretched out next to him, putting his head on Blake's shoulder and kissing his cheek.

"I knew you'd see it my way."

SURE. SURE Blake would see it his way.

He had no choice.

The next day, while he was practicing the new album with the guys, Cheever and Trav moved his dresser upstairs, and his paint stuff too. The dresser went in Blake's room. His paint stuff went in the suite with the most light.

The day after, the guys woke them up in the morning with Cheever's bed, which they put in one of the other suites, laughing even as they set it up, because they didn't see it getting a lot of use.

The day after that, Cheever spent the day setting up his studio, with drawers for his supplies and a computer desk and an easel. Blake watched him, frowning, thinking he'd have to move it all back, but he didn't say anything. It was June. He could have the happiest three months of his life if he just let Cheever do what he wanted. September was a lifetime away.

By the end of the week, Cheever Sanders had been in Blake's bed every night, laughing, pushy, and voracious, and Blake was starting to sense that this wasn't going away.

He yearned for it to not go away.

At the end of two weeks, Mackey was out of bed and on crutches, slowly but surely regaining some of his mobility and independence. He sat in on the practice sessions, listening, making suggestions, talking promotion with Trav. And while Blake knew he was writing his own stuff and practicing his own instruments in a limited capacity—including the piano, which was new to him—he seemed determined to let Blake fly with this project on his own.

Blake found himself settling more and more into the role of leader, much like Mackey had been. Unlike the first album, in which he'd pretty much taken the studio musician's vision and ran with it, he found he was taking the control the band had given him and making the album his own. For ten years, he'd made himself "useful," and he was proud of that. Kell, Mackey, the twins, even Briony and Shelia and the children, they'd all gotten very good at depending on him. For someone who had grown up only being able to look out for number one, he thought that being there for other people was as good as Blake Manning got.

But as they worked on this album, with Cheever in his bed, being bossy, being charming, telling him he was special, he found that telling the guys what to do—as well as some of the studio musicians he'd needed to hire to make his vision true—became easier as he went. He wasn't just the guy who was dependable anymore. He was the guy who helped make the music, helped make the sound that could make the spirit soar. And the sound that was coming out of the studio....

Oh, it pleased him. It made him happy and sad; it hooked him in the stomach and made him want to sing. It did all the things to him that good music had always done, and it was *his* music.

Cheever sat in through the recording sessions sometimes, sketching the guys when they were happy or pissed or thoughtful.

But it was more than that. Blake could tell, just by the way his eyes would move as Stevie would snark or Jefferson would make peace or Kell would problem solve with one or two pithy sentences, that Cheever was learning his brothers from the beginning again, figuring out how the boys who'd raised him had grown up as men. All of them had grown up in Mackey's shadow, but Cheever—and Blake, looking through Cheever's eyes—could see that they had grown strong enough to face the sun all on their own.

Blake would find himself just staring at Cheever sometimes, charmed and fascinated by this young man who seemed so completely himself, so completely at ease, after Blake had seen him at his worst.

It actually gave him hope.

People could learn. They could grow. They could transform. They could take their experiences, good and bad, and use them to become a better, stronger, kinder person.

Seeing Cheever in the process of doing it made Blake proud—proud of Cheever and proud of himself.

He'd done that too. *He'd* gone from being a coke whore to a rock star to an actual human being. Maybe Blake wasn't all of the bad things he'd once been. Cheever certainly wasn't.

Blake stopped questioning Cheever's presence in his bed, in his life, and, little by little, started to accept it.

A month after Cheever Sanders had simply asserted his way into Blake's bed, Mackey got his wrist cast taken off and got a brace in its place. And his leg cast was replaced with a waterproof walking cast. His back still hurt—anybody could see it, but pretty much every room in both houses had a special orthopedic chair meant especially for Mackey to take the strain off, and he spent about ten minutes every hour doing strengthening and stretching exercises to help the rest of his muscles pick up the slack.

Blake and Cheever had remarked privately that Mackey's stomach muscles were becoming insanely ripped—people were going to think he'd gone to get swole instead of gone to heal his injuries.

But that, along with so many other things between them, remained private.

Private.

Like the little moan Cheever made when Blake ran his lips from Cheever's earlobe down the side of his neck.

Private.

Like the way Cheever possessed Blake easily, like he'd been born to top, like Blake was smaller, more delicate, precious.

Private.

Like the way Blake stayed up nights, perfecting each song on his roster, worrying, fretting, teasing, until he was sure it was worthy of the Outbreak Monkey brand, since his brothers were pouring their hearts into what should have been his own risk.

Like the time Blake went upstairs unexpectedly and heard a competent if not spectacular guitar player working the chords from one of Outbreak Monkey's biggest hits again and again and again until it was smooth as silk. He'd found Cheever sitting in his art studio, playing until his fingers blistered, trying so damned hard to be like his brothers without anybody seeing him fail.

Like the way Blake had cried while bandaging those blisters, because Cheever was perfect and beautiful, and he couldn't figure out the right words to tell him he was perfect and beautiful and make him believe it.

That sort of private.

So private that Blake was reluctant to ask Cheever to come up with Trav, Mackey, Kell, and Heather to take Katy to her grandparents' place to visit when they could put it off no longer.

"You're going without me?" Cheever asked as Blake packed his bag the night before.

"You can come!" Blake told him, trying to smile about it. "It's just... you know."

"But I love that kid!" Once Mackey had gotten back on his feet, Cheever had spent his morning hours helping Shelia and Briony and Marcia—Blake didn't doubt he loved Katy. If three days at Disneyland didn't bond you with a pack of children, nothing would.

"I know it!" Blake tried a winning smile. "Baby boy, this is just... I mean, Grant's parents are awful. And it's hard leaving her there. The only reason we can do it this year is that her mom's gonna be there. Otherwise, I honestly think Trav would be fighting it in court. It's hard. It sucks. And Mackey and Kell are gonna be tore up. They are every year. Jefferson and Stevie are probably having their own little pity party with her right now, since they're not going. It's no fun for anybody, you know? I just thought I'd spare you, that's all."

"You called me 'baby boy,'" Cheever said softly. "That's sweet. I like it when you do that, because you think just saying it makes you the grown-up, and we both know that's not what's going on here."

Blake grimaced, because, well, truth. "Your point is?"

Cheever blinked those green eyes at him with a little extra sass. "Don't make the mistake of thinking I can't handle this because I'm your baby boy."

As. If. The way Cheever took Blake apart in bed almost nightly? Not even a chance.

"That's not what this is," Blake said, trying to be the fucking grown-up for once.

"Then explain," Cheever asked, all steel and reason. "Explain so I don't feel like you don't think I can handle this, or like this isn't any of my business because I was too young to get in your club on the ground floor."

Blake threw a pair of socks into his duffel as if he was trying to pitch them through a window. "I just don't want you to have to hurt!

Is that so goddamned bad?" Great. *His* throat was thick and his eyes burned, but Cheever was looking at him with profound understanding, which usually meant Blake had lost before he even opened his mouth.

Cheever stood up from the bed and walked behind him, setting his hands on Blake's hips and kissing his neck at the shoulder joint.

"Feel better?" he asked silkily.

"No." Blake scowled.

"Want to beat up some more socks? I got a nice pair of boxer-briefs you can really go to town on."

"Go away."

"No." Cheever wrapped his arms tight around him and Blake's unyielding body relaxed just a smidge. "Why are you so mad?"

"Because if I don't stay mad, you are going to win, and it's a... a... Roman general victory, that's what it is!" And goddamn his online degree anyway, because he couldn't remember the actual fucking word.

"Pyrrhic," Cheever supplied, rubbing his lips along the shell of Blake's ear.

"That. You'll win, but you'll have to go back to Tyson, and you'll get to see all of those shitty things that made it such a fucking death trap in the first place, and you'll feel like *ass*. So you won't really win—you'll just get to watch the rest of us fall apart. Mackey and I don't even get to down fucking beer, you get that? There's no boozy happy 'we're so glad we survived' or, 'no, no, no, *my* hometown is shittier!' or any of that coping crap. We are just pissed off and mad and fucking mean. Kell and I got into a *fistfight* the first time we did this, and then, when we looked like hamburger, we like hung on each other and *cried*."

"Wow." Cheever sounded surprised, but he wasn't stopping that gentle seduction, which meant that Blake's words weren't sinking in.

"It's better now," Blake admitted. "'Cause for the first couple years, we were leaving her there until we got back for Christmas, and that always sucked. She smelled like cigarettes and wouldn't eat for the first three days. This is six weeks—and Sam is there most of the time, so Katy'll be happy. But we're still leaving our baby someplace that almost killed the bunch of us, and dammit, I didn't want you to see."

Augh! He needed to run, or to work the sandbag, or to lift a lot of weight all at the same time.

But Cheever kept his arms around Blake's waist and his lips moving gently on his ear, and his groin thrusting repeatedly at Blake's backside.

"This isn't about me," Cheever said softly.

"It is too."

"No, it isn't. If it was, you would have asked me."

Well, hell. "Do you want to come with us?" he asked, done.

"Yes. But that's not the point."

"What is?" And still, that gentle assault at his irritation, his defenses, all of the self-protective measures Blake had taken to not be a raw, exposed nerve that needed a bump of coke to get his sorry ass out of bed.

"You don't want me to see you ugly," Cheever murmured. "You don't want me to see you hurt."

"I don't want you to get hurt," Blake repeated stubbornly.

"I might," Cheever admitted. "I didn't say your reasoning wasn't sound. But you can either trust me to deal with it or you can't."

Blake pushed his finger between his eyebrows and rubbed, trying to loosen the knot of tension that wouldn't stop building right *there*, and Cheever kept kissing the back of his neck.

"You suck," he muttered. "You really, really suck. This trip is going to suck. Your brothers are going to suck. Trav's gonna suck. *I'm* gonna suck. And your mom's gonna beat us all to death with a tire iron before this is done. Mark my words here, Cheever, this is not going to be pretty."

"So if you're right and I'm wrong," Cheever murmured, sliding his hands under Blake's shirt, "what's your prize? How long do you get to say 'I told you so'? I just want to mark it on the calendar, you know, to make sure you're done before you take off on tour in September."

Oh God. Tour. Blake was going to have to leave Cheever here, probably back in the big house to help with the kids so he wouldn't be alone—but still. Cheever planned to make up that class that had set him over the edge, which cheered Blake no end, because it meant all sorts of things—things about follow-through, about taking responsibility, about doing what was right and fixing what you broke.

But it meant Blake would leave, and Cheever would rediscover his life—the one with the rich friends and the bright future and the hot guys in pretty cars who didn't have Blake's baggage. Cheever would have a do-over, and it was all Blake had wanted for the boy from that first moment he'd seen him in that squalid hotel room. Blake's feelings shouldn't enter into it, not even a little bit, not even at all.

"No 'I told you so,'" Blake said gruffly, relaxing and leaning his head back so Cheever could take his mouth. "Just you and me, square like we are."

Cheever didn't disappoint him, and after they knocked his duffel bag off the bed and had energetic, strangely tender sex, they repacked it again.

For two.

THE EXTRA plane ticket was not a problem, since they were flying out so early in the morning on what was essentially a commuter flight, but Blake *did* get some satisfaction listening to Trav bitching and moaning about finding an SUV that could accommodate six adults, a kid's seat, and luggage.

As they stood in line at the car rental, listening to Trav teach the person behind the counter manners and efficiency old-school style, Blake smacked Cheever in the arm.

"See what you did?"

Cheever didn't even look repentant. "It's a car rental place, Blake. He's not even swearing. I'm sure they've heard worse."

Mackey snorted, shifting from one foot to the other restlessly, probably because the plane had been hell on his back. "Yeah, this is tame from Trav. Don't worry. He always calls the place afterwards and apologizes, then gives them a big tip. And he's always real careful not to make anybody cry. Think of him like a real cranky teacher, that's all."

Blake snorted. "Don't let Cheever off the hook. I told him we'd be back in the morning, but he seemed to feel we should all share the suck."

Mackey watched as Kell took Katy for one more run around the lobby to try to burn off some of her energy after being cooped up in the plane all morning and then getting in the car for a good four-hour drive.

"Stupid," he said, rolling his eyes. "Runs in the fuckin' family. You sure you want to hook up with that?"

Blake lifted a shoulder, enjoying Cheever's scowl. "It's not like he's gonna knock me up with inbred assbabies, Mackey. Stupid's not catching unless you want it to be."

Mackey snickered, and Cheever leveled a killing look at Blake.

Blake returned it blandly, and Cheever shook his head and ran off to join Kell.

"Seriously," Mackey said, once he was out of earshot. "This always sucks so bad."

The year before, Kell had needed to pry Katy out of Mackey's arms before giving her to her glowering grandfather. Trav had practically scraped Mackey off the ground to get him in the car, and Kell had sobbed on Blake's chest like a little kid.

"Sam will be there," Blake soothed, and then he let out a sigh. "I know it's gonna be bad, Mackey. I think it's why he wanted to come. So he can... I don't know. Be part of the family misery ritual and understand it."

"I don't want him anywhere near that fuckin' town." Mackey followed Cheever with his eyes as he chased Katy between the seats, graceful and grinning and all that was beautiful about youth.

"You think I do?" Augh! Blake's stomach churned with self-blame, but Mackey just arched an eyebrow at him.

"You noticing the family resemblance yet?"

"Stubborn as fuck? Yeah." Blake sighed. "He's also a manipulative little shit who gets his way all the fuckin' time."

Mackey's deep chuckle was almost reassuring. "Yup. Well, we all had survival skills. Cheever's was figuring out how not to be ignored and to get his way. You complaining?"

Unbidden, the night before passed in front of Blake's eyes, Cheever, legs spread, as Blake stroked his cock and licked his head.

"I need you to trade places," Cheever had panted. "I have plans."

Blake had opened his mouth to dissent—to just this once have his way in bed, to suck Cheever stupid so maybe he'd listen to sense.

But Cheever had lifted his knees and pushed up, grabbing Blake's hair and pulling him gently, slowly, off his cock.

Blake whimpered, suddenly shaking with need, and Cheever nodded. "See? Now let me!"

And it wasn't even a question of *letting* him, not anymore. It was a question of *needing him.*

"Not until he's tired of me," Blake said in the present, the memory of being fucked senseless still tingling on his skin. "You want to hear bitching? You'll hear bitching then."

Mackey grimaced. "I was twenty-one when Trav walked into our lives and saved us all, and I ain't ever letting go. Give the boy some credit. We know what we want."

Blake had no answer to that, which was just as well, because Trav had finished taking the poor attendant apart and putting him back together again. It was time to go get their giant Suburban out of the parking lot.

THE TRIP up was fun—they sang songs with Katy, told her jokes, and when she got tired and needed to calm down, they let her play happily on her tablet. They stopped at a Black Bear Diner outside of Redding and ate, and bought her a teddy bear to add to her giant collection of stuffed animals that had all been packed in one of her suitcases. By the time they got to Tyson, with its depressing collection of old storefronts and apartments, followed by the Walmart and a winding road through the wealthy part of town, Katy was sleepy and ready to see her mother.

The Adams's family home always struck Blake like a fifty-fifty bar. The front part of the house was like a gracious Georgian mansion, with pillars and a great sweep of lawn on either side of the drive and giant shade trees peppering the landscaping, making it look old-school Southern and rich.

Blake knew for a fact that the back of the place was plain old red dirt, crab grass, and horse pens, and he knew that because he'd been there. Unlike when they were there to see Grant, Mr. Adams did *not* wave their SUV to the back lot to park. Trav steered the thing to the front and let Mackey and Kell help Katy out while Blake and Cheever got her luggage and Heather gave her some last-minute grandma hugs.

Once Mr. and Mrs. Adams came out, they wouldn't be staying long.

Samantha Adams turned out to be a blessing.

Originally, Blake had hated the woman. The whole reason Grant had stayed back in Tyson was because Sam was supposedly pregnant, but once Katy was born, anybody could see she'd lied. Katy had been born ten months after Outbreak Monkey blew town—plenty of margin for Grant to have escaped with them, if Sam hadn't trapped him to begin with.

It had been a shitty thing to do. Trav had called her on it, Mackey had called her on it—and something about that had been freeing.

She'd made mistakes. She'd done shitty things. Well, at that point, hadn't they all?

She took her opportunity—and the money Grant had left her in his will and that Outbreak Monkey was willing to gift her with for more time with Katy—and ran with it, getting her college degree and her law degree and opening a practice in Redding.

She had bettered herself.

The woman who came out to the front porch and greeted her daughter was poised and warm—not bitter and angry.

This was someone who had seen the damage she could wreak with her viciousness and decided *not* to do that to her child.

Blake could respect that—hell, *all* the boys could respect that. And Grant was gone, God rest him. All they had left was Katy, and they had to work as a team.

This time was different. This time Katy ran to her mama and hugged her and talked a mile a minute about *all* the things—the tour, her summer, her time with her cousins. She gave all her uncles hugs then, including Blake, who booped her nose, finishing with Cheever.

"This is my new Uncle Cheever," she said proudly. "He plays with us now. It's fun. We used to be scared of him 'cause he was so cool, like a movie star, but he's really just regular folk." Blake wondered where she'd picked that term up—maybe from the boys themselves.

Samantha's mouth quirked at the corners, making her look young at thirty-two when she'd been old at twenty-three. She squeezed her daughter's shoulder and greeted Cheever warmly. "Nice to see you again, Cheever. You probably don't remember me—"

"I do," Cheever said, bobbing his head respectfully. "You grew up pretty."

"So did you," she said dryly. "So nice of you to come up. I understand you and your girlfriend have been doing a lot of childcare—"

"Friend," Cheever corrected charmingly. "My boyfriend might have some words if Marcia and I started to date."

Samantha raised her eyebrows. "Oh! Well, good to know." She shook Katy playfully, and Katy grinned. "You could have warned me, Katydid."

Katy giggled. "But you *know* his boyfriend! It's Uncle Blake!"

"Oh!" Color rose to Samantha's face. "Okay! Well, now I know, and that's okay."

Blake felt his own cheeks burn. "Glad to have your blessing," he mumbled.

"Well, not that any of you need it. I'm just saying—it's the first time I've seen you with *anyone*, Blake. It's good to know you're doing okay."

"Thanks, ma'am." He winked at Katy. "A lot better since you agreed to be here," he admitted, and all the guys nodded.

Samantha sighed. "Well, we'll try to make sure this is how we start summer vacation all the time," she said. "But Trav, if you don't mind, I loved your suggestion about coming down for the holidays. Is there any way we can make that solid?"

"Absolutely!"

From the bowels of the house, they heard the sour tones of Grant's father.

"Samantha, don't keep that child out in the heat all day. She'll need a bath as it is!"

"You could always help with her luggage!" Samantha hollered into the house, then, more quietly to Trav, "I'll call you." Katy waved to all of them from behind her mother's back as Sam beat a hasty retreat.

The relief sliding off everybody's shoulders was a palpable thing.

"Oh God, that was better," Heather said as they boarded the SUV. "So, so much better."

"Blake's idea," Trav noted.

"Was not. That was all you." Blake didn't know why people insisted on doing that.

"Was too," Trav argued lazily. "Anybody want anything? I gotta stop for gas."

There was general discussion after that, with the consensus being everybody needed to use the bathroom and people wanted ice cream and sodas and a big bag of chips for the trip back to the hotel. Yeah, this had been relatively painless, but that didn't mean they weren't going to miss the girl.

Trav filled the SUV up, and they all raided the gas station minimart, which was pretty well stocked, given that there weren't a lot of towns out here. Cheever was the last to the bathroom, and he gave Blake his own pile of junk food and soda to purchase from the boy at the counter.

The boy was pretty, in a faded, straw-colored way, taller than Blake, with wide shoulders and a narrow waist and muscle tone that could easily melt to meat. Blake knew the look of a small-town hero who was about to age badly because that's how all the heroes in *his* high school had looked at twenty-two.

Blake grabbed his little bag of crap and his two sodas and made it back to the SUV, setting up his and Cheever's middle row, since Kell and

Heather had the back this time. He was sipping his soda, wondering what was keeping Cheever, when he saw him exit, with the blond high-school-hero kid on his heels.

Cheever's posture was ramrod straight, and his face had shut down, assuming that cool, remote expression Blake remembered from eight years of hating him for being so much better than them all.

He barely looked at the faded hero, and Blake frowned. "Cheever must really hate that kid."

Heather grunted. "Yeah, well, Aubrey Cooper was always a sneaky little asshole. Best thing I ever did was break up with that kid's father after Mackey came out."

"You dated his father?" Kell asked, surprised, and Blake's brain started to get fuzzy.

"What did you say his name was?"

"Aubrey Coop—*Blake*!"

Blake didn't remember much of the next ten minutes, but he'd never forget the killing haze that filled his vision.

Street Fighting Man

CHEEVER SHOULD have known he'd run into Aubrey Cooper sooner or later. He'd been so preoccupied with Blake—and how relieved everybody seemed to be that Katy had gone willingly, and her mother was there to take care of her, and they didn't seem to be abandoning her in hell—that he hadn't even seen the guy on his way into the bathroom.

On the way out, Aubrey had called his name.

"Cheever?"

Oh Jesus. "Hey, Aubrey." Cheever wasn't stupid. He wasn't going to throw a big old tantrum right here, and he certainly wasn't planning a confrontation.

"How you been doin', man? I missed you once you moved out of town." Aubrey smiled like they'd been the best of buddies, and Cheever's brain pulled a big self-protective cloak around itself.

"Not doing this," he said politely. "Excuse me, my family's waiting in the SUV."

"Not doing what?" Aubrey skirted around the counter, maneuvering his six-foot-plus football-player's frame with ease, and followed him out, the late afternoon sun hitting them both like a calculated blow. "Man, I'm just trying to say hi! We were real tight back in middle school—"

"Tight?" Cheever swung in a circle. "Tight? Aubrey, you *raped me.* Repeatedly. We weren't friends. We weren't boyfriends. You raped me and extorted me to stay silent."

Aubrey looked hurt. "Aw, you knew that was just boys playing rough, right? I mean, you'da said something if you didn't want it."

"No," Cheever told him. "Because I was desperate not to be picked on anymore. Man, what makes you think what you did was okay?"

"You wanted it, right?"

And oh my God. Aubrey's face was just... puzzled. Like he hadn't ever realized.

"No," Cheever said again. "Never. Being touched by you made me vomit."

And there it was. Shock. Hurt. Surprise.

It was everything Cheever had ever wanted to see in his tormenter, and now it just made him feel…

Sad.

"You know what?" he said. "Forget it. I've got a boyfriend in that car, and he loves me, and he knows what consent means, and he'll never hurt me. You're stuck here. Where you gonna find someone like that *here*?"

Aubrey Cooper looked like he was going to cry, and that gave Cheever some serious satisfaction.

Until a madman barreled out of the SUV and started beating the shit out of Aubrey, that is.

"Oh my God, *Blake*! Trav, get out here! Blake, *stop it*!"

Blake was straddling a stunned Aubrey, his fists battering at the boy's face—and he was shouting, and he was crying, and Cheever couldn't make him stop.

"Blake, dammit! Get off him—oh."

Trav got behind Blake and lifted him bodily off Aubrey, who was lying in a little ball, sobbing.

"Holy God, Manning, what in the hell—"

"Trav, you gotta let me kill him! Man, you gotta let me kill him. He hurt him! He hurt him! I gotta fuckin' kill him!"

Trav looked at Aubrey, pathetic and bleeding, and then looked at Blake.

And then he looked at Cheever, and Cheever could see when he made the connection.

"Dammit, keep hold of him!" Cheever snarled, but Blake had lunged out of Trav's grasp toward Aubrey again, only to be caught around the waist by Kell.

"Ten years ago, I would have killed him myself!" Trav snapped. "You weren't going to tell us this was him?"

"Dammit, Blake, back off!" Kell hollered, shoving him a few feet away and planting his feet in front of Aubrey. "We can't just go around beating people up! Man, there are cameras and wall-to-wall fucking people who just watched Outbreak Monkey walk into a minimart! You will go to fuckin' jail!"

"I'll go to fuckin' prison!" Blake snarled, trying to dodge around Cheever's mom, who had placed herself in front of him. He was having a hell of a time, unable to put his hands on her or even shoulder her out of the way, because he was basically decent and he loved Cheever's mom.

"No, you won't!" everybody screamed, including Trav, who had calmed down enough to join Kell, standing in front of Aubrey.

Mackey appeared at Blake's side, tugging at his arm. "C'mon, man. This guy, he ain't worth it. He hurt my brother. Don't let him hurt you."

Blake tore his arm out of Mackey's grasp, and Mackey winced, because the movement twisted his back. Kell and Cheever met eyes. "Blake, you're hurting Mackey!" Cheever said at the same time Kell said, "You fucking asshole, you're fucking hurting my fuckheaded little shit brother. Now stop it!"

The fight went out of Blake so quickly, he almost toppled onto Heather, who was screaming, "You are *not* going to prison, goddammit, because you will break my son's heart! Now *stay!*"

Now that he didn't have to defend Aubrey fucking Cooper, Cheever moved to where Blake stood, distraught and shaking, and put a hand on his bicep. Blake tensed, and Cheever pulled it away, then met Blake's red-rimmed eyes and tried again. This time Blake relaxed, just enough for Cheever to touch him.

"You sane now?"

Blake shook his head. "He hurt you," he mewled, and Cheever opened his arms and pulled him in.

"And you put me back together," he whispered.

"He hurt you."

"Never again."

"I can't fix it, baby."

"You already did," Cheever soothed, and the tremors that had rocked Blake were now rocking them both.

This was what love looked like when it hurt. Shit. Now he knew. He held Blake tighter, relieved when Blake's hands came up and clutched the back of his shirt, clinging for dear life.

"C'mon, Blake," Cheever whispered. "Let's get the fuck out of this town before someone posts a video, okay?"

Blake nodded into his shoulder. "He hurt you."

"But not for a long time."

Cheever was still coaxing him to the car as Aubrey stood up and started to scream, "I'm gonna tell my father, Cheever Sanders! He's gonna have your psycho boyfriend locked up! You better watch your rearview mirror, you little pissant—"

Cheever's mother walked up to him and punched him hard enough in the stomach to bend him over and make him gag.

"Augh!"

"You listen to me, Aubrey Cooper," she snapped. "You tell your father, you tell the sheriff, you tell any person in this town what just happened, and we'll open up an ad in the local paper telling the world that you assaulted my son. Cheever's all grown up now, and he's nobody's victim, and we don't give a shit who knows 'cause we're proud of him all the way through. But what's that gonna do to *you*, Mr. Hometown Hero? You go ahead and tell the world you treated my boy like...." And her voice broke for the first time. "Like you done, and we'll see who it hurts. I know your daddy. You tell him where your peter's been. He'll have you out on your ear so quick, your ear'll be a smudge on the sidewalk."

Aubrey could barely straighten up, and he cast Cheever a furtive, chickenshit look under his lowered brows.

"I didn't know," he protested. "I thought he wanted it—"

Heather slapped him, hard. "Fuck off."

Aubrey yelped, and she stalked to the car. "Get in the car, dickheads. I'm driving because I fucking want to. Trav, see that Cheever calms Blake down. Mackey, you're in pain, you still get the front. Everybody else, remember how to act civilized. God*dammit*, I need to get the fuck out of this town."

"I'M SORRY," Blake said into the dead silence of the car as it whizzed down I-5.

"It's okay," Cheever said automatically, looking at him with worried eyes. Blake sat, head leaning against the window, staring off into the flat topography.

"No, it's not." Blake thudded his head against the glass lightly. "I could have hurt everybody—Cheever, you were handling it. I... I just...." He let out a frustrated breath, and while they weren't touching, Cheever could still feel the fine trembling that didn't seem to have left him since they'd been outside the minimart.

"It's hard," Trav said, his voice tired. "You think there's people out there I haven't wanted to kill?"

Blake let out a humorless laugh. "We had to sit on you, that one time," he said.

"Yeah, you did," Trav said, and Cheever remembered that night, while they'd been visiting Grant before he died. He never knew what Stevie's father had done—but whatever it was, Kell, Blake, and Mackey had needed to tackle Trav before Trav killed him. Not even Cheever doubted the outcome if they'd failed. He also remembered how Stevie and Jefferson had just disappeared, because Stevie's father wasn't their bogeyman anymore—and now he understood. Aubrey wasn't his bogeyman anymore, but that didn't mean Blake didn't want him dead.

Here, in the present, Trav let out a breath. "But I should know better now. I should have kept a tighter hold on you, Blake."

Blake grunted. "Wasn't your fault I'm a fucking moron."

"Hey." Cheever bumped him gently. "You were trying to protect me. It's okay."

But Blake just shook his head. "I wasn't there the right way. You didn't need that. I needed to be... different. I'm sorry."

"No." A sense of dislocation hit him, as though he was looking at one thing when something else was going on. Like those paintings he'd done of Tyson, the ones in which only Blake saw the despair. There was something here Blake and Cheever were seeing differently. "You were—"

"Making it about me. It's about you. And you had it handled." Blake closed his eyes. "I'm sorry. I should have trusted you. You were great."

Cheever reached for his hand tentatively, remembering the way Blake had flinched before. He didn't now, even when Cheever felt the split skin of his knuckles, which must have hurt like a motherfucker.

"Trav," Cheever said, trying to keep his voice steady. "Do we have a first aid kit? He's bleeding."

"I'm fine." Blake tried to reclaim his hand.

"Shut up," Cheever said thickly. "Just... just don't talk to me if you're not going to let me fix the damage."

Blake didn't say anything else, but he let Cheever hold his hand. Trav produced a first aid kit like magic, out of his ass because he really *was* that guy, and Cheever pulled out some antiseptic wipes and started to doctor the splits. Blake barely twitched as Cheever worked, and Cheever wondered about how often Blake was used to nobody taking care of him at all.

Except Cheever's family, standing between him and jail time, shouting at him that prison was unacceptable.

That was love, right there, and Cheever was mad at himself all over again for not trusting them.

Trav pulled him out of his own spiral of self-hatred by calling his name.

"What?" he said, smoothing the back of Blake's now-bandaged hand with his thumb.

"I never asked if you wanted me to press charges."

Cheever snorted. "Yeah, no." Blake's hand tensed in his. "Could we even make them stick? We were both minors. It's been eight years. No. I...." And this baffled him. "He didn't even know what he'd done."

"I'll bet he'll be wondering tonight when he looks at his face," Kell said with some satisfaction. "Jesus, Blake, your technique ain't gotten any worse since you and Trav beat the shit out of each other outside of Albuquerque."

Blake let out a chuff of air. "Yeah, but I'll never level anyone in one blow," he said, and Cheever was willing to buy into it, just to get Blake to talk again.

"One blow?" he asked.

"Oh God." Trav covered his eyes. "That little club that belonged to Heath's friend. Jesus, that was... unusual."

"What was unusual," Mackey said from the front seat, "was the size of this guy. He was six-foot-ten, maybe three-fifty, and it was all fuckin' muscle. And he...." Mackey looked at his mother quickly.

"He decided he wanted a piece of Mackey," Kell said loudly. For Cheever's ears only, he murmured, "Guy told Mackey he wanted to use his ass like a Fleshlight. Blake had to tell Mackey what one was, and the guy shoved Blake against the wall and told him he had a pretty mouth, he was gonna use that too."

Cheever's mouth dropped open, and he saw the faint smile on Blake's lips. "What happened?" he asked, enthralled.

"Well, he was concentrating on me and Mackey, 'cause I guess he was hard up—"

"Rock star fetish," Mackey grunted. "Some guys like some grit with their dinner."

"*Mackey*!"

"Oh Jesus!"

"Mackey, for fuck's sake!"

"McKay James Sanders!"

Only Blake refrained from chewing him out, but his smile was a little bigger now.

"What did Trav do?" Cheever asked when the outrage had died down.

"I took care of the situation," Trav said, like that put an end to it.

Kell guffawed. "He coldcocked the guy. Giant fuckin' asshole was busy trying to grope Mackey and Blake, and Trav snuck up behind him with a—tell him, Trav?"

"A fucking bongo drum," Trav said in resignation. "It had a weighted bottom—the opening band had left it in the green room."

Cheever couldn't help it. He chuckled. "You knocked him out?"

"I stunned him," Trav corrected.

"*Then* Trav got him behind the knees with some ninja Army shit. And when he went down, Blake got him over the ear with a mic stand."

"The only other option was a guitar," Blake said softly. "Went with the mic stand."

"I was so fuckin' proud," Mackey gloated from the front. "Man, *that's* respecting the trade, right?"

"Can't fuck up a good guitar," Blake agreed, so seriously Cheever had to check his face to see if he was kidding.

Nope.

Apparently, Blake's indoctrination into Mackey's little cult of rock 'n' roll was 100 percent thorough. But that was the religion that had kept him from killing Aubrey Cooper today, and Cheever was going to be grateful.

"Of course not." Cheever brought his bandaged knuckles to his lips and kissed softly.

"I'm sorry," Blake whispered again.

"I'm okay." Cheever hoped it was the right thing to say, but Blake sighed and pulled his hand back into his lap.

"I'm glad," he said, his voice remote, and Cheever sighed and packed up the first aid kit to give back to Trav.

"Give him space," Trav advised. "It... it's hard. Being that guy."

Cheever grimaced. *Except Blake wasn't just that guy. Blake was the victim, and nobody put him back together. He was trying to be the hero, and the duct tape didn't always hold.*

The image of Blake trying to put himself back together with no help was so striking, Cheever had to close his eyes to see it.

The picture of a broken guitar player on the sidewalk gutted him, and every brush stroke, every line was etched so deeply in his head, he knew he could paint it tomorrow, in a week, in a month.

The words came with it, which only surprised him a little.

He pulled out his phone and started to text, wishing it was a tablet, wishing he had a pencil, but relying on words because that was all he had.

There you were in broken pieces
No one saved the day
You grabbed the duct tape and salvation
And fixed your problems anyway
You left fragments of your heart though
On the cracked pavement beneath
Not enough for you to bleed out
You're just unsteady on the beat
I'll hold you while you bleed on me
And I'll soothe away your pain
I'll use silk instead of duct tape
Which is serviceable and plain
I'll stop up all your leaky parts
I'll seal up all your cracks
But whether you're fixed or broke
I need you to come back
Just promise me no matter what
You'll still be coming back
I'll put together all your pieces
If only you come back.

He finished the lyric and looked at Blake, wondering if he'd want to see it. To his surprise, Blake was looking back at him, his eyes wide and shadowed.

"Texting?" he asked curiously.

"Writing," Cheever said with pride. For the barest moment, he contemplated holding the phone to his chest, but then he remembered what he'd just written, about putting Blake together. The only thing that would do that was trust.

He went back and titled it "Cement Ragdoll" and showed Blake his phone, biting his lip.

Blake's breaths got shakier and shakier, and Cheever grimaced as he used the back of his bandaged hand to wipe off his cheeks.

"Okay?" Cheever asked, because who didn't worry when they gave someone something close to their heart.

Blake nodded and sobbed again.

"Aw, man." Cheever reached out and pulled at his shoulder. "Baby, c'mere."

Blake fought it—oh God, he fought it. Even at the end, every sob ripping through his body was ragged and unwelcome. But Cheever held him through them all, until he rested, limp and spent, in his arms.

THEY HAD arranged to stay in a hotel outside of Redding, two to a room. Cheever and Blake had a king-sized bed, which made Cheever sort of proud, but Blake was silent as he brought in his duffel bag and dropped it on the luggage rack.

He started rooting through the bag immediately, coming up with his running shoes and clothes Cheever had thought were pure wishful thinking. But Blake changed swiftly, not talking, not even making eye contact.

He didn't break the silence until he put his hand on the doorknob, nylon hat in place over his forehead, running jersey swinging around his hips. "I'll be back," he said shortly.

"Blake, it's 105 outside!" Because this area hadn't gotten any less like the cauldron of hell in the summer over the last eight years.

"I gotta—"

"Water!" Cheever said desperately.

"Cheever, if I don't get out of this hotel in five minutes, I'm gonna be snorting drain cleaner and hoping it's coke," Blake said brutally. "Now I'll be back, I promise—just let me go now."

And he was gone.

Kell was next door, and Trav was across the hall, and Cheever pounded on Kell's door because it was closer.

To his surprise Kell popped out fully dressed in his running gear, and Trav emerged in his kit too, with a net bag of water bottles.

"He left already," Cheever said, near tears.

"Well, yeah," Kell said, starting his sturdy jog down toward the elevators. "'Cause he's smart."

They both disappeared around the corner, and Cheever sagged against his own door. He looked numbly into his hand and saw he had the key and wondered how in the hell that had happened. It was the only thing to go right since they'd left Tyson.

Mackey came limping out of his and Trav's bedroom as he stared, and Cheever caught a pair of board shorts in the face before he could even ask where his brother was going.

"Change," Mackey grunted, and Cheever saw he had his own pair on with a T-shirt over it. "I figured you wouldn't know the drill. Meet you at the pool."

Cheever had no choice, apparently. He changed and left again, meeting his mother on the way to the elevators. He blinked, because she'd done her makeup and fluffed out her hair.

"Mom?"

"Going to the bar," she said with a watery smile. "Trav won't drink 'cause of Mackey, Kell won't drink 'cause of Blake, and the twins just don't drink on general principle. It's tradition. Guys work out, girls go to the bar. It's been a long day, sweetheart—we all need our drugs."

The door opened, and his mother went toward the hotel bar and Cheever followed the signs to the pool, bemused.

Yeah, sure he was worried. But his poem had been pretty on point, actually. The band had their ways of putting themselves back together again. It was Cheever's job to let them do it without getting upset.

The pool was warm and overchlorinated, but it was water. Mackey was in up to his chest doing strength exercises, and Cheever started doing laps in the lane next to him. The physical activity was soothing, he realized. The day had been nonstop traveling and drama, and his own tension drained out of him steadily until he was pleasantly tired.

He pulled his heart rate up for a good ten laps and then cooled down, floating to a halt near Mackey without conscious thought.

"Feel better?" Mackey asked, doing what looked like yoga under the water.

"Yeah. You?"

"Got about two more reps. How was Blake when they left?"

Cheever let out a dispirited breath. "Two heartbeats away from using. Three from running off a cliff."

"That's why it's better to go in a group," Mackey said seriously, and Cheever gave a bark of laughter.

"What?"

Just ... just....

"There is so fucking much I don't know." Cheever swirled his hand in the strong-smelling water. "I guess Mom goes out and gets girl-drink drunk once a year. Who knew?"

Mackey chuckled. "Well, she's always been fond of Briony." He deepened his stretch. "Me too. She's the sister I was never smart enough to want."

Cheever grunted. Truth was, he'd been stocking Blake's refrigerator and leaving the note for the housekeeper because he was well and truly afraid of so much as asking for a soda in the big house.

Mackey chuckled harder. "Last ass-beatin' she gave you still stinging, right?"

"She's terrifying," Cheever said flatly.

"Yeah, well, whole reason we got tight was she wouldn't take my crap. Stands to figure she won't take yours either. But you brought one of those with you—the sister who just sort of fits into the family. She doing okay?"

Cheever thought of Marcia, who had always been so intense, so stressed, so determined to get her degree and do her parents proud. She'd helped Katy pack her stuffed animals that morning, and she'd made a little pile of them that Katy wanted to leave in Marcia's room so they wouldn't be lonely. Marcia had taken each one into her room and put it on her bed, reciting the name so she wouldn't forget. Yeah, she'd been sad because Katy was going, but she'd been so in her element, talking to that little kid.

"She's doing good," he said, smiling slightly. "I guess being surrounded by kids and cranky rock stars is actually her thing."

Mackey changed his stretch, dropping his shoulders, keeping his face barely out of water. "Yeah—Shelia and Briony's too. Who knew. You talk to her about Blake?"

Cheever stood straight and let the warm wind sweep over him. Redding didn't cool down in July. "Am I supposed to? She was like the rest of you all. I was like, 'Yay! Great guy! Seems to like me!' And you all were like, '*Don't break Blake!*'" He felt the same helpless frustration building up behind his eyes. "And apparently I broke him. Because...."

He felt Blake's sobs—not helpless, but not welcome either. There was no cleansing cry for Blake Manning, just this terrible certainty that he'd failed by crying at all. "Because that in the car… it was painful."

Mackey snorted, his breath blowing a little bit of water back. "You gonna let a little bit of pain stop you? 'Cause if that's the case, I'll be the first to tell you that starting the relationship was a bad idea. It's like the first time you have butt-sex, really. Going forward will hurt, but it will eventually feel good. Just stopping will feel better in your ass, but it's gonna fuckin' destroy your heart."

Cheever stared at him. "Oh dear God."

Mackey stood carefully and extended his arms over his head. "What?"

"That was the most awful analogy in… I mean, you make your living writing songs, for sweet Christ's sake!"

Mackey swooped his arms down his sides. "Does it work? Is it true?"

Cheever shifted uncomfortably. "I… well, you know. Ain't really done that, voluntarily." *Ain't. Fucking aces.*

Mackey dropped his arms and turned to stare at Cheever deliberately. "You…." He crossed his eyes. "Dear God. You have actually made me uncomfortable talking about sex. First time in your entire life, I wish Mom had gotten a cat instead. You and Blake been doin' the dirty, right?"

"Yes." Cheever swallowed. "I'm very comfortable topping, thank you."

"But you don't trust him to even see if the other way is a thing you'd want?" Mackey asked. "'Cause I gotta tell you, Blake's pretty fucking good at leading and planning and taking care of people and shit. I think he might not suck at it."

"He hasn't—" Cheever was going to boil the goddamned swimming pool. "—complained," he finished weakly.

"Well, no. Blake wouldn't. Because he'd do anything to make you happy."

"Well, dammit, Mackey, everything just got healed back there!"

Mackey scowled back. "Still hurt?"

"No."

"You all freaked out about doing it that way?"

Cheever had to think about it. "I don't really know?"

"Look, I'm not saying the magic fuckin' hoo-ha in the magic fuckin' whatsis is gonna fuckin' cure what ails you. And I damned sure ain't gonna tell you to do something that hurts or makes you feel uncomfortable. What I'm saying is you gotta trust a guy with the things that might hurt you before he trusts you with the shit that's been hurting him for fifteen goddamned years. And yeah, I'm sure he's told you. But there's telling someone like they practiced it in their head, like you learn to do in rehab, and there's telling someone like you really lived it and it really happened to you. Which telling you done?"

"The second kind," Cheever said, remembering being handcuffed to his bed and the way Blake had crawled in and held him anyway, falling asleep because he'd been taking care of everybody's business but his own.

"Which telling he done?"

Cheever sighed. "The kind like it happened to a stranger."

Mackey grunted and put his hands behind him, stretching out his chest. "Yeah. I know that kind. But you can bet your fuckin' life that's not what Trav heard when I was tryin' to get clean. And Blake's probably deliriously happy for you to take charge, by the way. You take charge, he doesn't have to worry about fucking up, which I know for a fact is his biggest goddamned fear."

"Yeah," Cheever said, so relieved to not be talking about sex with his brother that worrying about Blake was almost a blessing. "I'd agree with that."

"God, this conversation sucks. Any way you could have one of these with Marcia next time? I personally would raise her salary if I didn't have to do this again."

Cheever had to laugh. "You don't talk about sex with the guys?"

Mackey actually dropped his stretch to stare at him. "Are you fuckin' high? If you're fuckin' high, get out of the pool right now, because for all I know, you'll pee in the pool and I'll get a contact high and all this bullshit about taking the goddamned pain pill was a giant waste of time. No. No, I didn't talk to our *brothers* about sex, because Kell told me to use a condom the first time he saw a hickey on my neck. I wasn't gonna tell him his best friend put it there and we weren't using condoms because that was our rule with each other. There you have it. The one bit of advice I ever got. It is the tip of the motherfucking iceberg is what it is, the absolute minimum you can know about sex in any given situation, from Kell. Me, I'm giving you gold. You had better be taking notes."

"Note-taking commencing!" Cheever said, a little panicked. He tapped his forehead with his finger. "All up here."

"You are fucking hysterical. Does that mean I'm gonna be your go-to guy for this shit from here on out? Because I need to read some fuckin' psych manuals or shit if this is gonna be a thing. Fuckin' Marcia—she better be teaching those kids super honors English and how to fly and shit because she is falling down on the job."

"Do *you* talk to Briony about sex?" Cheever asked in sheer self-defense.

"Sometimes," Mackey told him. "For example, we had a very useful discussion about cocoa butter a few years back that has eased both our minds considerably. But you wanna know what I talk to Briony about? I will tell you. If someone pisses me off, I tell Briony. And she pets me and says I'm pretty and everybody else is a fuckin' moron. Does she mean that shit? Probably not. She's probably thinking, 'For fuck's sake, Mackey Sanders, get over yourself.' But she *says* that shit and that's all I need. 'Cause if I told Trav that someone pisses me off, you know what would happen?"

Cheever thought of Trav, trying to decide whether or not to pound Aubrey into the ground again. He'd been so collected. For him, it had been a conscious decision, made in the heat of battle without a flinch.

"He'd kill him or fire him?" Cheever was only guessing about the firing.

"Or kill him *with* fire," Mackey agreed. "So I whine to Briony, she tells me I'm pretty, and whatever pissed me off is not nearly so fucking dire. And I know for a fact I am a giant diva pain in the ass, but I try not to take that shit out on anybody else in my life because I did that to Blake and I'm gonna be apologizing for it for a long time. So me and Briony go on and slaughter each other in video games, and it's all good. And Trav already knows I'm pissed off, but if he doesn't have to fucking fix it, nobody dies or loses their job. And I haven't hurt anyone but the little assholes in the video game, and those assholes deserve it for not reading my mind."

It was a good system. "I...." Cheever swallowed. "I guess I haven't... you know. Talked to *anybody* in so long. Blake was the first person I felt like... like he wouldn't hate me. Wouldn't judge." God. Wasn't *that* pathetic. But then Mackey surprised him yet again, like Mackey had been surprising the world for probably his entire life.

"Yeah. Well, so was Trav. But you start with that one. And he's your rock. And you get your rock, and you can go swimming with other people to see if they're just as sturdy. Not everybody is. And some people you tell different things. But that's the thing with damage. Other people broke you. You're afraid. And nobody's gonna take all your weight, all the time. So you try to find the people you can count on, and know if they let you down, it's not always their fault. The whole world is like a bone with micro fractures. Be as careful as you can, and forgive yourself if you hit that bone just right. And then help that person stand up as best you can afterward. It's not a perfect system, Cheever. We are human fucking beings. We're gonna screw up. But we can't walk in the world without each other, and that's the goddamned truth."

Cheever's throat burned. "You know, if we weren't in the pool, I'd want to hug it out or something—"

"I am in massive amounts of pain. Touch me and die." He let out a long breath. "But yeah. Good talk, little brother. Go bottom like a champ. I'm gonna hope Trav's back so I can take my pain pill."

"You're not going to take it without him?" Cheever asked, heading for the pool steps.

"That's the deal we made. I'd take them if he'd give them to me. 'Cause I'm in pain and I'm frustrated and I'm not ready to trust myself just yet."

"You trust me?" Cheever was so proud he could offer.

Mackey followed him, walking slowly, dragging his feet— particularly the swimming cast—probably because his back hurt too much to lift them. "Sure," he said, his voice clogged. "That's real kind."

They made it up to the room, and Cheever helped Mackey into the shower, pulling his pain meds from Trav's shaving kit and setting them up on the bed stand next to a granola bar he found in one of the gas station bags.

He helped Mackey get dressed when the shower was done, his heart wrenching a little at the fine trembling in Mackey's limbs that came from going through a long day when your body was not 100 percent.

"Gah!" Mackey said as Cheever settled him under the blankets and against the pillows in his pajamas. "This sucks. I thought 'Hey, I'll be sitting most of the day. How bad can it be?'"

"Real fucking bad," Cheever said softly, offering him water. Mackey washed down the pill and started to munch doggedly on the granola bar.

"Yeah. That's about it. Hey, fetch my phone from the bathroom, would you? I didn't check to see if Trav called after the pool."

Cheever had checked *his* phone and hadn't seen anything. The sun had gone down as they'd gone inside the hotel, and the temperature had dropped to about ninety. Cheever wondered if they were trying to run all the way to the goddamned airport.

"Oh, hey!" Mackey let out a little smile as he scanned his phone. "They went for food. Trav says they're all bringing back takeout—Chinese, I guess. Says they went ahead and ordered for us. They'll be back in about half an hour."

Cheever closed his eyes in relief. "Oh good. I should shower—"

"Don't forget to moisturize." Mackey grimaced. "My skin's already dried out. Fuckin' hotel pools. Every fuckin' time."

Cheever brought him some body butter from his shaving kit and made sure he had the phone charger and enough water.

"Cheever?" Mackey said as he was leaving.

"Yeah?"

"You're growing up real good. Blake would be the first guy to tell you not to take his bullshit as your failing. And you know, if anything I say sounds like crap, blow me off." He tilted his head back against the pillows, obviously completely exhausted.

"Blow you off?" Cheever said, just to make him smile. "I finally figured out what good brothers are after the last eight years. This shit's gold." He made sure he had Mackey's eyes on him before he tapped his temple with his forefinger. "It's all up here."

Mackey smiled slightly and closed his eyes again. Cheever left.

HE HEADED directly for the shower, because damn, chlorine, and replayed the conversation under the spray.

Mackey was right, well, on a lot of fronts, but about trusting Blake as much as he expected Blake to trust him. He'd been hell-bent on seducing Blake at first, making it so good for him that he didn't even think about leaving. And Blake had just been so willing. So needy. It had been easy to take him over, to give him everything he seemed to want.

But he'd also seemed to want to pleasure Cheever, and Cheever hadn't let him. Cheever took a handful of conditioner and smoothed his hand down over his backside. Too scary, right? Not even physically scary, but emotionally scary. Letting someone into your body—some people would just do that, and it was no big deal.

Blake had confessed to rock star days when he slept with anything that moved.

But obviously, it *was* a big deal for Cheever. He hadn't been physical with anybody—voluntarily—until Blake.

Cheever needed to not just trust Blake because Blake let Cheever get his way.

Cheever needed to trust Blake because if Blake was in charge, he knew Blake would do it right.

Using the conditioner, Cheever fingered his backside, checking for soreness, checking for any residual swelling.

Nope.

Everything an asshole should be.

Tentatively, using the conditioner as lube—poor man's lube, but it helped—he tapped his fingertip in.

Odd. Very strange. Tingly. Even under the water, Cheever felt sweat wash his chest and his nipples and the back of his neck. Curious, he thrust his finger in a little deeper.

Mm. Okay. That wasn't... oh, hey, a little stretching....

Cheever leaned his forehead against the shower wall, spread his stance, and got serious. Damn. Oh... a little twinge there.... He closed his eyes and deliberately relaxed, pushing out against the intrusion instead of tightening in.

His finger wasn't wide enough.

Two was good. Two was perfect. Three was.... He shuddered and moved his hand to the shower wall, and then washed off all parts involved before shutting off the water.

Okay. Okay, then. Cheever's body was shaking with need, and his brain was in fuzzy-happy la-la land for the mental gymnastics that came with accommodating that need.

But one thing was pounding through him besides want.

The absolute certainty that this was something he wanted to share with Blake.

Yeah, sure, some people could share their bodies and not their hearts. But Cheever wasn't one of them—and Cheever had the feeling that Blake never should have tried to be. If someone couldn't see what a treasure Blake Manning's heart was, they didn't deserve to touch him.

He was still drying off, that thought branded in his brain like words of fire, when he heard Blake's tentative tap at the door.

Love, It's a Bitch

TRAV HAD forced a quart of Gatorade down his throat when they were done with the run, and then gave him enough Chinese food for six people to take back to the hotel room.

"Trav, I'm fine—"

Trav had simply fixed him with that no-bullshit glare that had pulled the entire band out of their own ass almost a decade before.

"I swear," Blake said weakly. "I ran it all out of my system, right?"

Well, they were all sopping wet with sweat. Usually Trav was the one who set the pace, but Blake was always at his fastest when he was running from his demons. Kell had been the one to beg for mercy, and that had been the only reason Blake had slowed down.

"You say that, but you never do. You just internalize it." Trav's glower always made him feel small. "You had reason to be upset, Blake. It's okay to admit that."

"Somebody hurt him," Blake said simply, and he didn't seem to be able to get over that.

"Somebody hurt every one of you guys," Trav returned. "Yes, Kell, even you, although not in the same way. You think I don't want to go back and beat the shit out of Grant Adams's dad? Because I know he was your boss, and we all know you would have driven your car off a bridge if you had to work for him for one more minute. Not one of you got out of your shitty childhoods without some holy-fucking-wow scars, and I hate the assholes who inflicted every one of them. So I get it."

Blake's knuckles stung, and his calves were cramping, and he was starting to hate his own smell. "You don't beat everybody up all the time," he muttered.

"Well, I had practice not doing that in the Army," Trav said with dignity. "Look, Blake, I'm sure he's worried about you. Just go back, take a shower, for God's sake, eat something, and talk to him. He loves you—anybody can see it."

Blake's brain shorted out.

Oh God. Cheever loved him? Cheever loved *him*?

But you love him back, moron.

After giving himself a few minutes for that bombshell to settle, Trav pulled into the hotel parking lot and was about to kill the engine, effectively rendering the rental into an Easy-Bake oven, even after dark.

"Blake, you back in your head?" Kell was asking worriedly. "Where the hell did you go?"

Blake sort of squinted at him. "I'm in love with your little brother."

Kell let out a strangled laugh. "Yeah, Blake. Color me shocked. Stunned. Jesus, go upstairs and eat, and drink the rest of that Gatorade, okay?"

Blake nodded, and Trav finally killed the engine. Blake hauled his share of the takeout and the bag of Gatorade to his room, and embarrassingly enough, had to knock because he couldn't access the wallet in the little pouch on the side of his running shorts.

Cheever opened the door, fresh from the shower, smelling so good, his hair slicked back from his face and his curls clustering below his ears.

Blake could have just stared at him stupidly for a good ten minutes, because he looked so damned good.

Cheever grinned at him, cheeks flushed, eyes dilated a little, like they did with sex, and Blake had a flash of desire so strong, he almost dropped the takeout and sank to his knees in the carpet. God, the boy was wearing little more than a towel. All Blake had to do was lower his head and he could claim Cheever's nipple, and tease and tease—

"Go shower," Cheever ordered huskily, taking the bags out of his hand. "Make it quick."

Blake nodded, all of that stupid heartache forgotten as he fought with the urge to run his lips over Cheever's bare skin.

He made the shower cold, the better to lower his core temperature and keep him from overheating, and he rinsed every crease and crevice extremely well. That image, Cheever's pale chest, his towel, the little cinnamon nipples pebbling, was coursing through Blake's body.

He hadn't been sure he could stand as he'd knocked on the door, but now he wasn't sure his erection would ever go down.

Still, he emerged from the shower, a clean towel around his hips, fully expecting to see Cheever in his pajamas, digging into dinner.

What he found instead was Cheever, buck naked on his back, a towel under his bottom, knees spread. He was plucking at those nipples with his fingertips, and his backside, between the spread knees, was slick and dripping with lubricant. The bottle was up on the bed stand, and Blake groaned a little when he saw it was opened.

Cheever's cock lay against his thigh, swollen and dripping and lewd.

Blake's erection tented the towel around his waist, and he groaned, loud and aroused, as he drank in Cheever's wanton offering before him.

Cheever opened his eyes at the sound and gave Blake a look so sultry, so filled with heat, that Blake actually dropped his towel.

"Do you want me?" Cheever asked.

"Oh God, yes."

"Come take me, then. I am dying for you, you know that, right?"

Blake crawled up between his legs, thinking about taking his cock, wanting to devour it whole. But Cheever tugged at his hair, letting out a little whimper.

"A kiss first," he begged. "I want everything, but first I want—"

Blake lunged up his body and claimed his mouth.

Sweetness. Oh damn. What had Blake Manning done in his life to deserve such sweetness? He couldn't rationalize it, not now. Couldn't explain it. Cheever's mouth under his was perfect, feeding into his need, satisfying his hunger for warmth, for kindness, for heat and edge, all in the same taste. Cheever wrapped his legs around Blake's thighs. The effect of their bare bodies sliding silkenly together electrified him. More kissing, more give-and-take of tongue and pleasure, and then Blake set about to eat him alive.

Hot kisses down his neck, nips, nibbles, sucks. He took the dreamed-about nipple in his mouth and pulled hard, glorying in Cheever's cry, in the way his legs tightened around Blake's hips, the way they ground against each other, dripping and hard.

Blake spent a long time there on his nipples, until after a particularly sharp bite, Cheever arched up and bit Blake's neck, hard.

"Suck me or fuck me!" he begged, raking his nails across Blake's shoulders. The hint of pain made Blake grind against the bed, pushing his abdomen against Cheever's cock, which spurted hotly with precome.

They didn't have a lot of time here. "Which one's it gonna be?" he asked, caught between the two heady promises. "Which one you want, Cheever. I'll give you anything—"

"*Fuck me!*"

Blake's head came up, and he made eye contact, sweat breaking out across his back, his forehead. "I'll be gentle," he promised, barely able to talk, knowing what this meant. These last two months, Cheever had taken him, and now he was giving that trust in return.

"Fuck gentle." Cheever half laughed. "Be thorough. God, I need you—there. Exactly where you're thinking. Please, baby, please."

"Okay," he grated. "But I'll die if I don't taste this first."

He slid down and took Cheever's cock into his mouth, loving it—how it stretched his lips, filled his throat. Cheever thrust up, like he couldn't help himself, dripping copiously, salty and bitter and good.

"I'm gonna come," Cheever moaned.

Blake pulled off for a moment, and took the opportunity to slide a finger down Cheever's crease, into his stretched, oiled entrance. Oh wow, his boy had been playing hard with himself. He was stretched and hot, and he clenched around Blake's finger greedily.

"Blake...," Cheever whimpered, and Blake licked up and across his cockhead one more time before rising up on the bed.

"You are just too delicious all over," Blake whispered, taking his mouth again. "And you sure do seem ready for me."

"I am. I trust you."

The words almost sent Blake over. He moaned and positioned himself carefully. "Tell me," he rasped. "How fast, how far—"

Cheever grunted and pushed down, opening up enough to glide over Blake's head. "Keep going," he begged. "Just... oh God... please... don't stop...."

Blake went slow, because he knew it was all about the stretch, and because he needed to be ready to pull out if Cheever changed his—"Oh!" His head popped all the way in and sweat washed Blake's body again. "How are you?"

"*More!*" Cheever demanded, and Blake slid all the way in. "Yes! Yes, that's *perfect*! Now *move*!"

Blake chuckled roughly as he began to slide out, then in. "Anything you want," he said, thrusting a little bit harder. Then a little bit more.

"*Faster!*"

Blake came to a stop, his muscles trembling, no hesitation left, just the boiling certainty of Cheever's body locked securely around Blake's cock.

"Slow," he said. Slow and long and deep. Until Cheever opened for him and every muscle relaxed. Until Blake found his sweet spot, obvious because Cheever arched off the bed and howled when he hit it. Until Cheever let out a breath and melted, still aroused but submissive, soft and yielding, riding the buzz until Blake broke and started hammering him hard, fucking him wide open.

Cheever lost his mind then, gibbering, begging, his face slack, limbs flailing. Blake caught his hands above his head and slowed a little more.

"Take it easy," he whispered. "I'll take care of you."

"So close!" he gasped.

Blake shifted to his knees and slung Cheever's thighs up over his shoulders. "Cheever," he said, making his voice strong.

"Blake?"

"Grab your cock, sweetheart. Yank just like you want it."

Cheever did, his low groan cueing Blake in to fuck him blind.

Sweating, pounding, hearing Cheever's cries rising, Blake took him up, up, to the clench of Cheever's ass on his cock sending him over, the sight of Cheever, head back, eyes closed, as he shot over his stomach and chest, searing behind his eyelids as he went.

He rutted for a moment, his cock awash in spend, Cheever's body loose and hot around him. Finally, he fell forward, both of them sticky and sweaty and neither of them repentant in the least.

"God!" Cheever blew out a breath, using his wet hand to push his hair out of his eyes.

Blake chuckled and freed it of the strands of hair, then licked it methodically, from fingertip to webbing, tasting Cheever's come.

"That was so good," Cheever mumbled, searching Blake's face. "Why didn't we do that sooner?"

Blake paused and sucked Cheever's thumb into his mouth, hard enough that he felt Cheever's ass clench again as his young body thought about arousal. He let the thumb go with a pop and began rocking without urgency, deep in Cheever's body.

"'Cause you weren't ready," Blake murmured. He felt a low headache starting behind his eyes, and his eyelids fluttered closed against it. Cheever's body felt so good.

Cheever lifted up to kiss him, and Blake opened for him, melting, closer to Cheever in that moment than he'd ever been to any human being.

"Ready now," he whispered, nibbling on Blake's lower lip and tugging on it.

"Again?" Blake's movements began to have purpose, and his cock swelled up all over again, his body beginning a tingling that didn't feel like it would stop.

"Oh God," Cheever moaned. "Yes. Just like… just like…."

Blake rolled his hips, tried again for Cheever's sweet spot.

Cheever's body arched off the bed while his head fell back, and a long, slow, prolonged orgasm rippled through his body, clenching Blake's cock so hard he couldn't stroke anymore, just stopped, convulsing in his own aftershock, both of them spilling together.

This time when Blake collapsed, he rolled off Cheever to his side, his head pounding worse than ever.

He closed his eyes against the light, and his next sound wasn't one of pleasure.

"Blake?"

"Ouch," he mumbled, throwing his arm across his face. "Too much light!"

"Goddammit!" Cheever muttered. "Didn't you have any water or anything?"

He rolled off the bed and slid on some underwear as Blake tried to piece together the events *before* he'd gotten out of the shower and saw Cheever naked and playing with himself.

"I brought some in with the takeout," he apologized as Cheever squatted by the desk, finding the bag underneath.

"Yeah, here." Cheever helped Blake sit up and handed him a bottle of blue Gatorade, still a little cold from the cooler. Blake started drinking—not gulping, just drinking at a reasonable rate.

"Thanks," he sighed.

Cheever came back with two ibuprofen tablets, which Blake downed immediately.

"So much."

Cheever sat down at the edge of the bed, sliding his fingers through Blake's hair. "Not sure whether to be mad at you for not eating or flattered for being that hot," he said, but he sounded smug, so Blake figured he knew which side of *that* fence he'd slid down on. "I wish you'd take care of yourself, you know?"

Blake kept his eyes closed, but he smiled a little. "All that matters is that I finish," he mumbled.

"Kell says you come out of concerts like this."

Augh! "It's embarrassing that you know that."

But Cheever kept stroking his hair. "Just… you know. Take care of yourself. Make sure there's something left for snuggling."

Blake turned over to his side. "We could snuggle now."

Cheever's soft laughter was his reward. "We could eat now."

"Killjoy." Blake grunted and tapped his hip. "Let me up. I'm going to shower again. Trav's getting us up at 5:00 a.m. so we can be at the airport on time."

"Ugh. Fine. You shower first, then start eating—"

"We could shower together," Blake asked hopefully, because he didn't want to let go of Cheever's supple, responsive body.

"No." Cheever's kiss was unexpected and welcome. "I still want you. And you need food. One of us has to be the grown-up."

Cheever stood up and helped Blake do the same, his hands kind and brusque. Blake found himself under the water, rinsing off the traces of lovemaking, exhausted and puzzled.

How did he get to be the grown-up again?

He didn't have any answers, but after they ate and brushed their teeth, they settled down to sleep, Cheever being the big spoon tonight, like always.

But not being the grown-up, surprisingly enough.

"Can I ask you something?" His voice in the dark startled Blake just enough to make him twitch. "Sorry—you were sleeping."

"No," Blake mumbled. "Go 'head."

"What made you fall for my brother?"

Blake's eyes shot open. "I could have used some warning for that."

Cheever's soft puff of breath was his only acknowledgment. "Sorry. I'm curious. I get that it was a long time ago—"

"Ten years."

"And that you and Briony are supercool and you love his kids—"

"Like my own."

"But... but why Kell?"

Blake grunted. "Your brother isn't bright"—and when Cheever sounded like he was going to agree vociferously, Blake kept right on going—"but he knows it." Oh yeah, that was sobering. "So he keeps at it. He kept studying. Briony helped him, and he listened to what she had to say, and that's how he got his degree. He knows Mackey's got, like, stupid talent, but Mackey worships the ground Kell walks on, so Kell just keeps trying to live up to that. He knows his brother isn't going to ever leave him out, and he's grateful. He tried to protect you and Mackey when you were kids, and sometimes, that was bad and backfired. But

mostly, it just came because he's your brother and he loves you. I...."
Blake's voice dropped, because he was never *not* going to love Kellogg
James. But he couldn't imagine having the same relationship with him
that he had with Cheever. "Any sane person would love Kell."

"Oh." Cheever sounded so disheartened, and suddenly Blake knew
what he needed. It was a truth, one Blake had known for a while now,
but he'd put off saying it because when Cheever left him.... September?
Would it happen when he left for tour? It didn't matter. If he said it,
Blake thought the leaving would hurt worse.

Well, nothing would hurt worse than when Cheever left him now.

"But it's not nearly the way that I love you," Blake said, closing his
eyes against the heartache he knew that would bring.

Cheever's arms tightened around Blake, almost convulsively. "I
love you too. Like so big. Like mountains and sunrises and stuff."

"And oceans," Blake murmured. "And deserts and planets." Every
word, every comparison, opened up a chamber in his heart that would
flood with pain when the time came, but he couldn't help it. He already
proved his one strength was pushing through and not leaving anything
for the end.

THE THOUGHT bothered him, though. During the short plane ride
home, Blake sat between Kell and Cheever, a wide-awake filling in the
rock star Oreo, and fiddled with his phone.

Cheever was leaning his head against the window, knees drawn
up underneath him, so sound asleep Blake wasn't sure he was going
to wake up when the plane touched down. He looked so vulnerable, so
defenseless, and Blake couldn't help thinking about the wounds they all
carried, and the way he seemed to love Cheever with no self-protection,
no guards, no plan B. At least when he'd been in love with Kell, he could
cover the ache with empty sex.

There wasn't another soul, another body that would fill this ache.
And he couldn't stop feeling, couldn't stop falling, because Cheever was
right there, and the promise might be a lie, but Blake was too ragged to
do anything but soak it up and believe.

He opened his notes app and started writing.

Mountains fall. Deserts bloom. Oceans turn to sand.
Moons decay. Stars explode. That leaves me where I am.

All alone in an empty room.

His head filled with chords, a delicate guitar riff, a breath of air before the next part. He tapped those in too.

I opened my heart, it filled with love, with sex, with power, with new.
With every door I pulverized, I knew I'd be missing you.
All alone in an empty room.

More power chords, the riff was bloody now—he tapped some notes to help him remember what it would be like, since he didn't have his guitar to learn it in his hands.

I know you're gonna leave me. It's like the night following the day.
I can't do much but hold on tight, until you go away.
Just don't leave me
All alone in an empty room.

He added some more notations, some ideas for drums, for the bass line, for the two guitars.

And then he sent it to Mackey, who was sitting in front of them with his mother and Trav. He didn't think Mackey had his Wi-Fi on too, but he must have, because about five minutes later, Blake got a text bubble.

THIS IS BRILLIANT. You can't sing it.

I thought for the new album. He frowned. Mackey was usually so supportive.

You will break my brother's heart. Jesus fucking Christ, have some faith.

Blake looked at the text and fought the burning in his eyes. Damn these Sanders boys. Who gave them the right to have a window to his soul? Every goddamned one of them, even Stevie.

"He's right, you know," Kell said softly, and Blake looked at Cheever quickly, to make sure he was still asleep.

"How'd you—"

"He sent it to me. Jesus, Blake, we're practically in each other's laps."

"It's a good song," he said stubbornly.

Kell looked at it, his lips moving as he read the riff. "Fine. I'll sing it."

Blake stared, but Kell wasn't giving in.

"No. I'm totally and completely serious. It's a great song. You're right. But you can have a great song out there to break my little brother's heart for the rest of his life, or you can have a great song out there that his older brother sings and he can give a rat's ass about. Briony knows I don't write shit like this. I give her cards that say 'Babe, you're awesome!' and she's happy. This is fuckin' poetry. Don't let it ruin your life."

Blake clenched his jaw against the ache in his throat, and Kell threw a brotherly arm over his shoulders. "Man, it's like that song you wrote me. It's great. We should do it on tour. But it guts me, because I know how much that hurts."

Oh fuck me! Blake took a shuddery breath and turned his face into his brother's shoulder. "You knew?" he managed to ask.

"You're not that hard to figure out." Kell kissed his hair. "But you're my favorite brother. I hate to see you in pain."

Blake took a deep breath and tried to pull himself together. By the time the plane touched down, his eyes were only a little red, and that could be blamed on lack of sleep.

Cheever woke up as the plane landed, dazed and out of it, and Blake could only be grateful as they steered him down the aisle and to the gate. He really wasn't sure what to say.

THEY MADE it home, and the rest of the summer passed in a blur of rehearsing the new album, then recording it, then—when Mackey was finally up for the two-hour set, which was the least he'd settle for—rehearsing to finish the tour.

Blake showed Mackey the song Cheever wrote, and Mackey came back the next day with complete instrumentation. Mackey said they should put it on Blake's album, but Blake refused.

"The fuck?" Mackey squinted at him.

"Think, Mackey. All that kid has wanted his entire life is to be a part of you guys. I mean, I know he spent eight years acting like that was the *last* thing he wanted, but trust me—it's the *only* thing he's wanted. Don't put his song on my album, where it's gonna get lost. Put it on Outbreak Monkey's, where he can be part of the band."

Mackey tilted his head. "That's a great idea, but I hate where you got it. This album? It's gonna be *great.* It's gonna be like, *Nebraska,* or like if Kurt Cobain hadn't self-destructed and Dave Grohl spent part of his time with the Foo Fighters and part of his time with Nirvana."

Blake stared at him. "Are you high? All this bullshit about not getting high, and what in the fuck are you taking for your back? Be truthful now—you finally caved and did edibles, right?"

"Shut the fuck up," Mackey snapped. "No. I'm not high. This is a quality fucking album. And that song you're gonna let Kell sing is going to make it."

Blake grunted. "Look, how about we keep that one on Outbreak Monkey's too. That way you can sing it."

Mackey glared at him. "*Trav!*"

Trav showed up at his elbow before he even stopped shouting. "What?"

"Would you make this asshole take credit for some of his own fucking work? Please? I am *killing myself* not to be a total douchewaffle and save all this shit for myself, but if he doesn't stop talking bullshit, I'm taking his songs and good luck trying to get people to remember he wrote them."

"Cheever wrote one of them," Blake argued. "With your help! And if you love the other one...." He swallowed. "I'd be... you know, honored if you sang it."

Trav gave him a crooked smile. "I think that's an awesome idea. Mackey, shut up and tell the man thank you. He just gave you some quality songs for the next album. Blake, all you need is one more, I think, and this one will be complete."

Stevie and Jefferson spoke up from their corner of the sound room, where they were leaning against each other and playing a game on their Switches.

"It's gotta be new," Stevie said, his eyes intent on his game. "None of the other ones are up to the quality of the tracks we've got laid down."

"Write our brother a better goddamned love song," Jefferson said, not even looking up.

Blake didn't even ask them how they knew about "Empty Room." He'd done the instrumentation on it and performed it so they could hear it, and they'd vetoed it immediately—on the grounds that it would break Cheever's heart.

"You guys—"

And now Jefferson *did* look up. "You love him?"

"Duh," Stevie said, eyes still focused. "'Course he does. Question is, does he have the guts to write something happy!"

"Look, guys, leave him alone," Mackey cautioned. "He can write whatever song he wants." Mackey leveled a gaze at him that brooked no argument. "But that doesn't mean that happy should be off the table, you understand?"

"We're going on tour in September," Blake said evenly. "He's staying here. Plenty of time for him to figure things out then."

"What makes you think he's not going to figure out he misses you and you're the one thing he really needs?" Mackey tilted his head in speculation.

"Because that would be a fuckin' first," Blake snapped. "Now let's work on getting this next song laid down, and I can go write some goddamned happy."

THE TRACK went down smooth as silk. It tended to do that when Mackey worked the sound board, because like everything else having to do with music, Mackey had a natural touch. They broke for dinner—separate dinners this evening—and Blake went upstairs to where Cheever was painting.

He was working on a landscape concept. Five different canvases, spanning California like it was one camera shot, looking westward. LA in the first canvas, panning to Monterey Bay, panning to the farmland of Bakersfield, panning to Sacramento, panning to Mount Lassen, which was only about eighty miles from Tyson itself. Yeah, the state wasn't entirely shaped that way, but Blake admired the idea—California was a big state, with definite landscape features, and a sort of unique demarcation along topographical lines.

Cheever was deep in concentration, his eyebrows drawn as he danced from canvas to canvas and sketched in details of each landscape, including the bleed from the left edge of the canvas into the focus landscape, and from the focus to the right side, which hinted at the landscape to come.

Apparently, this was supposed to be the assignment Cheever was working on when he'd produced those sickly landscapes of Tyson. Cheever wanted to go meet his teacher—the woman Blake had confronted when he'd been packing up Cheever's stuff—and show her what he could do with a clear and happy heart.

He'd already finished the "two sides of the same coin" pictures of Blake and the brothers, and those canvases were stacked up against the wall. More importantly, their digital downloads had already been sent to Heath, their producer, for approval. He was having a graphics department

do some shuffling, but Trav said he'd loved everything, from the concept
to the execution, and Cheever had made his first commission.

He was just like Mackey—so talented, it practically glowed off
his skin.

Blake watched him for a moment, in his element, humming happily,
and went to his desk by the fish tank.

"Hi, guys," he murmured. They seemed to be thriving. At least,
the giant bottom feeder hadn't died yet. He was still jumping out and
surprising the other fish—that was good.

Blake pulled out a pen and some paper, because the phone thing
had been an anomaly, and set about to write Cheever—but happy.

Spin me a world out of pencil lines
A universe of paint
A minute watching you at work
Shows me what I ain't.
Keep dancing in that world
I'll imagine I'm there too
And as long as we're in fantasy land
I'll be dancing there with you
Travel mountains to the valleys
From the valleys to the sea
Most fantastic thing I've ever seen
Is how you look at me
The mountains blaze like flame and fire
The sky is cobalt blue
That landscape isn't mine to admire
I've got eyes only for you.
You're the only world I'll ever need.
That's why I'm looking at you.

IT TOOK him an hour. Every note felt carved from obsidian. Every word
felt dragged from the center of his heart. But it was a happy moment for
Cheever and him, and maybe the boys would call it good.

He took out his guitar and played the intro, making notes on the
paper, then went back to instrumentation, keeping it as simple as possible

so the boys could help embellish. He finished, starving and thirsty, and looked up to see Cheever had put some orange juice on his desk and the sun had about gone down outside.

"Pretty," Cheever said, rubbing his shoulders. "What was it?"

"Love song," Blake told him, leaning into his caress.

"For me?"

Blake laughed. "Don't see anyone else here, do you?"

"Very funny. Just… you know. It sounded happy."

"I am happy," Blake said, his voice throbbing with hope. Cheever leaned over and kissed the crown of his head.

"I'm happy too."

Blake stood up and kissed him, leaving the rest of the song for tomorrow.

They were happy for now. The guys were right. The end would come soon enough—Cheever hadn't left yet. He needed to enjoy what he had.

MACKEY LISTENED to it thoughtfully, nodding. "Good," he said. "Good. Guys?"

"It's not permanent," Stevie said.

"Blake's still got one foot out the door," Jefferson said.

"Give it time." Kell smiled encouragingly. "I was pretty sure Briony was mistaking me for someone else until I knocked her up. Turned out, she really *did* love me."

"So that's the album?" Blake asked, not even daring to hope.

"Nope." Mackey pulled a rolled-up notebook out of his pocket, the cheap kind with the spiral wire that he got for twenty-five cents in the back-to-school sales. It's all he'd ever written on, even though they were a pain in the ass for a lefty like Mackey. "Trav, can you bring me my guitar?" He was leaning against a stool, and with a little difficulty, he hopped up on top of it.

"Here," he said, handing Blake the notebook. "Fix it, fuck it— whatever. But you need to hear it, whether or not you put it on."

The intro was a slow one, a couple of notes, a couple of chords, a build. So strong, so hooky, it gave Blake goose bumps.

Then Mackey sang.

You spent a year in my shadow
Then stayed
You deserved sunshine
You seemed to like my shade.
You won't take a thing from me
Brother, I give you my all
Don't be afraid
To turn your face to the sun
We're here to catch you
Turn your face to the sun
We grew up in hardpan
The lot of us thrived
There's more to living
Than just being alive
It's your time of softness
Flowers so sweet
You're still tough enough
For the fall
We're here to catch you
Turn your face to the sun
Blossom, thistles, and all.

The guitar trailed off, and Mackey glared defiantly at Blake.

And Blake gaped back.

"Dammit, Mackey," Kell muttered. "It's ten o'clock in the goddamned morning and you're gonna fuckin' make me cry."

Mackey rolled his eyes. "If that's your excuse for blowing up the bathroom, go ahead. We won't stop you. Blake? What you think?"

"You gotta sing it," Blake said, voice thick. "I'll do backup."

"Did you miss the goddamned—"

"No, man. I got the point." He stomped hard on his voice to keep it from cracking. "What is it about the last fucking months? It's like being back in rehab. Just every fucking thing dancing on my balls." He dragged his hand through his hair and tugged. "You're saying you love me. Like a brother. Saying you want me happy. Every goddamned thing I ever wanted to hear, you just fuckin' said." He swallowed. "I gotta go to the bathroom."

Kell blocked him. "Naw, man. Don't go to the bathroom. Stay here and ride it out."

Kell's bear hug grounded him, but then everyone else joined in—Mackey, Trav, Jefferson, and Stevie. Blake didn't have anywhere to go.

He had no choice, none at all, but to cry in their arms and know they'd be there when he needed them.

God, he was going to need them.

When the tears were over, he took a deep breath and wiped his entire face on the inside of his shirt. "Mackey, you're playing it, right?"

"We can do it together. Bruce and Stevie been doing it for years."

Blake grinned. "D'yall hear that? I'm Miami fucking Steve Van Zandt."

One of the biggest compliments in music. One of the best moments of his life.

BUT SAYING goodbye to Cheever in mid-September was one of the worst.

Cheever had been back to school for three weeks by then, and while Blake had expected it to take him away, mostly it was just one day a week he went somewhere else and came back with school stories to tell.

He was… fine. Happy, apparently. Facing school with aplomb. He talked about his professor—Professor Tierce—and how she seemed to like his work now, how she seemed so much more human.

It was so normal, like any couple with a future. Like any two people facing challenges and talking about them over dinner alone, or with family. Blake had always wondered about that—the day-to-day living with another human being in his life. Briony and Kell, Trav and Mackey, Shelia and the twins, they had made it look so effortless. "Hey, this is another person in our group, and we will talk and laugh and fight and watch TV and argue over where to go on a Saturday night! It's fine!" But Blake had never been able to make that work. Mostly because he'd never had the courage to try.

With Cheever, in his bed, in his house, in his life, it worked.

So preparing to pack up and leave on tour was a different sort of pain, one he didn't have a handle on yet.

"I'm moving back to the big house because why?" Cheever whined for the umpteenth time. His brothers whined too, because it meant they were moving his bed from the guest room *back* to the room Blake had made for him in the big house. But Cheever was *not* seeing the point.

"Because you won't be alone at night," Blake said. Then, nervously, he said, "But you'll still feed my fish, right?"

Cheever bit his lip and turned to cup his cheek. "'Course, baby. But it would be easier if I just stayed here, in our room."

Our room. He'd hung that picture, the one of kids on the beach, at the foot of the bed. He'd promised to put the California landscapes up there after his professor evaluated them. He'd even picked out an area rug for under the bed and had started researching pets.

Cheever was making this part of the big house their home over the studio, and Blake couldn't bear to think of what it would be like when he was gone.

"I don't want you alone at night," Blake said, then grimaced as he realized how that sounded. "I mean, you know, I would rather you be *alone* at night."

Cheever rolled his eyes as though nobody had ever heard of a cheating rock star. "Yeah, sort of my sentiments exactly. I'll call you at night, okay?"

Blake smiled a little. "Yeah. That'd be good. I'd like that."

But Cheever's sigh told Blake he wasn't fooled in the least. "You're expecting to never hear from me again."

"No!"

But Cheever waved him away. "No, no, I get it. It's bullshit, but that's something you'll have to see for yourself. Sure, I'll move across the street so you don't have to imagine me having sex with someone else in our bed."

Blake recoiled. "That's not what—"

"Or so you don't have to imagine me slitting my wrists." Cheever's words were blunt, but his tone was tender. "So you don't have to imagine the worst. I get it. I'm sorry I didn't see it sooner." He cupped Blake's cheeks and kissed him. "I said I love you. I meant it. Now go help my brothers before they lose their shit. I'm going to start rounding up clothes."

"That's gonna be rough."

Cheever kept his clothes all over—on the floor and the bed and the dresser and the windowsill and the towel racks and the rod that held up the shower curtain.

Oh yeah, he had a chest of drawers too!

"I know, right? I'll use your suitcases to haul them and then help you pack."

And just like that, his worries were dismissed, and the day was just another one in the life of a rock star.

Blake wasn't sure if he was reassured or panicked, but he didn't have time to do anything about either choice, so he just kept on moving. Right up until the morning the car came to take them to the airport.

The guys were all out on the lawn, waiting with their travel bags since their equipment had been hauled up north three days before. Their goodbyes were apparently done—except for Mackey's, of course, and Kell and the twins looked sad but resigned. It occurred to Blake that this was the first time they hadn't been able to bring their significant others, and his heart hurt for them.

Cheever followed Blake out of the house, because he was going to help wrangle the kids to school before he left for his own class, and because he just didn't want Blake to be alone.

The car pulled up just as they got there and Blake turned to him with a smile pasted on for good measure, but Cheever touched his lips and shook his head.

Abruptly Blake was back to the night before, when Cheever had taken charge. They seemed to switch fairly regularly now—depended on mood—but Cheever had topping from the bottom down to an art form.

Last night, he'd only had to stare at Blake with eyes that glowed with intent, and Blake had done what he needed. Blake's lips ached, his asshole ached, his cock ached, all with Cheever's determined and skillful use.

There was no corner of Blake's body—or his soul—left untouched by Cheever Sanders the night before, and there was no lying to him now.

"I'll miss you," he said soberly.

"I'll miss you too." Cheever didn't blink, didn't smile. This was deadly serious to him. "If I don't call, you need to. There is nothing more important that I could be doing than answering your call."

Blake grimaced. "Fair enough," he said. And then—because Trav had asked him the day before and he'd forgotten—he remembered to say, "Hey, you guys might get some press calls. The girls do sometimes. Talk to Trav first and make them make an appointment. Don't let them catch you flat-footed, okay?" Blake looked around their gated community. "This place is pretty safe. Guards don't let anyone through. But at school and stuff, you might be fair game." He shuddered, remembering all that Trav had protected him from, that might come back to haunt him. His mother had been suspiciously quiet for a couple of years. That alone sent shivers down his spine. "If anyone asks you something that's right out, hang up and call Trav."

Cheever nodded. "What if they ask me if I'm dating Blake Manning from Outbreak Monkey? What do you want me to say?"

Well, shit. "Whatever you're comfortable with."

Cheever arched an eyebrow. "Good. I'll tell them we're living together, and we're looking to get married in the next year."

Blake's mouth fell open, and Cheever kissed him, hard, all tongue, dominating. He pulled away, and Blake tried to put his brains back between his ears and think adult things.

"We can pick out rings when you get back," Cheever said, only slightly breathless. "So that's your answer too."

Blake closed his eyes and rested his forehead against Cheever's. "Baby boy, if you are here when I get back, that will be as happy as I ever expected to be. All the rest is icing."

"That's me," Cheever told him. "Icing."

In the background, Blake heard the guys loading into the car, and he sighed. "I'll text you when we get in," he said, and Cheever kissed his cheek. Then he turned and got in the car.

The car pulled away, and Blake leaned back in his seat, eyes closed, blowing out a slow breath.

"That was depressing," he muttered.

"Amen" came the rousing chorus.

"The kids love school," Kell said glumly.

"Go fuckin' figure," Stevie said, his voice sour.

Blake knew—Cheever had told him the same thing, and so had the kids. The days of touring as a family were over.

"Two years," Trav said into the silence, and Blake opened his eyes so he could join everyone in staring at him.

"Trav?" Mackey asked, voice uncertain.

"I talked to Heath. He wants one album from Outbreak Monkey, then he suggested that Mackey work as a producer for at least three projects, one of them a solo from Blake. We'll use the same jokers in the background." Stevie and Jefferson bumped fists, and Kell pumped his arm. "And then we give a tour every two years instead of every year. So we get to be home, get to raise kids. That way, if the kids are game to travel again, we can pack up a tutor and a nanny and go. If they're not, it's two months out, one month home, and two months out. Only big stadiums. Briony will have the option of training a journeyman to take over for her permanently."

Trav took a deep breath, as if he'd been planning that speech for a long time. "You guys good with that?"

"Mackey?" Kell said.

"Yeah?"

"If you hadn't married this man, I might have."

Mackey laughed a little. "Well, thank God I did, because that woulda caused all kinds of havoc. You guys okay with that? 'Cause I had no idea, but I'm so fucking relieved, I could almost cry."

"God yeah!"

"Shelia'll be thrilled."

"Seriously, Briony'll be pissed, but she might only have to miss one or two tours before she's back at the board."

Blake smiled quietly, happy that his brothers were happy but not feeling entitled to the same sort of excitement.

"What'd'you think, Blake?" Mackey asked suddenly.

Blake shrugged. "I think… I think as long as I'm with you all, it'll be okay."

"Well, yeah," Kell said. "But what about Cheever?"

Blake looked outside of the limo, depressed to see they were still on the 405. "Cheever's a hope," he said. "This is a good plan. This is long-term."

Everybody but Trav made the same grunt.

Trav was made of sterner stuff than that. "That's a chickenshit cop-out answer if I've ever heard one. *Pretend* Cheever's in on this, Blake. What do you think?"

"I think it'll give him time to pursue his art," Blake said, apparently playing this game to the bitter end. "And then, when we go on tour, he can come with us if he has time." And that actually felt good. "That would be nice. I'd… you know, like it if he could come."

Kell clapped him on the shoulder. "Hang in there, man. You'll figure out how to hope for the future eventually."

But he felt like he let his brothers down. And he worried for the rest of the trip to Seattle how to fix it.

Standing in the Shadows

AS SOON as the car pulled away, Cheever's shoulders drooped, his eyes burned, and his throat ached.

God, that sucked.

Not just seeing Blake and the guys leaving him—again. That had been hard, but he was a grown-up now, and he got it. They didn't want to leave *him*. It still hurt, but it wasn't anything he'd done.

But watching Blake try valiantly not to close down over the last week had about killed him. For a whole two months—after dropping Katy off at her grandparents' place and starting to pack for the tour—Cheever had seen what living with Blake Manning, whole and unfettered and happy, would be like.

Every dream Cheever had ever had about someone who loved him, someone who respected him, someone who needed Cheever's love and respect in return—every one of them had been fulfilled during those quiet, busy, wonderful two months.

The only shadow had been the one that Cheever had seen in Blake's eyes. The fact that he was going to have to leave was never far from his mind.

And because he was Blake, and stubborn, he'd sort of convinced himself that Cheever would want to leave him while he was on tour, and Cheever, again, got it. This was the big test. If Cheever could manage to be alone for the next two months, if he could not break Blake's heart now, Blake would believe in them.

Cheever knew he could do that, but he hated sending Blake away thinking his world was going to disintegrate and Cheever wouldn't be there to pick up the pieces.

With a sigh, he turned to go into the big house, because fuck, all his stuff was here now, wasn't it?

And that was something else he got, but hated. The studio house had been their home. Jesus, Cheever didn't even get to look at Blake's fish?

"Cheever?" Briony called as he opened the front door. "C'mere. We're in the kitchen."

Cheever grimaced. He'd managed to stay out of that woman's kitchen since that one ass-chewing in June. He'd been hoping to stay out of Briony's hair for the rest of their lives.

But as he walked through the house, he could smell waffles and—oh, seriously? Fried chicken. And the early morning babble had the forced cheer of adults who were teaching children how to keep going when they wanted to cry all day.

And Cheever had to remember he wasn't the only one who was grieving.

"Cheever!" Katy had returned right before school, and now she jumped off her stool by the counter and ran into his arms.

"Katy-bug!" He held her close and blew a bubble in her ear. She giggled and then deflated in his arms.

"They're all gone, aren't they?"

He looked up and saw Shelia looking exhausted and sick, cutting up chicken and waffles for little Kansas and Kayla, while Kyrie did the same thing for Kale. Briony was manning the waffle iron and the frying pan, and Marcia was on juice and wipe-down detail, looking a little sad herself.

They were all mourning, and they'd asked him to be part of it.

That was kind.

"Yeah, Katy-bug. But they sure didn't want to leave you all behind."

"We can go next year, right?" Katy asked, and Cheever looked up to Briony, who shrugged.

"Baby, you guys need to see if school works for you."

"I like school," she mumbled. "But who's gonna sing me to sleep? And teach me guitar?"

"I will," he said, hugging her tight. "And Briony and Shelia can too."

"No singing!" Marcia piped up. "At least, not from me. But I can tell stories. I know, guys, it's rough, watching the dads and the uncles go. But what, the moms are chopped liver?"

"I don't even know what that is!" Kyrie complained, and the tenseness in the kitchen eased up a little.

Cheever sat Katy down and ventured near the counter carefully. "Anything I can do to help?" he asked Briony, and she gave him a watery smile.

"Eat. Please. I cooked enough for…." She bravely fought a sniffle. "For all the guys. I wasn't thinking when I bought everything. Which is dumb, because I was planning to make the kids' favorite meal for breakfast when the guys left, but I… you know.…"

"Bought enough for the guys." *Ouch.*

Briony shrugged and wiped her eyes on the inside of the shirt, and Cheever couldn't stand it.

"Honey, here—go eat with the kids. I can turn chicken and use a waffle iron. I promise not to even open the fridge."

He stood up bravely and ventured back to where the stove was, and watched her very carefully cover the chicken and fork a waffle out of the iron to add to a stack of them on a plate.

"We can freeze those," she said, her voice thick. "Like the kind you buy in the store but, you know, gluten free and better."

"Yeah," he said, trying to booty bump her out of her kitchen so she could fall apart on her sisterhood.

"Don't forget to put cooking spray on the iron between waffles." Her voice was getting more and more clogged, and he very gingerly put a hand on her shoulder, thinking she needed to get out of there.

"Kell always forgets, and we have to clean it off with a chisel," she wailed. And then she turned into his chest and cried.

For a moment, he was baffled, hands out, because oh my God, Briony was falling apart! But he was a brother—he was *Kell's* brother, and apparently this came with the territory, and he wouldn't let his brother down.

He wrapped his arms around her and held her tight until her shoulders stopped shaking and she backed away, wiping her face and her nose on her Outbreak Monkey T-shirt from two albums ago, and waving at him.

"Chicken's burning!" she yelled, before turning and sprinting for the bedrooms.

"Shit," he muttered, lifting the lid to the chicken. He turned everything over for what looked like the final time. "You know what this means, don't you?"

"You're going to have to learn the refrigerator system," Marcia said knowingly. "Don't worry. We'll help you."

Cheever winked at her. "I was hoping you would."

She really had prepared enough food for an army. Cheever spent the next half hour frying chicken and cooking waffles, making sure Shelia stayed seated, drinking orange juice and eating, and… well, eating a lot of chicken.

"Protein," she said, swallowing. "Like, the first waffle was carbs, but now all I want is protein." She gave a delicate burp. "And fruit. Cheever, could you throw me an apple from the fruit bowl?"

Cheever complied, pleased when she caught it like a champ and then bit down. She shared it bite for bite with Kale, her youngest, who was the only kid not going to school.

Oh shit. "School! Marcia, take over for a minute. I gotta call Professor Tierce. I should have left a half hour ago!"

Fortunately, since the drive to the college was so long, that meant he was giving her an hour's heads-up.

He wandered into the hallway as the phone rang so he could have some privacy to leave a message. No one was more surprised than he was when she actually answered.

"Mr. Sanders?"

"Oh, hi! Professor! I'm sorry, I…. Something with the family came up, and I can't make it today. I just wanted to let you know. I already sent you digital files of the work I did this week, so after you see it, if you want to phone conference over it, I'd be grateful. It's…." He bit his lip. Besides the work on the album cover, he'd been very careful not to draw too many pictures of Blake, mostly because Blake was so self-conscious. But Cheever had come downstairs three nights before, and Blake had been asleep on the couch, slouched, his feet in front of him, guitar still cradled in his arms. Vulnerable, worried—his forehead was still creased—he wasn't classically pretty, no. But Cheever had sketched him, then used watercolors to soften the imperfections, make the strength around his jaw, his bony fingers, his lean but powerful body, beautiful.

"It's personal," Cheever trailed off, feeling stupid and lovestruck and defiant.

"It was lovely," his professor said softly. "It's… it's like everything you've done in the last month—an amazing improvement over what you were turning in last year. Is the subject the reason?"

Cheever grunted. "Well, duh. Anyway, he and my brothers left this morning, and usually they take the family on tour with them, but everybody's staying so the kids can be in school. So, you know, everyone's sort of a mess." Cheever had done a small series of the kids, so Professor Tierce knew his family situation.

"Well, that's to be expected. Were you planning to come in later today? You know I have class, but the rest of my day is free. If you want to get here around lunchtime, we can go out and discuss what you're going to do next year."

Cheever bit his lip. "I'd like that. Thank you." Truth was, he needed to see what the band was going to do next year, but that was hard to explain over the phone, especially to someone who thought the whole reason he'd held a razor to his wrist was because he didn't make it to graduate school.

"Excellent. I'll see you by my office at twelve thirty. I hope your family's okay, Mr. Sanders."

"Thanks, Professor."

Cheever hit End Call, then slid the phone into his back pocket and sighed. He turned toward the kitchen just as Briony emerged, face washed, wearing a different Outbreak Monkey T-shirt—this one two sizes too big, with the neck and sleeves ripped off. It had obviously been Kell's to start with.

"Everything okay?" she asked, sounding very much like she hadn't been crying her eyes out an hour before.

"Gonna be late. Had to tell my professor I'd meet her for lunch."

Briony grunted. "Nice. You're practically a grown-up." And if Cheever hadn't just seen her fall apart, he might have missed the little smirk that said she was kidding, just like the guys did.

"That's a lie," he said, "and you need to take it back."

She gave a weak chuckle. "Look, come in and help me clean up while Marcia and Shelia get the kids rounded up. I can show you how the refrigerator is organized so you don't have to run next door to get a soda or cookies for the next few months."

Cheever hadn't wanted to admit it, but that had been his entire strategy. "That's kind," he said, relieved. "Thank you."

They took a few steps. "I didn't mean to scare you so bad, that first day, you know that, right?" she said.

"You were terrifying." It wasn't anything he hadn't said to his brothers.

"Well, yeah. But so were you."

He opened his mouth in shock, but nothing but a squeak came out.

"Yeah, you. Think about it, Cheever. I knew… jack about you, except that you'd been a particularly shitty teenager. And that you'd hurt the guys—all of them—a lot. I know you didn't mean to. But… but Kell kept inviting you to car shows, and you'd say, 'Yeah, maybe,' and we'd all show up and you wouldn't. You'd text at the last moment, but… you know. It hurt. The twins would try ball games, Mackey tried *everything.* And then you showed up, going to live with us—hur-fuckin'-ray, right? And Blake was… was just this big oozy hole over you. And I couldn't stop you from hurting the guys. I couldn't stop you from hurting Blake. Honey, did you know he lost about twenty pounds at the beginning of the summer that he's only now starting to make up now? And all I could do was make sure you didn't hurt our kids, you know?"

Cheever nodded, trying not to be hurt. Everything she said was true. "I'm sorry," he said after a moment. "I… I know you know… well, sort of why I was an asshole—"

"I do," she acknowledged. "And we really do get it. And these last months, you've been great. The kids love you. But… but in that moment, all I knew was Blake was hurting because of you."

Cheever couldn't even laugh. He'd been so together all morning. "And now I'm hurting because he's gone."

She turned to hug him so quickly, he didn't have time to fend her off. He didn't cry, but that was only because he'd cried himself out three nights ago, sketching the lines of his first lover, the man who didn't think he was loved.

A ruckus drifted in from the front of the house, and Briony pulled away. "C'mon. Your mom's here to take everybody to school. Let's let Shelia off the hook before she falls asleep at the table."

As they were walking, Cheever remembered something. "Hey, did they ever figure out she's pregnant?"

Briony just laughed.

LATER THAT afternoon, he sat in a really fancy salad place and looked doubtfully at the thing on his plate.

"Doesn't look like a Caesar salad?" Professor Tierce asked, prodding her own with her fork.

"No, ma'am. Honestly, I'm just glad we had chicken and waffles for breakfast. If I catch a burger after I drop you off, I might not starve to death."

The professor had a great laugh, warm, round, fully committed. It made him glad she'd offered to take him on as a student to make up his grade. Getting to know her—her passion for art, her dedication to making her own art as perfect as possible—had given him some insight as to what kind of heart a true artist had.

And it had let him know he had a long way to go before he could consider himself a success at any art at all.

"If you're stopping for a burger, Cheever Sanders, I had better be in the car. In fact, I'm a little miffed you didn't bring me chicken and waffles."

Cheever grinned at her. "Next time Briony makes some, I'll pack you some in Tupperware," he promised. "Man, I have never had anything like it."

"Now who's Briony again?" The professor eyed her salad like an adversary and then carved off a piece of lettuce, a crouton, and some desiccated fish all together in one bite. She put the mess in her mouth and frowned speculatively.

"She's my oldest brother—Kell's—wife."

"And Shelia?"

That was a little tougher. "Well, she's Jefferson and Stevie's, uh… wife."

Her eyes widened, and she swallowed and then coughed until she cried. Cheever pounded her on the back a little and let her drink both her water and his. The waitress came over, concerned, and they met gazes and nodded. "Check please," Cheever said, without any further ado.

They beat a hasty retreat, and she grilled him some more in the car on the way to In & Out.

"So they all live in one house like a commune?" she asked later, as they were taking a walk around the college campus, finishing off their shakes. Cheever had to admire her—she had a round, voluptuous figure and gave zero fucks and fewer shits about downing a double-double with cheese and a large strawberry shake. He was sort of depressed that his own inhibitions had kept him from seeing what an amazing person she was, and how much she had to teach him about life, really.

You should never settle for a crouton and a leaf of lettuce when you could have a double-double and a strawberry shake.

"Well, they're sort of bummed," he told her. "Their families are getting big enough that Jefferson and Stevie's family needs their own house. Blake and I have been living upstairs in the house next door—the downstairs is a recording studio, but upstairs is really nice. I have my own painting suite. Or I will, when Blake gets home and I move back."

She chuckled. "You boys really do have stupid money, you know that, right?"

Cheever shrugged. "I do. I… I mean, I think I could be just as happy in a little apartment, as long as he was there. I… I know when I was a kid, and all of us lived in a two-bedroom apartment, I… I was happy. Because my brothers were there with me. This is the same thing. A place to sleep and a refrigerator. But, you know." He shrugged and looked around the college grounds. He'd never been one of the kids hanging out on the grass or playing Frisbee or hackey-sack. He'd always been too driven—to do a thing he loved but not the *only* thing he loved. "This was a good place to go to school. I shouldn't take that for granted."

"You sound a lot more grounded," she admitted, finishing off her milkshake with a slurp and tossing her cup in the nearest can. She held her hand out for Cheever's, and he gave it over, and she tossed it true. "Which is good." She paused, and made sure he was looking her in the eyes. "I really love what you're painting, Cheever. It's a lot more heartfelt than your other work." Then she looked away. "And you said you're getting commissions already—that sort of thing spreads. You'll be making money on your work, which is not something a lot of people can claim."

Cheever heard it in her voice then—and a year ago, it would have broken his heart. Five months ago, it had sent him screaming to oblivion.

Now it hurt a little; he wouldn't lie. But he'd seen it coming too.

"I'm not good enough," he said sadly. "Not good enough for the graduate program. Or to… you know. Be great."

"You're certainly good enough for the graduate program," she said, smiling gently. "And there are some real opportunities there—if you want them."

"You think I don't?"

She patted his cheek. "Someday, after some more living, after being in love a little longer and seeing the downs and not just the ups—"

Cheever thought of Tyson and rolled his eyes. "Or the *sustained* downs and not just the ups," she corrected, "after you've seen more, bigger things than just where you grew up, or where you're living now, you could very well be great. It's just... I get the feeling you're not done knowing who you are yet, Cheever. You fell in love, and that's great. And it could very well be forever. It was for me and my wife. We were eighteen, living in a shitty apartment and eating ramen and leftovers from the restaurant we worked in. We knew we'd live that way forever if we could just be together, and that hasn't changed. But she's on her third career. And I was going to be a street artist. But it turns out, she's *great* at teaching middle schoolers, and I wouldn't trade guiding young artistic voices for anything in the world, even fame, I think. I just.... You have some of that growing up to go, Cheever. And if you can do it and keep making commissions in the music industry, I don't know why you'd want to hang around here."

Cheever closed his eyes and turned his face to the sun until the ache in his throat subsided. When he looked back at his teacher, he could smile with all of his heart.

"The company," he said gamely.

She took his hand and raised his knuckles to her lips. "I will eat lunch with you any day, Cheever Sanders. Including next Monday, when I expect to see you in the morning to work with you some more. But do think about whether the graduate program here is really what you want. If you choose to put it off for a year or three, I will leave the recommendation in your transcript. You can get into our program anytime you want."

He bit his lip. "That's generous, Professor. Thank you. I'll have to think about it."

"See that you do."

But as they resumed their walk back to her office, where he dropped her off with a little bow—and a surprise hug from her—he knew what he was really thinking about.

He was thinking about him and Blake, taking a three-month hiatus from the family and the band and living in a little apartment in France. He was thinking about a month *with* the family and the band, playing in the surf in Hawaii. He was thinking about being a part of the tour next time, visiting cities, seeing historic sites, seeing museums. Or listening to bands and drawing concept art that made people think about music.

Maybe helping Briony with her lighting concepts, since he had a different background and could give her some suggestions she'd never thought of before.

Or even, whispered a voice he'd never listened to before, *making music too.*

He was thinking that his professor was right—and so was his mother, way back when he'd been in the mental health facility, pale and fragile and sad.

He *was* at a crossroads. And where he'd seen his path, all by himself, taking the road his family would never follow, that wasn't where his heart lay at all. He wanted to be on the bus with them. He wanted to be in their lives. He'd had chicken and waffles for breakfast that morning, and had wiped his niece's nose and hands and chin for fifteen minutes before she'd run out the door to get into his mother's car for school.

In a thousand years, he never would have thought of that as a magical, life-shattering event, and he knew logically that it wasn't.

But it was a part of his world now. And he didn't want to leave it to take that path by himself into the sunset.

It was a fucking lonely road, and he was getting used to the company.

BLAKE CALLED him at around eight o'clock, as he was sitting in front of the TV with Kansas on his lap, because Kell's son missed his father mightily, and Cheever was apparently a good substitute.

"Hey," he said softly. "You guys in?"

"Yeah. We're all eating in Mackey and Trav's room. We took a twenty-minute break to go call everyone, so expect—"

Katy's pocket buzzed at that moment, and Briony and Shelia both called out across the house from their own rooms.

"Guys! Dad's on the phone!"

Kansas hopped off his lap so quick, he left an elbow print in Cheever's ribs. Cheever grabbed the remote and put the TV on pause.

"Thanks for the warning," Cheever gasped, and Blake's tired chuckle on the other end of the phone told him everything he needed to know about timing.

"Sorry. I was trying to be first so you didn't get trampled."

Cheever warmed just hearing his voice. "It was a good thought. You guys all set?"

"Yeah. We're at this venue for three days, so we run a sound check tomorrow, and then it's all tour buses to Tacoma, and then Salt Lake City."

"And then Laramie and then Portland," Cheever repeated dutifully. "It's tattooed on the back of my eyelids."

"Ugh. That's funny—we always forget where the fuck we are. We get up in the morning and we're like, 'God, coffee? Where the fuck do you get coffee in...? Where the fuck are *we* anyway?'"

Cheever cracked up. "See—you need me on tour with you. I can help with that."

"I bet you could. Oh! Speaking of tours!" Blake outlined the new tour schedule, and Cheever listened happily.

"So next year, you guys stay here and work on other projects?"

"Yup. And the year after that, we work up a new album and go on tour. It'll be good, you know? You can paint and put together an exhibit or a show or whatever, and Kell and I can go find more artists and be home at night for the kids. It'll be... you know. Domestic." His voice dropped while Cheever was looking for words to adequately express his elation. "Or boring, I guess—"

"Shut up," Cheever said thickly. "I would follow you to the ends of the earth, okay? But this—oh my God, Blake. We can do so much here. We can do a world tour or.... Jesus. We can go to France. Just you and me. Or anywhere, with everybody. We can take my mom on a vacation. Do you know how often she *doesn't* go on vacation because nobody's there to go with her? No, man. This is amazing. How do the other guys feel?"

From the other room, Cheever could hear excited voices and cheering. Apparently, the wives and children thought it was a pretty damned good deal.

"They almost cried. Kell offered to have Trav's babies."

Cheever cracked up. "That was sweet of him, but probably unnecessary."

"Yeah, that's what Mackey said."

Cheever's smile went all the way to his toes. "Blake, there are so many good things coming. I'm so excited."

"Good." Blake's voice sounded so tender. "I'd do anything to make you happy, baby boy."

Cheever's eyes burned. "You know my professor told me she'd recommend me to the graduate program for next year, but...." He chewed on his lower lip. "She said maybe I'd want to go out and live a little first. You and me, we can do some living, right?"

"I really do want to," Blake rasped. "I'd... I'd do almost anything to be able to have that future, Cheever. You've got to know that."

"Good."

Cheever already knew that life was never as easy as planned, though. That conversation would haunt him in the weeks to come.

THE FIRST week crawled by. It was busy, yes, but there was no denying it—the biggest bright spot for the entire family was the mass phone call that came around eight o'clock, and comparing notes afterward. Katy would come in and talk about how Mackey wrote her a song about clouds and sang it over the phone, and Briony would tell Cheever privately that Mackey had been flat on his back for the trip and stuck looking out the window and bitching incessantly about how the sun hurt his eyes. Shelia would come in and add that Stevie and Jefferson used the sandbag after the show and Stevie sprained his wrist, and Cheever got to tell them all that Blake and Trav had to talk Mackey into taking a pain pill before his brothers strangled him in his sleep.

Funny how they had to look through six lenses to get an accurate picture, right?

At the beginning of the third week, Cheever got a phone call when he was in the studio house, practicing the guitar.

Since his conversation with Professor Tierce, he'd been driven to music, more and more. He'd penned a couple of songs, neither of which were nearly as raw and as good as the one he'd written for Blake. But he kept trying.

He'd heard the guys working up a couple of songs for the album—not even sure which album—and looking at him with furtive eyes. He knew Blake had written songs that nobody wanted Cheever to hear, and knew there were bloody, aching tears in Blake's heart still. But he also knew they were things that would heal with time. He'd pirated those songs, took pictures of the sheet music when the guys were breaking for lunch.

He was practicing them now.

Cheever was finding that he could say as much with music as he could with painting and sketching, and alone in the house that still held echoes of Blake's voice, he could learn the vocabulary his brothers had picked up on when they were kids.

He'd started singing the children to sleep as part of their nightly ritual since their daddies were gone, and including bits of nonsense from his own head. The kids—*these* kids—accepted that as normal, that someone would just sing random bits of rhyme in a tune pulled from the air.

Cheever felt like he could fall, in his own time, into the world of Outbreak Monkey, learn to swim in it, learn to dance.

And he felt so much closer to Blake in that room, with the guitar on his lap. It was almost like Blake was there, somewhere else in the house, and Cheever wouldn't be going back next door to sleep alone.

The phone buzzing in his pocket was a surprise.

"Blake?"

"Yeah—wanted to give you a heads-up. There was a blog interview. Your name came up. They'll be calling you for a quote. Trav gave 'em permission." Blake's voice changed pitch. "I'm telling him right now! No, he hasn't seen it yet!"

"Which blog?" Cheever knew the major ones, and he was pretty impressed. "Okay, so, just me or the whole family?"

"They'll be calling Briony. She usually speaks for everyone. But you're getting special treatment 'cause you're a Sanders. Just, you know, tell 'em what you're comfortable with, okay?"

"Yeah. What was the—"

"Shit. I gotta go, Cheever. They need some headshots. Gross. Anyway, talk more tonight!"

Cheever stared at the phone and then set down the guitar.

Shit.

Briony was unimpressed. "Yeah, I got a shit-ton of these when Kell and I got married. Suddenly everyone was going, 'Wait, your light board person was a *girl?*' and Kell was like, 'Derp. And she's pretty too. We done?' Anyway, there's gonna be speculation because everybody's pregnant—"

Cheever stared at her, and Briony grimaced.

"Everyone?"

Briony pulled fitfully at the long strawberry-blond braid that went to her ass. "Yeah. Everyone. Figure I'm about a month along. Kell wasn't gonna—said something about adopting, which was superfuckin' dumb because I obviously don't mind growing my own—but, you know." She smiled cheekily. "Wiles. I got 'em. Anyway, that shit's gonna come up. Especially since they're changing their tour schedule and only doing big venues mostly. Just, you know. Be honest." She paused and bit her lip. "And, you know, don't tell them anything Blake doesn't know already."

Cheever nodded. "Believe it or not, I picked that up already. I'm not fourteen anymore."

She sighed and leaned over the counter. "I know you're not. But… look, it's different. I've seen my name in those blogs, and I've seen the gossip. You know how Blake and Kell scout talent? They found this beautiful little pixie singer, Gracie King—"

"I know her. She's awesome. They found her?"

"Yup, playing in a shitty dive in Sacramento. Anyway, they got Heath to sign her, set her up on her way. Then, two weeks later, Kell was doing backup for her down in LA as sort of a, I don't know, 'welcome to the party' thing, and suddenly the blogs are plastered with photos of the two of them hugging it out backstage. I know what it was—I know my husband—but I'm getting five calls a day asking me if I'm okay with him stepping out on me. I was pregnant with Kansas at the time and as big as a fucking house. Then some papa-rats-i sneaks past the gate here, and there's me, big as a Volkswagen, swimming in the pool so my feet don't swell, and I'm asked for a quote as to whether or not Kell left me because I'd put on two hundred pounds."

Cheever groaned.

"It was thirty-fuckin-five pounds. I told them my husband would rather rip out the reporter's spleen and eat it than cheat on me."

Cheever chuckled, and Shelia, who had just settled Kale down to sleep and wandered in as Briony was going off, added, "And Mackey grabbed the phone and said he hoped the reporter died of syphilis with a chainsaw up his ass."

Briony nodded. "Yeah. Good times. Anyway, none of that made it into the blog, but they *did* print a retraction of the 'Kell cheating on me' story, which is the only reason Trav gives them the time of day. But what I'm saying here still stands."

"Be careful," Cheever said. "Stick to the facts. Don't exaggerate. But don't be hostile unless it's called for."

Both women nodded. "Exactly. If we give them a little bit of play, they give us a little respect. It's a good system. Also, if you need it, have someone on your side who will arrest the guy who trespassed to get pictures of you without your permission. I hope the fucker had a roommate the size of a tank, that's all I'm saying."

"Trav don't play," Cheever said, remembering the way Mackey's husband's muscles had strained as he tried not to pound Aubrey Cooper into the ground.

"No, he does not." Briony poured herself a giant glass of orange juice and pulled out a soda for Cheever. "Here. We gave you a little shelf on the side for sodas and milk. Also, there's a cupboard overhead for you, since you're tall. You see it?"

Labeled like everything else. "I appreciate it."

His phone buzzed with a push notice, and he checked it. "Hey, guys, wanna see the interview?"

"Damned straight!"

Briony and Shelia gathered at his shoulders, and Marcia came in from where she'd been straightening the kids' rooms to look over the counter.

The interview had been done in a lobby or a lounge or something— not too much background noise, all the guys on a couch, with Mackey sitting on the arm of it next to Kell, and Blake between Kell and Stevie.

They sat like guys who'd been together for nine years, like guys who'd been *family* for nine years. Close and not worried about who was touching who.

The reporter spent some time with Mackey, asking about his health, and he'd grimaced and confessed to hating pain like poison. The band chimed in and talked about his stretches and how they helped him each morning and night.

Then came the band's personal lives—and Cheever could see the difference there, between how they talked among themselves and how they had learned to talk to the press.

"So, guys, I understand you're all devoted family men. Mackey, you and Trav take care of your former bandmate's daughter when you're home, is that right?"

"That's right," Mackey said dutifully. "Katy's in our custody legally, but her mother is fully in her life. We just...." He looked at Trav, who nodded. "Her father died and wanted her with us as much as possible. We'd never planned on kids, but she's proof that shit can change."

"What about the rest of you guys? Kids still front and center?"

"We had to leave 'em behind for this leg of the tour," Kell said. "Everybody was starting school, and it just wasn't okay to take them out." He looked at his bandmates. "We all had a sucktastic school experience. It would be great if the kids had a better one."

"So, how many kids total?" The reporter was a young man, a tad scruffy, wearing a shearling coat in deference to the weather in—where was it? Laramie? But overall, a good-natured sort of guy.

"Changing every day," Jefferson grunted, and Stevie snorted.

"Changing in five months, anyway."

"Eight months for me," Kell muttered. He looked over his shoulder. "Nobody seems surprised."

"Women talk," Stevie said briefly.

"What about you, Blake. You jumping on the baby bus anytime soon?"

And Cheever could see it happen. He saw Blake open his mouth to say something noncommittal, and then everybody met eyes, and Mackey jumped on the grenade.

"Not if he keeps sleeping with our little brother."

Blake's mouth fell open, and Mackey met his glare head-on.

"Makes babies a different proposition," Blake admitted after an electric breath. "We might just be uncles for a while."

Mackey nodded like something had been decided, and the reporter let out a startled gasp.

"Everybody's fine with that?"

"Cheever's grown," Kell said. "All we asked is that they treat each other decent. So far, so good."

Color had flooded Blake's face, and Cheever knew—*knew*—he was thinking about the last time they'd made love. Blake had straddled Cheever, at Cheever's request, and had ridden him, panting and shouting, chasing his orgasm like a shooting star.

"Real good," Blake said weakly, and the band chuckled a little, like they hadn't seen the hard emotional work that went into their relationship, like every one of them hadn't worried about Blake and Cheever's well-being.

And *that* was the difference between real life and the press. One vaguely off-color joke and the press was satisfied.

In real life, Cheever was suddenly missing Blake in the pit of his stomach.

The video ended and everybody sighed.

"Fair enough," Briony murmured. Her phone went off, and she pulled it from her pocket and sighed. "Yup. Okay, guys, I'm first. Let's get this over with."

The girls each took about five minutes, but Cheever wasn't getting off the hook that easy.

After the reporter introduced himself, he started questions that got less and less comfortable.

"So you were, what? Fourteen when you met Blake Manning?"

Oh God. Cheever knew where this was going. "Yeah, he was just one of my brothers' friends for a long time."

"How long?"

"Until this May. I was going through a rough patch, and Blake helped me through it."

"So you and Blake didn't explore your romantic feelings for each other until you were at least eighteen?"

Fucking Jesus. "We didn't *have* any romantic feelings for each other until I was *twenty-two*. I was away at school a lot of that time. Like I said, just sort of part of the background."

"So what made you turn your sights on him?"

Oh. This narrative. Fun. "He's kind," Cheever said passionately. "And funny. And smart. And talented. Isn't that enough?"

Then the kick to the balls. "So you're serious?"

"Yes," Cheever said, and let Blake debate it. "He's a part of my family—not blood related of course. But he's a part of my family, and you don't start shit with someone like that unless you know it's going to be for real."

"So if you're so serious, why aren't you with the band on tour right now?"

"I had to finish up some schooling," Cheever said. "Technically I graduated in May, but I had a workshop class that I needed to take." He hoped Professor Tierce would forgive him for that, but he wasn't telling this asshole that he almost flunked out of school because of razor blades and blow.

"And your degree is in…?"

"Art. I did the cover art for Blake's next solo album." Cheever stuck his tongue out at the phone. The guy had mentioned Blake's album in the interview—hopefully this wasn't too much information.

"So you're not going to try to join the band?" The comment was half snark and half sour grapes—he'd been hoping for some dirt, and Cheever hadn't given him any, but it hit a chord in Cheever's stomach.

"Don't you get it?" he taunted. "We're *all* in the band. That's my family up on the stage. My brothers, my lover. My sisters got left here at home this time around. We're a part of each other's hearts. They've been asking me to join the band since I was a little kid. I just finally realized it was my destiny, that's all."

"Oooh…. That's a good line. I'm gonna use that."

Oh hell. "You do that," he said sourly. "Can I go now?"

"One more thing. How does it feel to know your destiny is in the hands of a former prostitute?"

Cheever almost swallowed his tongue before he could hang up. *"Briony!"*

BRIONY'S FIRST course of action was, of course, to call Trav. Cheever would have rather not, but then, he was fully aware he was in over his head.

Trav called him back directly. "Did he say anything else?"

"No. Because I hung up on him."

"Good boy." There was a pause. "I'm going to assume Blake told you about his past."

"Yessir. But this—this was what? Fifteen years ago?"

"A little longer. He was barely sixteen when he ran away. I'm not sure what the reporter's source is, and I need to find out. Look…." And Trav's military crispness softened. "Look, he's going to get weird about this. You know he is. Just… just don't let anything he says while he's a thousand miles away be locked in stone, okay?"

Ugh. "Yeah. I know. Gah! Does he know this is floating around yet?"

"Nope. And try not to mention it, okay?"

Oh right. "Are you shitting me? I know you're absolutely shitting me, because that works in this family *never.*"

"Look, just… just hold on to it until I can get some background, okay? Man, I could give a *fuck* what the fucking press says, but someone's trying to hurt my boys with this, and until I have a target and a baseball bat, I don't want them to see me swinging."

Cheever had to take some deep breaths. This was Trav—he should have known. Trav would have Blake's back.

"Roger that," he muttered. "Just... I'm not gonna lie to him."

"Understood. Just don't go there unless he asks. Please?"

"Yessir."

"And good call on the hang up. That was not on the approved list of questions."

"Well, the guy was trying to make Blake out to be kind of skeevy. He kept asking me how old I was when we got together, like he'd been hitting on me since I was a kid. I set him straight, but, you know...."

"Yeah. They're off the approved list no matter what. Thanks, Cheever. Good job, son."

Cheever felt himself preening a little. Well, Trav was the ultimate father figure, so it wasn't a mystery. "Thank you, sir. Uhm... you know. Take care of him, okay?"

"It's my job." And he hung up.

Cheever rested his head against his fist for a moment and thought that yeah, it might have been in Trav's job description, but he defied anybody to say Travis Ford didn't take his work to heart.

"What'd he say?" Briony asked from his side.

"Said it sounds hinky. He's gonna look into it, and we should maybe not tell Blake until he knows something solid."

"Fuck," Briony muttered. "Fuckity bugger. I'll tell you what, Cheever, you better fasten your seat belt. It's gonna be a fucked-up ride."

CHEEVER MADE it through his phone call with Blake that night, pacing in the kitchen, but his stomach ached with anxiety as he waited for everyone else. Marcia was helping the kids get ready for their baths as the wives had serious convos with their husbands, and he actually raided his cupboard for Oreos since there was nobody there to see him eat.

"Oh, you bastard," Briony muttered as she emerged from down the hall. "Give me."

Cheever handed her the pack—she'd been modeling good eating habits for the kids, but every mom needed a vice.

"I hear sugar," Shelia snapped, stalking from the same direction. "Give me!"

Briony took a handful and handed Shelia the rest. She'd had an ultrasound that afternoon. The biggest thing on her agenda was *supposed* to be telling the twins she was *expecting* twins.

"What's our sitch?" Cheever asked, when everybody had downed at least three double-stuffs.

"Trav had an emergency meeting with the guys while you were on the phone with Blake," Briony said. "He asked them if anybody had heard from Blake's mom."

Cheever held his hand to his mouth. "I'm gonna puke," he muttered.

"Don't you fucking dare," Shelia snarled. "You go, I go. I go, Briony goes. Nope—you suck it up and hold your nausea like a woman! Jefferson told me Trav was calling a lawyer who specialized in extortion. He mentioned something about somebody trying to blackmail the band."

"Trav's not gonna like that," Briony said.

"None of the guys will like that," Shelia agreed. "The only reason the guys would agree to it would be to...."

They both looked at Cheever furtively.

"To protect Blake," Cheever said, those Oreos not sitting any easier.

"Okay, this sucks." Briony groaned and rested her head on her fist. "And it sucks worse 'cause we're far away. But maybe we should wait to see what Trav says before we panic, okay? I mean, we can't panic."

Cheever nodded and held out his hand. "One more Oreo," he promised. "I won't panic until I puke."

HE DIDN'T sleep that night. At one in the morning, Marcia came into his room wearing baby-doll pajamas and Hello Kitty slippers, as casually as if they were still in rehab.

"Look, if you're going to toss and turn, you should at least be considerate about it and do it quietly."

"Augh!"

"Look, Cheever, what's the worst that can—"

"He will break up with me," Cheever said, because even Shelia and Briony knew it was true. "He will say, 'Oh, Cheever, you are young and have your whole life ahead of you, and I am just weighing you down.' And then he'll find an apartment, let the twins and Shelia have the studio house even though it's a dumb idea, and just sort of fade out of everybody's life until they have to get back together for the next tour."

"Yikes!" Marcia made herself comfortable at the foot of his bed, and he was just so damned glad she was there. "Don't you think he'll fight for you at *all*?"

Cheever dragged a hand through his hair. "You don't get it. It's not that he's afraid to fight for me—it's that... God, Marcia. He's been told his whole life that he's not worth it. And he loves me. Don't you see the logic? If he's not worth it, then the best thing he can do for me is cut me loose."

"But he *is*," she said softly. "We both know it. What can you do? I mean... if you guys were in the same room, you'd just sort of will him into submission. We've all seen you do it. But how do you... I don't know. Fight that? I mean, painting him didn't do it. He hates to look at himself."

"I wrote him a song," Cheever said softly, resting his cheek against his knees. "The band's working it up live, but it's already recorded. He wrote me.... God. I mean, he's written me some really gorgeous love songs, right? But there's this one—I'm not even supposed to know he wrote it. But there's no hope at all in it. It's about the world self-destructing around him and he's alone in an empty room. And my brothers are right. If I had to hear him sing that, it would kill me."

"Well, you should play it for him," Marcia muttered, scowling. "See how *he* feels hearing it. Too bad you couldn't."

Cheever stared at her. "I could, though," he said thoughtfully. He reached for the guitar—one of Blake's old ones they kept at the house— that rested by the bed. "Want to hear it?"

"Sure," she said, sighing. "You've been getting really good."

Cheever grinned at her. "Not good enough for the band," he said, finding his fingers on the strings and tuning.

"Who says? I mean, we've all heard their first album. *They* weren't good enough for their band. The only one who could play was Mackey, really."

Cheever thought about it and worked his way through the opening chords. "That's true. I mean, you know. Maybe I could...." He bit his lip and repeated the chords—right this time. "Maybe I could show up for a couple of songs." This part was tricky. He finished and breathed a sigh of relief. "I'd give anything to be there right now."

And there. He was in the place where the music came from. It was the same place his art came from, but a little harder to get to—less practiced. It had been getting easier these last months, every time he picked up the guitar.

He launched into the opening lines of "Empty Room" and became lost in it. It was a beautiful song—but a brutal one—and he wanted to do every note justice.

He finished, and Marcia let out a quiet sob and wiped her face on her knees.

"Okay," she said, voice clogged. "That was gorgeous. Now play me something with hope, you bastard!"

Cheever laughed a little and launched into "Cement Ragdoll," the one he'd written on the plane. He finished that, and Marcia flipped him the bird.

"I said hope."

"Seriously," Briony said, yawning from the doorway. "Play a love song."

Cheever played the beautiful one Blake had written about him, the one about him painting and Blake accepting. It was delicate—almost too delicate for rock and roll, but when he'd finished with the final notes, he looked up for approval.

"Now do the coffee shop one," Shelia said, and Cheever wrinkled his nose, but still kept riffing.

"You should be in bed."

"I need something to make me not cry. I'm pregnant, dammit. Give me hope."

Cheever thought about it and then played the song Blake had written about Kell. And the song fell in place—it wasn't about Kell at all, really. It was about hope. It was about loving someone so much that how they took that love didn't matter. The love itself was the thing.

He finished, and Shelia and Briony both wiped their eyes on the insides of their sleep shirts.

"It's perfect," Briony said. "So, here's what we're going to do tomorrow, after we get the kids to school."

She launched into a rather gutsy plan, leaving Cheever breathless. "But wait—"

"Look," she said bluntly, "even if he doesn't use this opportunity to bolt like a jackass-rabbit, you still need to do this, you understand? This is one-hundred-percent commitment. Not just to Blake, but to the band. To the family. You showing up at their next stop—"

"Which is where?" Shelia asked.

"Portland." Cheever hadn't forgotten.

"Portland's a nice place," Shelia said. "Lots of coffee shops. Briony, you bring that up to Trav, okay?"

Briony nodded. "Good idea. So Cheever, you show up in Portland while this shitstorm is breaking, and you do this, and you'll make fucking history."

"I don't care about making history," Cheever said, feeling a little overwhelmed. "I just want Blake to be okay."

"And that's why it must be done," Briony said with satisfaction.

Cheever chewed on his bottom lip and had a thought. "If that's true, then we need one more thing," he murmured. "Briony, I'm gonna need your help on this too."

HE WAS in the tattoo parlor when Blake called the next day, death metal thundering through the speakers, a forty-something woman with a platinum mohawk inking his right bicep with precision. It *felt* like the sting of one persistent bee, over and over again, and Cheever was doing lots of Lamaze breathing to keep from twitching. When he saw the name on the phone, he looked at his tattoo artist and wrinkled his nose.

"Please?" he begged, and she rolled her eyes and yelled across the store.

"Hey! Toad! Fuckin' music!"

Toad—a scrawny kid barely Cheever's age but covered with black ink on his practically green-pale skin—nodded and lowered the volume.

"Blake?"

"Hey, baby boy." Oh, that wasn't a good sign.

"How's Portland?"

"We leave this evening, get there tomorrow morning. I hate sleeping on the bus."

Cheever grunted in appreciation, and Blake continued.

"You gotta know—I mean, Trav said you might know something about it, but we're gonna have a press conference tonight before we get on the bus."

Oh God. "How bad is it?"

Blake's voice was practically breaking, and Cheever's heart just fucking hurt. "It's bad. Someone got hold of my mom and gave her proof of what I did to make rent when I was a kid. She's threatened to just tell before, but now she's got pictures."

Cheever closed his eyes and swallowed. *Oh, Blake.* "How bad—"

"In the photos, you can see my face and the coke mirrors, and you can tell if I'm circumcised," he said grimly. "And she apparently tried to get hold of Trav back in May, right after Mackey fell off the fucking amp, but she couldn't. Anyway, my mother's trying to blackmail us— me. If I don't pay up, she's going to the press about me... you know. Bein' a fuckin' whore." Cheever closed his eyes against the self-loathing practically dripping from the phone.

"Baby—"

"Anyway, Trav and the boys ain't havin' it. They told Trav to fuckin' announce it to the world and they'd back me, which is really kind. I don't want that shit hanging over my head. But it's gonna come out, Cheever. It's gonna come out, and it's gonna be ugly. And I just told the whole world we were together. So, you know, I'm calling to say that when shit breaks, you can tell people you didn't mean it. Tell 'em I was a phase or something. Tell 'em I tricked you or—"

"Fuck that, Blake Manning. Fuck that, and fuck *you* for even thinking I would do that."

"Cheever," Blake pleaded. "You don't want any piece of this. Man, the shit she's got on me—I don't know who I blew, but she's got the pictures, she's got dates and times—"

"And I don't fuckin' care," Cheever snapped. "You think I don't want a piece of it? I want *all* of it. I want her to wave that shit in my face and see what I have to say to her. You were sixteen fucking years old and living on the goddamned street, and you managed to do it for years. I fucking *dare* her to come at me with that shit. I fucking dare her to come at any of my family—"

"You don't have to do this!" Blake snarled, feral, in pain.

"I *want* to! You think you're breaking up with me over this? Fucking bullshit. Don't you dare break up with me over something you were straight up about from the very beginning."

"Cheever!" There was the break, the complete crumbling of his voice, and Cheever's heart with it.

"We're not broken up," Cheever said, hard and without mercy. "You're not a defenseless kid. You're not alone. You got my brothers backing you. And their lovers. And our mother. And me. You just hold on until tomorrow. In fact, tell Trav not to have that press conference until tomorrow afternoon, you hear me?"

"What in the—"

"Look, you tell him or Briony will. You put off the fucking press conference until I get there."

"You're not coming up here—"

"The fuck I ain't." Cheever let some softness seep into his voice. "Blake, have some faith. A little bit of hope. Some joy in us. I know you got that. So use it. Be strong, baby. You don't ever got to be alone again."

"I gotta go," Blake mumbled, his voice clogged.

"I love you. Don't ever forget it again."

There was a long silence, and Cheever wondered if he was going to deny it. But Blake was strong—stronger than he knew. "I'll never forget it. Love you too."

And then he was gone.

Cheever ended the call and looked up at his tattoo artist, who'd been holding off with the needle until Cheever stopped gesticulating wildly to make his point.

"Blake Manning?" the woman said, not blinking.

"Yeah."

"Your boyfriend's Blake Manning."

"Yes, ma'am."

"Tat's free," she muttered, and then she went back to work before Cheever could even ask what Blake had done for her.

It didn't matter.

What mattered was that *this* was the man who thought he wasn't good enough.

Very carefully, Cheever texted Briony about putting off the press conference.

It was time somebody made the grand romantic gesture for Outbreak Monkey's second lead guitarist.

It was time Blake knew he came first.

2000 Light Years from Home

BLAKE GOT off the phone with Cheever and *thunked* his head against the hotel bathroom wall.

"You doing blow in there?" Kell called, and Blake grimaced.

Not that he hadn't been tempted in the extreme this past day, but no.

"I was on the phone!" he called back. "You gotta go?"

"I blew up the one in the lobby. If you're not naked, get the fuck out of there. I'm worried, and we need to talk."

Without the wives on this trip, they shared a room like back in the old days, and Blake hadn't minded. He and Kell had a rhythm, a language. They could sit in the same room for hours playing games on their phones if they just needed to chill out, or they could hook up a computer and watch super-violent movies. Kell was particularly fond of the *Taken* franchise, and Blake had a thing for *Mission Impossible* and the two *Equalizer* movies.

Comfort flicks.

Blake was going to need one of those once they got on the bus. He always slept like shit on the bus, anyway.

"What are we talking about?"

"The economy and the next election. You know what we're talking about. Now get your ass out of the bathroom, you big coward, and let's talk like men!"

"I was going to use the show—"

Kell broke into the room.

One minute, Blake was sitting on the toilet seat, fully clothed, and the next, he watched as Kell Sanders—built like a lean tank from all the working out they did—shattered the bolt through the door frame, and then had the nerve to look at it in surprise.

"Holy God," Blake said, staring at the splintered wood and twisted metal in awe.

"I need to take a picture of that," Kell said, reaching for his pocket. "Briony will never believe me." He finished his snapshot and then turned to Blake, who was still staring at the door. "Now, are we going to face this situation like grown-ups or do I have to ship you home to my little brother in a monkey cage?"

"Cheever's gonna meet us in Portland," Blake said, his stomach roiling. "I tried to talk him out of it, but—"

"Good. Not that you tried to talk him out of it, but I'm glad he's showing up. You need him. Now let's talk about *you.*"

"What's to talk about?" Blake asked bitterly. "Sometime in the next two days, Trav's gonna get up in front of a camera and tell the entire fucking world that I sold my ass for rent. And your kids and Jefferson and Stevie's kids, and Katy, and your mother, and...." He swallowed. "And Cheever—you're all going to get to see it in the tabloids for a news cycle, and the little kids will hear it at school, and then it will go away, leaving a—" He shuddered. "—a greasy, filthy residue that they just won't be able to wash off."

"And that's what we need to talk about." Kell poked the doorknob with his finger. "Because it's bullshit." The doorknob fell onto the tile with a clatter, and Kell picked it up and snagged the one from the other side before it could fall too. "I'm keeping this," he said with conviction. "It's a trophy. It's going down in the weight room with the other stuff on our fuck-me shelf. It'll go right between Trav's bongo drum and that seat from Denny's that collapsed when Jefferson sat down too hard."

"You do that. Just let Trav know about the deposit." They hadn't trashed any hotel rooms since their prerehab days, but the guys did seem to leave a trail of havoc in their wake—there was a lot of stuff on that shelf.

"'Course. Now, back to bullshit. You think we see you any different? I mean, you told us. We know. The kids don't, but then, the kids don't know we did all the fucking drugs and women back in the day either, 'cause you don't tell your kids that shit and you hope they never find out. But you know something? Even that's bullshit. 'Cause what if Kyrie comes home high one day? What'm I gonna do? Yell at her like I never did that shit? Or tell her how bad it got, and how much I don't want that for her? 'Cause parents aren't perfect. That's one thing that saved us all—the fact that Mom knew *we* weren't. She knew we weren't perfect, and she let us know she wasn't either. All she could do was love us for who we were. And that *includes* you, you dumbass! My mother *met you* in rehab, and not once did she ever think, 'Hey, here's a guy my sons love like a brother—I should tell him we're better than him.' So this... this *thing* you're carrying around on your shoulders, like you don't deserve love, like you don't deserve *us*, you need to drop that thing quick. It's like that play, the one with the play inside. If every man gets treated like they deserved, every man would deserve to get beat up. Don't treat people like they deserve, treat people like we *want* to be treated. *I* want to be treated like my fuckups don't define me, and that's how I want my brothers to be treated too."

Blake stared at him, his mouth open. "Kell, did you just paraphrase *Hamlet*?"

Kell wrinkled his nose and juggled the parts of the door. "Maybe?"

Blake swallowed. Kell Sanders just mentioned Shakespeare and broke a door for him. It was possible, *just possible*, that Cheever knew *exactly* what he was doing with Blake Manning and loved him for real.

"I'll think about it," he said softly. "I'll… I mean, he's coming out tomorrow. He's your brother. It's not like I can refuse to see him."

Kell snorted. "Oh my God. Like, he gives you one look from those moon eyes of his and you'll be, like, 'See you all later, I'm going to get laid!'"

"Not this time," Blake said, not even bothering to deny that's how it usually worked. "This time, he needs to see me for who I am!"

"'Cause you do such a good job of that? You're the *worst* at seeing yourself for who you really are. Now just do us all a fucking favor and let him love you!" Kell sighed and set the doorknob on the counter. "Let *us* love you. What part of 'you were young and alone and fucked-up' do you think we don't understand?"

"Have you seen him?" Blake asked helplessly. "He's so pretty… so young. He could be on a yacht, painting billionaires or something. He could be sleeping with royalty. What the hell is he doing with me?"

Kell grimaced. "Well, do *you* want to sleep with royalty?"

Blake thought about it. "Not really."

"Who do you want to sleep with?"

Blake scrubbed his face with his palms. "Cheever."

"Go figure."

"Fuck."

"Yeah, well, fuck us both. I wouldn't trade Briony in for an entire club full of bunnies. 'Cause when the tits and ass are over, what the fuck would I talk about with them? Briony, she's my life."

Blake's phone buzzed, and judging by the way he jumped, so did Kell's. They checked their messages in the sudden silence in the bathroom, and Kell said, "Fuck me. I gotta talk to Trav. Who's on your phone?"

"Cheever," Blake lied. "He's got a flight."

"Awesome. Start packing. I'll start hauling shit when I'm done with Trav."

Kell stormed out of the motel room—after snagging the doorknob—and left Blake staring at his phone.

He didn't recognize the number, but whoever her sources were, they were pretty fucking accurate.

Just pay up, sugar, and I'll hand over the film. I'm not trying to make your life hard, just need a little green to be flush.

Needed a little green to feed her coke habit. Blake hadn't picked up self-medication on the streets. No, he'd *practiced* it there and had gone on to perfect it in the hotel rooms on the road.

He'd picked it up when he was a kid, watching his mother's nose bleed over a frosted mirror. The last time she'd tried to contact Blake and ask for money, Trav had put a restraining order on her, and it had worked. Blake had been afraid of her, and she was never far from his mind. But when he didn't hear from her for a long time, somehow, he'd managed to convince himself she'd passed away between then and now.

The thought hadn't troubled him much, honestly.

He needed to put her off, though—at least until Trav made his announcement. *Talking to my manager. He controls the cash. Will let you know tomorrow.*

I know where you'll be.

Well, it probably wasn't hard to figure out. They had a sound check tomorrow morning at the Zoo Amphitheater (Outbreak Monkey—get it?) for one of the venue's last concerts of the season. The concert was at seven, and they had a green room call at six. He and Kell were going to a nearby coffeehouse around one to hear a band that had been getting big in LA over the summer and had come home to roost. So, again, no big surprise.

Not if I see you first. Not original, but it got the point across.

Don't you want to see me and catch up?

I'm blocking this number now. Talk to Trav.

God. God fucking dammit. But Kell was right in some ways. Blake deserved better than this. Deserved better than to have *her* as his past. He might, someday, deserve to have Cheever in his life.

He might even deserve to have him now.

Easy words, but they were harder to believe after sleeping in the bus all night and pulling into Portland feeling numb and cranky. The twins went on a coffee run, coming back to the Zoo Amphitheater with a jumbo-sized thermos of something that tasted exquisite but had enough caffeine to kick you in the balls. They also brought Voodoo Doughnuts, including the bacon maple one that Blake craved.

Blake thanked them absent-mindedly and went back to making sure the equipment was online. They'd discovered that Nigel, their lead roadie this time around, wasn't nearly as detail-oriented without Briony running around backstage.

"That's all we get?" Stevie asked, threatening to yank the bacon-maple bar out of his hand. "A thanks guys."

Blake purposefully keyed his expression down from "Fuck with me, I dare you," to "You're family, so I can't eat you."

"I'm sorry, guys. I was distracted. It was real nice of you to go out for—"

"Spare us," Stevie said, letting go of the doughnut. "You need to calm down, you know that, right?"

"I was expecting Trav to make the announcement last night. Why today? Kell and I have that scouting trip—"

"Don't worry. He's called the reporters to meet us across the street from the coffeehouse—there's a little park. It'll happen right after the band plays," Jefferson said, as bored as usual. "Just, you know, be in the now. We still gotta play a gig tonight."

Blake grunted. "Don't I know it."

Mackey accepted no excuses, but then, neither did any of them. Music was the fucking thing. The only thing. Blake took a bite out of his doughnut and pulled himself into the present.

There was no place else for him to be.

THEY MANAGED a nap and a shower before their scouting trip, but there was no word on when Cheever's flight got in.

"What if he gets here while we're onstage?" he asked. "She's out there, Kell—I mean…." He shuddered. "I just don't want her to talk to him, is all. Like she could—"

"What?" Kell demanded. "What could she tell him you probably haven't drawn in excruciating detail? You know something? When I was fifteen, I got a giant zit on my back."

"Ew. Gross."

"It hurt like a motherfucker. My *mom* had to pop that thing. It was disgusting. She almost threw up."

"Is there a point to this, Kellogg, 'cause you are straining the bonds of friendship right here."

"Yeah. Until this moment right here, not another soul knew about that, because my mother's a decent person and would have let me erase that from my memory right there. That's her fuckin' job. The only dirt your mother's got is the filth on her nicotine-stained fingers, you hear me? You been living right these past years. She can't touch you. She can't touch Cheever. She can't fuckin' touch us. So let's go scout this band and hope they don't suck, and then we'll play the gig, 'cause every gig we play gets us one step closer to home. And I gotta tell you, I miss my wife, I miss my kids, and I can't wait to settle down for a couple of years. You?"

"Missing the fuck outta my fish," Blake said, and Kell smirked.

"Missing the fuck out of my brother's big fish, that's what you're missing."

Jesus. "Please go back to mangling Shakespeare."

"Buddy, you wish. Now let's go hear a baby band!"

They walked out of the hotel with some speed on their heels, and Blake was surprised to find Mackey, Trav, Stevie, and Jefferson waiting to follow them when they got outside.

"The hell?"

"Shut up," Mackey said companionably. "We're not talking about this."

"About what?"

"That's the spirit. Trav says this place is known for baby bands and coffee. Please God, let there at least be coffee."

"Who are we listening to again?" Stevie asked.

"Lasagna Kid," Kell supplied, looking both ways and then leading across the street. Blake noted that their security force—a fiftyish, super-fit woman named Deborah and her son, Crane—had attached themselves at the intersection.

"Do we, uh… need security?" *Oh my God.*

"Press meeting afterward," Trav told him crisply.

Well, yeah, but security? This wasn't right before a concert, or when they were trying to fight their way onto the bus after. This was, well, a coffee shop in Portland.

"Overkill," Blake muttered.

"You're the one who was worried about her coming to see you," Kell muttered back.

"Oh God. Yeah. Okay. I gotta remember Trav's got it covered."

"Right?"

He was unaccountably nervous.

They got to the coffee shop, though, crowding around the table that the proprietor—a dapper, graying man in his fifties with a "Dad" smile—had reserved for them as gracefully as possible.

"I didn't know you all were coming until the last minute," he apologized. "Our Saturday coffee hour is usually pretty full—I'm sorry." He looked apologetically at the table next to him that had an extra chair and snagged it.

"Me and Kell can go stand in the back," Blake offered, embarrassed at the attention.

"No, we can't," Kell said with uncharacteristic brusqueness. "Jefferson, you and Stevie—"

"You'd have to pry us away with a crowbar," Stevie said flatly. "Nope. Trav, can Deborah and Crane maybe…?"

Trav rolled his eyes. "They can stand at the door with me. Mackey, you stay put, but save that seat."

Mackey did as ordered, sinking gratefully down into the surprisingly comfortable basic square-backed chair.

"Yeah," he said to the owner—his nametag said Callum and the place was called Callum's, so the odds against him being the owner were nonexistent. "Sorry, we'll smash. We know each other."

"Yessir," the man said. "Who are you saving the seat for?"

Mackey didn't look up, which was telling in itself. "My mother. I reckon she'll be here about the middle of the first set."

"Oh yeah—okay. I got it."

"We can't stay for both sets, Mackey," Blake said hurriedly. "Kell and I only promised—"

"We'll stay," Mackey said mildly, and then, only then, did Blake get the feeling something else entirely was going on.

Still, he was not prepared.

Lasagna Kid was actually a really wonderful band for a coffeehouse. They'd never play a coliseum, and they'd probably work best with a monetized YouTube channel rather than a big-time record contract, but Kell and Blake had some contacts for them to help them cut a decent CD at a bargain basement price and an agent who made a living on small bands, because the world needed all the music, not just the kind that played to stadium seating. They finished an enjoyable set, and Kell tapped Blake's knee and stood to go over to them as they broke down their equipment. He was talking quietly to their front man—a stunningly gorgeous, androgynous person dressed in a crisp white dress shirt and black slacks—offering cards and a smile and a handshake and encouragement. At one point, the singer looked over at Blake and nodded. Kell looked at him and back, nodding too.

Right then, Heather Sanders walked into the room, and Blake's attention was called to the door in surprise as she greeted Deborah and Crane and then hugged Trav.

"Your mom's here," he said out loud in general.

"Yup." Mackey didn't move.

"Wait—where's Cheever? She must have come up with—"

Three things happened at that exact moment.

Heather came to sit down with them, putting her hand on Blake's shoulder first and kissing his cheek warmly.

Another woman—the same age as Heather but dressed in fuchsia-and-eggplant-colored leather, with spikes around the wrist and neck, and sporting far more bitter wrinkles—*tried* to get through the door, only to be turned away by security, who had apparently been briefed on Blake's mother, including the last known photograph.

And the lead singer for Lasagna Kid set a stool down in front of the mic and spoke to the rest of the coffeehouse.

"We appreciate you all not leaving," they said in a modulated voice between alto and tenor. "But maybe that's because you saw our famous audience." They led a round of applause, and Blake and the others all waved sheepishly. It was inevitable, but then that's why they were here.

"So, Outbreak Monkey came here to give unselfishly of their time, and we understand their newest member, Cheever Sanders, is here to give us a little show of his own. Everybody, welcome a one-man act, Cheever Sanders is Monkey Shines."

"Holy God." Blake completely forgot about his mother, screaming obscenities outside the clear glass of the coffeehouse as Crane hauled her to the corner, probably to deliver her to a police officer when one arrived.

The point was, *he forgot about her.*

Because Cheever stood there on the stage, having come up from the other side, near the coffee bar.

And Jesus, he looked good—auburn bangs curling right above his eyebrows, little sideburns crisp under his ears. He was wearing low-waist jeans and a tight white T-shirt with the sleeves ripped off, which was a little cold for Portland, but Blake got the point immediately.

"That little shit," Kell said happily, coming back to the table. "I didn't know about the tattoo."

The Outbreak Monkey tattoo was in the same place as Blake's, on the bicep. And it was the exact same monkey. Cheever Sanders, the man who'd tied Blake's insides into a heart-shaped knot since May, was sitting on a stool in a coffee shop, wearing the band tattoo, and playing the guitar his brother had bought him for his birthday. Yes, Blake remembered.

And he was playing with the strings and looking at the audience from under those bangs, pleased and flirty and just so goddamned pretty Blake could cry.

"So hey. Y'all probably saw my brothers and my boyfriend there."

More applause—but uncertain. Oh Jesus. Blake knew the tentative breaths of a group of people waiting to see if he would suck in a paper bag or not. Cheever was so vulnerable up there, so open, but by God, he was owning the fucking stage, wasn't he?

"Yeah. You all know *they're* good, but how's their little brother?" The audience laughed, and Cheever fingered a moderately difficult riff. "Well, I been practicing." More laughter, but Blake's stomach was still clenched.

He'd been where Cheever was. Blake's stomach, chest, asshole wouldn't stop clenching until this was over.

"I came up to Portland 'cause my boyfriend—Blake Manning? You guys know him?" Some appreciative hooting. "Yeah. He's having a shitty moment. Those happen. The kind that make you doubt yourself. But he's, like, the best person ever, so I think maybe he'll learn to have a little faith, you think?"

Affirmative noises then, and Blake saw a dozen phones out, getting ready to make this viral.

"Anyway, it was just really important that I come out here for him, you know? So he's never afraid I'll leave him alone in an empty room."

And with that, he launched into the song, the song he wasn't even supposed to know about, singing it with such soulfulness, such pain, Blake wasn't sure his heart would ever start beating again. He made a sound—a whimper?—and Heather turned to him with a tissue, as Cheever Sanders unmade Blake Manning and then rebuilt him with just one goddamned song.

Then he did "Cement Ragdoll."

Then he did "Painted Love"—Blake's love song for him, for sweet God's sake.

And then… oh Jesus. He finished up with the love song to Kell. And Blake heard it, saw the way Cheever looked him in the eye and owned him during that song.

It wasn't Kell's song anymore. It wasn't Cheever's. It was hope. That song was the hope song between the two of them that Blake would always deserve love.

By the time Cheever was done with that song, he had the audience in the palm of his hand—and the audience had grown.

Oh shit. Blake recognized a lot of those people, and Trav's hand on his shoulder confirmed it. "Goddammit. We were supposed to go across the street after this."

Cheever stood and smiled, gesturing to Outbreak Monkey with a nod. "Okay, all, that's about it. Come see my brothers and my boyfriend play tonight. I'll be in the wings."

"You'll be on the stage, you lazy asshole," Mackey called. "'Bout time you earned your keep!"

Cheever's smile went ear to ear, and the applause erupted thunderously.

So did the questions—and the lights from the phones.

"Cheever, did your brothers know you were coming out?"

"Cheever, how long have you and Blake Manning been seeing each other?"

"We noticed the tattoo, Cheever. Are you really going to be part of the band?"

Cheever paused in the act of exiting the stage. "I've always been part of the band—I just never took my place. But I'm taking it now. Trav, you want to handle the rest of it?"

Trav grimaced, and Blake could tell this wasn't planned. Trav looked over at Callum, the coffeehouse owner, who grimaced back good-naturedly, shrugged, and gestured Trav to the stage.

Heather Sanders was right on his heels.

"What's your mother doing?" Blake asked.

Kell shrugged. "Whatever it is, you'd damned well better appreciate it. I have to room with her for the next week, do you know that?"

Blake glared at him sourly. "I'd say it serves you right. You fucking knew?"

Kell's chuckle was low and evil. "Well, not when I broke down the bathroom door."

"Fuckin' hate you."

The pat on Blake's shoulder was both condescending *and* patronizing. "Sure you do. Now stand up and tell Cheever we're all impressed. You know how baby bands get when the big boys are watching."

There were neither words nor side eye enough to capture how much Blake wanted to rip the legs out from under Kellogg Sanders's chair right then, so Blake took his advice instead.

Oh God, he could smell the performance sweat from Cheever's body as he drew near. Blake stumbled to a halt, overwhelmed for a moment, and Cheever closed the distance, spanning Blake's waist under his leather coat possessively.

"How'd I do?" he murmured.

Blake couldn't look at him, but he couldn't hold back his proud smile either. "So damned good."

Cheever leaned in and cupped the back of his head. Blake couldn't help it. He smelled so good, felt so good. He leaned forward and breathed in lightly, smelling the heat and the soap and the sweat in the hollow below Cheever's ear.

"Glad to see me?"

It was hard to swallow. It was hard to *breathe*. "You got no idea," Blake rasped. "God, Cheever, it's like the world was spinning and you're the only one who can make it stand still."

Cheever's arms on his shoulders were everything. He gave a little moan and a shudder and melted into that embrace. If the world had ended right then, he would have been locked in Cheever's hold, and happy.

"Then let me," Cheever whispered. "Let me be that guy. I won't let you down, Blake. I promise."

Blake nodded, his face against Cheever's throat. "You were amazing," he said. "Best damned talent we ever scouted."

Cheever's soft laugh filled him. "Think Mackey meant it? 'Bout me playing?"

Blake's eyes burned. "I think they've been waiting for you to join the band your whole life."

"Me too."

Blake really could have stayed there forever, but at that moment Trav—who had been talking quietly to the coffee shop owner and the bloggers—checked his phone first and then tapped on the microphone.

"Okay. So the original plan was for this announcement to be done in that little park across from the coffeehouse. But as it turns out, the whole world showed up here for Cheever Sanders's debut, which is nice and all, but we don't want to put Callum Chutney out, so here's the deal. Every damned one of you buys coffee. Callum's got a few employees coming, and if I give this damned announcement and watch so much as one of you walk out when I'm done, I will never contact your news organization again. Are we clear?"

There was a lot of nodding then, and a lot of gravitating to the coffee line. Trav grunted in satisfaction.

"Good. Now Heather Sanders, the mother of… well, Outbreak Monkey, really, but four of the six guys who make it up now, would like to speak. I figure she's earned it, and I'll run cleanup, so save any questions for me."

"Six? Trav, does that mean Cheever's a member of the band now?" someone piped up.

"Did you not just hear them? And he's got a tattoo!" There was uneasy laughter, and anybody who didn't know Travis Ford might assume he was kidding. Blake met Kell's amused glance, because no, Trav did not play.

"Anyway, first person who shows disrespect to Miss Heather will be looking for a new job tomorrow. I'm not kidding. I'm not exaggerating. And depending on how badly she's disrespected, finding a new job might be something you will never achieve. Are we all clear?"

More of those terrified nods. Wow. Trav was looking for blood tonight.

"Okay now. Miss Heather? You ready?"

"Thanks, Trav." Cheever's mom smiled prettily. "So, I'm the single mother of four grown boys," she said into the microphone, nodding in surprise at the applause.

"When Kell, my oldest"—and the asshole waved, smiling smugly— "was a kid, he tried to run away to his best friend's house. I drove my car and found him and made sure his best friend could get to our place anytime he needed to. When Jefferson, next in line, did the same thing, I pretty much grabbed his friend by the ear and dragged him to my place because we didn't want Stevie where he was at." Her face grew pinched then, and the air in the room grew sober.

"When Blake Manning ran away at sixteen, nobody went looking for him. Nobody found him. He left his mother's car at a bus station and told her where it was, then disappeared, and she thought that was fine. Today, she wants Blake to give her money, and if he doesn't, she's going to show us all pictures of what he did to survive, when he was sixteen and alone. Now before any of you start asking exactly what that was, let me ask *you* something—is there *anybody here* who wants to watch an underage boy have sex for money? Because if that floats your boat, get the hell out of my sight. Blake won't deny it happened. He's been straight with me and my boys. I'm asking you, does anybody here need the pictures as proof? Is that something you need to see?"

The coffeehouse was absolutely silent, and Heather nodded decisively.

"I didn't think so. So that woman is outside, ready to sell her pictures to the highest bidder. We're not stopping her. Blake's got better things to do than let her poison his life right now. He's got a solo album coming out and a wedding to plan—and that woman's got no place in any of it. So, if we see those pictures show up on your blogs, we'll know you paid for them, and we'll know what kind of publication you work for. If you want to print the truth, you go ahead. But you remember—that boy was on his own at sixteen, trying to survive. And no one was coming after him to make sure he was okay.

"I'm coming after him today, because he's mine now, and I need to make sure he's okay. He and my boys did more than survive together. They *thrived.* If anyone here wants to paint him as a bad person because he lived through the bad to get to the good, that's on you. That's not on him, that's not on my boys, that's not on me. He's our family, and that's all I wanted to say."

The coffee shop owner raised a tentative hand into the electric silence. "Ms. Sanders?"

"Mr. Chutney?"

"You still single?"

"Yessir."

"Thank God. That's all I wanted to know."

Heather's cheeks—pale with rage—washed a delicate pink. "That's kind," she said graciously. "Anyone else?"

Another hand went up. "You said he's planning a wedding, Ms. Sanders. To whom?"

"My youngest boy—you just saw him onstage. Who'd you think he was going to marry after a performance like that? That was history, young woman, there's no denying it."

"No, ma'am. Will Blake be answering questions himself?"

"No!" Cheever said at the same time Blake said, "Depends on the question." He stepped reluctantly out of Cheever's embrace.

"Is it true you told your bandmates about your past, sir? Because that's quite an admission."

Blake looked at the guys, who looked steadily back. Heartened, Blake turned to the reporter. "Yes, ma'am. I told Mackey when we were in rehab—if you all remember, that was about nine years ago. The first time my mother tried to blackmail us, which was right about then, I told Kell and the twins and Trav, in case she didn't keep it to herself."

"What made her go away then?" someone else asked.

"Money," Blake said bluntly. "I was a mess—hell, we all were back then. There was lots of shit we couldn't have dealt with back then that we'd knock out of the park now. She came round this time, and we decided we weren't going to let her have that power over us anymore. I mean, it's gonna be a sucktastic news cycle, I won't lie. But she don't got anything they don't know."

"But what about your fans?"

"The fans who knew I been to rehab? The fans who were there when I came out as bi? Fans who still know every word to my little solo album, 'cause something in me meant something to them? I ain't worried. People who respect art know that a lotta times, it comes from pain. Hopefully they'll be glad I survived. Not everybody does. Lots of kids just disappear into that life, and I wasn't one of 'em. Maybe someone living that now will hear this, hear one of my songs, and think, 'Hey, I can get clear.' It's why we make music and paint pictures. So humans know we're not alone."

"But Mr. Sanders—"

"I think that's a place to stop," Trav said. "In fact, I hope you all got that on film, because that there is a helluva quote. Nicely done, Blake."

"Kell was talking about Shakespeare," Blake said. "Like, if he can paraphrase Shakespeare to calm me the fuck down, I figured I could maybe talk pretty for a press conference, right?"

There was general laughter, and then one impertinent soul called out, "So, Cheever, when's the wedding!"

"We'll tell you a month after the honeymoon!" Cheever called back, and then he grabbed Blake's hand and tugged. The guys stood up to block for them, and Cheever pulled him past the door.

"Where we going?" Blake asked softly.

"Elevators back by the bathrooms. This place is under a hotel, did you know that?"

Blake tried to think about what the building looked like and couldn't. "No, sir—shit."

His mother was standing inside the door, glaring at him.

"You think you're pretty smart, don't you?" she snarled, trying to break out of Crane's grip. "Letting me in, just to watch you shit on my chances for cash!"

Crane grunted. "We just wanted you to see how much the guys don't care," he said. "Now come on. I see a cop car outside with your name on it."

Blake opened his mouth to struggle for words, but Kell got there first. "Lady," he said quietly, "he has nothing to say to you. Now go outside and let the nice officer arrest you."

"Blake!" Virginia Manning tried to get his attention, her beat-down eyes trying hard to make contact. "Son, I'm your mother. You gonna throw me in jail?"

"Better jail than to the wolves, Mama," Blake said. His chest ached. "Did you hear what Mrs. Sanders said? She chased her boys down and made them happy. She came all the way up here to defend me. Jesus, Ginny, you couldn't even fuckin' leave me alone."

She gaped, and Cheever pulled. "He's getting glassy-eyed," he murmured to Kell. "Let's get him out of here."

And Blake found himself hustled to a small bank of elevators back behind the bathrooms. "Go figure," he said, looking around at the familiar layout. "This really is a hotel."

"Yeah, well, I'll bring your clothes to the concert. Green room at six," Kell said bluntly.

"Cheever, don't break him," Mackey insisted. "And don't break you. From now on, you're the only one singing that god-awful 'Empty Room' song. Great song, Blake. Pretty much wrecked us all. Well done. Anyway, you get two solos and a backup, middle of the set, to calm everyone down before we go kicking ass again. You good with that?"

Cheever grinned. "I'm in the fuckin' band."

"Monkey Shines, my ass," Mackey said sourly. "Nice fuckin' tat."

That grin didn't get any smaller. "Thanks. I can stay in the secret clubhouse now? Do I need a password?"

"Cheever fuckin' Sanders," Stevie and Jefferson said together, going in for hugs.

"Justin," Blake mumbled as the elevator opened. "Cheever Justin Sanders."

"Yeah." Cheever hustled him in. "That there is my cue."

Once they were in the elevator, Cheever folded Blake into his arms like origami, so perfect Blake couldn't figure out how to unfold. His brain had blanked—everything, plans, responses to the last hour, even joy over seeing Cheever again—was just one big static charge between his ears.

"Almost there," Cheever murmured, waiting for the elevator to ding. There weren't that many tall buildings in Portland—this one went to the eighth floor, but Cheever had apparently checked into a suite. Blake had a moment to notice the clothes—mostly tank tops and slacks—strewn around the couch and closet as they entered, and it would hit him, later, that Cheever had thought hard about those new jeans and that ripped white T-shirt.

He'd wanted to fit in with the band.

But now Cheever's words were shaping his reality.

"Undress," Cheever growled. "Get on the bed."

Oh God. Something concrete to do. Blake pulled down the covers and dropped his clothes in a puddle on the floor, even his boots, which he kicked off after undoing the laces.

Naked, he crawled onto the bed on his hands and knees, needing something, anything, to ground him, to keep him from losing all coherence and becoming a sobbing wreck in the bathtub, forgetting how far he'd come.

Cheever's rough hands at his hips maneuvered him, turned him around on his back, and Cheever draped his naked body over Blake's, warm and electric. Blake clung to him, lifting his head so they could kiss, Cheever's mouth tender on his, grounding.

"I need you to see me," Cheever murmured, sliding their bodies together. He smiled slightly. "It wasn't easy, what I just did."

And like that, Blake remembered that Cheever had been both vulnerable and magnificent, a born performer, one who'd practiced a lot more than he'd ever admit.

"You were so good," Blake said, kissing his neck. It was never easy, doing that thing onstage. Maybe it wasn't supposed to be. "I was so proud of you. God, Cheever, you were so bright and shiny up there, like a supernova, but I couldn't look away."

"Your songs," Cheever said, grinding up against Blake's thigh rhythmically. "They were your songs—your words, your music, your heart. Don't ever forget that."

Blake's arousal was ramping up, fueled by their bare skin, by Cheever's tender kisses on the corner of his mouth, by his words, kind and generous.

By the feel of the two of them, touching, complete.

"God, I love you," Blake breathed. "I love you so much. I can't imagine what I did to have you like this in my life."

Cheever claimed his mouth, demanding now, urgent and hard. He pulled back and reached between them to stroke Blake's cock tightly, smiling when Blake let out a gasp.

"You just had to be you." Cheever stroked him again and wiggled a little, so he sat between Blake's spread knees. He let go and positioned himself, oiled and slick, and Blake groaned.

"You gonna let me in?" Cheever asked, pushing forward.

"Yeah."

"All the way in?"

"Fuck me!"

"Into your heart!" Cheever demanded, thrusting inside.

"*Love me!*" Blake cried, undone by the burn, the ache, the overwhelming pleasure of the pain of having Cheever in his body.

"Forever." Cheever pushed the last few inches home, and Blake groaned. God, he was so big, huge, pushing out all the other things in Blake's head, leaving no room for anything but the explosion of nerve endings, the fullness of Cheever Sanders in his body, in his heart.

"Okay," Blake gasped.

Cheever pulled out and thrust in again, hard and without mercy.

"*Forever*," he insisted.

"Forever!" Blake accepted. "Augh! God, Cheever! Fuck me forever!"

Cheever's chuckle, filthy and uninhibited, rumbled down where their bodies were joined, and Blake's fingers dug into Cheever's shoulders as he tried to hold on to himself.

"I'll love you forever too," he whispered, battering into Blake's asshole again. "I'm gonna fuck you right into now."

Oh God! Again! And again and again!

Blake's fingernails dug into his shoulder muscles, his back, as Cheever pulled Blake relentlessly into the here and now.

Blake's crest, when it came, crashed over him like a thunderclap, bowing his spine as he all but screamed his release into the air around them. His semen, splashing hotly between them, forced another cry, because it was vital and real, just like the man fucking him, buried in his ass, was as vital and real and perfect as any song Blake had ever known.

Cheever thrust a few more times, swelling, trapped by Blake's orgasm and shooting hotly into Blake's body. Oh God. They were together—one. Blake started to shake as he came down, fine trembles taking over his body as his climax faded.

They were together.

"Baby?" Cheever asked, rubbing his lips over Blake's sweaty forehead.

"I'm okay," Blake said in wonder. He could barely open his eyes, he was suddenly so exhausted, but this needed to be said. "I'm okay."

"I knew you would be," Cheever murmured, keeping up the kisses, the tenderness, the soft touches. "You always were."

"You're fucking amazing," Blake mumbled, falling asleep, their bodies still joined. He fought it for a minute. "I got a green room call—"

Cheever chuckled. "*We* got a green room call. Nap now. Don't worry. We got time."

And the wonder of that was, they *did* have time. They had time to be together, to work together—even to work apart if they needed to. They had all the time in the world.

Cheever slid out of Blake and rolled him into his chest.

"God, I love you," Blake said, because he couldn't not.

"I love you too."

"We really getting married?"

"Yup. I'll plan that later."

"Yeah. Today was pretty big all on its own."

Cheever laughed and held him, and for an hour Blake dozed, knowing he was as safe as he'd ever been in his life.

THEY TALKED when he woke up, quietly, reliving Cheever's performance, the things he'd need to pick up being with the band, the ways they could use him in Outbreak Monkey, how much he'd have to practice to stay.

"Mackey doesn't fuck around," Blake told him, playing with his curls as Cheever lay with his head on Blake's shoulder. "You sure you want a piece of this band thing?"

Cheever nodded and looked up at him. "I still want to make art," he said. "I can do that during the hiatus, while I practice and get good enough to really be part of the band. But I want to be a part of what you do, a part of what my brothers do. I know I'm lucky—but I want to work with my brothers, my husband. This family thing may be new to me, but I gotta tell you, I really love it."

Blake kissed his forehead. "Good. Your family is the best thing to ever happen to me. And you love me, and that's the other best thing. And we get to have them all rolled up into one."

"Mm." Cheever shifted and kissed his mouth. "We got time for one more round," he purred. "Because if I'm your other best thing, I want my share of time."

Blake laughed but Cheever didn't. This time Cheever straddled Blake, lowering himself slowly, head back, the long line of his throat exposed as he enjoyed every moment of Blake's length.

This time he rode Blake relentlessly, until Blake had no choice but to come.

This time, Blake knew where he was, who he was with—and, as usual—knew that Cheever was in charge.

Blake trusted himself in Cheever's hands. Cheever would never let him down.

Emotional Rescue

THEY WERE showered and dressed and only running a little late as they charged backstage and to the green room. Blake was wearing the dress shirt, jeans, and boots he'd worn to the coffeehouse, because they were only a little rumpled. He'd told Cheever to stick with the white T-shirt and jeans.

Well, simple, right, until Cheever had time to adapt.

The guys rolled their eyes a little at their late entrance, and Mackey started bitching right off.

"You think you're a real rock star now?" he asked. "You did a cool thing and suddenly you don't need to practice, no coaching?"

"Sorry, Mackey," Cheever said automatically. "We fell asleep."

Mackey rolled his eyes sourly. "Is that what the kids are calling it these days?"

"No! It's true!" The second nap had caught them both by surprise. "I think it's just been a rough couple of days."

"Yeah, well, sleeping on the bus is never a treat. Blake, you good?"

Blake nodded, his game face in place, and Cheever suddenly realized he looked a little pale.

"No, he is not. Dammit, we got any fucking Gatorade and ibuprofen back here?"

Kell groaned. "*That's* what was worrying me—yup. He's got that look." He stood and went to a mini-fridge in the corner while Mackey had Trav scared up some ibuprofen.

Blake thanked the guys softly while he downed the Gatorade and the medicine. "You didn't need to do that," he said.

"'Course we did," Cheever told him, liking how at peace Blake looked, how solid, how focused. "Need to make sure you got some gas for the end."

"What happens at the end?" he asked.

Cheever cupped his cheek and ignored Mackey, giving him directions that he probably sorely needed. "We don't know yet. We still got a lot to go."

"That's real wise fuckin' words," Mackey snapped, breaking into their little bubble. "But it's time to be rock stars now. Can we do that?"

Cheever put his focus on Mackey. He had the tattoo—now he needed to earn it. "Yessir," he said, no bullshit intended. "What's the plan?"

Mackey smiled, in his element. "Okay—we got the lineup written for you on the whiteboard. You're out there offstage, watching for all of the green songs. The red songs are when we need you to either be ready or you're singing them yourself. No blended instrumentals this time out. We'll work up a couple of songs tomorrow during sound check rehearsal. Tonight, you're just there for introduction, your songs, and we'll play behind you, so don't be surprised, and the finale, when you and Kellogg'll double up on the part. You good?"

Cheever grinned at his irrepressible brother, who'd cast such a long shadow he'd kept the scorch of life's hells off Cheever's back until he'd had time to grow.

"I'm great, Mackey. I'm a fuckin' Sanders. How bad can I be?"

Mackey grinned, all teeth. "Baby brother, we can get real fuckin' bad. But not tonight. Blake? You all doctored up?"

Blake's grin was just like Mackey's. All teeth, all feral energy, all the kid who'd fought his way out of hell and was still throwing punches 'cause he liked the swing.

"Ready to go get bloody, Mackey."

"Righteous. Reckon they're about ready for us now."

The crowd roared, the sound filtering backstage, and the energy level in the green room spiked to "nuclear."

Cheever grabbed his guitar and followed his brothers as they headed for the stage, startled when Blake caught his elbow.

"Cheever?"

"Yeah?"

"No matter what happens up there, I love you."

Cheever nodded soberly. "No matter what happens here, in real life, I love you too."

Blake grinned. "We're gonna kick ass."

"And you're gonna have some gas for the end," Cheever said.

"'Cause the end is just the beginning." Blake nodded, and Cheever's heart soared over the stage, over the zoo—they could smell elephant shit from the green room—and over Portland, all the way back home to LA.

"Damned straight. Let's go start something."

They hit the top of the stage, and Cheever's mother was back there with Trav, overseeing the equipment and generally giving the guys their space. For a moment, Cheever couldn't see anything backstage, though—his eyes were still adjusting to the brightness of the lights.

That was their future up on the stage, the glorious unknown with a thousand places to go.

His family there, like they always had been, trying to give him the world, and his lover with them, who needed Cheever to make sure he saw the same promise as Cheever.

In his whole life, Cheever had never guessed there'd be so much to live for.

He couldn't wait to get started, with Blake by his side.

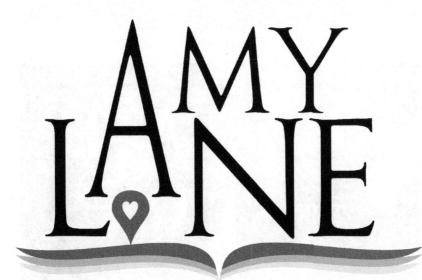

Choose your Lane to love!

Orange

Amy's Dark Contemporary Romance

A Beneath the Stain Novel

In a town as small as Tyson, CA, everybody knew the four brothers with the four different fathers—and their penchant for making good music when they weren't getting into trouble. For Mackey Sanders, playing in Outbreak Monkey with his brothers and their friends—especially Grant Adams—made Tyson bearable. But Grant has plans for getting Mackey and the Sanders boys out of Tyson, even if that means staying behind.

Between the heartbreak of leaving Grant and the terrifying, glamorous life of rock stardom, Mackey is adrift and sinking fast. When he's hit rock bottom, Trav Ford shows up, courtesy of their record company and a producer who wants to see what Mackey can do if he doesn't flame out first. But cleaning up his act means coming clean about Grant, and that's not easy to do or say. Mackey might make it with Trav's help—but Trav's not sure he's going to survive falling in love with Mackey.

Mackey James Sanders comes with a whole lot of messy, painful baggage, and law-and-order Trav doesn't do messy or painful. And just when Trav thinks they may have mastered every demon in Mackey's past, the biggest, baddest demon of all comes knocking.

www.dreamspinnerpress.com

Racing
for the
Sun

AMY LANE

"I'll do anything."

Staff Sergeant Jasper "Ace" Atchison takes one look at Private Sonny Daye and knows that every word on paper about him is pure, unadulterated bullshit. But Sonny is desperate, and although Ace isn't going to take him up on his offer of "anything," that doesn't mean he isn't tempted.

Instead, Ace takes Sonny under his wing, protecting him when they're in the service and making plans with him when they get out. Together, they're going to own a garage and build race cars and make their fortune hurtling faster than light across the desert. Together, they're going to rewrite the past, make Sonny Daye a whole and happy person, and put the ghosts in Ace's heart to rest.

But not even Sonny can build a car fast enough to escape the ghosts of the past. When Sonny's ghosts drive them down and run their plans off the road, Ace finds out exactly what he's made of. Maybe Sonny was the one to promise Ace anything, but there is nothing under the sun Ace won't do to keep Sonny safe from harm.

www.dreamspinnerpress.com

AMY LANE
STRING
BOYS

Seth Arnold learned at an early age that two things in life could make his soul soar—his violin and Kelly Cruz. In Seth's uncertain childhood, the kindness of the Cruz family, especially Kelly and his brother, Matty, gave Seth the stability to make his violin sing with the purest sound and opened a world of possibility beyond his home in Sacramento.

Kelly Cruz has loved Seth forever, but he knows Seth's talents shouldn't be hidden, not when the world is waiting. Encouraging Seth to follow his music might break Kelly's heart, but he is determined to see the violin set Seth's soul free. When their world is devastated by a violent sexual assault and Matty's prejudices turn him from a brother to an enemy, Seth and Kelly's future becomes uncertain.

Seth can't come home and Kelly can't leave, but they are held together by a love that they clutch with both hands.

Seth and Kelly are young and the world is wide—the only thing they know for certain is they'll follow their heartstrings to each other's arms whenever time and fate allow. And pray that one day they can follow that string to forever… before it slices their hearts in two.

www.dreamspinnerpress.com

DREAMSPUN
DESIRES

Search and Rescue

WARM HEART

Amy Lane

Survive the adventure. Live to love.

Following a family emergency, snowboarder Tevyn Moore and financier Mallory Armstrong leave Donner Pass in a blizzard… and barely survive the helicopter crash that follows. Stranded with few supplies and no shelter, Tevyn and Mallory—and their injured pilot—are forced to rely on each other.

The mountain leaves no room for evasion, and Tevyn and Mal must confront the feelings that have been brewing between them for the past five years. Mallory has seen Tevyn through injury and victory. Can Tevyn see that Mallory's love is real?

Mallory's job is risk assessment. Tevyn's job is full-on risk. But to stay alive, Mallory needs to take some gambles and Tevyn needs to have faith in someone besides himself. Can the bond they discover on the mountain see them to rescue and beyond?

www.dreamspinnerpress.com

AMY LANE lives in a crumbling crapmansion with a couple of growing children, a passel of furbabies, and a bemused spouse. She's been a finalist in the RITAs twice, has won honorable mention for an Indiefab, and has a couple of Rainbow Awards to her name. She also has too damned much yarn, a penchant for action-adventure movies, and a need to know that somewhere in all the pain is a story of Wuv, Twu Wuv, which she continues to believe in to this day! She writes fantasy, urban fantasy, and gay romance—and if you accidentally make eye contact, she'll bore you to tears with why those three genres go together. She'll also tell you that sacrifices, large and small, are worth the urge to write.

Website: www.greenshill.com
Blog: www.writerslane.blogspot.com
Email: amylane@greenshill.com
Facebook: www.facebook.com/amy.lane.167
Twitter: @amymaclane

Made in the USA
Middletown, DE
18 November 2022

15484724R00186